DADDY'S GIRL

ALSO BY LISA SCOTTOLINE

DADDY'S GIRL

Lisa Scottoline

HarperCollins*Publishers*

HarperCollins books may be purchased for educational, business, or sales promotional use. For information, please write: Special Markets Department, Harper-Collins Publishers, 10 East 53rd Street, New York, NY 10022.

FIRST EDITION

Library of Congress Cataloging-in-Publication Data is available upon request.

ISBN: 978-0-06-083314-5
ISBN-10: 0-06-083314-9

07 08 09 10 11 ID/RRD 10 9 8 7 6 5 4 3 2 1

For teachers everywhere, with gratitude

I am all the daughters of my
   father's house,
And all the brothers too.

—WILLIAM SHAKESPEARE,
Twelfth Night, ACT 2, SCENE 4

DADDY'S
GIRL

Nat Greco felt like an A cup in a double-D bra. She couldn't understand why her tiny class was held in such a huge lecture hall, unless it was a cruel joke of the registrar's. The sun burned through the windows like a failure spotlight, illuminating two hundred empty seats. This class filled only nine of them, and last week the flu and job interviews had left Nat with one very uncomfortable male student. The History of Justice wasn't only a bad course. It was a bad date.

"Justice and the law," she pressed on, "are themes that run through William Shakespeare's plays, because they were central to his life. When he was growing up, his father, John, held a number of legal positions, serving as a chamberlain, bailiff, and chief alderman."

As she spoke, the law students typed on their black laptops, but she suspected they were checking their email, instant-messaging their friends, or cruising the Internet. The classrooms at Penn Law were wireless, but not all technology was progress. Teachers didn't stand a chance against sex.com.

"When the playwright turned thirteen, his father fell on hard times. He sold his wife's property and began lending money. He was hauled into court twice for being usurious, or charging too much interest. Shakespeare poured his empathy for moneylenders into Shylock, in

The Merchant of Venice. It's one of his most complex characters, and the play gives us a historical perspective on justice."

Nat stepped away from the lectern to draw the students' attention, but no luck. They were all in their third year, and 3Ls had one foot out the door. Still, as much as she loved teaching, she was beginning to think she wasn't very good at it. Could she really suck at her passion? Women's magazines never admitted this as a possibility.

"Let's turn to the scene in which Antonio asks Shylock to lend him money," she continued. "They agree that if Antonio can't pay it back, the penalty is a pound of his flesh. By the way, future lawyers, is that a valid contract under modern law?"

Only one student raised her hand, and, as usual, it was Melanie Anderson, whose suburban coif and high-waisted Mom jeans stood out in this clutch of scruffy twentysomethings. Anderson was a forty-year-old who had decided to become a lawyer after a career as a pediatric oncology nurse. She loved this class, but only because it was better than watching babies die.

"Yes, Ms. Anderson? Contract or no?" Nat smiled at her in gratitude. All teachers needed a pet, even lousy teachers. Especially lousy teachers.

"No, it's not a contract."

Good girl . . . er, woman. "Why not? There's offer and acceptance, and the money supports the bargain."

"The contract would be against public policy." Anderson spoke with quiet authority, and her French-manicured fingertips rested on an open copy of the play, its sentences striped like a highlighter rainbow. "Antonio essentially consents to being murdered, but murder is a crime. Contracts that are illegal are not enforceable."

Right. "Anybody agree or disagree with Ms. Anderson?"

Nobody stopped typing emoticons to answer, and Nat began second-guessing herself, wondering if the assignment had been too literary for these students. Their undergraduate majors were finance, accounting, and political science. Evidently, humans had lost interest in the humanities.

"Let's ask some different questions." She switched tacks. "Isn't the hate that drives Shylock the result of the discrimination he's suffered? Do you see the difference between law and justice in the play? Doesn't the law lead to injustice, first in permitting enforcement of the contract, then in bringing Shylock to his knees? Can there be true justice in a world without equality?" She paused for an answer that didn't come. "Okay, everyone, stop typing right now and look at me."

The students lifted their heads, their vision coming slowly into focus as their brains left cyberspace and reentered Earth's atmosphere. Their fingers remained poised over their keyboards like spiders about to pounce.

"Okay, I'll call on people." Nat turned to Wendy Chu in the front row, who'd earned a Harvard degree with honors in Working Too Hard. Chu had a lovely face and glossy hair that covered her shoulders. "Ms. Chu, what do you think? Is Shylock a victim, a victimizer, or both?"

"I'm sorry, Professor Greco. I didn't read the play."

"You didn't?" Nat asked, stung. "But you always do the reading."

"I was working all night on law review." Chu swallowed visibly. "I had to cite-check an article by Professor Monterosso, and it went to press this morning."

Rats. "Well, you know the rules. If you don't do the reading, I have to take you down half a grade." Nat hated being a hardass, but she'd been too easy her first year of teaching, and it hadn't worked. She'd been too strict her second year, and that hadn't worked either. She couldn't get it just right. She was like Goldilocks and all the beds were futons.

"Sorry," Chu whispered. Nat skipped Melanie Anderson for the student sitting next to her, class hottie Josh Carling. Carling was a tall twenty-six-year-old out of UCLA, with unusual green eyes, a killer smile, and a brownish soul patch on his square chin. A Hollywood kid, he'd worked as an A.D. on the set of a TV sitcom and he always wore an Ashton Kutcher knit cap, though it never snowed indoors.

"Mr. Carling, did you do the reading?" Nat knew Josh's answer because he looked down sheepishly.

"I didn't have time. I had a massive finance exam to study for. Sorry, for reals."

Damn. "Then you're a half-grade down, too," she said, though her heart went out to him. Carling was in the joint-degree program, so he'd graduate with diplomas from the law school and the business school, which guaranteed him a lucrative job in entertainment law and a spastic colon.

Nat eyed the second row. "Mr. Bischoff? How about you?"

"I would have done the reading but I was sick." Max Bischoff looked the part, with credibly puffy eyes, a chapped ring around his nostrils, and his library pallor paler than usual. "Yesterday, I ralphed all over my—"

"Enough." Nat silenced him with a palm and quizzed the rest of the second row, Marilyn Krug and Elizabeth Warren. They hadn't done the reading either, and neither had Adele McIlhargey, San Gupta, or Charles Wykoff IV.

"So no one else in the entire class has done the reading?" Nat blurted out in dismay, and just when she thought things couldn't get any worse, in the door strolled Vice Dean James McConnell, Faculty Vampire.

Nat stiffened. She wasn't sure what McConnell did except hire and fire people, and she had already been hired.

McConnell was in his sixties, with a silvery wave of hair that rolled sideways across his head. Today he was dressed in a dark wool suit with a bloodred tie, unusually formal for this school's faculty. Everybody here dressed academic casual, which was like business casual only with footnotes.

McConnell entered the lecture hall, took a seat, and crossed one leg over the other, scrutinizing Nat from behind his tortoise-shell bifocals. Nat imagined how he saw her. She was thirty years old but looked thirteen because she was only five foot one, with her mother's sparrow-thin bones. Her features were nice in a forgettable way; large brown eyes, a slightly upturned nose, and a small mouth. She had thick, straight hair, a deep red brown, which she wore shoulder length in an overpriced cut. Today she had on a tailored black pantsuit, but nevertheless came off more middle school than law school. Her childhood nickname was Gnat for a reason.

She saw her career flash before her eyes. She was only an assistant professor and was up for tenure next year, and McConnell must have come to evaluate her. Did he hear her say that nobody had done the reading? For a minute, she didn't know what to do. She didn't want to lower the grades of the entire class, especially for the students without job offers. But she couldn't let them get away with it, not in front of McConnell. The vice dean watched her, puckering his lined mouth in appraisal.

Do something, Gnat! She squared her shoulder pads to show that she deserved her job, despite all evidence to the contrary, and said, "Well, then, class, you leave me no alternative."

The students gulped collectively. McConnell half smiled and folded his arms.

"Mr. Carling?" Nat pointed to him. "Please come up here and bring your book."

"Uh, okay." Carling rose, slid his paperback from his desktop, and climbed the steps to the stage with a too-cool-for-school smile.

"Come here, please," Nat said, motioning him over to where she was standing.

Carling crossed the stage, scanning the high-tech lectern, with its touch-screen controls and multicolored display.

"This is *sick* up here."

When Carling was beside her, Nat reached up and took the wool hat from his head.

"May I borrow this?"

"Sure." Carling refluffed the layers of his sandy hair, looking at the class from the stage. "I could get used to this, yo."

"Now stay there, please." Nat scanned the lecture hall. "Mr. Wykoff?" She pointed to Charles Wykoff IV, an all-Ivy lineman from a Main Line family, via Dartmouth. Wykoff had a big baby face, a fringe of crayon-yellow bangs, and guileless blue eyes that telegraphed Legacy Admission. "Please come up and bring your book. And Ms. Anderson, please come with him."

"Sure." Anderson happily made her way to the steps. Wykoff followed her, mystified.

"Hurry up, guys." Nat hustled over as the students made their way to her. She positioned Wykoff by his shoulders, solid as bowling balls under a faded Patagonia fleece. "Good. Now, Mr. Wykoff, you be Bassanio."

"Ba-what-io?"

"Bassanio. He's the hunky boyfriend in the play you didn't read. Open your book. You've got lines." Nat turned to Anderson. "Lady, you're Shylock."

"Terrific!" Anderson grinned.

"Whoa, we're putting on a *skit*, in *law school?*" Carling asked in disbelief.

"Not a skit, a play," Nat answered. "It's William Shakespeare, not David Letterman."

"*Pssh.* What's next? Milk and cookies? Nap time?"

Wykoff guffawed. "Damn, I left my protractor at home."

"Guys, would you rather I lowered your grades?" Nat didn't wait for an answer. "You'll read this play, one way or another. By the way, Carling, you're Antonio."

"But he's gay!"

"So what?" Nat turned on her heel. "And how do you know that, if you didn't read the play?"

"I saw the movie. Jeremy Irons borrows the money from Al Pacino because he's in love with a *dude*."

"Way to miss the point, Mr. Carling. Don't discriminate in the class *about* discrimination."

The students laughed, and Nat startled at the unaccustomed sound. They'd never laughed at any of her jokes before. In fact, all nine of them were paying attention for the first time ever. Behind them, McConnell leaned back in his seat, but she couldn't stop now. She took her place downstage.

"Everybody," Nat said, "please turn to act one, scene two, the big courtroom scene. I'm playing Portia, one of Shakespeare's best female characters, except that she fell for the wrong guy. She's about to save the day, and in this scene, she disguises herself as a man, like this." She shoved Carling's wool hat on her head and hurried to the lectern for her purse.

"You look hot, Professor Greco!" Elizabeth Warren hollered, and the class laughed.

"You ain't seen nothin' yet." Nat rummaged through her makeup bag, found her eye pencil, and drew a crude mustache on her face with two quick strokes, courtesy of Clinique.

"Awesome, professor!" San Gupta shouted, making a megaphone of his hands. The class broke into applause that echoed in the cavernous hall. Somebody in the back of the room wolf-whistled, and Nat looked toward the sound. It was Angus Holt, whose blond beard and ponytail qualified him as Faculty Freak. Angus taught in this room after Nat's class, but she didn't know him except to say hello and goodbye. She smiled, then caught sight of McConnell in the foreground, which gave her an idea.

"We need a judge." Nat rubbed her hands together.

"I'll do it!" Max Bischoff volunteered, forgetting he had typhus.

"Pick me! It should be a woman judge!" Marilyn Krug shouted, and Adele McIlhargey chimed in, in an unprecedented traffic jam of class participation.

"Wait a minute, gang." Nat waved them off. "Vice Dean McConnell, would you please be our judge this morning?"

The students turned around, surprised to see McConnell sitting in the back. The vice dean frowned at the sudden attention, cupping his earlobe as if he hadn't heard, but Nat wasn't buying.

"Vice Dean McConnell, we'd love for you to play the Duke of Venice. Right, class?"

"Yes!" Everybody shouted, smiling, and Nat started a cheer.

"McConnell! McConnell! McConnell!"

The students joined her, and as if on cue, Angus Holt lumbered down the sloped aisle of the lecture hall. He scooped up McConnell on the way and escorted him to the stage, amid laughter and clapping.

"Special delivery, Professor Greco!" Angus handed over a slightly winded vice dean.

"If it pleases, Your Grace." Nat extended her arm to McConnell with an Elizabethan flourish.

Gotcha.

CHAPTER 2

After class was over, Nat said goodbye to McConnell, who had rendered judgment on Shylock and presumably on her, too. She grabbed her stuff to leave, but by then Angus Holt's class was entering the hall, pouring down the center aisle, laughing and joking like they were at a party. They kept coming and coming, and soon she found herself swimming upstream against a student tsunami of water bottles and Coach purses. She watched, astounded, as one by one they filled every seat in the lecture hall. Nat had never seen so many students in one place, except at graduation.

She started up the aisle, where Angus stood surrounded by a circle of clinic students, identifiable by their unruly hair, so collectively curly it hovered above them like a cloud. She didn't know much about the clinic, except that it taught students to work as lawyers for the public good, while avoiding the abstract legal issues that bored everyone but her. Whatever Angus was doing, it was working. Faculty Freak trumped Faculty Comic Relief.

"Natalie!" he called out, waving to her. His student circle broke up and went to their seats, and Angus strode down the aisle in jeans and Frye boots.

"What do you teach?" Nat asked, looking up at him. He towered over her by a full foot and wore his blond hair parted messily down the middle. His thick, uncombed ponytail trailed over his shoulders and the knitted cables of his fisherman's sweater.

"Issues in Constitutional Law. Why?" Angus's eyes flashed a bright, amused blue. His nose was straight and his grin omnipresent, even if buried inside a mellow-yellow beard, and he smelled vaguely of patchouli, or marijuana.

"Because . . . this room, it's full. It must be a great course. You must be a great teacher."

Angus smiled modestly. "Not at all, and by the way, I love your mustache. Most women shy away from facial hair, but I say, go for it."

Nat had forgotten. Her hand flew to her face and she almost dropped her purse and papers. She spit on her fingertips and wiped her upper lip.

"You're just smearing it around." Angus laughed, his teeth white and even. "Forget it, it doesn't matter. That was a cool move with McConnell."

"Thanks." Nat gave up on the mustache. "Did he say anything when he left? I thought I saw him speak to you on the way out."

"Don't worry about it. You love your course, and it shows."

It's my passion, which I suck at. Rather, at which I suck. "Did McConnell say that? Am I fired?"

"All he said was that he found the class 'unusual.'" Angus made quote marks in the air. "Don't sweat it. Of course you're not fired."

"Easy for you to say. You have tenure. I have nine students."

"How do you do in your other classes?"

"I fill the room when the courses are mandatory. And they're 1Ls, so they're too terrified not to listen."

"You know what your problem is? You're not getting to the right students. You need marketing."

"Marketing, of justice?" Nat recoiled. "They're law students. They should be interested in justice."

"No, they're interested in law, and there's a difference. Isn't that your point?" Angus looked down at her, smiling. "For example, how many of your students want to practice law?"

"I assume all of them."

"I bet you're wrong. In my non-clinic classes, like this one"—Angus gestured around the noisy hall—"many of the students are going into business. They just want the law degree."

"Really?"

"Absolutely. Didn't you ever ask them? Talk to them about their future? Their plans? What they want out of life?"

"No." Nat reddened. She had office hours but no one came in, and she communicated with her students mostly by email. She probably kept too much to herself; that's what her father always said. She felt guilty that she didn't network, especially now that it had become a verb.

"You need to reach the students who want to be trial lawyers. Students who feel justice at gut level, like the students in my clinic. They'd love your seminar." Angus nodded. "Tell you what, I'll spread the word, and maybe you can stop by sometime and promote yourself."

Yuck. Nat shuddered.

"Anyway, can I ask you a favor? I need your expertise."

"My expertise is legal history. Who are you suing? Julius Caesar?"

"You're funny."

You're high. Two male students walking in stared at Nat's mustache.

"You know how the clinic works. We give the students hands-on experience outside the classroom, through externship programs. One is at a local prison in Chester County. I'd like you to lecture there, with me."

"At a *prison?*"

"It's safe. Minimum security. Inmates who take my class have to be selected, and most of 'em are only in for DUIs or pot possession."

Bingo. "What would I lecture on?"

"Tell 'em exactly what you told your class today. It was a *great* class." Angus sounded genuinely enthusiastic. "Tell 'em that true justice is tempered with mercy. That the Duke was wrong to bring Shylock to his knees. That law and justice are not always the same thing."

"But Shakespeare? To prisoners?"

"'Hath not a Jew eyes?'" Angus knit his furry blond brows, and his tone stiffened. "Maybe prisoners can relate to Shakespeare better than Ivy Leaguers can. Nobody knows the difference between law and justice better than prison inmates." He checked the clock. "I should get started. So, you free tomorrow morning?"

"It's *tomorrow* you're talking about?"

"One of my students got sick, and I need to fill that spot. I'd really love it if you came along. Please?" Angus slapped his hands together in mock prayer, and heads turned, one by one.

"I don't know." Nat tried to think of a way to say no. She wasn't teaching tomorrow and she couldn't lie. Faculty schedules were online.

"Please, Professor Natalie? I'm begging you." Suddenly Angus dropped to one knee and raised his hands in supplication. His students giggled and pointed, the whole room beginning to take notice, and Nat laughed, disarmed. It was fun and embarrassing, both at once.

"Okay, yes. Stop."

"Cool! Pick you up at nine." Angus popped up with a broad grin, and the students clapped and hooted with approval, which he seemed to absorb and reflect like the sun itself, beaming down at her. He soaked in the attention, and Nat could see that there were no failure spotlights in the life of Angus Holt.

She turned and fled.

CHAPTER 3

Nat shook off the cold night air, set the Whole Foods bag down on the mahogany console, and slipped out of her gloves and toggle coat. The big house radiated light and warmth, its elaborate crystal chandelier in megawatt blaze and probably the gas fireplace fake-burning, too. Flowered wallpaper she'd never seen before covered the entrance hall, so fresh she could almost smell the paste. The Courtney Road house was her parents' most recent McMansion, and she had stopped counting at twelve. Greco Construction had custom-built all of them, starting with their first twin in Ocean City, N.J. As family fortunes increased, they'd sold and built bigger each time, and there was always a For Sale sign planted on the front lawns, permanent as an oak tree. Nat grew up thinking that their family name was Builder's Own Home!

She hung up her coat in the hall closet, the hinges of its louvered doors still stiff, and she knew that even the tiny defect would not escape her father's punch list. The aroma of roasting filet mignon and baked potatoes wafted from the kitchen, mingling with a clove-and-orange room fragrance, her mother's signature Open-House spray. Tony Bennett sang in the background but was drowned out by boisterous laughter and a raucous argument; her boyfriend, father, and three brothers armchair-quarterbacking the Eagles. In the spring, they'd armchair-quarterback the Sixers, and in summer, they'd armchair-quarterback the Phillies. You could say they had a passion. Not for sports. For armchair-quarterbacking.

"No way!" came a voice from the great room. "You can't run a team that way, with a player thinking he runs the show. Coach runs the show. Management runs the show, calls the shots. Owner runs the show. Not a dumbass wide receiver."

Dad. Big John Greco, enunciating the standard management-rights line, not at all influenced by the fact that he ran a successful construction business and a family obsessed with football.

"Aw, come on, Dad! They never shoulda let him go! He was the best receiver in the league. They let too many good players get away. Started a long time ago, with Corey Simon and Ike!"

John Greco, Jr., still known as Junior. Junior was Operations Manager at Greco Construction and had been an All-American quarterback at Villanova, like Dad. He'd just missed the NFL draft, also like Dad, and was heir to the CEO throne, to be vacated when Dad retired, which was never.

Nat was just about to join them when Jelly, their huge Maine coon cat, ambled across the Oriental like a moving ottoman. He stopped and stretched, extending his front legs with their mop feet, then leaned forward sleepily and extended his back legs. Nat would never understand how he slept with this noise level. It was survival of the fittest chez Greco, even for the pets.

"Get over it! It was years ago now! They lost who they could afford to lose."

Tom Greco. Tom was the second son and had been an offensive lineman at Villanova until an ACL tear ended his football career. He'd graduated with a degree in accounting and was now the company CFO, which they said stood for Chief Fuck-Off. The joke was that nobody worked harder. In the world.

"Hey, Jellybelly." Nat bent down and scratched the cat, which she'd named for the Jellicle cats in the Eliot poem. Gray wisps sprouted from his ears, his coat was dense and striped, and only his funky teeth gave away his age, which was sixteen. He had been her Christmas kitten, the perfect gift for a bookworm who loved to curl up with a new Nancy Drew, a waxed sleeve of Ritz crackers, and a glass of cold milk. From early on, she preferred reading to sports and had ended up warming the Greco bench. Not that she minded. There were worse things than being The Smart One.

"I AGREE WITH TOM! IT'S DONE AND DONE. GET OVER IT, JUNIOR! ALWAYS, WITH THE T.O. THING. LET IT GO!"

Paul Greco. The third son and the baby of the family, he couldn't speak softer than three billion decibels, in case he didn't get enough attention. He'd excelled at high school football but didn't get enough playing time at Penn State, so was forced to settle for golf and a three handicap. He'd been a rabbit on the pro tour until he quit to become property acquisition jock at Greco.

"Funny how you don't hear from Rosenhaus anymore. I gotta admit, I miss the guy. Remember T.O. at the podium with him and some reporter asked that great question? How funny was that? I'll never forget it. What'd he say?"

Hank Ballisteri. Nat's boyfriend of three years, a commercial realtor who did business with Greco Construction and who had impressed Big John enough to get invited to every family function, where he and Nat had met, as part of her father's master plan. Tonight was Hank's thirty-third birthday. She'd wanted to take him out alone, but he'd closed a big deal with her father and a client today, so it made sense to celebrate his birthday en famille. It reminded Nat of a poem about birthdays. She scratched Jelly, and while he purred, she tried to remember the poem. She couldn't hear herself think for the shouting. It sounded like they'd started celebrating early.

"'WHAT HAVE YOU DONE FOR YOUR CLIENT BESIDES GET

HIM FIRED?'" the men yelled in unison, then burst into loud laughter. Jelly startled at the sound, curling his tail into a question mark, then skittered off like a monkey. Hank shouted, "Hey, stop, that's my birthday present! Gimme that! Hands off my stick!" They burst into new laughter, and the fight was on. "I WOULD NEVER TOUCH YOUR STICK, YOU LOSER! YOU COULDN'T PAY ME ENOUGH TO TOUCH YOUR STICK!"

Nat picked up her shopping bag and went through the sample-house living room, sinking into the dense burgundy carpet and following the noise to the great room. She crossed the threshold into a *House & Garden* version of country casual, except for the horse-play between Hank and her brothers. The boys were fighting over a wooden cue stick, bumping the coffee table. All her brothers had her father's huge, heavy-boned frame and his thick, dark hair, deep brown eyes, and largish noses and lips, as if Big John had called all the genetic plays. The family resemblance was so strong their brawl looked like a fistfight among overgrown triplets.

"Hey, watch it!" Junior swung a cue stick at Paul and Tom, who grabbed the narrow end and struggled to wrest it back.

"I got dibs first game!" Tom called out, holding the cue stick until Hank wrestled it from him. The others jumped in, the four of them in silk ties and oxford shirts, making a corporate scrum and almost knocking over her mother as she walked past with an empty china platter.

"Paul, put your back into it!" Her father stuck out his tasseled loafer and almost tripped his youngest son, which was when Hank noticed Nat.

"Hi, babe!" he called from the melee. "We're gonna play pool with my new stick!"

"Happy Birthday, Hank." Nat waved. "Now you have to grow up. All of you."

"No, stop!" Tom shouted, as Junior broke free with the cue stick and ran for the door. Nat stepped aside at just the right time, from years of practice.

"That's mine!" Hank bolted after Junior, chased by Paul and Tom, an express train of flying ties.

"I'll take you all!" her father yelled, hustling to bring up the rear. At sixty, he was still quarterback-broad in a smooth blue shirt, Hermès tie, and dark pressed slacks. He had conventionally handsome features, round brown eyes with deep crow's-feet, and thinning hair a shade too dark to be completely credible. He ran past, trailing Aramis.

"Hi, Dad," Nat called out, but he had already gone. The room fell abruptly quiet, as if the life had gone out of it, leaving the women alone with Tony Bennett. Nat trailed her mother as she made her way back to the kitchen. Ivory-enameled cabinets lined the walls above a built-in plate holder and a tile backsplash in floral curlicues. "New tile, Ma?"

"It's an upgrade."

"Pretty."

"Did you get the cake?"

"Chocolate with red roses, and two kinds of cheesecake, plain and cherry." Nat picked up the Whole Foods bag, crossed to the glistening Sub-Zero, and made room for the bag, sliding it inside. "How can I help?"

"I'm fine. Table's almost set. I just need the napkins."

Nat folded the napkins, seven in all. "No girlfriends tonight?"

"The boys came straight from the settlement, so no. It's enough work with just us, believe me."

Nat felt a twinge. "I feel guilty that you're doing so much."

"Don't be silly. I was home all day. Your father didn't need me."

"Well, thanks." Nat came over to the granite counter, next to her mother. The former Diane Somers had been a flight attendant when she met John Greco in the first-class cabin of the now-defunct Eastern

Airlines, and they were a match made in heaven, or at least, at 35,000 feet. Then, her mother had been tall, honey-blonde, and pageant-pretty. Today she was only more beautiful. She had azure eyes set off by photogenic crow's-feet, her nose was small and straight, and her mouth generous. She'd smoothed her hair back into a chic pony-tail, her makeup was perfect, and her forehead remained uncreased, though she'd never admit to Botox, even to Nat. Especially to Nat, who asked again, "You sure I can't help?"

"No, I enjoy it." Her mother layered beefsteak tomatoes on a plate, then began to cut a wet, spongy ball of mozzarella, in a routine Nat knew by heart, the way daughters always know their mother's go-to dishes.

"I gather that you guys gave Hank a new cue stick."

"Paul picked it out. It's got his initials on it."

"That was very nice of you."

"We're very nice people," her mother said defensively, and Nat let it go. As much as she loved her mother, she could never get close to her. Diane Somers Greco had transferred her awe of first-class business-men to her family life, and when she'd called herself a "man's woman," Nat knew what she meant. That a daughter, born third, would always finish fourth.

"How've you been, Mom?"

"Not good." Her mother shook her head, her tone agitated. "I'm just sick about Paul."

"He makes me sick, too." Nat leaned against the counter, and her mother didn't laugh.

"He's got this cold and it won't go away. I'm afraid it's pneumonia, walking pneumonia." Her mother sliced the mozzarella, holding the cheese between clear-lacquered nails and expressing the slightest bit of water from it with her fingertips. "He was playing racquetball and he couldn't catch his breath."

"He was probably just running hard."

"I don't think that's all it is."

"So tell him to go to the doctor, get some antibiotics."

"He won't. He says he's fine." Her mother kept slicing, and whitish water leached from the mozzarella.

"I'm sure he'll be okay. Don't worry, Mom."

"How can I not worry? He was a preemie."

Twenty-six years ago. Nat let it go. She had long ago accepted that Paul was her mother's favorite, though she herself was the runt of the litter.

"I looked on WebMD, and it only made me more nervous. It's not good for people to know everything. I say, a little knowledge is a dangerous thing."

"A little knowledge is better than no knowledge, Mom. You just have to keep it in perspective."

Her mother layered the mozzarella ovals on the tomato plate, and Nat knew she'd said the wrong thing. A moment passed in which Tony Bennett had the world on a string, but she didn't. She tried to get back in the game.

"What does Dad say?"

"He says not to worry."

"Then he's right." Her father never worried; it wasn't the Greco way. He regarded every football injury as proof of the boys' toughness. He and her mother had run the Booster Club at the kids' high school, organized the awards dinners for the coaches, and used whatever house they lived in as the unofficial locker room. Everybody knew the Grecos. They weren't a family, they were a cult.

"Well, this should be a very nice dinner." Her mother chopped fresh basil and sprinkled the bright green strips on the platter, and Nat handed her the wooden grinder, knowing her mother would want fresh-ground peppercorn on top.

"Great job, Mom."

"Thanks, dear." Her mother lifted the platter and took it to the dining room table, an elongated cherry oval set with Villeroy & Boch china. Once back in the kitchen, she picked up where she had left off. "We're happy to do it. You know we love Hank."

Nat smelled what was coming, and it involved grandchildren. Time to change the subject. "Mom, guess where I'm going tomorrow?"

Suddenly a loud crash came from the living room, then the inevitable tinkle of glass, followed by cursing and laughing. The women's heads snapped around to the sound.

"On no," her mother said, already in motion toward the door. "What'd they break now?"

Just so it wasn't the cat. Nat followed on her heels.

At midnight, Nat and Hank got back to her apartment in Center City, where she undressed as she walked to the bathroom, finished there, and padded nude into her bedroom. The only illumination was a sliver of gray moonlight that slipped through the curtain and the halogen lamp on Hank's night table. They lent a soft glow to the room, with its pale blue walls, gray-blue rug, neat pine dresser, and an armoire that hid the TV. Over the brass bed hung a muted watercolor of a cat who looked like Jelly, sitting on a lemony table with his tail curled neatly over his front paws. It was signed and numbered. Nat had bought it in a downtown gallery, prima facie evidence of her having grown up. Books sat in stacks on both night tables, and Nat loved every inch of this room, especially when Hank slept over, which happened more often, of late. She crawled into bed next to him and pulled the blue flannel comforter up to her chin. It was too cold to be comfortably naked, but she owed him birthday sex.

She turned over on her side, propped herself up on her elbow, and eyed him as he dozed. His nose was strong and perfect, ending in flat lips, which she found very kissable. The bedside lamp picked up the shiny, dark filaments of russet running through his brown hair. She stroked his hair gently, finding it silky to the touch. Hank had the best hair, which was completely wasted on him, since he mistakenly thought there were more important things in life. Like golf.

Nat smiled to herself. She saw Hank Ballisteri as the chocolate Lab of men; overgrown, active, and affable. A Penn State econ major and born salesman, Hank connected instantly with people, complementing her perfectly. She knew enough not to go for you-complete-me love, but she did enjoy knowing that she could delegate her social life to him, at least for the foreseeable future.

Her cold toes found his under the covers, and he wiggled back, their customary toe-hello. She leaned over and kissed him on his slightly oily cheek, since he never washed his face at night, and he shifted onto his back, smiled lazily, and opened his eyes, a rich, large brown.

"Thanks for a great birthday party," he murmured.

"You're welcome. I was cooking all day."

"You did buy the cake."

"True."

"I love my new pen. I hope I don't lose it."

"You won't. You're thirty-four now. Thirty-three-year-olds lose gold pens. Men your age, never."

Hank smiled with pleasure and fatigue. He reached up and touched her hair. "I love you."

"I love you, too. And my family loves you even more than I do."

"The lamp was Paul's fault, no matter what he says."

"I know. Forget about the lamp." Nat inched close to him and warmed her breast on the side of his arm. "I'm nude, by the way."

"I noticed."

"I want extra credit."

"For not wearing that disgusting sweatshirt to bed?"

"Exactly." They both smiled, and Nat stroked his chest under the covers. "You too tired?"

"For what?"

Actually, Nat wanted to tell him about the vice dean and the trip to the prison, but men never stay up to talk about work. "For Happy Birthday."

"Now that's worth missing Conan for," he said, rolling over and giving her a deep kiss.

After they had made love, Hank fell fast asleep, but Nat tossed and turned. She couldn't stop thinking about her seminar or the prison trip. She regretted saying yes to Angus. She should have just begged off. She even had work to do, writing another article that no one would read. What would she do at a prison? More important, what would she *wear*? How do you dress to look terrible?

Nat turned over and shut her eyes. She would have switched on the light and read but then she'd never get to sleep. She tried to relax, breathing in the sweetness of the dark bedroom, with the chill of winter safely at bay and the man she loved slumbering beside her. In time, she drifted off, and at the threshold of sleep, she remembered the birthday poem.

My heart is gladder than all these, because my love is come to me.

Nat and Angus were driving in his sunflower-yellow VW Beetle along a one-lane road that wound up and down through the snow-covered hills of the Pennsylvania countryside. Angus had been pleasant company on the drive from the city, and Nat was relieved to note that he didn't smell like a controlled substance this morning.

"It's gorgeous out here," she said, looking out the car window. The mid-morning sun climbed a cloudless sky, late to work as it lingered behind the barren branches of winter trees. They drove past a field of snow, its glazed veneer broken in patches from horses, which stood together under worn blue blankets, nosing the snow from habit or in vain hope of grass. Their long necks stretched down with a quiet grace, and chalky steam wreathed their muzzles.

"This is southern Chester County, the Brandywine River Valley. Wyeth Country." Angus downshifted around a curve. "The Wyeths live around here, and the Brandywine River Museum's not far, in Chadds Ford. Ever been to the museum?"

"No."

"I go there all the time. It's dedicated to the Wyeth family. They have Andrew and his son Jamie, and N.C., the grandfather. Newell Convers Wyeth, the patriarch. I love his stuff."

"Why?"

"The colors. The light. The superheroes. He was more into people than landscapes. He started out as an illustrator of adventure books. Old N.C. was a painter of knights and pirates, and I can relate."

"To the knights or the pirates?"

"To the painter," Angus answered, and Nat smiled. She sat enveloped in her toggle coat, unusually near him in the forced intimacy of the small car. Up close, he had intelligent, if narrow, blue eyes and heavy eyebrows of a darker gold shade. His thick hair, barely contained by an orange rubber band, still looked uncombed, and he wore the same clothes as yesterday; a faded blue workshirt, its wrinkled collar sticking out from underneath a thick fisherman's sweater, worn with jeans and boots. He barely fit in the driver's seat and looked as incongruous in a VW as a Viking.

"That house is a funny color," Nat said, as they passed a Colonial-scale home, its gray stone shining oddly green.

"It's the copper in the stone, leaching through. Have you ever been out this way, in Chester County?"

"No, but I do a chapter on the Fugitive Slave Act in my seminar."

"What's that have to do with Chester County?"

"Chester County was an important stop on the Underground Railroad. On a map, you can see that it's just north of the Mason-Dixon Line. The Quakers down here, especially from the Longwood Progressive Meeting, brought thousands of slaves north."

"Longwood? That's not far, about half an hour." Silence fell for a minute, then Angus said, "I thought I knew everything about this area. I was trying to impress you with my Wyeth lecture."

"I was impressed." Nat smiled. "I think the Progressive Meetinghouse still stands. I read that it's part of Longwood Gardens."

"So why don't we go, after the prison?" Angus shifted gears around a curve, and his hand accidentally bumped her knee.

"I can't. I should get back to work."

"We can get back by two, even if we grab lunch."

Did he just ask me out? "I don't have time. I'm working on an article."

"But how can you pass up the chance to see it? You teach it."

"I teach *The Merchant of Venice* without going to Italy. That's why we have books."

"No, that's why we have clinics," Angus shot back with a grin. "How about Saturday? We can take in the Wyeth museum, find the meetinghouse, and then have dinner. A day o' fun!"

His hand bumped her knee again, and this time, Nat wondered how accidentally. She stole a glance at his left hand. No wedding band, but maybe he didn't wear one. She had thought he was married. For school gossip she always relied on a colleague, who'd gone on sabbatical this year. Maybe delegating your social life wasn't such a hot idea.

"I can't go. I have plans."

"What about Sunday?" Angus hit the gas, and Nat shifted in her seat so her knee wouldn't get bumped. She didn't want her bumpage to lead him on, and, anyway, enough was enough.

"Aren't you married?"

"Not anymore. We divorced about a year ago." Angus kept his eyes on the road, and if he was upset, it didn't show.

"I'm sorry. I didn't know."

"I didn't advertise. She dumped me for a Republican." He smiled, then it vanished. "So how about it? Would you like to go out?"

"Thanks, but I'm seeing someone."

"I should have known." He braked at the stop sign, his lower lip puckering somewhere inside his beard. "Cool move by me, huh? Am I rusty or what?"

"You're fine," Nat said, touched by his openness. He really was a nice guy. Then she thought of something. "Is that why you asked me to go to the prison?"

"No. I thought my class would benefit from what you had to say. But I admit I was looking forward to the drive—way too much." He glanced over. "I thought what you did in your class was so cool, and it's too bad we don't know each other, even though we have so much in common."

"We do? Like what?" Nat asked, keeping the incredulity from her tone.

"For one, we're both outsiders at school."

"Are you kidding?" She scoffed. "No one is more inside than you. I saw your students gazing at you adoringly."

"Those are my clinic members, and the clinic is its own little world, didn't you notice?"

"No, I'm in my own little world."

Angus smiled crookedly. "We have the same problems. The truth is it's tough to attract students to the clinic. How do you get a kid to go into public interest law when he has student loans of a hundred grand? It's a lost cause."

"Which is what you love about it."

"Exactly. Like you and your class. Don't you like the idea that you're doing something important, even if no one else recognizes it?"

Nat understood. He was right; they did have that in common. She let an awkward moment pass.

"My clinic needed marketing, too. I had to explain to the students what's so great about what we do, so they would see the benefit to them. I told them that they could get into court and actually represent people." Angus paused. "In our situation, I would explain to you the many benefits of dating me."

"You'd market yourself?"

"If that's what it took."

"It's not happening," Nat said with a smile, and Angus laughed, which broke the tension.

"Are you and this lucky guy serious?"

"Yes." *But don't tell my mother.*

"So, okay, Professor Holt strikes out. If you two break up, will you take me off the wait list?"

Nat flushed, flattered. "Yes," she answered, and they took off through the countryside. She could have been imagining it, but he seemed to drive faster after she turned him down. They traveled up and down hills, through forest and pasture and over the Brandywine Creek, and in time, rounded a sharp curve. On the right was a brick building with a bright green roof behind a Youth Study Center sign, but they drove on. Tucked uphill behind a grove of tall evergreens appeared an older wooden sign that read, CHESTER COUNTY CORREC-TIONAL INSTITUTION in white-painted letters that were oddly rustic for a penitentiary.

"End of the Wyeth part." Nat instantly regretted that she'd come. She should have been back at school, teaching class. Her students needed sleep.

"I know, right?" Angus said matter-of-factly. They drove up to a tall, white guardhouse, and out of its skinny door stepped a young, blue-uniformed guard with a black rifle slung over his shoulder. The guard leaned into the car window, which Angus had rolled down. "Hi, Jimmy."

"Hey, Teach!" the guard said, grinning broadly. He had brown eyes under the patent-leather bill of his cap and sported a small, dark mustache over unevenly spaced teeth. "You brought a new student? Hi, honey."

"Keep it classy," Angus said, mock-stern. "This is Professor Greco. She's lecturing here today."

"Oh, jeez." The guard shifted his cap up, instantly sheepish. "Sorry."

"It's okay." Nat waved him off, and Angus thanked the guard and hit the gas. Nat asked, "Don't we have to show him any ID?"

"Nah. He knows me."

"I have to show ID in a store, when I use a credit card."

"Like I said, minimum security." Angus shrugged, but Nat didn't get it.

"More minimum than J.Crew, yet not so minimum that the guard doesn't carry a gun."

"Exactly." The VW traveled up a single-lane paved road to a small, elevated parking lot. Freshly plowed snow sat piled around the perimeter of the lot, decreasing the number of spaces. Angus continued, "Inside, none of the guards is armed. I should say C.O.s. Corrections officers. They don't like when we call them guards. They're nice guys, most of 'em."

"They don't have guns inside?" Nat's tone said, *You told me it was safe.*

"No. It's standard in prisons. Most of the C.O.'s treat the inmates with respect, but still as a group. Like a lower caste, not like each one is an individual. The C.O.s have to, to manage them. But in my class, I try to make up for that."

Nat sensed that Angus was climbing a soapbox, but she didn't mind. Passion did that to people. She'd sound the same way if anybody asked her about Abraham Lincoln. She loved reminding her students that he was a lawyer. Nobody believed her.

"Rehabilitation is essential here. These men are inside for only two years, so they're getting out again. They're in for misdemeanors and nonviolent offenses. Petty larceny, burglary, fraud. Chester County offers drug and alcohol counseling, and job training like heating and air conditioning, auto repair, even haircutting."

Bad to worse. "With scissors?"

"Sure, and the inmates who work in the kitchen use knives."

"Great."

"Don't worry." Angus steered the car into the parking lot. "They hang up the scissors and knives in glass cases, on pegboards painted with the shape of the tool, and when the inmates are finished, a C.O.

locks the cases." He found a space, and Nat noticed that many of the cars were idling, with white plumes of exhaust puffing from their tail-pipes.

"What's up with the cars?"

"They're inmate families, waiting for visiting hours to start." Angus put on the emergency brake and looked over at Nat with a smile. "Let's rock. Bring your driver's license but leave your handbag. Only legal papers are allowed. Do you have lecture notes?"

"Yes." Nat retrieved her accordion file, and they got out of the car. She stepped into the cold and clasped her file to her chest like a security blanket, surveying the scene.

The prison complex was situated on a large, flat tray of snow-covered land, which looked as if it had been created by cutting the top off of one of the hills. A tall blue water tower stood behind the compound. The prison itself was a sprawling brick edifice shaped like a T, with a public entrance and largish windows at the bottom of the T, in front of a circular driveway. The no-joke end of the prison was the body and top of the T, where the windows were ugly slits. Double rows of cyclone fencing topped with razorwire surrounded that section. The compound was discreetly screened from the surrounding neighborhood by a man-made forest of tall, full evergreens, encircling the entire property.

"It's something, isn't it?" Angus asked. His breath made a cloud in the cold air. "Lovely setting for a place with no windows."

"It's crime and punishment."

"So they say."

"Didn't you bring a coat? It's freezing out."

"Too manly. Let's go." Angus touched her back, and they walked up a long plowed road, their shoes crunching in the salt and ice patches. They reached the circular driveway, which was lined with black prison vans and a grimy Chevy pickup loaded with lumber and covered with a blue tarp that flapped in the wind. Behind the truck sat a construction trailer with a plastic sign that read, PHOENIX CON-STRUCTION, some white propane tanks, and a pallet of cinderblocks. Ahead lay the prison entrance.

Nat tried to shake off her nerves, and Angus slowed their pace as they passed a dark blue sedan with its engine running. Two men in dark suits and ties sat in the front seat. Angus pointed. "Look, *federales*."

"What?" Nat asked, but he was already walking up to the car and knocking on the driver's window.

"We don't need no stinking badges," Angus said as the window slid down, and the driver laughed. He wore Ray-Ban sunglasses and held a slim can of Red Bull.

"The original army of one!" the driver said, and Angus flashed a peace sign.

"Ha! I prefer the loyal opposition."

"Who're you suing today, Holt? Somebody miss yoga?"

"Don't give me any ideas," Angus shot back, and they laughed as the window slid back up. Angus touched Nat's elbow, and they resumed walking. "Those poor guys, they're federal marshals, bored to tears. That's the truest thing about this place. This prison, any prison, whether it's a supermax or a playpen. The inmates, the C.O.s, the staff—they're just so damned *bored*. Everybody who's ever been inside will tell you. Every day, it's the same as the last."

"Why are marshals here?"

"The prison takes in federal prisoners on a courtesy hold. They got one guy here, all by himself in maximum security. The marshals maintain an official presence until he goes to trial in Philly."

"What'd he do?" Nat asked, as they reached the entrance, a windowless metal door painted red, a strangely cheery color against the industrial brown of the facility. "I mean, allegedly."

"Oh, he did it." Angus smiled wryly. "It's Richard Williams. Distribution, murder, the whole enchilada." He pulled open the door and waved her inside.

"Thanks." Nat stepped into a tiny room with bars all around, like the elevator to hell. She told herself not to be afraid.

Or, at least, not to let it show.

CHAPTER 5

Once inside the prison, Nat and Angus produced ID, left her coat in a locker, and were ushered through three sets of locked, barred doors, called sally ports. Bulletproof glass covered the bars, which were painted the same cherry red as the entrance. They checked in at the command center and were funneled together through a metal detector and cattle chute to a final set of locked doors, which a female C.O. unlocked and pulled open, greeting Angus with an attitudinal smirk.

"Yo, Holt. Nice suit." The C.O., an African American, had large brown eyes and looked fit and trim in her navy blue uniform. A strand of dark hair curled like a shiny fishhook in front of her ears. "News flash. Jerry Garcia's dead."

"That never gets old." Angus grinned. "Tanisa Shields, meet my colleague, Natalie Greco."

"Hiya." Tanisa shook Nat's hand, but her gaze didn't leave Angus. "Take a lesson, Holt. This girl knows how to dress."

"But I'm wearing my lucky sweater," Angus said, and Tanisa snorted.

"Yeah. Lucky I don't set it *on fire.*"

Nat stayed happily out of the fray. She'd changed her clothes five times this morning, mentally going from nun's habit to pup tent to down comforter. She'd finally settled on a brown tweed pantsuit, white tailored shirt, and a Hermès scarf in granny pastels. Hank would have approved of the outfit, but he'd left for work early and never got to see it, or to hear that she'd be at a prison today. That, he might not have approved.

"You gotta lose that beard, too." Tanisa clucked. "Looks like you got a damn *dog* stuck to your chin." She slammed the bars shut behind the three of them with a ringing *clang*, then locked the door with a large, crude key.

"I love a woman in uniform," Angus said, but Nat wasn't laughing. *I'm locked inside.*

Tanisa turned on the rubber heel of her patent work shoe and led them into a wide hallway that appeared to run the length of the building, presumably the body of the T. A black male C.O. stood against the wall and he acknowledged Angus with a nod. The lower half of the wall was mint-green cinderblock, and the top half bulletproof glass, which exposed the inside of the rooms that lined the hallway. A floor of polished concrete shone dully, and the air felt hot and dry, overheated.

"Stop right there." Tanisa stiffened her arm, holding them back, and Nat felt herself tense. A line of red lightbulbs protruding from the ceiling flashed on suddenly.

"What's going on?" Nat asked, and Angus turned.

"At the end of the hall are the residential pods, and whenever the C.O.s move the inmates across the hallway, the red lights go on. Wait a sec."

"Okay." Nat exchanged looks with the male C.O., who gave her a reassuring wink. In the next minute, inmates in white T-shirts and loose blue pants shuffled as a group from one side of the hall to the other, talking and laughing. Even though they were far away, a few spotted Angus and waved to him, and he waved back.

"My kids," he said softly.

Tanisa chuckled. "Then you need a new family."

Angus said to Nat, "It's only in the movies that a prison eats and exercises together. Inmates live, eat, and exercise in the same pod, which is corrections-speak for cellblock. That's why they're remodeling this facility, to build new pods."

Nat nodded. The inmates kept crossing the hall, the red warning lights flashing.

Angus continued, "They keep movement between pods to an absolute minimum and break up gang members among the pods. Here it's mostly Hispanic gangs, then Aryans and African Americans."

"I didn't know there were that many Hispanics in Chester County." Nat had always thought it was whiter than white out here, but she could see from the moving stream of inmates that her demographics had been wrong.

"They come up from Mexico to work on the mushroom farms and fancy horse farms. Some are gangbangers. It's East L.A. come to Chester County." Angus patted her shoulder. "Don't worry. The gangbangers live in RHU, the rehabilitation unit farther down the hall, far from our classroom."

Good.

"That's the processing room, where they handle intake and paperwork for the inmates." Angus pointed to the left, near them. "Here's our classroom, next to it is the infirmary, and behind that extra pods, temporarily converted to infirmary space. They're short some beds."

"This gonna be on the test?" Tanisa asked, and Angus smiled.

"How's your son, by the way?"

"Better, thanks." Tanisa turned away, lowering her arm as the stream of inmates ceased and the bars were locked behind them. The red lights blinked off. "Okay, time to make the doughnuts."

"This way, Natalie," Angus said, and they walked a few steps and entered an empty room off the hallway, its bottom half cinderblock painted white and its top the bulletproof glass. Bucket chairs in white plastic sat scattered around a white Formica table, and on the wall hung a greaseboard. On the board, ACTIONS was scribbled in black Sharpie, with an arrow leading to CONSEQUENCES. It seemed so clichéd that if Nat hadn't seen it, she never would have believed it.

"I'll go get 'em." Tanisa turned, leaving the door open. "Be right back."

"The heat's good, at least," Nat said after the C.O. was gone, just for something to say. The air in the room was hotter than the hallway, bringing up the smell of institutional disinfectant and body odor. She understood now why the inmates wore only undershirts and she instantly regretted her wool suit. Tweed was so supermax.

"It's because of the construction. Excuse me a sec." Angus took off his fisherman's sweater, yanking it over his head until his ponytail popped free. He tossed the sweater, inside out, onto the table. "Parts of the building are open, and the cold air gets in, so the thermostat overcompensates. It's been like this all winter."

"Tanisa will guard us during class, right?" Nat asked, but just then inmates began to file in through the open door—about fifteen men in T-shirts and blue scrub pants, worn with a variety of nondescript cotton sneakers. All shapes, colors, and sizes of men were represented; inmates had mustaches, plastic glasses, neck tattoos, and a gold chain or two, but they were all about the same age range, in their thirties.

"Good morning, gentlemen," Angus said with a smile, stepping to the head of the table. "How you all been?"

"Fine," answered a thin inmate, taking the first chair. The other inmates answered "good" and "good to see ya" with obvious warmth as they walked around the table and settled into their seats.

"See y'all," Tanisa said, then left, and no other C.O. came to replace her, which was when Nat got her answer.

Yikes! She and Angus were going to be unguarded, and the inmates weren't wearing handcuffs. Again, if she weren't living it, she wouldn't believe it was done this way. Angus rolled up the sleeves of his work-shirt, and Nat held her papers to her chest, sweating through two layers of clothes and one security blanket. She avoided eye contact with the inmates, who seemed to look away from her, too, their heads down and manner subdued, like a class that hasn't done the reading. Ever, in their whole life.

Angus rubbed his hands together. "Gentlemen, I thought we'd do something different today, because by now you most definitely need a break from the Personal Choices lecture."

They all chuckled, and Nat braced herself to get started.

"This is Professor Natalie Greco, and she teaches a class called the History of Justice, in which she talks about law and justice. Is that something you gentlemen have any views on?"

"*Hell,* yes!" a heavy inmate called out, and they all laughed.

"Good. Now, before we get started, I see two new folks in the group." Angus gestured toward the end of the table, where two inmates sat, one burly and tattooed, and the other slimmer and wearing glasses held together with Scotch tape. "I'm sorry, do I know you two?"

"Kyle Buford," answered the burly inmate. Crude blue tattoos blanketed his overdeveloped biceps.

"Pat Donnell," said the one with the broken glasses.

Angus frowned slightly. "Who admitted you gentlemen to the class? I don't remember getting your files."

"I dunno," Buford answered, and Donnell nodded. "They just told us to come and start today. I guess we were next on the list."

"I'll look into that, but welcome. Please, everybody, go around the table and tell Professor Greco your name. We'll make like summer camp, only it ain't summer and it sure as hell ain't camp."

The inmates laughed again and introduced themselves to Nat one by one, which put her more at ease. Their names, their voices, and their smiles transformed them from anonymous inmates to people, and it perked them up, too. Their aspect seemed collectively to change, eyes brightening and chins rising, and they shifted forward in their seats, as if they'd reclaimed their identities. She remembered Angus saying that he treated the inmates as individuals, and she could see its effect.

"I almost forgot. Before we start, some old business. Remember we spoke last week about the staph infection issue?" Angus paused, and heads nodded. "I wrote the warden a letter, and he says there will be no transfers because of MSRA."

"Come on, bro!" an inmate said, scowling, and the other inmates started grumbling. One called out, "You can *die* from that sh— *thing!*"

"Sorry, but that's the best I can do." Angus held up an authoritative hand in his loose workshirt, its baggy elbows thinned to a soft, washed blue. "MSRA is a common bacterial infection in prisons. Also in hospitals and schools, by the way. They're not gonna start transferring your ass outta here. This is the newest prison in the county. None of them is as clean as this one."

"That's 'cause they got *me* cleanin' it," a younger inmate called out, a gold crucifix looping his neck. Everybody laughed, even Nat.

Angus continued. "Allegheny County is where those two guys died, and you're better off here. Wash your hands as much as you can. The warden did agree that anybody with an open cut has an expedited pass to the infirmary. Just let one of the C.O.s know."

"How much we owe you, mouthpiece?" the inmate with the crucifix asked, and everybody laughed.

"Nothing, and please, don't shake my hand." Angus shoved his hands in his pockets, and they all laughed again, including the skinny inmate in the front, who raised his arm cautiously.

"Can I ask a question, Angus?"

"Sure, what?"

"Isn't Damian coming today?" The inmate was so thin, the bones of his sternum showed through the V-neck of his undershirt. "I wrote up some facts for my petition. He said he wanted it."

"No, sorry. Damian's sick. Give it to me, and I'll make sure he gets it." Angus picked up the brown folder that the inmate slid across the table, opened it, and skimmed some papers, typed in old-fashioned Courier font. "Looks good, Jim. Great job. You had a public defender at trial, right?"

"He had a *pubic* defender!" interrupted Buford, the tattooed inmate.

Yuck. Nat stiffened.

Angus looked up with a deep frown. "That's enough of that, Kyle. We have a guest today."

"Only jokin', man." Buford looked away, his reddish blue eyes scanning the others for approval.

"We don't joke like that here," Angus snapped. "You're new, but you know better. If you wouldn't say it in front of a C.O., you don't say it here. Please apologize to our guest."

"That's okay," Nat interjected, wanting it to be over. "It's all right."

"Ready to start then?"

No way. "Sure." Nat stepped forward as Angus stood aside, setting her accordion file on the table but not feeling brave enough to get her notes. She could teach the lesson by heart, though it would be hard to stay on message with Buford's eyes boring holes into her underwire.

"Well," Nat began, "thanks for having me today. Before I start, let me ask you a question. Has anybody read *The Merchant of Venice*?"

The inmates' expressions went uniformly slack, which she should have expected. At the end of the table, Buford chuckled and shook his head. Angus folded his arms and glared at him.

An inmate raised his hand. "I think we read it in high school. It's from Shakespeare, right?"

"Yes." Nat smiled, then got a better idea. "Let me ask you this instead: How many of you know what a shylock is?"

"You mean a shy?" the heavy inmate asked.

"Like a dude who lends you money?" another chimed in, and every hand shot up around the table, the inmates' faces quickly reanimating. They *wanted* to learn, she just had to figure out a way to reach them.

Buford lifted his illustrated arm. "I'm hot for teacher," he said, then burst into laughter.

"That's it." Angus stepped forward, his expression grim. "You're outta here, and I'm making sure that—"

Suddenly a siren outside the door burst into an earsplitting alarm. Nat jumped at the sound. Angus whirled to look out the door. Eyes flew open around the table. The inmates started leaping out of their chairs, shoving them and each other aside and shouting, "Lockdown!" "Go, go, go!" "It's the lockdown siren. We gotta go!" Inmates bolted for the door, bottlenecking at the threshold.

The announcement system burst into sound: "We are in lockdown! Repeat, lockdown! All inmates proceed to their pods without delay! All inmates proceed directly to their pods!" The male C.O. who had been standing outside the room took off down the corridor.

"What's happening?" Nat yelled, beginning to panic.

"Stay with me!" Angus grabbed her hand, yanking her out of harm's way just as the inmates rounded the table, heading for the door.

"Move, lady!" they shouted.

"Go, go, go!"

"We gotta get outta here!"

"Haul ass!"

Suddenly Nat felt like she'd been hit by a truck. It was Kyle Buford, barreling into her. The impact threw her backward, knocking the wind out of her. She tried to get out of his way, but he was in her face, so close she could smell his breath. Then she realized that Buford wasn't trying to get to the door, he was trying to get to *her*.

Nat screamed as Buford wrapped his arms around her, squeezing her tight and tackling her. She fell backward and banged her head and tailbone against the concrete floor. Pain arced through her head and back, momentarily immobilizing her as Buford clambered on top of her. Tears of fright sprang to her eyes. She couldn't catch her breath. His body was a deadweight. She couldn't believe this was happening. It was chaos. Everything was unfolding too fast to process.

Angus grabbed Buford by the shoulders, but the inmate twisted around and elbowed him viciously in the mouth, sending him staggering backward. Nat punched out with her fists. Buford grabbed a clump of her hair and slammed her head into the concrete. Her head exploded in agony. Her hands stopped punching and fell back against the floor. Buford was on her, trying to kiss her, his tongue thrusting into her mouth.

No please don't!

Nat flailed out but couldn't stay conscious. The siren sounded far away. The loudspeaker announcement blared from another place and time. Angus grabbed Buford again, but the inmate threw himself back down on Nat, covering her like a mad dog, clawing her shirt open.

God! No!

Buford reached her bra and grabbed her breasts. She hit him but then went weak. Her head thundered. She couldn't stay awake. She couldn't stop him. The room went dark.

CHAPTER 6

L ET HER GO!" Angus shouted, and the sheer terror in his voice brought Nat back from the brink. Her eyes flew open. Angus grabbed Buford by the neck and roared like a raging animal as he wrapped his hands around the inmate's tattooed throat and squeezed, choking him. Nat punched and kicked, twisting this way and that, trying to squirm away.

"You little *bitch!*" Buford shouted, his spittle hot on her face.

"Get off!" Nat screamed in fury, then reached up and bit Buford hard on his unshaven cheek. The inmate howled and reared back, and Angus jumped in and punched him, then hit him again and again. Nat felt Buford's grip loosen, and with one mighty heave, she pushed him away while Angus yanked him from above. Nat scooted backward like a crab as Buford turned to punch Angus, who hit him first, connecting squarely with the inmate's temple.

"Natalie! *Run!*" Angus yelled, a split second before Buford recovered and hit him in the neck. Nat watched in horror as Angus's eyes bulged and his face contorted in agony. His hand flew to his neck, and he staggered backward. "GO!" he managed to yell.

Nat scrambled to her feet as a bloodied Angus picked up a bucket chair and swung it at Buford, but by then she was bolting out of the classroom. She darted into the hallway. The prison had gone into battle mode. The sirens blared. The loudspeaker barked. She smelled smoke. A SWAT team in bulletproof vests and dark full-face visors poured into the hall and thundered in formation toward the RHU.

"Help!" Nat grabbed the sleeve of a SWAT guy running by, but he didn't stop.

"Gotta go!" he shouted over his shoulder. Yelling and screams erupted from down the hall. There must be a riot in the RHU. It was every man for himself. Nat ran to the entrance door and yanked on the bars. They didn't budge, locked.

No! She banged on the bulletproof glass of the command center. No one was inside. She couldn't get out. She had to find help. She prayed that Angus was holding his own. Where the hell was help? She didn't know the prison layout. She turned around wildly and screamed at the sight. A C.O. and an inmate were fighting in one of the other rooms.

Nat ran the other way in fear. Her blouse billowed open and she closed it on the run, spotting a hall of doors. She ran down it, shouting for help over the cacophony of sirens and alarms. She tried the first closed door, but it was locked, then the next and the next. All were locked. Her heart raced. She felt warm tears welling in her eyes. This was taking too long. Buford could kill Angus. She ran down the next corridor, amazed and relieved to see a door opening.

"Help!" Nat ran for it just as a stricken and bloodied C.O. came out of the room, leaving the door open on a horrifying scene.

"They've gone crazy, they've all gone crazy." The C.O. was physically shaking, and behind him, another C.O. lay on the floor, a makeshift knife plunged into his chest. A muscle-bound African American inmate lay curled next to the C.O., blood soaking his T-shirt. Both men looked dead, and the C.O. at the door was in shock.

"You have to help me!" Nat grabbed his shoulders. "My friend's being attacked!"

"What? Where?" the C.O. asked, his dark eyes focusing as he came to his senses.

"The classroom near the entrance." Nat pointed behind her. "Angus Holt. We were teaching. And another C.O. needs help in the hallway."

"Shit!" The C.O. took off running, just as Nat heard a moan from the room and looked toward the sound. The C.O. on the ground was still moving, the homemade metal knife protruding grotesquely from his chest. He turned his head toward the door and stretched his hand to her, across the floor.

He's still alive. Nat ran into the room and knelt beside the man, horrified. She could barely look at his chest. She knew to leave the knife in place. She'd read it somewhere. He'd lose more blood if she pulled it out. Blood soaked the pocket of his blue uniform, but not from the knife. He had another stab wound.

Nat pressed her hand over the wound. Hot blood burbled through her fingers, and she felt sick to her stomach. The C.O.'s face had gone ashen. She had to stop the blood flow. She yanked her silk scarf off her neck, wadded it into a ball, and pressed it as hard as she could against his wound. If she could stop the blood, she could keep him alive until help came.

"It's okay, it's okay," she said, over and over. Her heart hammered. She prayed that the other C.O. had found Angus. She couldn't leave this one. He focused on her. Then his blue eyes rolled back into his eye sockets. In the next instant, she felt his hand squeezing her forearm as if in a death grip.

"Hang in, please, hang in." Nat felt her tears welling again. She pressed harder with her scarf. Its silk ran red with fresh blood, warm under her cupped palm. The C.O.'s lips were moving. Blood bubbled from his mouth and leaked down the side of his face. He tugged on her arm. He was trying to say something.

"Tell . . . my wife," he whispered. Blood hiccupped from his mouth, a sight so grisly Nat almost cried out. He said, "*Please*. Tell her."

"I will, I will. I'll tell her you love her," Nat said, finishing his sentence, her words rushing out in a choked sob.

"No, no," the C.O. moaned, shaking his head. "No. It's . . . under the floor."

What? Nat blinked, shaken. What did he say? Between the sirens and her shock, she could hardly hear him. She leaned over, her ear to his mouth. "What did you say?"

"Tell . . . her." The C.O. struggled for breath. "Tell her it's . . . under the floor."

"Okay, I'll tell her, I promise." Nat pressed hard but blood soaked the scarf. In the next second, the C.O.'s eyelids stopped fluttering. His blue eyes fixed. The grip on her arm loosened abruptly. His hand fell back, the fingers still bent.

"No!" Nat knew CPR. She couldn't let him die. She bent over, pinched his lips open, and huffed into his mouth, tasting salty, hot blood. Two breaths, then she straightened up and pressed with all her might on his chest.

One, two, three, four. "Please, come back!" Nat bore down, pressing hard. The scarf fell off him. Blood bubbled gruesomely from the other wound. She kept pressing and counting. The C.O.'s eyes didn't move. He didn't react to her shouts. She finished the count of chest palpitations and bent over again, trying to breathe life into him.

She kept pressing. She heard a sickening gurgling from his throat, and in the background, faraway shouts. Suddenly, an explosion resonated in her chest. What the hell was going on? Where had that come from? The RHU? What had blown up?

Nat struggled not to panic. She kept pressing, but the C.O. didn't move. She bent over and huffed a short, powerful breath into his mouth, then stopped. The poor man was dead. She had to let him go. She had tried her best. She had to get to Angus. The explosion.

"I'm so sorry," she whispered. She wiped her eyes, streaking warmth across her face. Blood. She scrambled to her feet and ran from the room and into the hallway. A siren blared a continuous state of emergency. The lockdown announcement blasted over and over. Smoke wafted down the corridor, layering the air with gray streaks.

She ran down the hall, veered around the corner, and sprinted for the classroom. Thick smoke billowed down the hall, singeing her eyes and filling her nostrils. She took a breath and felt herself gag. There was a fire in the prison, and she was locked inside. So was Angus. They would all burn to death.

Suddenly there came the deafening blast of a percussive explosion. Nat was thrown to the floor. The side of her face hit the concrete. Her knees slammed down hard. She rolled in shock and pain into the cinderblock wall.

"NATALIE!"

Nat opened her eyes to see Angus running through the smoke to her. He reached her, knelt down, and scooped her up in his arms.

"Your Grace." He grinned, his forehead bleeding, and Nat felt a rush of relief that approached delirium. Behind him was the C.O. she'd sent to him.

"This way!" the C.O. shouted. "Move!" He hustled them to the barred door at the entrance, where another C.O. in black SWAT gear met them, unlocked the door, and hurried them all out of the prison and into the cold.

CHAPTER 7

Wrapped in a thin blue blanket, Nat sat on a gurney in the back of an idling ambulance, while an EMT dressed the gash on her cheek. He was thirtyish, with prematurely salt-and-pepper hair and earnest brown eyes behind steel-rimmed glasses. He wore a bunchy nylon jacket over his blue uniform, which bore a bright patch Nat didn't bother to read. She had forgotten the EMT's name. She had been here an hour, and her thoughts were still scrambled. She felt shaken, sad, and so exhausted she was almost sleepy.

"One more minute." The paramedic dabbed goopy Neosporin onto her cheek, his hands encased in latex gloves of pale purple.

Ouch. "Thanks."

"How's your head? Better?"

"Yes, thanks," Nat answered. The throbbing had almost stopped. Her knees and butt felt tender. She pulled the blanket closer, covering her torn shirt; the ambulance was drafty. The parking lot outside the prison was serving as a makeshift infirmary and staging area for the cops and press who swarmed the compound.

"Okay, let's cover this baby up." The paramedic unlatched a stainless steel drawer, retrieved a box of butterfly bandages, and opened it. While he worked, Nat spotted Angus through the ambulance's back window. A gauze bandage covered part of his forehead, and he still had on his bloody workshirt. He was talking with two tall state troopers in stiff, wide-brimmed hats set at a slightly forward angle. They wore gray uniforms with black insulated jackets and heavy gun belts. Angus gestured to the troopers, who squared off, arms folded identically, at a distance from him. He was clearly pissing them off, so he must have been feeling better.

This is my lucky sweater.

Nat sipped water from a Poland Spring bottle. Was it even the same day that Angus had said that? She tried to block out the image of the C.O. bleeding to death on the rug, blood hiccupping from his mouth. She hadn't even known that was possible. She had never seen anybody die before. She couldn't shake the memory.

"Okay, you're all done." The paramedic pressed the butterfly bandage gingerly into place. "You'll be sore for a while, but I don't think anything's broken. Like I said, just to be on the safe side, I'd get to the hospital and talk to a doc. Any concussion can be serious. You're a little lady to be in such a big fight."

"Thanks." Nat was only half listening as she watched Angus. He was gesturing more emphatically, and one of the troopers was gesturing back. It looked like a sixties rewind, the longhair vs. the cops.

"Last point I should mention." The paramedic closed the bandage box, slid it back into the drawer, and latched the drawer. "You should get yourself an AIDS test. The blood on your hands can't all be yours."

Nat looked down at her hands, clutching the blanket. Dried blood stained the wells between her fingers, had found its way into her cuticles, and delineated the lines on the back of her hand, like a macabre ink drawing. Now she knew what fresh blood smelled and even tasted like, and she wished she didn't. Maybe her mother was right. Maybe you don't need to know everything.

"You have any questions, about the dressing or anything?"

"Yes."

"Okay, shoot."

"There was a C.O., a guard, inside." Nat swallowed hard. "He had a knife in his chest . . . and another wound. I found him. There was blood . . . everywhere. I know CPR. I did CPR on him."

"Oh, it was a guard's blood? Well, officially I'm telling you to get the test, but between us, you don't have to worry. The guards are tested for AIDS in their annual, so you should be fine."

"No, it's not that. I tried to help him, but I couldn't." Nat didn't know why she was even telling him this. "I wonder if I could have tried something else, or done something better than I did—"

"I see," the paramedic said softly. "I know what you're worried about, and you shouldn't be. I saw him when they carried him out. He didn't have a chance. That shiv in his chest, there was nothing you could have done." He placed a hand on Nat's arm to comfort her, but it reminded her of the C.O.'s death grip.

"What could I have done better, or different? You're an expert. What could you have done?"

"There was nothing I could have done."

Tell my wife. Nat tried to block out the words. The whisper.

"Don't blame yourself." The paramedic eased back onto the black-padded bench seat across from the gurney, and he gazed at her in a steady, centering way. "Believe me, I've had to let a lot of really nice people go. Old people. Someone's mom. Or kids, really little ones. You'll never get used to it. Natural deaths I can deal with. But violent death, it's the worst. Car accidents are the worst. Pool drownings, the worst." He shook his head. "It's all the worst."

Nat knew what he meant, now. It was the carnage. Human beings, butchered like so much meat. The C.O. and the inmate, lying dead.

"We don't get a lot of this out here, not as much as Philly. But we get some business from Chester, that's for sure. Considering the knife wounds that man had, it was a miracle he was alive when you found him."

Tell my wife. "He . . . talked to me."

"You heard his last words?"

Nat nodded. She couldn't speak. Maybe the C.O. was waiting to tell somebody. Maybe that was why he hadn't yet died when she got to him.

"Now I understand. Now I get it. Okay." The paramedic sighed, leaning over on his haunches in his bunchy jacket. "That's happened to me more than a few times, and it's tough."

Nat struggled to remain in control. For a minute she felt as if she were talking to a priest. Or Dr. Phil.

"This is how I look at it," the paramedic said after a moment. "What happened to you, it's sacred. You heard a man's most personal, intimate words. But it's kinda goofy because you're a stranger."

Nat nodded.

"That's how you feel, right? It's goofy?"

Random, her students would have said.

"Listen, once a man dying in a car wreck told me he had a daughter no one knew about. He wanted to keep it secret but he had to unburden himself. To someone, even a stranger." The paramedic paused, his forehead creased with the memory. "Sometimes they give you a message for someone they love. For their wife, or their son. I used to feel like I wished I hadn't heard it, like it was a burden. I almost quit this gig."

Tell my wife.

"But I was talking to one of my buddies, and he said, 'just flip it.' Think about it different, because there was a reason they told it to you. It wasn't a burden, it was a gift." The paramedic patted her arm again. "Okay?"

"Okay," Nat said thickly.

"If he gave you a message for someone, deliver it. You can't avoid it, anyway." The paramedic smiled, almost ruefully. "In my experience, the loved one will seek you out and give you the third degree. Be prepared for that. They'll want to know, 'What were his last words?' 'Did he say he loved me?' 'Was she thinking of me?' 'Did she suffer?' They'll ask you everything." He shook his head. "My last piece of advice? Don't pretty it up. Don't tell 'em what they want to hear. You're just the messenger. Tell the truth."

Tell my wife.

"I got a question from one widow, after her husband died in a car accident. She wanted to know if he'd said the name Sonya. I told her, 'No, I'm very sorry, he didn't say your name.' She said, 'Good. My name's Lillian. Sonya's his girlfriend.'" The paramedic laughed, and Nat managed a smile, because he was trying to cheer her up.

Tell my wife. The words were still there when she stopped laughing. They weren't going away anytime soon.

"If you go to the hospital, they can give you something to calm you down a little. Help you with the pain, too." The paramedic gave her a final pat. "Drugs, I can't dispense. Advice, you don't need a license for."

"I'm fine, thanks." Nat looked out the window to see Angus striding to her ambulance, ahead of the two state police troopers. She wondered who had won the argument, because nobody looked happy. She rose unsteadily. "Here they come. The cops and my colleague."

"Stop. Sit down a minute." The paramedic eased her back onto the gurney, which wasn't difficult. "You can talk to them here. I'll go out and see if anybody needs me."

"Do you need the ambulance?"

"Nah, anybody's who's going to the hospital has already gone. If I get a call from dispatch, I'll throw you out."

"Thanks for your help," Nat said, and the paramedic rose, crossed to the door, and left, letting in a blast of frigid air.

Angus stuck his head inside, and Nat gasped.

CHAPTER 8

Up close, Angus's face was a wreck. Under the gauze pad, his right eye puffed up, a rosy color. A nasty bruise blanketed his left cheek, and black stitches puckered his lip. Blood spattered the front of his workshirt. "How's the patient?" he asked, his blue eyes concerned, nevertheless. "You all right?"

"Better than you, I think."

"Oh, you mean this?" Angus pointed at his mouth with a puffy grin. "Only when I laugh. But we have a more pressing subject than my rugged good looks." He leaned into the ambulance, his long arms braced on each door, effectively blocking two state troopers behind him. "Got the staties with me, since they don't have local police out here."

"No local police?" Nat didn't understand.

"It's common in rural areas. They can't afford a local force, so they rely on state police. They interviewed me but they still want to talk to you, to support the charges against Buford. I told them this isn't the place or the time."

Nat shuddered. Buford. His breath. His hands.

"Tell me you don't feel up to talking to them, and I'll tell them to take a hike."

"Mr. Holt, that's not your call." The trooper's dark eyes flashed under his wide brim, though his voice remained under control. "You're interfering with police business. It's important that we interview her while her memory's still fresh."

"Show a little sensitivity, would you? She's a crime victim, and you don't need her statement. I'm an eyewitness. I gave you my statement." Angus raised his voice, but the trooper ignored him and turned to Nat.

"Ms. Greco, we understand that this is difficult, and we're prepared to make it as easy as possible. We'll interview you here, rather than asking you to come down to the barracks."

"It can wait until tomorrow or the next day," Angus interjected, but Nat waved him off.

"I can give it now. Let's get it over with." Nat didn't want a fight. She'd seen enough fighting for a lifetime.

"They're being ridiculous." Angus pursed his stitched lips. "You should be going to a hospital, not giving a statement to support a charge they can file right now."

"It's fine, thanks." Nat wrapped the blankets closer around her. "Come in, please, everybody."

Angus harrumphed under his breath and stepped into the ambulance ahead of the troopers, ducking his head to fit inside. His boots clomped on the corrugated-metal floor as he crossed to Nat. He sat heavily beside her on the gurney, which squeaked under his weight. He bristled with pique, but when he looked over at her, his eyes softened. "I'm so sorry, about all of this. I wouldn't have brought you here if I had thought it was unsafe."

"I know that." Nat heard the guilt behind his words.

"I can't apologize enough. I'm so sorry."

"We're both okay, and that's what matters," Nat said, meaning it.

"Take this, by the way." Angus set an insulated black jacket onto her lap. "For the ride home. I got it from Tanisa. She wanted you to have it. I'm not sure when you're getting your coat back."

"Thanks." Nat took the jacket, happy to learn that the C.O. was safe. In the meantime, the troopers were climbing into the ambulance and closing the doors behind them. They also ducked to walk inside, and the ambulance bounced at the additional weight. They seated themselves on the padded bench opposite Nat and Angus, like the double date from hell.

"I'm Trooper Bert Milroy, with the state police," one trooper said. He was maybe forty years old, with a handsome face, cool blue eyes, and a long, bony nose, red at the tip from the cold. He gestured at the trooper next to him, who had thinner lips and looked younger with faint acne scars on his cheeks. "This is my partner, Trooper Russ Johnston. We'll keep this short, because I know it isn't easy for you." The trooper leaned over, slid a steno pad from his back pocket, and flipped back the cardboard cover. "Do you feel well enough to speak with us? Did you want to go to the hospital or anything?"

"No, thanks." Nat raised a hand, in the blanket. "First, can you tell me what happened in there? Is it really over?"

"Absolutely." The trooper slid a Bic pen from his inside pocket. "The disturbance took only sixteen minutes to put down."

"Sixteen minutes?" Nat almost laughed. "It seemed like a lot longer."

"It was," Angus interjected flatly.

"But what happened?" Nat asked. "There was a riot in the RHU, right?"

"Not a riot. A disturbance."

Angus chuckled. "Let the spinning begin."

The trooper paused, pointedly. "As I was saying, Ms. Greco, inmates in the RHU got into an altercation over a gang issue. Three were killed and four seriously injured."

Tell my wife. "A guard was killed, too."

"Yes, and two others seriously injured."

"What was his name, the C.O. who died?"

Trooper Milroy flipped through his notes. "Ray Saunders, I believe. No, Ron. First name's Ron. His wife was just notified. As I was saying, the prison SWAT team put it down in record time, preventing further loss of life. We've arrested four individuals in connection with the murders. Charges will be brought against Mr. Buford as soon as possible"—at this, the trooper shifted his ice blue gaze to Angus—"but we dot our *i*'s."

Nat tried to process it all. "There was fire. I saw smoke."

"A few of the inmates set their mattresses on fire."

"I heard explosions. What was that?"

"The SWAT team."

"The SWAT team uses *bombs?*" Nat was confused.

"No, the explosions would be the stingers from the SWAT team," the trooper answered.

"What's a stinger?"

"A device that is fired at the floor and explodes in thousands of rubber pellets—"

"Not that many, Bert," the other trooper said, and Trooper Milroy frowned, annoyed.

"Okay, not thousands, but a lot, and they sting. They stop a man in his tracks without lethal force. The SWAT team performed superbly." Trooper Milroy raised his pen. "Now, please tell us, in your own words, exactly what happened from when you and Mr. Holt began your class this morning."

Nat took a deep breath, and between sips of water, began a scary instant replay. She got to the part where Buford ripped her shirt and began to think that maybe Angus had been right, she wasn't ready to tell this yet. Her mouth went dry, and she was strangely afraid, even surrounded by police. She felt an instant kinship with every woman who had ever been the victim of violent crime. Questions entered her mind, about what could have happened. How do you live through something like that? What would Hank say? Her father? What if it had happened in front of Angus? Would she have been able to look him in the eye at school, and vice versa? By the time she finished the story, she'd drained her water bottle.

"What happened after you ran from the classroom?" Trooper Milroy asked, scribbling.

"I ran to get help."

"Did you find any?"

"Yes. I found a C.O. coming out of a room. I asked him to help, and he came."

"Can you be more specific?"

Nat paused. She was thinking of the other C.O., who now had a name. Ron Saunders. The blood. His fixed stare. She went into a stall.

"Ms. Greco?" the trooper asked, and Angus turned to her, his gaze sympathetic.

"Natalie, you want to stop now?"

"I'm okay," she said, but Angus was frowning.

"Wait a minute." He turned to the troopers. "What difference does it make what happened after Buford attacked her? You just got her statement to support the charges against him. The ADA has plenty to make his case."

Nat considered this, listening. He was right. They didn't need the information, and she didn't want to tell them what Ron Saunders had said, especially not in an official statement. His last words belonged to his wife.

Trooper Milroy said, "Mr. Holt, we need to have a complete statement if we want to avoid putting her through this twice. If our statement is complete, there's no need for prison officials to speak with you, or the D.A." He faced Nat. "Ms. Greco, it's for your benefit."

"I still don't see the relevance, legally." Angus shook his head, adamant. "She went and got help. She told the C.O. where I was. Buford was kicking the crap out of me until he got there. This woman saved my life."

"I did?" Nat asked, surprised. She hadn't thought of it like that. She hadn't had the time to think of it at all. "You almost got killed trying to save mine. I was returning the favor."

"Ms. Greco, we do need to finish here." Trooper Milroy cleared his throat, testy.

"You're finished!" Angus said, but Nat waved him off. She had made a decision.

"Trooper Milroy, ask away. Let's get this done."

"Okay, what happened after you found the C.O.?"

"I told him where Angus was, and he ran off. Then I saw that there was an inmate and another C.O. lying on the floor of this room. It was very bloody."

"What room?" the trooper asked, his head down as he wrote. The wide brim obscured his features.

"I don't know. I just hit doors until one opened. I noticed that the C.O. on the floor wasn't dead. I know CPR, so I tried to save him but I couldn't."

"You administered CPR?" the trooper asked.

Angus looked at her in surprise. "You did that, Natalie? That's amazing."

"Not really. It didn't work. I used my scarf to stop the flow of blood . . . but it didn't work. Nothing I did worked." *There was nothing you could have done.* "Then I left and went to see if Angus was okay. There was an explosion but the C.O. got us out. And that's it, my statement." Nat sipped from her water bottle, forgetting it was empty. She wasn't a good liar, and Milroy eyed her hard.

"That's all?"

"Yes," Nat answered firmly, and the trooper nodded, closing his steno pad.

The Beetle's engine thrummed and its tires rumbled against the frozen asphalt. Nat and Angus rode back through the countryside, with neither talking much. She didn't tell Angus what Ron Saunders said before he died, because it wasn't his business, either. She watched the Wyeth trees and bay horses whiz by. It seemed impossible that such beauty could exist fewer than five miles from such carnage. She couldn't ever explain what had happened to anyone who hadn't lived it, much less to Hank. She realized with a start that he didn't know where she was. He'd gone out of town today, to a job site with Paul. She reached into her purse and retrieved her cell phone.

"Do you mind if I make a call?" she asked, and Angus shook his head.

"Not at all. Tell him I said hi."

Nat smiled and pressed her speed dial for Hank's cell, but she got his voicemail, so she said, "It's me. Call when you get a chance, on my cell. But don't worry, I'm fine." She snapped the phone closed.

"Good move. Voicemail isn't appropriate for major felonies."

Nat half-smiled. "Agree."

"I hope we're not on the news. I didn't give any interviews, and nobody asked me about you." Angus shook his head. "I'm so sorry this happened."

"It's okay. At least it wasn't a student."

"Either way, it's awful. I'll figure out a way to make it up to you, but right now, I'll just get you home. You're not going back to school, are you?"

"No. I just want to go soak in a bathtub and get lost in a big, thick book."

"You read in the tub?" Angus smiled. "My sister used to do that."

"Sure, it's the best place. All my favorite books have bumpy pages. A day like this calls for period fiction. Everybody wearing frills and all the talk over teacups."

"Okay, then tell me where you live, and I'll get you to your tub."

"Thanks."

"Do you guys live together?"

"Sort of."

"What's your boyfriend's name, by the way?"

Nat told him, but all the time, she was thinking of a different name.

Ron Saunders.

CHAPTER 9

Nat closed her apartment door and stepped into the cozy living room, never happier to be home than at this moment, even as a Major Homebody. She ran a loving eye over the cushy beige couch and matching chairs, which fit neatly on a square sisal rug. Soft, indirect light flooded the room from the window, which overlooked a scenic fraction of the Schuylkill River. Bookshelves surrounded the room like literary insulation. A pile of novels sat stacked on one teak end table, her Priority To-Be-Read pile, and the other end table held her Secondary To-Be-Read pile. A mug sat so often next to the stack that it had made a faint ring on the coaster, like a wedding band.

She dropped her purse at the door, kicked off her pumps, and padded down the hall to the tiled bathroom, large enough for only a downsized tub, toilet, pedestal sink, and two Emergency To-Be-Read piles. One pile sat atop the back of the toilet, and the other on the floor next to the tub, mostly paperbacks, which floated better.

She turned the bathwater on, letting it run while she took off Tanisa's jacket. She made a mental note to return the jacket and tried not to think about blood or last words. She shed her ripped shirt and bra without dwelling on how they'd gotten that way, then slipped off her pants and underwear, eyeing the stack of paperbacks beside the

tub. Josephine Tey, Wilkie Collins, Dorothy Sayers. It was a familiar crowd, but Nat needed a mood elevator. She reached for the new
Janet Evanovich, then caught sight of her naked body in the mirror
and dropped the book. Hideous scratches crisscrossed her breasts
and stomach. Red raised welts swelled like fingernail rakes, leaving
snakes of bruises.

Buford. His nails. His hands. On me.

Nat grabbed the bar of soap and a white washcloth, and began
washing her chest. The water was cold but she wasn't waiting for
hot. The scratches stung, and she scrubbed harder, anywhere and
everywhere his hands had been, the sting and the cold water a tonic.
She didn't stop until her chest had gone so red she couldn't see the
scratches anymore, then she grabbed a soft white towel and patted
her chest dry, covering the sight, even from herself.

Nat needed a bubble bath and two great chapters to restore her to
normal. She'd washed her hair gingerly because of the bump on the
back of her skull, and her head had started throbbing again. She'd put
Neosporin on her ugly scratches, changed into a soft white T-shirt, a
blue J.Crew cashmere sweater, and jeans, then padded into the spare
bedroom she used for a home office.

Books lined the room, a costly collection of first-edition mysteries, including her Erle Stanley Gardner. Nat loved to collect, getting
a thrill from the penciled-in prices on the flyleaves or the occasional
embossed stamp. She haunted library sales and loved when she scored
the older books, from the day when people actually signed books out
of the library in their own handwriting. She scanned with satisfaction her row of faded blue Nancy Drews. Today she was doing some
amateur sleuthing of her own. She took a seat behind the computer
and logged onto whitepages.com, selected Pennsylvania, and typed
in "Ron Saunders."

Twelve listings, read blue letters in the bold boxes. She skimmed
them and eliminated the addresses that were too far away. Two were

from towns she didn't recognize, but one was in Pocopson, at 524 Roselawn Lane. She remembered seeing the Pocopson Township sign on the way to the prison. This was probably the C.O.'s house. The listing supplied the home phone number, too.

Nat eyed the information and imagined what was going on there, right now. Saunders had a wife, maybe children. Family and friends would be coming over to mourn. It would be a house of pain. She had a message to deliver, and for consolation, she could offer only an explanation as to why she couldn't save the man. She eyed the phone next to her computer, then picked up the receiver.

Don't pretty it up.

She set it back down again.

"Honey? You okay?" Hank burst through the door, his long topcoat flying and Paul right on his heels. He had returned her call at the end of the day, and she had filled him in about the riot, so he'd skipped a business dinner and come straight home. He threw open his arms when he saw her. "A *prison riot?*"

"Hey, babe." Nat set down her book, rose from the couch, and met him in the middle of the living room, where he put his arms around her and pressed her against his chest, his wool coat reassuringly scratchy, retaining a wintry cold. She sank into the security of his embrace and breathed in the night air, mixed with cigar smoke.

"What were you doing at a prison? Is this a joke?"

"I was teaching, and a riot broke out."

"YOU MEAN THE PRISON RIOT ON THE NEWS?" Paul planted his hands on his hips, his camelhair coat spread open. He was wearing an Italian suit, a silk print tie, and his most outraged expression, usually reserved for missed pass-interference calls.

"Since when do you teach in a prison?" Hank held her off and eyed her cheek wound, horrified. She'd unbandaged it as per directions, to let it breathe. "Baby, who *hit* you? One of the criminals?"

"It's a long story." Nat wasn't going to tell him about Buford in front of her brother. She released him and tucked her hair behind her ear, so it wouldn't get stuck in the Neosporin, like lip gloss. "I was going to tell you last night I was going, but I didn't get a chance."

"WHO SENT YOU TO A PRISON, NAT? ARE THEY NUTS?"

"It's part of a clinic program. I went with the clinic director, and can you ever lower your voice?"

"I HAVE A COLD. MY EARS ARE STUFFED."

"You always talk loud, Paul."

"THAT'S HOW I ROLL. WHAT'S A CLINIC? ISN'T THAT FOR POOR PEOPLE?"

Nat gave up. "It's an externship program at school, run by my colleague Angus Holt."

"SO WHERE THE HELL WAS HE WHEN MY SISTER WAS GETTING HER HEADLIGHTS PUNCHED OUT? I SHOULD KICK HIS ASS! WHAT KINDA NAME IS *ANGUS*, ANYWAY?"

Nat's head started to throb again. She knew it would go like this if Paul came home with Hank. Her brothers had always been insanely overprotective, evidently saving for themselves the right to beat her up.

Hank brushed her hair back gently. "Where were the prison guards, babe?"

There weren't any? "They were busy. It's no one's fault."

"OF COURSE IT IS!" Paul waved a finger. "IT'S THIS CLINIC GUY'S FAULT OR WHOEVER RUNS THE PRISON. WE SHOULD SUE THE SCHOOL!"

Nat suppressed an eye roll. "Good idea, in my tenureship year."

"THEY DON'T DESERVE YOU IF THEY SEND YOU THERE. WE DON'T PLAY THAT." Paul flipped open his cell phone, and Nat read his mind.

"Don't call Dad."

"WHY NOT?" Paul pressed speed dial. "HE'LL CALL SOME-BODY IN LEGAL."

"I *am* somebody in Legal, and I'm not suing anybody. Please, Paul, hang up."

"TOO LATE. HE'S ALREADY FREAKED. HE WANTS YOU HOME."

"I am home. I live here now, having reached the age of majority."

"Honey, talk to your parents," Hank said, putting a hand on her shoulder. "They're worried. I spoke to them before I called you back."

"Who worried them?" Nat blurted out, anger flaring in her chest. She had been hoping for a quiet dinner at home and a good talk, but that idea was circling down the drain. "I didn't call them. I called you. And why'd you call them before me?"

"Don't be silly." Hank pressed the phone into her palm. "Please. Talk. It'll only take a minute."

"TELL HIM YOU'RE FINE. HE'S CONCERNED. HE LOVES YOU."

"I told them I'd call as soon as we got in." Hank looked apologetic, but Nat was upset all over again. She'd need another bubble bath to recover from everybody's love and concern.

"Dad?" she said into the cell phone.

"What the hell happened?" Her father's voice echoed Paul's, or maybe it was the other way around. "They said there was a riot in a prison. Were you caught in that? What were you doing there in the first place?"

"I'm fine. I just have a cut on my cheek."

"A *cut!* How many stitches did it take? You got a good plastic surgeon, I hope."

"I didn't need stitches."

"Which hospital they take you to? Don't tell me one of those butchers in Philly. They only know from gunshots."

"I didn't go to a hospital. I don't need stitches. It's just a little cut."

"On your face, no cut is little. You don't want a scar. You're not one of the boys."

Oh please. "Dad, it won't scar."

"I'm calling your mother's skin doctor. Dr. Steingard, from the club. She's the best. Leave now, you can be at her office in an hour. It's in Paoli on Lancaster Avenue, the same building as the dentist. We'll meet you there."

"Dad, I'm fine. Please, don't call the doctor."

"Your mother's worried sick, between you and Paul. Go to the doctor, so she can sleep tonight. We'll meet you there, then you and Hank can come home and have a nice dinner."

"Dad, listen, I have to go. I don't need to see the doctor. Love to you both." Nat handed the phone back to her brother. "I'm not driving out to the suburbs."

Paul said into the phone, "DON'T WORRY, DAD. WE'LL MAKE SURE SHE GOES. SEE YA SOON."

"Why'd you say that?" Nat exploded. "I'm not going!"

"DON'T YOU THINK SHE SHOULD GO?" Paul looked at Hank, who turned to Nat in appeal.

"Honey, what's the harm? You'll get a specialist to look at it. If you don't need stitches, you don't have to get them."

"It's not the stitches." Nat felt like screaming. "It's that I'm fine."

"THEY'RE ON THEIR WAY ALREADY. SO WILL THE DOCTOR BE. YOU CAN'T NOT SHOW UP."

"Babe?" Hank said, cocking his head. "Make your parents happy. It's better to be safe than sorry."

"TRUE THAT," Paul added.

Nat sighed inwardly. Sometimes she loved that Hank got along so well with her family, and sometimes she hated it. On the days she got caught in a prison riot, she hated it.

"Okay," she said, going to get her coat.

• • •

They got back to the apartment from The Greco Show around midnight, overfed and exhausted. Hank had gone to bed already, and Nat lingered in the bathroom. She needed time alone. The lightbulb panel flooded the small room, and she examined her infamous cut in the mirror. It looked the same as it had four hours ago, having survived the poking and prodding of the Main Line's best plastic surgeon, who ultimately decided that it required no stitches and reapplied a veil of Neosporin.

Nat felt a knot of resentment tighten within her chest. She reached for the electric toothbrush Hank had bought them for Christmas and pressed the green On button, starting the frantic motion of the brush and its generally menacing bzzzz. She buzzed her teeth, pining for her old low-tech toothbrush. She needed silence after all the Greco noise.

At dinner, she had told them the sanitized version of what happened at the prison, or at least the first few lines of it, which proved more than enough for the family attention span. She had also prevented litigation against the University of Pennsylvania Law School, the Department of Corrections, the Commonwealth of Pennsylvania, and two United States congressmen, to be named later. She switched off the electric toothbrush and shoved it back into its holder, which was already collecting white Colgate crust, and then she couldn't delay any longer. She slipped off her cashmere sweater and T-shirt, down to a lacy white bra, and eyed anew the scratches on her chest.

The shock value had gone, but not completely. Red welts still strafed her chest, and droplets of dried blood dotted her bra, across her breast to the nipple. She took off her bra, put on the soft Penn sweatshirt hanging on the back of the door, and left the bathroom, trying to figure out a way to tell Hank about Buford. Sooner or later he'd have to see her chest again, and she wasn't exactly sure how he'd react, or even how she would, the next time they made love. She didn't think she'd be unduly traumatized, but then again, she felt relieved that his birthday had been yesterday.

She entered the bedroom, lit only by the circle of halogen on Hank's night table. He lay with his back to her, naked to the waist, and his silhouette emphasized the round, muscular cap of his shoulders, the curve of his bicep, and the sexy way his torso tapered to his trim waist. He'd dated a lot before they'd met, so much so that Nat sensed her father's mild surprise when Hank went for her. She slipped into bed behind him and shifted over for a toe-hello.

"Babe?" she asked, then heard a soft snoring sound. She propped herself up and peeked over at him. His eyes were closed, and he breathed into the down pillow. She didn't have the heart to wake him and didn't relish telling him anyway. It had been a long day, and she'd forgive herself the conflict avoidance. She rolled back over, pulled up the covers, and checked the glowing bedside clock. 12:23. Twelve hours ago, she'd been sitting in an ambulance, talking to a paramedic.

Goofy, isn't it?

Nat pushed the thought away. It was too late to call the Saunders house.

She reached uneasily for a book.

CHAPTER 10

Nat's hair was still damp from her morning shower when she found herself sitting in the reception area outside Vice Dean McConnell's office, having been summoned by an early-morning voicemail. She was wearing a black-and-white knit suit, striving for that Soon-to-Be-Tenured look, and a pink silk blouse with a neckline high enough to hide her scratches. She'd come in early because she couldn't sleep anyway, and every time she'd moved last night, she felt a new pain in her ribs. Her head ached from the bump in the back, and she'd put a flesh-toned Band-Aid on her cheek, hoping everybody would think she was hiding a zit. She had to teach today, and answering questions about the prison riot wasn't her idea of class participation.

She glanced around the room, which she hadn't been in since her first day on the job. This section of the school had yet to be renovated, so ugly oblong fixtures shaped like flying saucers still marred the ceiling. Oil portraits of past deans hung on a scuffed wall, and the rug was a worn blue. A navy couch sat flush against the wall, flanked by two club chairs in a coordinating navy print, one of which Nat occupied. Two black desks and cubicles were situated against the opposite wall, both of them empty. It was too early for the dean's or the vice dean's secretary to be in, and McConnell was keeping Nat cooling her heels while he chatted on the phone. She remembered power games like this from her days at Morgan Lewis, which she'd left because she didn't like the rough-and-tumble of litigation or big-firm politics.

"Morning, Natalie." It was Angus's voice behind her, and when she turned around, her ribs reminded her that twisting was a bad idea.

"Ouch."

"I hear that." Angus walked around her chair and plunked down on the couch, catty-corner to Nat. His eyes shone bright blue, even if one was still swollen, and his grin couldn't be stopped by a few black stitches. "How you feelin'?"

"Terrible."

"I'm sorry." His smile vanished. "I really am."

"Don't start. How do you feel?"

"Same." He had on a fresh gauze bandage, and the bruise on his cheekbone had turned a darker red. She wondered how he had gotten his sweater over his head, this one a rough-hewn Ecuadorian knit in heather gray wool, which he wore with jeans and new cowboy boots with a pointier toe. She wondered if he'd gotten blood on his Fryes, but she didn't ask. He leaned close to her. "McConnell called you, too, huh?"

"He said come 'immediately.'"

"I got 'right away.' Where is that boy?" Angus craned his neck toward the open door to McConnell's office and spotted him on the phone. "What's he doin' in there? Buyin' staplers?"

"We're being called to the principal's office."

"I know, right? Now that he thinks he's the Duke of Venice, he'll be unbearable." Angus chuckled. "Called you last night but you weren't in."

"I didn't get a message."

"Didn't leave one. Didn't think Mr. Greco would like it."

Nat smiled again. "You could have. He doesn't have a jealous bone in his body."

"Sensible guy." Angus smoothed a ropy blond strand back into his ponytail. "Didn't know you were in so early or I would've called here this morning. I'm worried about you. You had a helluva day yesterday."

"I'm okay."

"Really?" He frowned under his bandage.

"Please, enough."

"Just so you know, I've suspended externships to the prison." His mouth made a grim line. "None of my students is going out there until I understand exactly what went down, and why Buford and Donnell were in my class. I want to know why they were cleared. It's strange because—"

"Angus? Nat?" McConnell appeared suddenly at the threshold and motioned to them, so they rose and followed him in, where he gestured them to the two tan leather chairs across from his desk. "Please, sit down."

"Thanks, Jim." Angus offered Nat the first chair and took the other after she'd been seated. She glanced around the office and determined that it hadn't changed since her intake interview four years before, or even since 1795. Foxhunting prints blanketed the walls, and the wing chairs were all old leather with dull brass tacks. A lamp with a black shade had a base like a small brass bugle, and the end tables were of walnut. Case reporters, law reviews, and legal periodicals stuffed the bookshelves, and McConnell's large walnut desk sat stacked with papers, correspondence, and even a few leather-bound books, which made his black laptop look anachronistic.

"Thank you both for coming." McConnell sat down behind his desk. "I'll be handling this matter in Sam's absence."

The dean is gone?

"As you may know, he's on vacation. He left last week."

I knew that.

Angus said, "There's not much to handle, Jim. I take complete responsibility for what happened at the prison, and I've already suspended the externship program there, pending an investigation. I'm very sorry for the injury to Nat, as well as any adverse publicity to the school."

McConnell nodded. "Perhaps we should back up a minute. Why don't you tell me what happened?"

"Sure," Angus said, and Nat maintained her professionalism as he recounted a brief version of the attack, the riot, and the aftermath. At the end of the account, McConnell's lined face had fallen into even deeper lines. He patted his blue-and-green rep tie, then his silvery wave of hair, in thought.

"This is a very serious situation."

"It was, but it's over." Angus gestured to Nat. "She had it the hardest of all, and she'll need time to recover, physically and emotionally. You should give her a week off."

Nat interjected, "I don't need it, thanks." *I need a month.*

McConnell turned to eye her, smiling almost warmly. "You've been through quite an ordeal. I assume you won't be performing Shakespeare anytime soon."

"No." Nat managed a smile that telegraphed the Professional-Grade Toughness required of Chevy trucks and tenured professors.

"I must say I love the works of Shakespeare, and you were quite correct to emphasize the elements of law and justice." McConnell paused. "Of course, you must know that we can't continue to offer the seminar if it remains at its current low subscription levels."

My baby! "But I developed it myself, and I teach it in addition to my other courses." *Read, for free.*

"I understand that. But the school has other needs, if you have extra time." McConnell peered through his tortoiseshell bifocals to consult some papers on his desk. "Scott is going on sabbatical to finish his textbook, and we could use someone to teach taxation, which would demonstrate your versatility as a scholar and legal educator."

I'd rather date Kyle Buford. "I'd love to, in addition to the seminar."

"That's not what I had in mind, but we can discuss that later." McConnell turned to Angus. "Back to the problem at hand. This incident at the prison arose from one of your clinic's externship programs. Currently, how many externship programs do we have?"

"We're up to six. We have externs in the civil practice clinic, entrepreneurial, mediation, child advocacy, transactional, and public interest."

"Civil practice is the most subscribed, is it not?"

Angus nodded proudly. "Yes, our students counsel the indigent in housing, social security and disability, health law, education, child custody and support, and consumer law."

"Chester County Correctional Institution is the only externship program in which something like this has occurred, is that correct?"

"Yes, of course."

"I see." McConnell cleared his throat. "Well, in addition to the harm incurred by you two faculty members, my concern, of course, is the harm to the school. Its reputation and its potential exposure."

"Exposure?" Angus repeated, but Nat knew what McConnell meant, because she had learned a few things at Morgan Lewis:

Time for even the lawyers to lawyer up.

McConnell said, "Waiting for me this morning were messages from the parents of several of your clinic students, who had been out to the prison in the past. They're understandably concerned that their sons and daughters have been exposed to danger, or could be in the future. I assured them that, as of this morning, the externship program to the prison has been cancelled."

Angus looked as if he'd been slapped, his mouth partway open. "I've suspended the program. I'm not canceling it."

"The parents are demanding as much."

"The parents don't run my clinic."

"If you send a student out there and he gets hurt, you expose the school to an array of negligence actions."

"I've already taken the appropriate measures to protect those students, and I care about them, too." Angus shifted forward in his seat, his face flushing red even under his bruise. "The program is suspended."

"I'm afraid that's not your decision."

"Nor is it yours," Angus shot back. "I'll take it up with Sam."

"He can't be reached."

"I have his cell."

"Good luck trying it. He's in Kenya with Carolyn and the kids, on a safari. In his absence, I make the decisions."

"Jim, this is absurd!" Angus shouted, and Nat worried he'd pop a stitch. "There has never been an incident before at Chester County, and our best students have served in the externship program there, counseling inmates for over eight years."

"That benefits the prison, not us."

"Wrong. The students have learned more about criminal defense than they can ever get in a classroom. They represent real inmates on real cases. They draft all the pleadings, find all the experts. That's invaluable experience."

"They can learn it within these walls, Angus." McConnell tented his fingers. "I cannot ignore the concerns of these parents. As a result, effective today, I will be running all of the clinic externships programs, and you are relieved of your duties with regard to them."

"You're *firing* me?" Angus exploded, jumping to his boots.

"What?" Nat blurted out, astonished.

"Don't be so emotional, Angus." McConnell remained calm, his gaze even and unblinking behind his bifocals. "I'm not firing you. You will continue to teach your non-clinic classes, meet with clinic students, and run the in-house clinical programs. I'm merely assuming supervision of our externship programs. I have to make sure they're run with due regard for the welfare and safety of our students."

Nat interjected, "Vice Dean McConnell, Jim." *Whatever*. "Angus has the clinic under control, and if we overreact as an institution, it will only aggravate the situation."

Angus nodded. "Jim, you don't even know what the programs are. How can you begin to run them? This isn't about programs, this is about people. Real students who work ongoing lawsuits for real people."

"I know how to run a tight ship, no matter what it is. If you ask me, this happened because it's been loosey-goosey for far too long under you."

Angus looked stricken for a moment, as he realized he had lost. Nat felt terrible for him. His long hair, cowboy boots, and his image were coming back to haunt him, and she saw him in a different light. He'd been right when he said he was in his own little world. The students may have loved him, but McConnell had barely tolerated him, and with this, he had just declared war.

"I'll take it up with Sam, when he gets back," Angus said, struggling to rein in his anger. "He knows how important those programs are to the school. He's the one who raised the funds for them and for our renovation."

"Thank you," McConnell said, but Angus was already leaving the room, storming through the open door.

Nat watched him go, and her heart went out to him. He'd developed and grown those externship programs himself. The clinic was his passion, and he'd been very good at it. She turned back to McConnell just as the phone on his desk started ringing.

"Thank you for your time, Nat," the vice dean said, dismissing her with a wave before he picked up the receiver.

Nat got up stiffly and left the office, shaking her head. Only she had been naïve enough to think that academia would be politics-free.

It was all the books they had lying around that fooled her.

CHAPTER 11

Nat sat, allegedly concentrating, in her small modern office. She'd called Angus twice but he didn't call back. She went to see him after her morning classes but he was gone. McConnell had already sent around an email advising everybody that he was assuming supervision of all externships, which set the faculty and students buzzing. Colleagues who had never spoken to Nat had stopped in to fish for juicy details. She'd begged off, saying she had to research her article, and corroborated her alibi by papering her desk with handwritten notes and placing a takeout Dunkin' Donuts cup next to her laptop, which had long ago gone into hibernation, code for "you're not working hard enough, girl."

She checked her desk clock. 12:05 p.m. She had brought Mrs. Saunders's phone number to the office but hadn't gotten up the nerve to call her yet, though she came close at 10:23 a.m. and 10:43 a.m. She'd wanted to talk it over with Hank, but he'd left early again. She couldn't decide whether to call. She felt as if it were either urgent or too soon, which made no sense.

Her gaze wandered over the wooden chairs in front of her desk, then strayed to the wall-mounted bookshelves of yellowish oak, happily crammed with law books, case reporters, and legal nonfiction. Llewellyn's *Bramble Bush*, Holmes's *The Common Law*, Breyer's *Active Liberty*. The sight of books didn't comfort her the way it usually did, and she couldn't stop thinking about Mrs. Saunders, Angus, or yesterday. No reporters had called her, for which she thanked God. Still. She hit a key to wake up her computer and logged onto phillynews.com. She had to look everywhere to find the story: **Disturbance Put Down in Record Time at Chester County Correctional Institution.**

Nat almost laughed. What had Angus said? *Let the spinning begin.* She clicked the link and the story came on, barely a paragraph on her laptop screen:

> Prison officials quelled a disturbance at SCI Chester County yesterday, in the record time of sixteen minutes, though not before the deaths of a corrections officer and three inmates. The disturbance began with a mattress fire in the RHU, or the rehabilitation unit, but was suppressed with the use of high-tech "stingers," percussive devices that fire nonlethal rubber pelts when deployed. Killed were corrections officer Ron Saunders, 38, of Pocopson, and inmates Simon Upchurch, 34, of Chester, Herman Ramirez, 37, and Jorge Orega, 32, both of Avondale. Charges in connection with the incident are pending.

Nat frowned. The article made it sound as if all the deaths had taken place in the RHU, which they hadn't, and that Saunders was a casualty of the melee, rather than having been murdered in a different place. Did the difference matter? She skimmed the article again and noticed a related article link, and clicked it. **The Very Model of a Corrections Officer**, popped onto the screen. It was a sidebar about Saunders. She sipped cold coffee and read on:

Ron Saunders died as he lived, serving others. When inmates started a fire in the RHU, the rehabilitation unit where violent inmates are housed, Saunders was the first to respond to the call. That urge to serve others got him killed, even in a minor disturbance. Saunders was a veteran corrections officer with an eleven-year record, and also served as a volunteer firefighter for Pocopson Township and was well known in the community for his good works. He leaves behind a wife, Barbara, and three children, Timothy, John, and James. A private memorial and viewing will be held in his honor, and the family has requested that in lieu of flowers, donations be sent to the Boys' and Girls' Clubs of West Chester, Pa.

Again, Nat didn't get it. The sidebar also made it sound as if Saunders had died in the RHU. She shook her head, which started to pound again. Saunders's wife was named Barbara and he had three kids. Nat couldn't put it off another minute. She grabbed the notepaper with the number, picked up the phone, and called the Saunders house. Her heart began to hammer, and the call connected with a loud *click*.

"Yes?" answered a woman who sounded older.

"Hi, my name is Nat Greco. I hate to bother you, but is this the home of Ron Saunders, who worked as a corrections officer?"

"Yes, it is."

"Please accept my condolences. May I ask, is Mrs. Saunders at home?"

"She can't come to the phone. I'm her mother. You're not a reporter, are you?"

"No, not at all. I teach at a law school. I was at the prison when the riot broke out." Nat swallowed hard. "I happened to be with Mr. Saunders, at the time he . . . when he . . ."

"*You're the one*," the woman said, her tone hushed. "We heard that there was someone with him. Were you there, when he died?"

"I tried to save him." Nat felt shaky all over again. "I'm sorry, so sorry, that I couldn't."

"No, no, no, dear, that's all right." The older woman's tone turned soothing. "I didn't mean it that way. Barbara, my daughter, was so pleased that Ron wasn't alone when he passed. I feel exactly the same way."

Nat breathed easier. "I was wondering if I could speak with Mrs. Saunders sometime. I could talk with her over the phone or in person, whenever it's convenient. Whatever she wishes."

"I know she'd love to meet you and talk with you. You're her last connection with Ron. Would you mind coming out to the house? I'm afraid she's not ready to travel, and the children are here."

Poor kids. "Of course, I'll come there."

"When can you come? I know she'll want to see you as soon as possible. We were just talking about it, praying that you existed and that it wasn't just a rumor."

"I can come whenever you wish. Anytime this week is fine."

"How kind of you. How about today?"

Gulp.

"It would be such a comfort to Barbara, and she needs it. If you could manage it, anytime this afternoon would be wonderful. Though I'm sure you're very busy."

"No, I'm not. I'm in the city, and I could leave now and be there in an hour or so. I have your address."

"See you then. We're here all day."

"Thank you," Nat said, hanging up. *No time like the present.* She logged onto maps.com, got the driving directions, and was printing them when she heard a knock. She looked up. Angus was standing in the threshold of her office in his thick sweater, wearing a sideways grin. If he was upset about the meeting with McConnell, he was covering it well.

"So this is your office, huh?" he said, looking around. "Nice vibe. Pretty. Light. Quiet." As he scanned the shelves, Nat slid the driving directions discreetly from the tray. Angus gestured at the large window behind her chair, which overlooked Sansom Street, with its trendy shops and restaurants. "You have the hip and cool view. The White Dog is my favorite restaurant. Free-range law professors our specialty."

"What's your view like?" It struck Nat that she had no idea where Angus's office was. She really had to get out more.

"I'm in the basement, but it's gorgeous. We have our own place, all remodeled. You should see it."

"Don't tell me, lemme guess. Posters of Che Guevara. Lenin. Woodstock. Birds on guitars."

"How did you know?" Angus laughed, but Nat didn't want to banter anymore. He had to be hurting inside.

"You okay?"

"You mean since my demotion?"

"You weren't demoted."

"Emasculated, then."

Nat smiled, and Angus laughed, nevertheless.

"I'm fine. I called Sam's cell, but there was no answer. He has to go to the veldt to get away, where there's no possibility of fund-raising."

Nat cocked her head. "I feel bad for you."

"Don't worry. Sam gets it. He knows how important those externships are, and I built them. He'll set it right when he comes back." Angus shrugged. "Did you see the newspapers?"

"The account is hardly complete, or accurate."

"I know, right? I get that they don't want to alarm the community, but it's ridiculous."

"If I hear about those stupid stingers one more time, I'll scream."

"Hey, you wanna grab lunch?" Angus asked, but Nat hesitated.

"Uh, can't. I was just going out. I have an errand to run."

"Okay." Angus's face fell somewhere behind his beard. "Rain check, then?"

"Sure."

"I'm not hitting on you."

"I know that."

"I'm over you."

"Good for you."

"In fact, I barely liked you, until you stood up for me with that tool McConnell."

Nat laughed, and Angus's grin returned.

"You should stop by my office sometime. You're wrong about the décor. No Che Guevara posters."

"Jessica Alba?"

"You got me." Angus laughed. "Walk you out? I'll grab a falafel from the truck."

"Okay." Nat went in her desk for her handbag, feeling guilty for not telling him about Saunders. He was the only one who could really understand what yesterday had been like. Then again, if she told him, she'd be admitting that she'd lied to the police. On impulse, she closed her office door and showed him the seat across from her desk. "Sit down a minute, would you?"

Angus sat down, mystified. "You gonna emasculate me, too?"

"No, but I have to tell you something. The whole truth and nothing but." Nat went back to her desk, sat down, and told him the story of finding Saunders, alive despite his wounds. As Angus listened, his bright eyes grew somber, and Nat managed not to cry. "The thing I didn't tell you is that, before he died, Saunders said something to me. His last words. It was a message for his wife. I didn't want to tell the cops. It's not their business."

"I understand." Angus rubbed his beard. "It's not mine, either."

Exactly. "But I have to tell his wife. That's where I was going just now. Out to the Saunders house."

"In the subs? *That's* the errand?" Angus smiled. "You're a terrible liar, Natalie. You acted so guilty, I was worried you were having an affair, and I'm not even your boyfriend."

Nat laughed. It felt good to joke around with him. A shaft of sunlight moved onto his hair, bringing out golden highlights she hadn't noticed before. Either he had washed it last night or he was a total hunk and probably not a drug addict. She had a new respect for him, after yesterday and this morning.

"I also think that you're extraordinary, for trying to save him."

"I could have done more."

"No. That's not fair." Angus shook his head. "You can't ask so much of yourself. You'll lose sight of what you did accomplish."

"Like what?"

"Like simply being there when he died."

It's what his mother-in law had said on the phone.

"You know, sometimes it's enough just to be. Just be. Don't fix. Don't perform. Don't control. Just *be*." Angus paused "I know, it sounds so Zen."

"Faculty Steven Seagal."

"Forgive me, I was a religion major. I almost went to divinity school."

"Really?"

"I know, right? Anyway, so you're going out to the house now? I think that's the right thing to do. You have to do it, and in person. It's the man's last words before he left the planet."

"I agree."

"You want me to go with you? I know the area better than you do. I'll give you some privacy when you talk to his widow."

"Are you free?"

"I have to make some calls, but I can do it on the way. You shouldn't have to go alone, and I'm the one who got you into this. It's the least I can do."

Nat smiled, touched. "Falafel's on me."

CHAPTER 12

The country sky was ice blue and so cold that even the sun was keeping its distance. The Saunders house was the only one on this winding road, and it was surrounded by an expanse of frosted white snow, broken only by dark, barren trees, their branches heavy with snow. Nat parked her red Volvo down the street from the house, finding a space only at the end of a long row of salt-sprayed parked cars. She twisted off the ignition and eyed Angus, sitting in the passenger seat.

"It looks like she has a houseful," Nat said, stating the obvious. "I wonder if it makes sense to do this now."

"The mother asked you to come today." Angus flashed her an encouraging smile. "You'll do fine."

"Thanks, Coach." Nat reached behind the seat for her purse, and they got out of the car. There were no sidewalks, so they walked in the street, which had been recently plowed. Snow sat piled along the side of the road in powdery triangles, clean as spooned sugar. Nat held her camelhair coat closed at her neck, missing her serviceable wool toggle, which she'd left at the prison. Angus shoved his hands in his jeans, with only his sweater and his beard to keep him warm.

They made their way up the street, their breath frosty, their shoes crunching road salt and ice. Nat's stomach tensed as they approached the house, a modest white rancher with forest green trim and a tan garage door. The driveway, on the left side of the house, was parked up with an older Honda and a Toyota SUV, and in the side yard, a snow-covered metal swing set waited for summer. Nat took the lead as they walked up the side of the driveway. She could hear noise as they got closer to the house.

"Don't worry," Angus said as they reached the white metal door, its screens replaced with storm windows, and Nat knocked. A minute later, the door was opened by a young woman with strawberry blond hair, wearing a black knit top and jeans. Her gaze shifted from Nat to Angus; she was plainly frowning at their wounds. In other circumstances, Nat would have gone with "trick or treat."

"I'm Nat Greco, and this is my colleague, Angus Holt."

"Oh, jeez, of course. Nice to meet you," the woman said, chastened. She extended a hand to them both. "Jennifer Paradis. Please, come in." She stood aside, opening the door wide and motioning them through. "My mom's expecting you, too. She's in the kitchen."

Nat thanked her and they followed her into a warm, paneled living room crammed with people. Men stood talking, holding clear plastic glasses, and women gathered together, balancing paper plates that sagged under roast beef sandwiches on hamburger buns and thick squares of casserole. An oversized projection TV played *SpongeBob SquarePants* on mute, though a bunch of kids watched it anyway, sitting rapt in a circle. Two little girls sprawled nearby on the brown shag rug, their legs splayed carelessly as they crayoned in coloring books. Nat and Angus made their way through the crowd, and heads turned as they passed. Angus's ponytail and big bruise drew more than a few stares, but the mourners smiled at Nat as if they knew her.

"They're all C.O.s," Angus murmured under his breath, and Nat saw a balding man waving from near the TV. He threaded his way to her and shook her hand.

"I heard you tried to save Ron. He was a good friend of mine, and I thank you for your efforts. We all do."

"You're welcome." Nat's voice caught, with surprise. They walked on and entered a small eat-in kitchen filled with the delicious aroma of baked ham. Pyrex dishes of scalloped potatoes, macaroni and cheese, spinach lasagna, sliced eye roast, and other comfort foods covered every surface, though they did little to comfort at times like these.

"Mom, she's here," Jennifer said, and an older woman in red reading glasses, a black cardigan, and black stretch pants looked up from the double sink, where she'd been draining a can of Acme pineapple slices.

"Ms. Greco, my goodness, excuse me." She set down the can and tugged at a beaded lorgnette, so that her glasses tumbled from her nose and to her soft chest. She dried her hands hastily on a thin dishcloth and took Nat's hand in hers, clasping it. "I'm Clare Cracy, Barb's mother. Thank you so much for coming, and for what you did for Ron."

"You're welcome, and my deepest condolences." Nat introduced Angus again, as one little boy chased another into the kitchen, yelling for his Game Boy. Jennifer took off after them.

"My grandchildren have a lot of energy. We feed them too well." Mrs. Cracy smiled, then looked again at Nat and Angus. "Goodness, the two of you are the walking wounded."

"We're fine." Nat was feeling tense again. "Is your daughter around?"

"Barb's upstairs resting, but she wants to see you."

"If she's not up to it, I could come back another time."

"No, she's waiting for you. Come with me." Mrs. Cracy faced Angus, gesturing to the food. "I'll come right back and fix you a ham sandwich. It's honey baked."

"I've eaten, thanks." Angus winked at Nat. "I'll wait for you here."

Mrs. Cracy led the way from the kitchen and back through the crowd, and Nat felt every pair of eyes on her as she climbed the shag-carpeted stairs and disappeared from their view, into the darkness of a second-floor hallway. Leading her, Mrs. Cracy said, "We keep the lights off because Barb gets migraines when she's under stress. It's the second door, up ahead."

"Poor thing. How terrible."

"She's had them since she was a little girl. Light is a big no-no. No caffeine or chocolate, either." Mrs. Cracy continued down the hall, and Nat almost bumped into her when the older woman stopped short and opened a door. "Barb, honey?" she whispered. Over Mrs. Cracy's shoulder, Nat could see that the bedroom looked unusually dark, with blackout shades drawn almost all the way down, flanked by white sheers.

"Yeah, Ma?" a weak voice said.

"She's here. How're you?"

"Good, so far. It's holding off. Let her come in. Are the kids okay?"

"They're fine. That Game Boy is worth every penny."

"Can I see her? She's there?"

"Right here." Mrs. Cracy put a gentle hand on Nat's elbow and guided her forward.

"Hi, Barb. I'm Nat Greco." She entered the bedroom, feeling completely intrusive.

"Come on in. I'm the Princess of Darkness." Barb Saunders propped herself up on two pillows on a king-size bed, in a form-less gray sweatsuit. She finger-raked her short light hair in the darkness. "Mom, you can go. Thanks."

"You need more water, honey?"

"Got plenty." Barb motioned to Nat. "Please, come in. I'd turn on a lamp but I get migraines. I'm trying to hold one off."

"I'm so sorry." Nat entered the room, hovering by the bed as the door closed softly behind her. The bedroom was simply furnished, with an oak chest of drawers on the left wall and a long mirror above it. Photos and a brown jewelry box sat on the dresser, a man's white T-shirt spilled from a plastic hamper onto the shaggy rug, and a child's plastic helicopter lay on its side nearby. A roll of toilet paper sat on the bed and wads of it dotted the floral bedspread. Nat didn't want to think about how long Barb Saunders had been crying. She said, "I hate to bother you today. So soon."

"No, please. You're the only one I wanted to see. As soon as I heard about you, I was praying you'd call." Barb gathered the toilet paper balls and patted the bed beside her. "Would you mind sitting here? My head hurts too much to sit up."

"This is fine. Don't bother yourself." Nat perched awkwardly on the edge of the bed. In the dim light she could see the roundish face of a pretty woman, with puffy eyes, maybe blue, and a small, upturned nose that also looked slightly swollen. Her mouth was a Cupid's bow, drawn with grief at the corners. "I'm so sorry about your loss."

"Thanks. Oh . . . boy." Barb's hand went to her forehead, and Nat could see her wincing in the dark, her forehead buckling in apparent pain.

"Are you okay?"

"Hold on. Are you wearing perfume?"

"Yes." Nat didn't have to think. She always wore perfume. Today, her Sarah Jessica Parker.

"Oh no." Barb held her forehead again and eased back onto the pillows.

"What. What is it?"

"Smells like that, they help bring it on."

"Your migraine? Oh, no! I'm so sorry." Nat jumped up instantly, backing away. "Maybe this isn't the best time. I can come back."

"But I want . . . to talk to you. I just want to hear how . . . it was for him, at the end. You were with him, right? At the end? I mean . . . the very end?"

"Yes, I was with him." Nat felt stricken, standing off from the bed. Could she do one damn thing right? "Listen, I think I should come back."

Barb let out a low moan, in frustration and pain. "I waited too long to take the Imitrex, and now it's not working."

"This is too much of a strain. Let's not do this now. Let me come back another day. Whenever you want me to. I want to talk to you, too."

"Tomorrow's the viewing, then the funeral. But how about the day after that?"

"Sure, fine." Nat would find the time. She'd be here. The toy helicopter. The widow in pain. Saunders's undershirt still in the hamper. It all hurt, and she hadn't even known the poor man. She backed toward the bedroom door. "I'll come back. It's no problem."

"Get my mom, would you?"

"Sure thing. See you." Nat opened the bedroom door and hurried into the hall.

Relieved, and dismayed, that she had to go.

CHAPTER 13

Nat and Angus threaded their way to the front door to leave, having gotten Mrs. Cracy upstairs to tend to Barb. The crowd in the living room had grown, and Nat had almost reached the door when she spotted a familiar man among them. At first she couldn't place him, then she flashed on the same face in a different place and time. His brown hair in disarray. His eyes stricken with fear and shock. It was the C.O. who had come out of the room where Saunders and the inmate lay dead.

Nat willed the crowded living room back into focus. The C.O. was short but brawny, dressed in a blue flannel shirt worn under a black down vest, and he stood near the door with an Asian woman. His wavy brown hair looked as if it had been combed with water, his brown eyes were bracketed by crow's-feet, and he had a faint red bump on his right cheek, near his eye. Angus must have seen him first, because he was already making his way to him. The C.O. started to shake his hand, but Angus wrapped him in a bear hug that only caused the man to stiffen. The crowd craned their necks.

"Natalie, meet Joe Graf." Angus looked around to Nat, his eyes bright. "This man has a right hook you wouldn't believe. He dropped Buford. I mean *dropped* him."

Nat introduced herself. "I owe you, too, Mr. Graf. Thanks so much for getting me out of there yesterday. I don't know what would have happened without you."

"I was only doin' my job." Graf barely smiled, his mouth a tight line, as if he were self-conscious about his teeth. He turned to the petite Asian woman beside him who had a sorrowful expression. "This is my wife, Jai-Wen."

"Pleased to meet you. Sorry it had to be on such a sad day." Nat shook her hand, and the woman murmured a hello in accented English.

Graf shook his head. "I got Ron the job, you know. We worked together eleven years."

"He is our best man." Jai-Wen's eyes shone with a film of fresh tears. She had a tiny black brush of a ponytail and wore a burgundy coat with her jeans and white snow boots. "I can't believe he gone. Me and Barb always worry that something happen to Joe and Ron, and all the husband."

"Let's take this outside," Graf said abruptly. "I need a smoke anyways."

"Great, sure," Angus said, as they said goodbye to Jai-Wen and went outside. They hit the cold air and closed the door behind them. Nat walked down the steps to the snowy front walk, and Angus shoved his hands in his pockets again.

"Cold enough for ya?" Graf reached inside his coat and pulled out a pack of Winstons with a green Bic lighter inside.

"Ten degrees colder than in the city." Angus shifted his feet.

"Always that way." Graf shook a cigarette out of the pack and lit it, blowing a cone of acrid smoke. "Everybody wants to know what happened yesterday. Lotta people 'round here work at the prison. It affects everybody."

"I'm sure," Angus said. "I never thought there'd be a riot there, or what happened to Natalie. I'm lucky you came when you did. I'm bigger than Buford, but I couldn't take him. I tell you, that dude is *strong.*"

"He lifts, is why. Always in the weight room."

"Tell me about it." Angus didn't smile. "I knew he was trouble from the jump. What I don't understand is how he got in my class. He and Donnell, they were never in before. Machik is supposed to send me all the applications and he didn't send me theirs."

"Have to talk to him 'bout that." Graf took another drag, sucking deeply.

Nat wanted to change the subject. "Joe, I want you to know that I wish I could have done more for Ron, and I'm sorry."

"He was just doin' his job, that's what gets me. That's what's unfair." Graf shook his head, coughing out a puff of smoke. "Nothin' shoulda gone wrong. We were bringin' Upchurch into the office to write him up for weed. Then the siren went off."

Nat remembered, shuddering. The siren. The lockdown. Buford.

"Next thing I know, he pulls a shoe shank, a piece of metal they get outta shoes, and he stabs Ron in the chest." Graf's eyes narrowed to slits against the smoke and sun. "Upchurch was a troublemaker, but I never figured him for a killer. Then he tries to stab me, and we fought, and I was able to turn it on him."

"I'm very sorry," Nat said, shaken.

Graf kept his head down, smoking and saying nothing, and Nat and Angus exchanged quick glances. Suddenly Nat wished she smoked, too. It would get her through this conversation, but then she'd have to die.

Graf cleared his throat and finally raised his head, his flat lips unsmiling. "Heard you did CPR, Ms. Greco."

"Please, call me Nat. I did. I tried CPR, but there was nothing I could do."

"That your scarf they found on him?"

"Yes. I used it to stop the blood, but it didn't help."

"You tried that, too?" Graf managed a shaky smile. "What'd you think you were doing?"

Nat blinked, surprised at the hostility edging his tone. "God knows. Staunching the blood flow. I learned it in camp."

"Camp?"

"Summer camp." Nat knew how stupid it sounded, but it was true.

"You were with him a long time. I looked behind me, but you weren't there. When I figured out what you were doin', it gave me a little hope." Graf dropped his head, blowing another cone of smoke, and Nat watched it curl up and disappear like a ghost in the cold wind.

"I tried for a long time. He was too far gone."

"I never woulda lef' him if I'd known he was alive."

"Of course you wouldn't." Nat realized that Graf must be feeling the same guilt she did. Asking an identical array of what-ifs. "It doesn't matter if I tried to save him or you did. Just know that everything was done to save him, and it didn't work."

"Talk is that I lef' him to die, but I didn't. I thought he was dead."

"Of course you didn't. I mean, he was dead."

"Nobody thinks you'd do that, Joe," Angus added. "You're a hero. You saved us both."

Graf snorted, smoke puffing from his nostrils. "That isn't the way some people see it."

Angus frowned. "What do you mean?"

"No offense, professor, but I got you two out and lef' behind one of my own."

"No, that's not true," Nat interjected. "He was dead, and I came and got you and begged you to go get Angus. You *had* to go. I mean, I was desperate. If you hadn't gone, Angus would be dead, too."

"That's what I figured." Graf nodded, squinting hard. "I mean, Ron *looked* dead. The wound was to the heart, direct, which is why I went out. I was kinda in shock when I saw you. You were screamin' that you needed the help, so I went. I didn't think to look back, like you did. I didn't think to listen for his heart. I shoulda."

"I didn't, either," Nat said, trying to make him feel better. She had unwittingly made a fool of Graf, in trying to save Saunders.

"People sayin' he wasn't dead. That he begged you to help him. Not to let him die."

Nat stiffened. Had he heard something? Had the paramedic told him? "No, he didn't. I only went to him because he moaned, but that's it. He didn't say anything to me."

Angus looked over, and his blue eyes telegraphed, *Good girl.*

"Didn't think so," Graf said flatly, and Angus put a comforting hand on the C.O.'s shoulder.

"Don't work her over, Joe. It's good she was there with him. She tried to save his life."

"Yeah, right. It's good she did what she could." Graf eyed Nat through the smoke. "Sorry. I do thank you, as Ron's best friend, for what you did to save his life."

Nat smiled, relieved. "You're welcome."

"Hope you didn't try to save the nigger that killed him, too."

Whoa. Nat paled, caught unaware.

"There's no call for that," Angus said quickly, but Graf's head snapped around to him.

"What do you know about it, professor? What do you know?" Graf pointed at Angus, the half cigarette burning between his fingers. "You come in once a week, kissin' their ass, talkin' about their rights. You don't have to take their shit. What do you really *know*?"

Angus put up his hands grimly. "Don't shoot, Joe. I'm not what's bothering you today."

"You are, too! What about *Ron's rights*? Huh? What about *his* rights?" Suddenly Graf threw his lit cigarette at Angus, who dodged it reflexively. Nat jumped, and the butt fell to the ground.

Angus pointed a stiff finger at Graf. "I'll cut you a break, Joe, because you're having a bad day. Next time, I won't."

"I'll hold my breath," Graf shot back, but by then Angus had taken Nat by the arm and was hustling her down the driveway toward the street.

When they were out of earshot, Angus asked, "You okay?"

No. "Yes."

"I didn't see *that* coming."

"Me neither. Maybe he didn't mean it. He's obviously upset."

"No, he's obviously a racist. By the way, how'd it go with the widow?"

"Sort of okay." Nat didn't elaborate. She was too busy running away.

"Good. You mind if we make a stop? It's not far."

"Where?"

"It's not a date," Angus said with a tense smile, and they hurried to the Volvo, where he answered her question.

CHAPTER 14

The ride to the prison was barely long enough to get the heat going in Nat's car, much less for her and Angus to process Graf's reaction. She pulled up to the white guardhouse, and the same young guard emerged. This time his cap was on straight, and he wore his most official expression.

Nat lowered the window. "Hi, it's Nat Greco and Angus Holt."

"Sorry, we're in lockdown."

"It's me, Jimmy." Angus leaned over to show his face, and the guard's dark eyes widened.

"I heard you got into it, but jeez! What you got there? You get *cut*, too?"

"No, just a few bruises and a fat lip."

"Bastards! I heard it started over cigarettes. They're *animals*." Jimmy's eyes flashed with contempt, and his gaze shifted to Nat, then quickly away. She read his mind—*I heard you almost got raped*—and flushed, unaccountably embarrassed. Jimmy returned to professional mode. "Anyways, sorry, I didn't recognize the car. I gotta ask you guys for ID. I'm on orders. Tryin' to keep out the riffraff, you know."

"I hear you." Angus shifted to get his wallet out of his back pocket, and Nat retrieved her driver's license, then produced them both.

"Hold on. I gotta write down the number, and I don't have a pen on me." Jimmy turned away, muttering, and went back to the guard-house.

"This joint is jumpin'." Angus eyed the prison in the distance. "No pun."

Nat craned her neck. State police cruisers, a boxy mobile crime lab, and other unmarked black sedans were parked in the driveway, blocking it completely. The parking lot was full. "What's going on, do you think?"

"Evidence gathering, in connection with the murders. They'll take photos, review surveillance tapes, listen to audiotapes, if they have them—though I doubt this place has that kind of hardware."

Jimmy returned with their IDs. "Here you go."

"Thanks." Nat took hers, slid it back in her wallet, and handed Angus his.

"Warden in, Jimmy?" he asked.

"No, he lef' a while ago."

"How about the deputy warden?"

"Went with him."

"Machik?"

"He's in."

"Thanks. See ya."

"Hope you feel better," Jimmy said, stepping back from the car. "Botha you."

Nat parked where she could, and they got out and walked up the road. Men in dark overcoats lingered on the icy driveway near the official cars, talking with state police, their hats low on their fore-heads. Nat assumed that the men in overcoats were federal marshals because she recognized one as the marshal they'd seen yesterday, in the driver's seat of the sedan. He waved when Nat and Angus approached.

"Nice shiner, Holt," he called out, his voice carrying in the frigid air. "You owe me money."

"What for?" Angus called back.

"I bet you wouldn't get out in one piece, and you did." He laughed, and so did Angus and the other men—everybody but Nat. She could feel her heartbeat speed up the closer she got to the prison.

"I know, right? Who woulda thought?" Angus caught Nat's eye, and his grin vanished. "Gentlemen, this is Natalie Greco, my colleague."

"Good to meet you, Natalie. I'm Edward Sparer." The marshal shook her hand heartily, and then his gaze fell to her Band-Aid. His expression darkened instantly, and she knew he was thinking the same thing as the guard at the gate.

"Where were you guys yesterday when I needed you?" Nat asked lightly, and they laughed, the tension broken.

"Just glad you're okay," Edward said, smiling. "All's well that ends well, huh? Now, Holt, we don't care about."

"Thanks, honey," Angus said. "So what's the deal? How long they gonna be in lockdown, you know?"

"They're not saying but I think just today. We're already standing down."

"You're always standing down."

"Your tax dollars at work."

Angus snorted. "How much am I paying you to babysit that thug?"

"Ha! You mean to freeze my ass off sittin' in a car in the middle of East Jippip?" Sparer shot back, and they laughed. "Not *nearly* enough. I'm *dyin'* for a decent cheesesteak."

"When's his trial?"

"February 8. Hey, Williams was a good boy yesterday. Bided his time by himself, nowhere near the RHU."

"You must be very proud." Angus clapped him on the back, they all exchanged goodbyes, and Nat and Angus continued on their way through the parked cars. Angus took her arm and led her up the steps to the metal door with the cheery red paint, hit a buzzer, and showed his face through the window. The door was opened by a plump, middle-aged woman with a lipsticked smile. She was majorly made up, and her ersatz red hair was coiled in old-fashioned pin curls.

"Angus! How are you?" she said, eyeing his bandage. The pancaked foundation on her forehead almost cracked with concern. "You poor thing! What did they do to you? Come in, come in!"

"Thanks, Joanie." Angus gave her a brief hug, then introduced Nat to her. Her name was Joan Wilson. "I understand that Kurt is in. Can I talk to him for a few minutes? It's important."

"I'll check and see, but don't get your hopes up. It's busy here today." Joan clucked and waddled off like a mother hen. Nat looked around the office area, which she hadn't been in yesterday. An entrance hallway led into a wider, paneled hall lined with wooden office chairs. One end table held a cheap lamp and some wrinkled magazines. An American flag stood in a holder next to an Employee of the Month plaque, and a softball trophy on a side table made the place look more like a dry cleaner's than a prison.

"Angus?" Nat was trying to suss out where she'd found Saunders. "This hall looks as wide as the one that runs through the prison. Is it?"

"Yes. Same hall, only we're on the unsecured side." Angus pointed to the right. "Conference room there." Then, to the left. "There're offices over there. The warden's office is behind us, then the deputy warden's. Then Kurt Machik's office, down the hall where Joan went. He's the assistant deputy warden."

"Thanks." Nat visualized the layout. They were at the bottom of the prison's T shape, and the stem of the T was the long hall that ran the length of the prison. She tried to imagine where the room was in which Saunders had died. Close to here, somewhere near the bottom of the T. That was where the bodies should have been. Not near the RHU, which was all the way down the hall, at the top of the T. How could anybody mix that up?

"Angus!" a voice boomed, and Nat turned to see a tall, thin man with a gaunt face and brown eyes behind rimless glasses emerging from his office and closing a door behind him.

"Hey, Kurt. Thanks for seeing us." Angus introduced Nat for the fortieth time that day. "Ms. Greco is the woman who was attacked by Kyle Buford yesterday, during my class."

"Goodness! I'm very sorry." Kurt Machik frowned so deeply, his forehead pinched in the middle, as if his thin skin didn't fit his cranium. His hair was brown with grayish temples, cut short as a bristle brush, and he wore a dark suit, a white oxford shirt, and a dark blue tie with a tie tack in the shape of a musical clef.

"Can we talk in your office, Kurt? I think this should be private."

"I was just about to get lunch. Would you two like to join me?" Machik turned to Nat stiffly, swiveling from the hip like a robot. "I know it sounds early, but we start at six in the morning here, so lunch is at ten thirty."

"I'd rather not," Angus interjected, but Machik shook his head.

"I have no other free time. My day is wall-to-wall, given the unfortunate events of yesterday. Follow me, please, and watch your step. The construction makes life a little difficult."

They followed him past a box of tiles and went around a corner into a homey dining room. A long table occupied the middle of the room, covered with a tablecloth of red-checked plastic. White cabinets and white countertops surrounded the room. A microwave sat on its own stand, and a white refrigerator bore a sign reading: HANDS OFF MY SLIM-FAST, GEORGE! Hot chicken soup bubbled up from a large pot on a sterno rack, its aroma filling the room and steaming the windows. Sunlight filtered through lacy curtains, and the view was of the construction trailer and, behind that, a grove of towering, snow-covered evergreens.

"May I get you some soup, Ms. Greco?" Machik asked, holding up a paper bowl.

"Please, call me Nat. Thanks, sure."

"Good. There's a garden salad over there and some hamburgers."

"Who does the cooking?"

"The inmates." Machik handed Nat a paper bowl of soup.

Yikes. "Thanks." Nat took the soup, sat down at the table, and grabbed a white plastic spoon from a coffee can covered with red contact paper. She took the first sip of soup, which tasted salty but delicious, at least for felons' fare.

"What's the verdict?" Machik asked.

Guilty, what else? "Great, thanks," Nat answered, while Angus pulled up a chair and sat down heavily, tucking a stray blond strand behind his ear.

"Kurt, I'm angry about what happened yesterday in my class. Did you approve Buford and Donnell getting in? Nobody is supposed to get in unless I approve them."

"I don't recall approving them." Machik chewed his hamburger. "You know you have a waiting list, and I usually take whoever's next on the list and send you the inmate's file, for your approval."

"That's my point. I looked through my files last night, and I have a file on each inmate and a letter, mailed to me at the law school, telling me who would like to enter the class. Those letters are signed by you. I didn't get any letter for Buford or Donnell."

"An actual signature or a stamped signature?"

"I think stamped. But what, are you blaming Joan now? Whether it's signed or stamped, I got no letter."

"As I said, I don't recall approving those two."

"Somebody had to, and you're the only one who processes the

approvals. How can you not recall?" Angus's tone hovered at barely civil. "It couldn't have been that long ago. Norris and Bolder, the inmates they replaced, were released a month ago. So if you approved it, you approved it this past month."

"Not necessarily. I line up the approvals before the openings occur. It could have been a long time ago, and lots of paper crosses my desk in a month or two." Machik didn't sound rattled, but he did set down his prisonburger. "I am not certain how it happened, but I will check into that for you."

"For *me*?" Angus raised his voice. "How about for you? How about for Natalie? How about you're concerned that she could have been killed, or I could have? How about that you care about a legal aid program that's now jeopardized? How about you care about these inmates, for God's sake?"

"I've said I'll look into it, and I will. You have my word."

"Kurt, it's outrageous. It endangered not only us, but everyone, especially since it happened during the riot."

"It wasn't a riot."

"Oh, please." Angus leaned back in his chair. "Don't bullshit me. I was here, and the way it went down meant that neither of us could get out when the lockdown was announced. If Natalie hadn't sent Graf over to where I was, I'd be dead."

"I understand your position and I will address it. I will. I promise. I'll get back to you." Machik turned to Nat. "Obviously, I have yet to get a full report on what happened, and I assure you that as soon as our investigation is complete, we'll supply you with one. Would you like me to send one to your lawyer, too?"

"My lawyer? I don't have a lawyer." Nat felt a kick under the table, coming from Angus.

"You don't?"

"She means not yet," Angus interjected. "And why do you assume I wouldn't sue, Kurt?"

"I know you care about the institution. You've given our inmates a lot of your time over the years."

Angus paused. "Tell you what. I'll give you a written release if you get me that report by the end of the week."

"No can do, Angus."

"Try."

Machik sipped from a plastic glass of water, which flexed in the center from the pressure of his long fingers.

Nat said, "I have a question. The news implied that the bodies of the inmates and the C.O., Ron Saunders, were found in the RHU. But that wasn't true."

Machik sipped more water. "I'm not sure exactly what was reported."

"The article quoted the warden."

"Perhaps he thought that was correct, at that point. I'm not sure when he was interviewed."

"How could he have thought that? I found Saunders's body myself, and it was nowhere near the RHU. It wouldn't be an easy mistake to make, especially not by someone as familiar with the prison layout as the warden." Nat gestured to the wall behind her. "The room they were in would be right on the other side of that wall, if I'm oriented correctly. There would have to be blood all over the rug, maybe even on the walls. I could show you."

"Not today. We're in lockdown, so I can't permit you back there. But I'll tell you, confidentially, that we don't always give a detailed press release, for obvious reasons."

"What reasons?"

"It's for the safety of the community. So we don't set off a panic."

Angus asked, "Don't you think they have a right to know?"

"Frankly, no." Machik stood up slowly. The mood in the room had changed, and Nat and Angus stood up as well. "I do have to get back to work. I'll talk to the warden and let you know."

"When is lockdown ending?" Angus asked. "I have a client with an appeal at the end of the week. I need to meet with him to file his papers."

"Unsure. Call before you come." Machik picked up his plate, his burger half eaten, and shook Nat's hand. "Again, I'm very sorry about what happened to you. I've enjoyed meeting you."

"It's mutual," Nat said, but her lying wasn't improving.

CHAPTER 15

It was Domestic Initiative Night, and Nat stood at the sink in her kitchen washing a bundle of floppy watercress, waiting for Hank. He'd called to see how she was, and she'd said she'd tell him over dinner, but he was running late. She poured chilled chardonnay into a thin crystal glass and slipped an audiobook into the CD player: Frank McCourt reading his memoir *Teacher Man*. She set the watercress in the strainer, took a sip of cool, tangy wine, and breathed a relaxed sigh as soon as McCourt began to speak, his charming Irish lilt reverberating like Gaelic music in the galley kitchen.

"Here they come. And I'm not ready. How could I be? I'm a new teacher and learning on the job."

Nat gathered wet watercress from the colander, put it in the salad spinner, slapped on the lid, and set it whirling. Each simple task carried her further from weeping widows and prison officials, from razorwire and stab wounds. The salad spun dry, and she took another sip of wine, eyeing the view outside the kitchen window. The cityscape under a curved moon, rocking in a black sky.

She took the dry watercress out of the spinner, arranged it on two white china plates, and scooped a perfect mound of lobster salad on top of each, light on the mayo, with chunky celery and fresh lemon.

She slid a wooden mill from the shelf and ground fresh pepper on each salad, releasing the pungent scent of the peppercorns and adding the finishing touch. She carried both salads to the table and assessed the setting with a food critic's eye. Round cherry table. The tasteful glow of two ivory candles, smokeless. Real linen napkins, also ivory. Red chunks of lobster adding just the right boldness. The stage was Revelations About Scary Scratches.

She cleaned up the sink, put away the dishes, and wiped down the black granite countertops until they glistened darkly. She took a self-satisfied sip of chardonnay, finally feeling at peace in the quiet apartment, the atmosphere enhanced by the sensibility of a writer as fine as Frank McCourt. On the audiobook, he was managing to articulate her own thoughts about her profession, though he'd never met her. Which, of course, was the magic of books.

"Honey!" came a shout from the front door. It was Hank, at the top of his lungs.

"TURN ON THE TV! RIGHT NOW! IT'S IMPORTANT!" It was her brother Paul, even louder.

Paul's here? "What's going on?" Nat set down her wineglass, alarmed. Something must be on the news. Maybe about the prison. She crossed to the TV, a silver Samsung on the counter.

"IT'S GOING INTO DOUBLE OVERTIME!" Paul shouted, barreling toward her with Hank, and the three almost collided as the men thundered into the kitchen, racing to the TV.

"Babe, where's the remote? Quick!" Hank hoisted his briefcase and gym bag onto the counter, knocking over her wineglass. It shattered upon impact, sending the chardonnay spilling onto the counter and over the side.

"Hank! Be careful." Nat grabbed a paper towel.

"Oops. Sorry, sweetheart! Why is it so dark in here? Where's the clicker?"

"FORGET IT!" Paul stood at the TV, punching the Power button.

The sleek TV sprang to life, and a square of supersaturated hues glowed in the candlelit kitchen, flickering frantically as Paul kept hitting the channel changer on the cable box like a video game.

"Don't break the TV, Paul," Nat said, her tone big sister circa 1986, even to her. She pressed the paper towel into the spill, then reached for another to wipe the floor before the wine soaked between the boards.

"HE SHOOTS, HE SCORES!"

"All *right*!" Hank slapped Paul high five, as Nat rose with the wet towels and tossed them into the wastebasket. Shards of thin glass were strewn across the counter, glinting in the candlelight. She'd never get it all up in the dark.

"Don't cut yourself, guys." Nat flicked on the overheard lights, blinked against the brightness, and unrolled another towel.

"Sorry, sweetheart," Hank said, touching her shoulder. The TV set his profile aglow, his features flickering blue and red. "But this is the most incredible game ever."

Nat hit the Off button on the audiobook. "When will the game be over?"

"TRAVELING! THAT'S TRAVELING, REF!" Paul pointed at the TV with the outrage of Émile Zola.

"And why is my crazy brother here? Hank?" Nat could see that Paul's cold was just fine.

"Pass, you turd!" Hank joined in, yelling at the TV. "Pass! God, he's such a hot dog!"

"PASS! NO, REF! WHERE'S THE FOUL, REF! WHAT ARE YA, STUPID?"

"Hank?" Nat raised her voice over the game. "Can you answer me?"

"Sorry. Our meeting ran late. What's for dinner? We're starved!" Hank's attention remained riveted on the TV. "Fade away! Yes!"

"We? Paul is staying for dinner?" Nat didn't worry overmuch

about hurting her brother's feelings. His ego was congenitally bulletproof.

"If we feed him, he'll go," Hank answered, glued to the game.

"YES! THREE POINTER! WE'RE ON THE MOOOOOV-VVEEE!"

Nat poured herself a new glass of wine. She took a sip, mentally going to Plan B. She'd offer Paul some extra lobster salad, and then she and Hank could eat alone after he'd gone. At least Hank was hungry. Even in the bright light, the lobster salad looked delicious.

"I'd kill for a burger," Hank said to the TV, his eyes dancing across the basketball court.

"BURGERS WITH CHEESE! PICKLES! THE WORKS! YES!"

Nat blinked. "I made the perfect lobster salad."

"We had lobster for lunch, babe. " Hank threw his arms in the air. "Oh, come on, Iverson! You gotta make that shot!"

Lobster for lunch? "Who has lobster for lunch?"

"YES! WHAT A SHOT! C-WEB! SO SMOOTH! DIDJA SEE THAT? SWEET!"

"We took clients to the Palm."

"Why is Paul here?"

"We took one car. He's dropping me off. Do we have any burgers?"

Nat sighed inwardly. *At the prison. Wanna go?*

"Shoot, you lard ass!"

"A.I. WITH THE FADEAWAY! YES! I SWEAR, THIS IS GOIN' INTO DOUBLE OVERTIME!"

Nat went to the refrigerator for ground beef.

Later, after the Sixers beat the Celtics in triple overtime, and Paul and his mouth had finally gone home, Nat and Hank sat at the table, she behind a cup of Celestial Seasonings and he a bottle of Heineken. She told him the lite version of the Buford story, then about Saunders's death and his last words, and the visit to his widow.

"That's terrible, babe." Hank eyed her, his brown eyes rich with sympathy, and his usual grin gone for good. "You could have been really hurt."

"I know."

"I mean, this Buford character, what if he had gotten out of control? You could have been killed."

Tell me about it. "Honestly, I feel as if that's almost behind me. What's in front of me is telling the wife."

Hank scratched his head, mussing his red-brown hair. "'It's under the floor'? What did he mean by that?"

"Maybe his will, or some money? I don't know, but I hope she'll understand when I tell her." Nat sipped her cooling tea. "I dread going out there again."

"Then why don't you just call? Tell her over the phone."

"I told her I'd go back."

"Women." Hank smiled and took a swig from the green bottle, then Nat filled him in about the visit to the prison and the press release, which was where they disagreed. Hank set down his bottle. "I don't think they need to put in the press release where the bodies were found."

"Why not?"

"First off, it's disgusting. Second off, no company would explain every gory detail in a press release, especially if it makes them look stupid."

"But they're not a private company. They're a prison, a state-run facility. They account to the public, not to a president or CEO."

"I don't see what difference it makes."

Nat thought of Angus. "Don't you think the neighbors have a right to know? The question is, who decides?"

"But what's the point of telling the neighbors? It'd just get them all upset. They were never in danger."

"But it's not the truth."

"So what?"

"There is no 'so what.' The truth is its own end. They created a false picture. I was there, and it was chaos."

"Well, the good news is it's over." Hank cocked his head, his grin returning. "You talk to the widow, then you and this guy—what's his name?—Angus, you'll stop running around and get back to work."

"We're not running around."

"What're you doing then?"

"Following up."

"Not your job, babe."

"You jealous?"

"You know the answer to that." Hank smiled, because she did know.

"Even though he has a long blond ponytail and asked me out?"

"And I bet you told him no. You love me, and we both know it. How could you not?" Hank rose with the empty bottle. "By the way, that cut on your cheek? It looks hot, bad girl."

Nat managed a laugh. *Then you're gonna love my chest.*

"Did Angus get hurt, too?"

"Yes, on his face."

"Good. Remind me to hit the guy if I ever meet him." Hank snorted. "Bring a little excitement to those boring law parties."

"Don't be silly."

"He takes you to a prison, then gets you to save his lame ass? He needs a girl to rescue him?"

Nat frowned. "You didn't really say that, did you?"

"Bottom line, it's true, isn't it?"

"The prisoners work out all the time, Hank. Angus is a law professor, and he did fight for me." *I just didn't tell you that part.*

"Hell, you were tougher than he was. A true Greco! Ha!" Hank rose, but Nat was feeling defensive. And guilty for not telling Hank the whole truth about Buford. He would see, in bed.

"Ready to go up?" she asked, rising.

"Now you're talking." Hank threw an arm around her, and the wall phone started ringing.

"If that's Paul . . ." Nat reached over and picked up the receiver. It was a man's voice, but not Paul's. "Hello?"

"Professor Greco?"

"This is she."

"Mind your own business. Stay outta Chester County, bitch."

CHAPTER 16

The next day, Nat was trying to focus on teaching her seminar but wasn't succeeding. She'd dressed in a new navy suit to get herself going, but her energy lagged. She'd hardly slept, from worrying about the phone call and fighting with Hank. He'd thought the call was warning her not to go see Barb Saunders, but she thought the call was about the prison, maybe from Buford's friends or family. They went to bed again without making love, which meant that Nat hid her scratches under her sweatshirt for another night. It was strange and new, to be keeping so much from Hank.

"So, as you know," Nat continued, "*Brown v. Board of Education* struck down the doctrine of 'separate but equal' in public education. The case was a landmark in the history of justice. It's hard to believe, but there was a time in this country when it was considered just for black and white children to attend separate schools, as long as the schools were allegedly equal."

Nat eyed her students, who looked unusually attentive, despite their compulsive IM-ing. Anderson, coiffed and prepared, was paying rapt attention, and so were Carling, Gupta, and Chu. They'd heard about the prison riot, and Nat's new Band-Aid was proof that she'd been there. She wondered if Angus had gotten a call last night, too. She'd phoned him before her morning classes, but he hadn't answered.

"The Supreme Court in *Brown* recognized that discrimination creates a permanent underclass of human beings, an anathema to the constitutional principle of equal protection under the law." Nat's heart wasn't in it, and she sounded flat, even to herself. "I hope you see *Brown* as a logical follow-up to our discussion of Shylock and the effects of discrimination."

"Professor Greco?" Carling raised his hand. He had on a black knit cap, very Josh Hartnett.

"Yes?"

"How about we put on another skit? I'll be Brown and you be the Board of Ed." Carling grinned, and the class laughed.

"No, thanks." Nat didn't even mind the joke. Then she got an idea. "Mr. Carling, did you do the reading for today?"

"Of course. I had to, after last class. I couldn't take the chance with my grade."

Whatever works. "Then why don't you come up and present the case?"

"For reals?" Carling's grin broadened, and eight other mouths fell open.

"Why not? You guys present cases in your other classes, don't you?"

"In the big classes, sure."

Ouch. "So let's give it a try here. We're small but we're mighty. You said you could be a teacher. Go for it."

"Sweet!" Carling practically leapt from his seat, and the class started talking among themselves, their faces reanimated over the lids of their laptops. Wykoff and Gupta high-fived each other, for reasons known only to young men.

"Everybody," Nat said, "please give the professor your full attention." She left the stage as Carling sauntered up with his case materials. He wore a Sean John sweatshirt and baggy jeans that slid down as he strode to the lectern, where he eyed the touch screen with lust.

"Cool buttons, yo."

"Leave them alone." Nat took a seat.

"Good morning, boys and girls," Carling began, and Nat hoped she hadn't made a mistake.

"Call on me, Professor Carling!" Wykoff shouted. "I did the reading!"

"Me, too!" Marilyn Krug yelled, but Carling waved them into silence.

"Please, kiddies, no calling out." Carling's eyes found Nat's, and she shot him a thumbs-up. He squared his shoulders. "We begin our discussion today with *Brown v. Board of Ed.* Now, in *Brown* . . ."

Nat listened as Carling delivered a respectable discussion of the case, which she footnoted when necessary. In the meantime, she worried about the phone call and yesterday's meeting with Machik. She couldn't wait to talk to Angus.

After class, she found the clinic, tucked away by itself in a corner of the lower level, and pushed open its glass door onto an elegant suite of offices, located off a large reception area furnished with cherrywood tables and chairs and matching chair rails. Couches and club chairs in muted mocha hues coordinated with the tan walls and a patterned carpet, and the recessed lighting was subdued and soft, more Ritz-Carlton than Public Interest. A few students hung out, talking and looking at legal papers, and Nat saw more than a few fisherman's sweaters, complete with ponytails, jeans, and cowboy boots. It was clearly the team uniform, and Angus was the counter-culture captain.

"Is Professor Holt in?" she asked a female student who'd stepped forward to meet her. The girl had large brown eyes, dark hair that reached to her waist, and a white Indian tunic over her jeans.

"He's in, but he can't be disturbed," she answered, eyeing Nat up and down.

"I'm Professor Greco. I work here."

"I know that."

Not today, child. "Excuse me." Nat saw three doors over the girl's shoulder, one of which read, "Clinic Director," and made a beeline for it.

"Stop. You can't bother him." The girl hurried after her, but Nat knocked on the door.

"Angus, it's Nat."

"Natalie?" The door opened. Angus was on the cell phone, wearing a colorful Ecuadorian sweater, jeans, and a new gauze bandage. He motioned her in, shut the door behind them, and flashed her the one-minute sign. She sat down in one of the mesh chairs across from the rough-hewn pine table he used as a desk. There was nothing on it except for an Amnesty International mug of pens and sharpened pencils, an orange iMac, and three stacks of correspondence, each document bearing a yellow Post-it. The desk was immaculate, especially for a socialist.

Angus said into the cell, "Look, we can file an entry of appearance and brief electronically. All you have to do is appear before Judge Pratter, make the motion, and explain that the extern can't be there because the program's been suspended."

Nat looked around, surprised to find she'd been completely wrong about his office. Books, case reporters, and law reviews stood straight as soldiers in clean oak bookcases. Accordion files sat on the credenza in alphabetical order. There was no Che Guevara poster; only tastefully framed reproductions of pirates, sea captains, and knights, painted in vivid washes of watercolor. The signature was N. C. Wyeth. Nat amended her psychological profile of their collector: a socialist with a Hero Complex.

"Then get an associate to do it, Jake. What's your pro bono commitment this year? This family has no heat and it's twenty-five degrees outside."

Diplomas hung discreetly near the window, one from Williams College, another from Harvard Law, and one for "Sally" from The Doggie Obedience School of Delaware County. Black notebooks sat stacked on a table, next to a Bose iPod player and a cube of jazz CDs and mix tapes. A white Sony TV on a shelf played on mute, and on the screen, the female hosts of *The View* were interrupting one another in merciful silence.

"Great! Thanks, bro." Angus closed the phone and brushed back a stray hair. "Sorry to make you wait. I'm trying to get these appearances covered with no notice, and it's impossible."

"Can't the kids help? Why is Daddy making all the calls?"

"These they can't help with." Angus leaned against the credenza. "I'm cashing in every chit I have. That last guy was the managing partner at Pepper and my law school roommate."

"Who's Alanis Morrisette out front? She almost didn't let me in."

"Deirdre? She's a little protective."

"She's a little in love."

"Admiration is not love." Angus cocked his head. "Why are you so cranky? We didn't get beaten up or yelled at today—though it's still early."

Nat realized she'd sounded oddly jealous. "I got a phone call last night, from a man who told me to stay out of Chester County."

"I got the same call. Did you star-69 him?"

"He was out of the service area."

"Same here." Angus frowned. "But why'd he call *you*? You're a victim. You're not representing anybody out there."

"If I got a call, it's not related to a representation. It's related to the riot and maybe to Barb Saunders."

"Right. Weird."

"It could be one of Buford's friends or family. He may not want me to testify against him."

"Possible, but not likely. He won't come to trial for a year or so."

Angus shook his head. "I still don't get why he called you. You're not the one who has business in Chester County. I am."

"I am, too." Nat hadn't filled him in about yesterday. "I'm supposed to go to Barbara Saunders's this week. I didn't tell her anything when we went out there. She wasn't up to it."

"So are you saying that's why they called you? You think someone's trying to prevent you from telling her? Why would they?"

"No, not that. Only she and I knew I hadn't told her yesterday."

"Oh." Angus paused, lost in thought. "What about Joe Graf? He's not a fan of ours."

"Did it sound like him to you?"

"I don't know his voice that well."

"Me neither," Nat said. "Why wouldn't he want us out there?"

"Maybe we're a reminder that he didn't help Saunders, or it makes him look bad. Who knows? I'm supposed to go back to the prison today. They're letting me see my client. I wonder if Graf is back on the job."

"I doubt it. Are you still going?"

"Of course, I have to. But you don't." Angus folded his arms, bulky in the thick sweater. "Why don't you call Barb Saunders, instead of going there? It's good enough under the circumstances. Or write her a letter."

"Why don't I just email? 'Re: Your Husband's Last Words.'"

Angus smiled. "What does Mr. Greco say to your going out there?"

"Hank? Same as you." *Or, we're not speaking.*

Angus's cell rang, and he checked the display. "Sorry, I have to take this." He opened the phone. "Frank, thanks for getting back to me. My extern program is on hiatus, and I need a litigator to get me a continuance from Padova today, at two. Can you help?"

Nat looked away. On TV, *The View* had given way to the local news at noon. An anchorwoman came on, and the scene switched to a living room. A young woman talked into a station-logo microphone as she sat teary-eyed on a couch. The living room looked familiar. So did the woman.

"He picked up a possession charge," Angus was saying. "Coke, second offense. But he's a good kid. He got caught doing a line in the bathroom at a club, Privato. Oh, yeah? Then don't go back, or don't pee."

It took Nat a second to recognize the woman on TV. It was Barb Saunders's sister, Jennifer. The living room was in the Saunders' house. It must be a follow-up story to Ron Saunders's murder at the prison.

"Angus, look." Nat got up, crossed to the TV, and hit the Volume button.

"Hold on, Frank." Angus glanced at the TV screen. "Lemme call you back, bro."

The voiceover said, "The widow and her three children were at the funeral when the burglar struck, absconding with two computers, cash, and jewelry. It seems heartless that someone would take advantage of such a terrible tragedy, but state police say it isn't uncommon. Burglars read the obituaries, too, and know that homes will be empty at that time."

"She was *burglarized*?" Nat watched as the camera panned a ransacked living room. Children's DVDs and picture books had been torn from shelves. The drawers of the computer workstation had been dumped on the floor. The couch had been slashed, its pink stuffing yanked out. It looked like the room had been searched. As if someone had been looking for something.

It's under the floor.

The anchorwoman reappeared. "In other news, a warehouse fire in the city's Tioga section . . ."

"What the *hell*?" Nat lowered the volume, trying to process the information, and Angus crossed to his computer.

"Let's get the full story," he said, and Nat joined him at his laptop.

He hit a few keys and found the news article. The headline read, **Chester County Widow Burglarized During Funeral**, and the story confirmed the TV account, adding that $378 had been stolen from the Saunders home. Nat felt a clutch in her chest for Barb, having to endure so much. Then she had a darker thought.

"Something odd is going on," she said. "This isn't a random act. It has to be connected to the riot, and maybe the phone calls."

"You know, call me crazy, but I don't think that was a burglary. I think that person was looking for something."

Bingo. "What makes you say that?" Nat wanted to test his rationale. He didn't know yet about the message Saunders had given her.

"The couches were slashed. No burglar slashes couches. I see that in our drug cases. Drug dealers keep cash in the cushions. It's the first place a rival gang looks, or the cops."

Two heads are better than one. "I should tell you what Saunders said to me before he died. He said, 'Tell my wife it's under the floor.'"

"Are you serious?" Angus's blue eyes widened, now that the swelling had gone down. "Whoa."

"Exactly."

"So you think whatever they were looking for is under the floor?"

"Maybe. But what could it be? I was thinking maybe a will or some money. Now you have me thinking drugs or drug money."

"Maybe Saunders was crooked."

"I can't believe it." Nat thought of Barb, the modest house, and the kids with the Game Boy. "I know there are crooked prison guards, but I can't believe it of him, of that family."

"You don't know anything about Saunders, or what he did while he was alive. Drug money can corrupt anybody." Angus handed her his cell phone, which was still warm. "Call Barb Saunders now. With this burglary, break-in, or whatever it was, she needs to know that something is under her floor. Assuming the burglars didn't find it already."

"Agree." Nat opened the phone, dialed information, and got the number, which rang and rang. Then the Saunders's answering machine came on, catching her short. It was a man's voice on the recording, and she realized it was Ron Saunders's. Shaken, she waited to leave a message, but the machine was full. "No answer," she said, uneasy. "I'll keep calling. Sooner or later, I'll get through."

"She must be avoiding the press calls." Angus puckered his stitched-up lip. "If you want, I'll stop by the house and tell her on my way back from the prison."

"So you're really going?"

"Of course. I've gotten threats like that before. It's an occupational hazard. Most of them are from landlords. Those guys are power trippers of the first order. That's why Donald Trump is the way he is. It's not the money, it's the ownership of the planet."

"What if I went with you?"

"Why?" Angus's expression turned grave.

"I want to see what's going on out there. Check it out. It's all so fishy, and I care about Barb." *Also, I'm feeling a little Nancy Drew.*

"That wouldn't be staying out of Chester County."

"No, but it's daytime, and I'm with you."

"I don't like it."

"You're not the boss of me."

Angus smiled. "What will Mr. Greco say?"

"He isn't, either." *Plus, I won't tell him.*

"I promise to protect you better this time. I have to."

"Why?"

"Because you're my friend, and I don't have that many."

"Aw. How about Deirdre?"

Angus rolled his eyes, and Nat got up to go.

CHAPTER 17

The day was cold and overcast, but the drive still starkly beautiful, the white snow and black trees washed with gray by a pewter
sky. Angus spent most of the ride on the cell phone, and Nat tried
again to call Barb Saunders, but had no luck. She'd try calling again
later rather than going over there. She didn't want to barge in yet.
She focused instead on the scenery, trying not to think about Barb
Saunders or the phone call last night. She had as much right to be in
Chester County as anybody else. Not that she didn't check the outside
mirror—a few hundred times.

Angus pulled up to the entrance, and Nat could see that the prison
was back to business as usual. They didn't have to produce their IDs
for Jimmy, who was back in good humor. In the parking lot, families
sat in minivans with the engines running, waiting for visiting hours.
Angus parked, and they walked in the cold up the driveway, now
unobstructed by mobile crime labs or black sedans. They waved to
the marshals and entered the prison the way they had that first day,
going through the sally ports. Nat left her camelhair coat in the locker
room before they entered the prison proper.

Tanisa met them with her characteristic smirk. "Well, I'll be
damned. You lived, freak."

"So did you!" Angus scooped her up in a bear hug, and she left the floor, kicking her black work shoes.

"Oh *hell* no! Put me down!"

"Thanks for the jacket," Nat said, hugging her impulsively.

Tanisa reared back, laughing. "I'm on the job, white people! What the hell's got into you?"

"We're happy, that's all," Nat answered. "I would've brought the jacket back but I didn't know I was coming out here today. I'll get it to you."

Tanisa waved her off. "Don't think on it! It's a present to you, girl. I heard what you did to try and save Ron. That was above and beyond."

"Thanks."

"I'm feeling so bad about him." Tanisa locked the door behind them, shaking her head. Her hair fishhooks peeked out from under her cap. "He was salt of the earth. I couldn't take off to go to the funeral this morning and now I'm hearing about the burglary. You believe that?"

"Terrible."

"I feel so bad for Barb and the kids. How much can a woman bear?"

Nat thought of the dark bedroom. "Do you know her?"

"Met her coupla times. Real nice. Went to pay my respects last night, but she was sick upstairs."

Angus said, "I'm just happy you made it through, Tanisa. I was worried about you."

"*Hmph.* Take more than a few shit cans to break me down."

"What do you mean?"

"You didn't hear that? How they started the mattresses on fire?" Tanisa wrinkled her nose. "Been saving up their *shit* for God knows how long and threw a match into it. *Nasty!* What if they had that damn bug that was going around, the one that kills you? They tried to throw burning shit at me, I'd throw it right back—and add some of my own!" Tanisa's smile vanished. "Anyway, we're back in business. Who you seeing today, Angus?"

"Willie Potts."

"I think he's waiting on you. I'll go see." Tanisa escorted them through the metal detector, and in a minute they'd pass into the secured section of the prison.

Nat felt her stomach tense in the heat and smelled the close, anti-septic smell. In a second, they'd be in the wide hallway, just a few paces from the classroom where Buford had attacked her. She steeled herself and followed Angus past the control center, then stopped. Everything was different. The hallway had been completely reconfig-ured. It had been narrowed by half, and a bright white wall blocked off the corridor through which she'd run to find Saunders. The new hall ran the length of the prison. Nat stood, stymied, and identified a new smell. Fresh paint.

"Where are the staff offices?" Angus had already spun around, his confused expression mirroring hers.

"This is where the hallway used to be." Nat ran a hand along the wall, then looked at her fingerpads. Drying white paint dusted the whorls on her fingertips, like fingerprints in reverse. "They've walled off the way to the room where Saunders and the inmate were killed."

"Oh, yeah, they're remodeling," Tanisa said, returning with an inmate. He looked about twenty-five years old, a slight African American man with his hair shorn close to his head.

"Hey, Willie," Angus said quickly, shaking the man's hand. "Why don't you go sit down, and I'll be right over."

"No sweat." The inmate left for an informal meeting area near the classroom.

"Tanisa, didn't there used to a hallway here?" Nat asked.

"Yeah, but it's gonna be a new set of staff offices. It was gonna be Phase Two but they moved it up to Phase One. The muckety-mucks musta wanted their new offices sooner."

"When did they change the schedule?" Nat asked, just as she spotted Machik walking toward them down the skinny new hallway. His dark suit jacket flew open as he walked, but his striped tie remained in place, under its musical clef.

"Angus! Natalie!" he called out, waving to them.

Tanisa turned. "Hello, sir," she said as he approached.

Angus shook his hand. "Kurt, what happened to the old staff offices?"

"Hello to you, too." Machik turned to Nat. "How's your cut, dear? Improved, I hope."

"Great, but I'm as confused as Angus. Where's the room where Ron Saunders was killed? Is it behind this wall?"

Machik maintained his smile. "It's being rebuilt. It'll be a set of offices, a suite. When it's all finished next year, we'll have two new pods, an enlarged infirmary, and three new classrooms."

"So the room we were talking about yesterday doesn't exist anymore?"

"I suppose not. They got back to work yesterday."

"Because of the riot?"

"It was a disturbance."

Persistence pays.

"Not at all, it was always part of the plan."

"Phase One or Phase Two?" Nat asked.

Machik's eyes narrowed behind his glasses. "How do you know those terms?"

Nat thought fast. She didn't want to get Tanisa in trouble. "I'm a builder's daughter. Greco Construction, ever hear of it?"

"Why, yes, I have," Machik said, surprised.

"Well, that's my family. Most construction has a Phase One, which includes framing, piping, electrical, HVAC, and a Phase Two. Drywall, primer, paint, and the like. Phase Three is flooring, carpeting, the details. They're practically terms of art."

Tanisa's eyes shifted from Nat to Machik and back again.

"Phase One," Machik answered.

Why is he lying? "If they demolished yesterday, I bet the rug with the blood on it is still in a Dumpster. It's blue."

"I believe they emptied the Dumpster this morning." Machik frowned. "I fail to see why you're so interested in this issue."

I'm interested because you're lying. "Two men were killed in that room. I know. I was there. It's a crime scene."

"Natalie, Ron Saunders's murder was a tragedy for us, the first of its kind at this facility. My wife and I, as well as the warden and his wife, Elena, attended his funeral this morning. Now we have to move on. We have a prison to run. This was a crime scene, but the murderer is dead. There's no one to prosecute." Machik stiffened. "We have another crime scene in the RHU—which, by the way, we are preserving, for at least another day or two—and that's where we're devoting our resources and efforts. Understand?"

"I understand," Nat answered, but she didn't. She didn't understand why Machik would lie about the scheduling of the construction, or why they'd want to cover up the room in the first place. None of it made sense. She said, "Did you hear that Barb Saunders was burglarized?"

"Yes, I did. Terrible shame." Machik turned to Angus. "Now. Angus. If you're here for Willie Potts, he's waiting for you. He's got to be back in his cell in fifteen minutes."

"Why?" Angus frowned. "We just got here."

"We're moving him." Machik checked his watch. "Folks, I've got work to do. Tanisa, please show Angus and Natalie to Mr. Potts."

"Yes, sir." Tanisa motioned to them.

Angus turned to Machik. "Joe Graf in today?" he asked.

"No. He deserves the day off, don't you think?"

"Sure," Angus answered, meeting Nat's eye.

CHAPTER 18

Sorry about the delay, Willie," Angus said. He introduced Nat and set down his accordion file on a white Formica table, one of six built into the painted cinderblock wall. The tables stuck out in a line, and at each were plastic bucket chairs on either side, more fast-food restaurant than prison except for the uniformed C.O. standing against the far wall.

"'S'all right," Willie answered, nodding. He sat behind a wrinkled manila folder. "How's your lip, Angus?"

"Fine. Where were you during the riot?"

"Hiding under my desk."

They laughed, and Angus turned to Nat. "Willie works in the processing room, which used to be across the aisle."

Willie added, "They got us down the hall now, trying to hook up all the computers. It's crazy. All those wires, like spaghetti."

"Why they stripping you out, Willie?" Angus asked, as he opened the folder, went through the papers, and pulled out an affidavit.

"My cellie's having some problems with the Mexicans."

Angus turned again to Nat. "A strip-out is when they take all the inmate's belongings out of his cell, either to search for contraband or move him. I think I told you they move the inmates around, to cut down on gang rivalries. No chance for a fight, but no chance for a friendship, either."

"I'm my own friend," Willie said. "That's the best policy."

"I hear you. Okay, we don't have much time. I prepared this affidavit along the lines we discussed. It's what you told me last week. Why don't you read it and sign it?" Angus slid the paper to Willie, addressing Nat again. "Willie was picked up for his second DUI and is just about to finish up his stint."

Willie looked up. "I got eleven days left."

"He completed the alcohol rehab program here and now he teaches it. He's been clean and sober for how long now, pal?"

"Six hundred and eight days."

"Congratulations," Nat said, wondering what it was like to count your life in days. Days of sobriety. She was lucky, addicted only to books.

"We're filing an appeal for Willie on Friday, to get him pardoned, so his record won't show his DUI conviction. His experience in the office qualifies him for a number of jobs on the outside, but he needs to get his driver's license back so he can drive."

"This looks great, Angus. You got a pen?"

"Hold on." Angus rose and said to Nat, "Excuse me. Be right back. They're not allowed to have pens, and neither are we."

"Sure." Nat shifted as he left, then realized she was sitting alone with a prison inmate. Two days ago, this would have scared her, but after the riot, it didn't. *Ironic.* "So, you must be so thrilled to go."

"I can't wait. See my wife and kid, my grandmom." Willie beamed. "But I got no regrets. This place did a lot of good for me, and so did Angus. He helped me get the job in the office. I learned Microsoft Word and Excel, too."

"What do you do there?"

"I keep all the records, so they know when everybody's bit is up, and also infirmary visits, dental, write-ups, what have you."

Write-ups. Where had she heard that term? Then she remembered. Graf had said that just before the riot, he and Ron Saunders had had the inmate in to talk about his write-up. "What's a write-up?"

"When we get disciplined, say. They write us up."

"Do you, in the office, get a copy of a write-up each time an inmate is disciplined?"

"Yes, ma'am."

"Please, call me Nat. How does that work?"

"The C.O. fills out a form and gives it to me through the window in the processing office. I log it in, and that's it." Willie shrugged his shoulders, knobby in his thin T-shirt.

"Then the C.O. tells the inmate?"

"No, the other way around. The inmate gets the write-up first, before the C.O. gives me the other two copies. I log it in and file one in the disciplinary file and the other in his inmate file."

Nat tried to remember what Graf had said. "Then does the C.O. talk to the inmate about it?"

"Sometimes. They bring him to the security office, make sure he understands what the deal is."

Hmm. "Do you remember seeing a write-up for an inmate who was killed during the riot?" Nat had forgotten his name. She'd been so focused on Saunders, no other death mattered.

"Ramirez?"

"No."

"Upchurch?"

"Yes. Did you get a write-up for Upchurch, maybe the same day of the riot or the day before?"

"I don't think so, off the top of my head."

"Do you usually remember the write-ups that come in?"

"Mostly. This ain't that big a place. No gangstas except in RHU."

Nat remembered something Graf had said. "Did Upchurch ever get written up for marijuana?"

"Upchurch, a write-up for weed?" Willie squinted, confused. "I don't remember that. He got written up for insubordination, runnin' his mouth."

Why would Graf have lied about that? "Did he get written up for insubordination right before the riot?"

"I don't remember, not off the top of my head."

"Did he get written up a lot for insubordination?" Nat thought back. Graf had said Upchurch was a troublemaker.

"All the time."

"By Ron Saunders?"

"No." Willie glanced behind him, but the C.O. stood well out of earshot, against the wall in the corridor. "Upchurch had no problem with Saunders. It was Graf used to write him up. Graf was always in his grille."

Whoa. "More than the other C.O.s?"

"Oh, yeah. Picked on him."

"How do you know that? Did you know Upchurch?"

"No, he wasn't in my pod. I knew his name on account of his write-ups, from Graf."

"How do you know that Graf picked on him, and not the other way around?"

"Most of these C.O.s, they're all right." Willie checked over his shoulder, then leaned closer, lowering his voice. "But if Graf was the one got killed, nobody woulda shed a tear."

"So why would Upchurch kill Saunders and not Graf?" Nat whispered, but just then Angus returned with Tanisa and a male C.O., interrupting the conversation.

Angus handed Willie the pen. "You got a minute to sign. They need you at your cell."

Rats! Nat bit her tongue. Angus had the worst timing in legal history.

"Okay." Willie accepted the pen and signed his name.

"Do you have any questions?"

"You think it'll work?" Willie stood up and handed the affidavit to Angus, who took it and slipped it back in the folder.

"We're doing everything we can, pal."

Tanisa said, "Willie, John will take you back. I gotta get rid of these lawyers."

"Okay." Willie left without a look back, as Tanisa escorted Angus and a preoccupied Nat to the exit door by the new wall. They waited while Tanisa unlocked the door. The C.O. fell unusually silent, the only sound the clinking of the crude keys.

"Thanks, Tanisa." Angus touched her arm.

"Yes, thanks," Nat added. "I owe you that jacket."

"Forget it." Tanisa kept her eyes downcast as she unlocked the second barred door and held it open for them to leave. "I'm the one who should be thanking you."

"It was nothing," Nat said, getting her meaning. She retrieved her coat, and she and Angus walked down the corridor, through the sally ports, and out the door. They stepped out into the brutal cold. Nat looked up beyond the razorwire to the sky above, which had darkened to a charcoal wash. Spiky evergreens, burdened with snow, cut a jagged horizon, and a vast white field surrounded them like a chilly embrace.

"So they walled off the room." Angus shoved his hands in his pockets. "I don't get it."

"I think they're hiding something," Nat said. They walked down the driveway and waved to the marshal, who was on a cell in his car. "I learned a lot of juicy stuff from Willie."

"What'd I miss?"

"Tell you in the car." Nat shot him a wink.

"Having fun?"

And Nat had to admit, to her own surprise, that she was.

•   •   •

They sat in traffic, going nowhere on the road that wound back through the Brandywine countryside. Cars were lined up ahead as far as Nat could see, their taillights burning red and their exhausts exhaling plumes of white smoke. She used the time to call Barb Saunders and succeeded only in leaving a please-call-back message. She fidgeted in her long coat and checked the darkening sky. At this rate, she'd be late getting home, which would necessitate an explanation to Hank. She didn't remember what happened when Nancy Drew explained things to Ned. She hoped it was a happy ending.

"This traffic is crazy," Angus said. "Must be an accident. It gums up the whole works."

"It's the single lane that's the problem."

"I'll get off this road as soon as I can. I-95 isn't that far. Or, how about we stop and get some dinner, then try after it's cleared." Angus looked over. "That's not an ask-out."

"Still, not a good idea. I have to get home."

"I hear you." Angus shifted into second. No hand bumped into her knee, which was cold even in stockings. He said, "Let's review. Graf told us that he and Saunders had written up Upchurch for weed, but Willie says that didn't happen. I believe Willie. He's smart."

"Okay, so why do you think Graf lied about the write-up? Or do you think he just misspoke?"

"No, he didn't misspeak. He lied because he didn't want us to know he had bad blood with Upchurch."

"Agree, and that makes me suspicious." Nat turned it over in her mind. "Plus, it doesn't make sense that Upchurch would attack Saunders, if he had an issue with Graf."

"No, it doesn't. It looks bad." Angus shook his head, his eyes focused on traffic. "I hate what I'm thinking."

"What?" Nat asked, but she knew.

"That Upchurch's murder didn't happen the way Graf says it did."

Angus's tone was grave. "Machik must know that, and that's why they're hiding what went on in that room. They've destroyed the crime scene, so there's no way even the blood spatter can be preserved. They must have done an autopsy on Upchurch—they do in every homicide—and I wonder what it shows."

"What do you mean?"

"An autopsy can tell a lot about the way a knife fight actually went down. You know, like the angle of the knife wounds, even which wounds came first, almost reconstruct it."

Nat turned it over in her mind. "Graf told us that Upchurch attacked Saunders and then attacked him, and that he, Graf, was able to save himself by turning the knife on Upchurch."

"Right, but that doesn't make sense, according to what Willie told you. If Upchurch was going to stab anybody, it would have been Graf. You know, I've dealt with plenty of prison brutality cases and excessive force cases, in my time."

"And?"

"What if Upchurch pulled the knife on Graf, and then Saunders defended Graf? Maybe Saunders even stepped in front of Graf to save him. Then Graf saw his friend cut down and simply executed Upchurch, in the heat of battle. C.O.s are human beings, like soldiers. Think Haditha or My Lai."

Nat considered it as the Beetle rolled an inch or two and the sky got darker.

"It's entirely possible that Upchurch was no threat to Graf at the time he was killed," Angus continued, sounding intrigued. "For all we know, Upchurch could have been on his knees, begging for his life. That's the kind of thing an autopsy would show. The angle of the knife would be different, depending on whether the blow was struck from above or from the same level."

"Why stop there, if you're spinning hypos?" Nat asked, her thoughts clicking ahead. "What if there was no attack by Upchurch at all? What if Graf murdered Upchurch in cold blood? Planned the whole thing. Even planted the knife on him, after the fact?"

"What?" Angus looked over, his blue eyes widening. "Why would Graf have done that?"

"I don't know. For the same reason he bullied Upchurch. There was animosity between them."

"That's a stretch, Natalie. We don't know enough to go there."

"But what if?"

Angus thought a minute. "Then how does Saunders end up dead?"

"He's a casualty, like you said, of war. Graf sacrifices him. He's just there to provide the story that Upchurch attacked him and he acted in self-defense."

"*Graf* kills Saunders?" Angus's lips parted. "That's crazy! They were best friends. You heard him."

"We've established that he's a liar."

"And a jerk and a bigot. But that's not the same as a cold-blooded killer. That's not how C.O.s work, anyway. They're tight, like cops. Like soldiers, too, come to think of it. Loyal to each other." Angus's car traveled another inch on the clogged road. "You know, we're forgetting something. There's one sure way to find out what really happened in that room."

"How?"

"They have video surveillance all over the prison. Did you see those silver orbs on the ceilings, with the mirrors? There're cameras inside them."

Nat hadn't noticed.

"I know they have videotapes of the riot. The troopers told me they turned them over to the Chester County D.A., as evidence. So they must have videotapes of that room, too."

Nat straightened in her seat, imagining a videotape of a brutal double murder and of her trying to save Saunders's life. Did she want to see it? Could she even watch?

"Which room was it, exactly?"

"I don't know. One of the staff rooms." Then Nat remembered. "Willie said they take inmates into the security office to discuss their write-ups."

"Good," Angus said, nodding. "That's what we need to do. Get those tapes, from the security office." The Beetle finally reached the corner, then Angus took a right off onto another road. Traffic flowed freer, and Nat felt her own gears rev up.

"So how would we do that? They'll never give them up voluntarily."

"If I didn't owe Graf my life, I'd subpoena them."

"What do you mean?"

"I'd file a suit on behalf of the inmate who was killed, Upchurch, for deprivation of civil rights and unreasonable use of force, along the lines of my theory that Graf killed Upchurch needlessly, in return for Upchurch's killing Saunders."

"Upchurch's estate would be the plaintiff, right? And his family?"

"Yes, I'd have to find them."

"So this would be one of those lawsuits where the burglar sues the homeowner. The kind that endears lawyers to the populace."

"Thank you." Angus's eyes glittered with mischief. The Beetle zoomed ahead, and Nat's spirits lifted when she spotted a sign for I-95. She had a shot at keeping her hunky boyfriend, which was a good thing. Angus said, "In my younger days, I'd be all over it, but I'm so corporate now. I need a good relationship with that prison, for the clinic."

"But I don't. I can sue the prison, for admitting Buford and Donnell to your class. For failing to adequately safeguard the other inmates, and us. They'd raise an immunity defense but it would be a first strike."

"Not bad." Angus nodded. "That's what Machik is worried about, and he deserves it."

"So we tell him we're going to file, then we give him my settlement demand." Nat shifted forward as a plan began to form in her mind. "We ask for a copy of the videotapes in return for my complete, signed release. Essentially, we offer him a free settlement. If he says no, we know something's very, very wrong. Who turns down a free settlement? And if nothing incriminating is on the tape, he'll make the deal."

"That's a great idea! It blocks him in." Angus thought a minute. "But why will we say you want the tapes? What do we give as a reason?"

"We say it'll help me process the trauma of the event." Nat wasn't half kidding, but Angus laughed.

"You're an evil genius. Do you intend world domination?"

"Not at all. Tenure, merely."

"Done and done." They took off, and the Beetle hit the ramp for I-95. They reached the highway, three lanes of flat road headed north into Philly, and the traffic moved fast. The reflected light of cars, houses, and buildings muddied the sky. It was almost nightfall. They whizzed past billboards of pretty people, their supersize smiles illuminated by spotlights from beneath. The Beetle switched into the fast lane, and Nat figured that now she might even get home before Hank.

"Now we're moving," she said happily. She checked her cell phone, but there were no messages from Barb Saunders.

"This is way better." Angus looked annoyed in the rearview. "Except the dude behind me is a tailgater."

"Ignore him. He'll pass."

"How nonviolent of you."

"It's this talk of knife fights." Nat shuddered.

Angus accelerated, but the car behind them blasted the Beetle's interior with light. Nat turned around and squinted into headlights, which were higher than usual, above a large chrome grille.

"It's tall, like an SUV," she said.

"I think it's a pickup. He's been weaving through traffic. Must be a drunk. I can't believe Willie ever did stuff like this." Angus accelerated again. White reflective lines on the highway flashed by as one. Road salt made *tick tick* noises as it hit the Beetle.

"Slow down." Nat gripped the stiff rubber hand strap. "Make him go around you."

"Get off my ass, pal!" Angus shouted at the rearview, and the Beetle's interior finally went dark. The lane to their right opened up, and the pickup darted into the empty spot.

"Good." Nat relaxed. "I'll give him a dirty look."

"Nobody messes with Professor Greco."

Nat looked over and saw it was a black pickup, its F-250 letters and a Calvin decal in view. The Beetle and the truck sped side by side through the twilight. The asphalt glistened in the headlights. A veneer of black ice on the road winked darkly. In the split second before the accident happened, Nat saw it like déjà vu. The pickup hit the ice. She screamed. The pickup sideswiped the Beetle in a dark flash of metal, sending both vehicles skidding into the guardrail, spraying sparks and making a hideous scraping noise.

PHOOM! The Beetle's airbags exploded. A hot plastic cushion burst into Nat's face and pressed her back into her seat. The car slid forward, out of control. She kept screaming, praying for the Beetle to stop. She couldn't see anything but plastic. She couldn't hear anything but her own yelling. Everything was heat and fear and a funny smell.

Finally, the Beetle came to a slow, jerky stop. Angus must have engaged the ABS brakes. Nat's face plowed into the pillow. Her shoulder collided with the passenger window. Powder was everywhere. Then the accident ended as soon as it had begun. Nat's airbag began to deflate, and she looked over.

Angus was slumped against his collapsing air bag, motionless.

CHAPTER 19

The examining room was small and ringed with white metal cabinetry. Against one wall was a stainless steel sink, underneath an array of cleanser dispensers. A steel basket on the wall near the examining table held a blood pressure gauge and its rubbery black cord. The vital-signs monitors remained off, their black screens etched with frozen green and red lines. A plastic IV bag that read "Baxter" hung from a steel hook on the wall, dripping saline into the crook of Angus's arm. He sank back into the thin pillow, his blue eyes reddish under a forehead dressed with a new gauze bandage. His cheekbone had sprouted another wound, he'd cracked a rib, and doctors were trying to determine if he had any internal injuries, besides a bruised ego.

"That jerk!" Angus said. If he felt weak, it didn't show. "I would've kicked his ass if he'd been man enough to stop."

"Peace, brother."

"Screw peace!" Angus scowled. "That guy coulda killed us!"

"I know, but calm down." Nat sat in a metal chair beside his bed, having sustained no injuries except an achy nose and a throbbing headache. She was oddly calm, either because Angus was so upset or because a car accident wasn't as scary as attempted rape. Airbag powder dusted her camelhair coat, and she'd lost a shoe in the accident. Her wardrobe couldn't take all this excitement.

"Drunk-ass jerk. A hit-and-run. That man should be shot!" Angus said.

"Aren't you against capital punishment?"

"Except for drunk drivers. I'm making an exception."

"What about Willie? And your principles?"

"Willie is the exception to the exception, and my principles hurt when I move." Angus shifted unhappily in the undersize bed, and the top of his hospital gown revealed a sexy tangle of red-gold chest hair that Nat had been trying to ignore.

"Please, relax. The doctor told you to stay still, remember? He's worried your spleen might be perforated."

"Gross! Will it leak spleen juice? In front of the girls?"

Nat smiled. "No, but if it's ruptured, he said you'll need a splenectomy."

"I *knew* I needed a splenectomy! I've been saying that for years. What's a splenectomy?"

"You don't want a splenectomy, Angus. You heard the doctor. It would have effects on your lymphatic system. You'd be susceptible to infections." Nat didn't remind him of what else the doctor had said. She was hoping it wouldn't be an issue. She sensed Angus hadn't focused on what the doctor was telling him during the examination. "I think they're going to admit you. You sure you don't want to call someone?"

"No one to call, except about work. I'll call the clinic tomorrow to file Willie's papers." Angus seemed to quiet, and his gaze shifted to Nat, lingering on her face a moment. "You sure you're okay?"

"I'm fine."

"Did you call Mr. Whatever?"

"Mr. Hank."

"What did he say?"

Arg. "That's not your business." Nat didn't want to think about how hurt Hank had sounded when she'd told him where she was and that she was with Angus. She felt like she'd cheated, though she hadn't. She should have told him where she was going. History taught that the cover-up was always worse than the crime. You would think that she and Machik would learn.

"First the riot, now this." Angus flopped back on his pillow. "Is this cosmic payback, Natalie?"

"For what?"

"My life's work."

"Of course not."

"My head hurts."

"Close your eyes." Nat reached over as he complied, and she dimmed the harsh overhead lights and sat back down. "Payback for what, anyway? You represent the tired, the poor, the huddled masses. You have karma to spare. *Pro bono* karma."

"Yeah, right." Angus opened his eyes as if he'd just thought of something, or his rib poked his spleen.

"What's the matter?"

"More what-ifs." He shifted up in bed, wincing. "What if this was no accident tonight?"

"You mean our accident?" Nat wasn't sure she understood.

"Yes. What if that truck meant to hit us? What if it was related to the phone calls, last night?"

Stay outta Chester County. Nat couldn't tell if Angus was paranoid or brilliant.

"Well, you two look familiar," a masculine voice said from the doorway. Nat turned. Two uniformed state troopers in black insulated jackets stood in the doorway, the same ones who had questioned her in the ambulance after the prison riot.

"Hello, again," Nat said, rising. She was still thinking about what Angus had said. What if it hadn't been an accident?

"Trooper Bert Milroy, Professor," the trooper said, sliding his black glove from his hand and shaking hers. His eyes looked tired, and his bony nose was still red at the tip from the cold, as if he hadn't warmed up in two days. He jerked a thumb at the younger cop who stood beside him, the one with the faint scars. "You remember Trooper Johnston."

"Nice to see you again," the second trooper said, as Trooper Milroy stepped toward the bed.

"How you doin', Holt?"

"I've been better."

"That was quite an accident out there tonight. You caused a pile-up. No fatals, fortunately. Four cars, you, and another totaled. That section of I-95 is still closed." Trooper Milroy slid his pad from his back pocket and extracted a ballpoint from under his jacket. "The other drivers report a late-model Ford F-250 pickup, maybe 2002, black, driving erratically. Can you corroborate?"

"Yes," Angus and Nat answered in unison, as the trooper flipped back a few pages, then scribbled as he stood, rocking back on shiny shoes edged with melting snow.

"Did you get a license plate, folks?"

"It was from Delaware," Angus answered. "I didn't get the number."

"Me, neither," Nat said

"One of the other drivers got it, so we'll go with that." Trooper Milroy turned to Nat. "Did you see the driver? You were on the passenger side, correct?"

"Correct, but I don't remember seeing him." Nat tried to remember. "The truck was higher than the VW. The window was dark."

"Smoked windows?"

"I don't know. It had a Calvin decal."

"I've seen those." Trooper Milroy made a note, then clicked his pen closed and slipped pen and notepad into his pocket. "Thanks, folks."

"Before you go," Angus said, clearing his throat, "Natalie and I were discussing the possibility that the truck was trying to hit us. Last night, we both got phone calls warning us to stay out of Chester County. Today we went out to the prison and got hit on the way back."

"It does seem very coincidental," Nat added, though she wasn't completely convinced.

"You think the pickup driver *tried* to kill you?" Trooper Milroy arched an eyebrow under his wide brim, though his tone remained professional. "We have no evidence of that, and you know better than to speculate. Night like this, with black ice everywhere, we got five accidents already. One fatal."

Angus said, "He tailgated us, dangerously so."

"Tailgating's common on that stretch, and our information is that he was switching lanes erratically. Other drivers corroborated it. That's a drunk."

Nat considered it. "He wasn't drunk enough to stay at the scene. He drove away. I don't even know how he did that, if his airbag went off."

"Could be he disabled it," the other trooper interjected. "My wife drives a little Ranger pickup and she had me disable our airbags, because it's dangerous with the baby, in his car seat."

Trooper Milroy shot him an annoyed look, and Angus scoffed. "This guy didn't drive like a good daddy."

"You say you each got phone calls?" Trooper Milroy asked. "What did they say?"

"A man warned us to stay out of Chester County."

"Did you report it to the Philly police, or to us?"

"What's the difference?" Angus frowned. "And if you think about it, the fact that the driver was acting drunk doesn't mean that he was. Maybe he was faking it, to throw everybody off."

"That's pure speculation," Milroy said. "We'll find this guy. Drunks never stop the night they have an accident because we breathalyze 'em. Dollars to doughnuts, he'll come in of his own accord tomorrow morning, with his lawyer."

But Nat had another question. There'd still been no return call from Barb Saunders. "Any suspects on the burglary at the Saunders residence, by the way? The house of the prison guard who was killed?"

"Sorry, that's not our case."

Suddenly, Hank and Paul appeared at the door, their hair messy and cheeks ruddy from the cold. Next to the uniformed troopers, they looked oddly civilian in their dark wool topcoats, worn over sweatclothes and basketball sneakers. Hank's brown eyes softened when he saw Nat.

"Babe, you okay?" he asked, excusing himself as he walked past the troopers. On the way over, he glanced at Angus, who nodded in acknowledgment. Nat cut short the awkward moment by stepping over to him.

"I'm fine." She gave him a warm I'm-sorry hug. He smelled the way he always did after basketball, his waning aftershave heightened by a faint sweat.

"Nothing broken?" Hank pulled gently away, assessing any damage.

"No."

"Thank God," he said, though Nat noticed he avoided her eye.

Paul introduced himself to the troopers, then started in. "I HEARD IT WAS A DRUNK DRIVER. HE COULDA KILLED MY SISTER! HOW THE HELL DID HE GET AWAY?"

"Don't worry, Mr. Greco. We have his plate and—"

"YOU HAVE THE LICENSE PLATE? THEN WHY DON'T YOU JUST ARREST HIM?"

"We're a little shorthanded tonight, with all the—"

"THEN WHY DON'T *YOU* GO? THE DRUNK DRIVER'S NOT IN THE HOSPITAL, OFFICER."

Nat stifled a moan. "Paul, please."

"GIVE *ME* THE DAMN PLATE NUMBER! MY FATHER WILL HIRE A P.I. TO FIND HIM. HE'LL BE HERE ANY MINUTE!"

Oh no. Dad? Here?

Trooper Milroy said, "My captain happens to be outside, if you want to speak with him, Mr. Greco."

"YOU'RE DAMN RIGHT I DO." Paul whirled around on his squeaky Iversons. "BE RIGHT BACK, NAT." The decibel level lowered as soon as he left with the troopers, but the tension level increased. The small room contained only Nat, Hank, and Angus. She told herself there was no reason for this meeting to be strained. It wasn't like the three of them were in a love triangle or anything. Still she was having an out-of-hospital-room experience.

"Hank, this is Angus Holt, from school," Nat said, attempting to dispel the undercurrents.

"Nice to see ya." Hank extended a hand, and Angus winced when they shook. Hank said, "Uh, sorry."

"No, I'm sorry about all this."

"Not your doing." Hank smiled in a polite way. "How long you gonna be here, buddy?"

"Day or two. I'm happy Natalie's not hurt."

"Natalie." Hank repeated. "Right. Sure. Nat."

Gnat. Terrific. Time to go. Before my head explodes.

Hank nodded once, then again, plainly uncomfortable. "Nat, did you wanna go or stay?"

"Go," Nat and Angus answered, in unfortunate unison. She added unnecessarily, "I'm discharged, so I can leave anytime. I was waiting for you, Hank." *Faithfully. And I wasn't turned on by his chest hair.*

"We'll call your dad and tell him to turn around. They must've got held up in traffic."

"Okay, let's go." Nat took her coat from the back of the chair, and Hank quickly stepped over to help her put it on, which he always did.

It felt heavier than usual, and she wondered if the wool was weighted down with guilt, like a new fabric blend. She said lightly, "Okay, well, hope you feel better, Angus!"

"Thanks," Angus said, like a normal person, because he wasn't insane.

"See you, buddy." Hank put a hand on Nat's back, guiding her out of the room. "Let's go home."

Home. It sounded so good. She could shower and change, and they could have a glass of chardonnay, and she could explain everything and make his hurt go away. Hurt that he wouldn't admit to her, or even to himself, buried beneath his easygoing guy-ness. They could sort it all out, alone together. They were overdue for a talk.

"Your parents are beside themselves." Hank pulled his cell phone from a pocket and pressed speed dial as they went through a wooden door and down a corridor to the wide automatic doors, which slid open. "We'll give 'em a call and we can all go home."

"Wait." Nat got hit by a blast of cold air. "By home, you mean my *parents'* house?"

"Big John!" Hank barked into the phone. "I got the horse right here. She's fine. Turn around and we'll see you at home."

Big John. Her father. Her brothers. Paul.

"HANK! WAIT'LL YOU GET A LOAD OF THIS!" Paul shouted, hurrying toward them from a police cruiser parked in the emergency lot.

My head hurts. And for some reason, so does my heart.

"I GOT TWO SIXERS TICKETS!"

"Excellent!" Hank called back, throwing a heavy arm around Nat, and she knew that this would be their last moment alone until midnight.

"We should talk about this." Nat leaned wearily in the doorway to her bathroom, still dressed, while Hank buzzed his teeth in his blue boxers and bare feet. He nodded, holding the electric toothbrush against his incisors. His lips drooped over the brush like a basset hound's.

"Would you turn off the brush?" Nat asked.

"I can hear you," Hank answered, but it sounded like *I ckn heor bu. Bzzz.*

"Okay, fine. I know you didn't want me to go out to Chester County, but I felt I had to, after we heard that Saunders's widow was burglarized."

Bzzz. "You didn't go see the widow, you went to the prison."

"I couldn't reach her. I didn't think it was dangerous because I was with Angus. He got the same call, by the way."

"You don't belong at the prison. You belong at the law school. You're a professor, not a criminal. Or a criminal lawyer."

Nat let it go. They'd had this conversation in the car. At least he was calmer now. "Let's agree to disagree."

Bzzz. "Whatever that means."

"I just wanted to say I was sorry for going out there with Angus today and not telling you."

Bzzz. "Okay." Hank steered the brush onto his top teeth, holding it in place for ten seconds, which she knew he counted off in his head. For a messy guy, Hank Ballisteri took his dental health very seriously.

"It does seem like there's a cover-up at the prison, and we may follow up on that legally."

Bzzzz. Hank nodded. Four, five, six.

"You know there's nothing going on between me and Angus. I work with him, and that's all. The accident wasn't his fault, obviously. If it *was* an accident."

"What?" Hank lowered the toothbrush at eight, his mouth foamy with greenish gel. "What do you mean if it *was* an accident?"

Oops. "I don't know, exactly." Nat wasn't sure yet, and it was late. "It does seem odd that I get a threat not to go to Chester County, then the next time I go to Chester County, I get in a car accident."

"You got hit in Philadelphia County, and of course it was an accident. That driver was drunk. Your dad would find him by dawn if the cops gave him the plate number."

"They're not going to give it to him. It's police business."

"If it's about you, it's his business."

"Honestly, no, it's not," Nat said, more emphatically than necessary. But that was the whole damn point. "If it's anybody's business, it's my business."

"Your father is crazy about you. You're his little girl. You should be grateful he goes to the mat for you." Hank frowned. "My dad couldn't be bothered. You don't know how lucky you are."

Grrr. "I need you to understand this. I love my family, but sometimes I get enough Greco. Don't you?"

"What? You are a Greco."

"I mean those Grecos. Don't you ever get tired of being with them? All together, all the time?"

"No." Hank switched the brush back on and started buzzing. One, two, three.

"But I'm thirty."

"What does that mean?" *Bzzz.*

"It means I'm glad you're so close to them, but . . ." Nat faltered. She used to love the way Hank had embraced her family, and vice versa. He had been her admission ticket into her own house, and with him, they accepted her in a way they hadn't before. But now she couldn't pull Hank and her family apart, nor could she make him understand why she'd want to. Bewilderment troubled his usually smooth brow.

"What am I supposed to do, Nat? Blow off your father, your brothers? Quit my job? They're my business partners. My friends. I love them."

"I love them, too."

"Do you?"

"Of course I do."

"You don't get sick of people you love."

"Yes, you do." Nat felt that knot in her chest tighten, and Hank turned away, switching off the brush and reapplying toothpaste. *Bzzzzzz.* One, two, three.

"What's important here is you and me. I'm sorry if you felt embarrassed that I hadn't told you I'd be going to the prison, and I don't have anything to hide. There's nothing going on between me and Angus."

"I know that." Hank spat into the sink, turned on the water, then moved onto his bicuspids. Five, six. "I still think he's a loser."

Ouch. "Why?"

"The beard? The ponytail? He's a joke."

Nat reached over and turned off the water.

"Why do you do that?" Hank frowned, buzzing his teeth. Seven, eight, nine. "You always do that when I brush."

"Because you take a long time to brush your teeth, and it wastes water to run it while you're brushing."

"You're worried about the water bill now?" Hank moved onto the next tooth and turned the water on again. "I'll pay you."

"That's not the point. It's the waste. It's all the water we have on the planet." Nat turned the faucet off, hard, and Hank looked down at her as if she were nuts.

"Babe, the *planet*, as you put it, is like, 99% water. We could never run out of water."

"It's still a shame to waste it. Don't you care about anything bigger than yourself?"

"Fine." Hank spat into the sink, switched off the toothbrush, and shoved it, unrinsed, into the plastic caddy. "I think that accident scrambled your brains."

"Thanks."

"Sorry, but you've been in a foul mood all night. At your folks' house. Here."

It was true, and Nat knew it. "Excuse me, but I was in a car accident."

"How about I give you some time alone?" Hank asked. "Why don't I go to my place tonight?"

Nat paused. She knew this routine by heart. They rarely fought, but when they did, it was simply separate and reconvene the next day, as if nothing had happened, at which point one or the other of them would say they had been tired, that's all.

"Well, Nat? Your call. You want me to go?"

No. Yes. No. Yes. "Okay, fine."

"Good." Hank brushed past her, banged around in the bedroom getting his clothes and sneakers, and trundled back into the hall half dressed. "Call you tomorrow," he said as he left.

Nat heard the door close, with a new note of finality.

CHAPTER 20

You wanted to see me?" Nat asked from the threshold of Vice Dean McConnell's office. He'd left her a voicemail in the morning and she'd come straightaway, déjà vu all over again.

"Yes, please, do come in." McConnell gestured to the chair she'd occupied last time, which Nat was starting to think of as hers. She sat down, brushed off her black wool dress, and crossed her legs in the black suede boots that added three inches to her height—and her confidence. She suddenly understood the appeal of cowboy boots.

"Thanks. Good to see you."

"I'm so sorry about the accident that you and Angus were in. It's been a difficult week for you. Both of you." McConnell leaned back in his old-fashioned leather chair. The window behind him overlooked Sansom Street, busy with passersby hurrying to work on this cold, gusty morning. Wind blew through the brittle tree branches, threatening to snap them like dry wishbones. Or maybe it was just Nat's state of mind. McConnell asked, "How is Angus? I haven't heard from him since last night."

"I'm not sure." Nat felt unsettled. She didn't like thinking of Angus in the hospital alone. "I called this morning, but there was no answer in his room, and they wouldn't give me any info over the phone, since I'm not family."

"He had some internal injuries, I understand."

"Yes. We'll know the extent today."

"Well." McConnell set some papers aside. "That's not why I wanted to speak with you. I got a call from the warden about you and Angus. Apparently, you two made inappropriate inquiries to a corrections officer regarding prison operations." McConnell consulted some handwritten notes on a legal pad. "A Tanisa Shields?"

"Huh? We didn't make any inquiries of her."

"So the warden is incorrect? There was no questioning?" McConnell frowned.

"We spoke, but it wasn't a questioning. It was a conversation."

"Nevertheless, she has been placed on suspension as a result."

"She didn't do anything wrong." Nat felt terrible. She'd gotten Tanisa in trouble after all.

"You lack standing, Nat. We don't operate the prison."

"But she's being punished for nothing."

"You're missing my point." McConnell's gaze hardened behind his bifocals. "The warden has requested that neither you nor Angus be permitted back into the prison, until further notice."

"*What?* He can't do that." Nat took it like a blow, for Angus. "He teaches that class, and there are prisoners with active cases."

"The warden has contacted Widener Law School, which agreed to take over the pending cases."

"But Angus cares about those prisoners. His class. They know him. They love him there."

"They'll get to know another lawyer. Clients change representation all the time." McConnell eased back in his chair, eyeing her as if from a great distance. He wore the same suit as yesterday, with a different rep tie. "May I speak personally to you?"

No. "Yes."

"It's almost your tenureship year, Nat. We'll begin meetings soon. Evaluations are being gathered as we speak." McConnell hunched forward again. "I've read your articles on legal history and I've always thought of you as one of our finest young legal scholars. We value true scholarship on this faculty. We're one of the best law schools in the country, and we made our reputation on the excellence of our academic credentials, not our clinical programs."

Thank you? Nat didn't like getting props at Angus's expense.

"I admit I didn't appreciate your seminar the other day, the dressing up and such. It's not my cup of tea. But I understand the need to be relevant. I'm not a relic."

Uh, yes you are.

"All this running around, at a county prison." McConnell sniffed. "This isn't like you, Nat. Not at all."

"Maybe I'm changing." *Who said that?*

"You may want to reconsider the wisdom of that, dear. Particularly at this juncture in your career." McConnell smiled politely, and Nat got the message.

Stay outta Chester County.

"Let me tell you a story," Nat began, standing on the stage before her seminar class. It was her third class of the day, but she felt amazingly energized, still jiggered up after her meeting with McConnell. She'd tried to reach Barb Saunders and Angus again, but no dice. For the time being, she set it aside.

"One day in January, 1962, a prisoner in a Florida jail sat down with a pencil and paper to write a letter. He was fifty-one years old, white, poor, self-educated, a drifter, and by all accounts, stubborn to a fault. He'd been convicted for breaking into the Bay Harbor Pool Room in Panama City, Florida, and stealing money from the cigarette machine and jukebox."

Anderson tapped away on her laptop, as did Carling, Chu, Gupta and Wykoff.

"Wait a minute, stop typing." Nat raised a palm. "Everybody stop typing and look up. It's a story. Just listen."

Anderson lifted her gaze, as did the others, one by one, reentering.

"Good. Thanks. As I was saying, the prisoner couldn't afford a lawyer, so at the trial, he asked the judge to appoint one for him. The judge said no and told him that under the law, the poor were entitled to a lawyer only in capital cases or in exceptional circumstances. The judge was right, because that was the law at the time. So the prisoner defended himself at trial, making an array of mistakes, such as calling as his witness the very police officer who had arrested him. He was convicted and sentenced to five years."

Wykoff frowned, and Chu blinked. Warren's hand never strayed to her keyboard, for IM-ing. *Kewl.*

"But the prisoner studied law books in the prison library, and no matter how many times the inmate read the Sixth Amendment, he couldn't square it with the judge's refusal to give him a lawyer. So he wrote his own habeas petition to the Florida Supreme Court, which was denied, and then, undeterred, he handwrote a letter to the U.S. Supreme Court itself."

Gupta and McIlhargey were paying attention, at least apparently.

"The Supreme Court took his case and, as was their custom, appointed him a lawyer, one who couldn't have been more different from the prisoner. Abe Fortas was the quintessential Washington insider, a major partner in a prestigious law firm. He drove a Rolls Royce, and his hero was Justice Brandeis. Fortas would say of Brandeis, 'He is an angry man—angry at injustice.'"

Bischoff and Warren were listening.

"Fortas got angry about injustice, too, and he argued the prisoner's case before the Supreme Court. He argued that the Sixth Amendment requires that the indigent be appointed counsel in all state criminal trials. The prisoner and the lawyer were asking the Supreme Court to revolutionize the law of the land. And the Court answered yes."

Nat spoke without notes because the case always hit home for her, though today she was powered by something extra. Something she couldn't quite put her finger on.

"In the end, the prisoner got justice. He received a new trial in the Florida court, and a lawyer was appointed to represent him. His lawyer discovered that the state's star witness, the policeman, had himself been arrested for beating up and robbing another man outside the very same pool room. The prisoner was found innocent. His name was Clarence Earl Gideon. The case was *Gideon v. Wainwright.*"

Gupta and Anderson exchanged glances, and a slow smile spread across Chu's face.

"In a November 13 letter to Abe Fortas, Gideon wrote, 'I believe that each era finds an improvement in law, each year brings something new for the benefit of mankind. Maybe this will be one of those small steps forward.'" Nat paused. "Clarence Earl Gideon believed that a single person could change the world, if he had justice on his side. He made history, because he was *right.*"

The huge hall fell silent. The students remained looking at her. Nat had given this lecture for two years and had never gotten this response. It thrilled her, affirming her, the class, and Clarence Earl Gideon, all at once. In the next instant, she put her finger on that something extra.

And finally began to learn something she had been trying to teach.

CHAPTER 21

Students in peaked Tibetan hats, red-and-white-checked keffiyeh scarves, and multicolored hand-knit sweaters clogged Angus's hospital room. They turned when Nat walked in, looking at her like she was the one dressed crazily, in confidence boots and a black Armani coat. Truth to tell, the coat was a little pretentious, but after losing her toggle coat and camelhair coat, Nat was down to her dress coat, reserved for funerals and foreign films.

Deidre lifted an untweezed eyebrow. "Hi, Professor Greco," she said coolly, standing nearest the bed. All the other students parted deferentially.

"Natalie! You're just in time for ice chips." Angus craned his neck from his pillow in his hospital gown. He sported a new bandage and wasn't on an IV any longer, but he still had the splint in the crook of his arm and that golden tangle at his collar.

"Hey, pal." Nat made her way to the bed, and Angus's eyes lit up.

"You look pretty."

Nat's cheeks warmed. "Thanks. How're you feeling?"

"Good news! I may get to keep my spleen."

"Juice included?"

Angus laughed, and so did the students, though they hadn't been present for the joke.

"I worried when I couldn't get through."

"No, I'm alive. I slept all morning. I think one of the nurses put a Rufie in my apple juice."

Deirdre shoved Angus's arm playfully. "That's sexist."

"Really? Guess what? You flunk." Angus smiled wearily. "Deidre, why don't you take everybody to the vending machines and give me a few minutes with Professor Greco."

"Woot, woot!" hooted one of male students, triggering new laughter.

Deidre quickly masked a scowl. "We'll be right back," she said, as they shuffled out en masse, laughing and talking.

"Hey, you," Angus said softly. The room fell quiet, and the window behind him showed an evening sky the color of frozen blueberries.

"Hey back at you." Nat pulled over a chair, vaguely uneasy. It felt as if something had changed between them, but she figured it was her imagination.

"Love the boots."

Or not. "Now I see why you wear yours."

"Why?"

"Attitude."

"No, laziness. Attitude, I was born with." Angus cocked his head, eyeing her. "You look so happy. What's going on with you, girl?"

Damned if I know. "I had a couple of good classes today, and even my seminar went really well."

"Good for you! Making inroads, huh? I knew you would. They're coming around."

"Maybe." Nat felt happy inside. "It's just nice, is all. To connect that way."

"It's why we teach, isn't it?"

"Exactly." Nat hadn't realized it before today.

"What was the class about?" Angus shifted up on his pillow, interested.

"Gideon."

"Great case. Wonderful movie, too, with Henry Fonda."

"I believe it, because it's a great story."

"All cases are great stories, I think."

Nat nodded. It was fun to talk about work without having to explain everything.

"So what happened?"

"So when I told them the story of the case, we actually had a moment. I don't even really know what happened myself."

"They *got* it."

"Yes, right." Nat thought about it. "I taught it, and they understood it, and for a minute, we met somewhere in the space between us, between me on the stage and them in their seats. It was like the lecture had an academic hang time." She shrugged. "That's the only way I can describe it."

"How about love?"

Gulp? "What do you mean?"

"It's love. It's not that the students love us or that we love them. It's that we both love the same material—whatever principle you're trying to teach them—and in turn, it connects us." Angus made a full-circle movement with his hand. "We actually share that moment in time. It's a connection of human minds, and souls."

"Right." Nat felt caught up in his words, then stopped herself. Was she losing it? She had to get off the topic. "Well. Anyway, did you really mean it when you said that the car accident might not be an accident?"

"Yes. It's not a coincidence." Angus shook his head. "We were warned off, and the next day we almost got killed. If we put it together with what we think about Upchurch's murder, it makes sense. Somebody doesn't want us digging any deeper, somebody associated with Graf or the prison."

Nat thought of her meeting with McConnell. "Then here's another coincidence, one you won't like." She told Angus the news that he was banned from the prison, and his cheeks flushed as red as his bruises.

"Damn him! That bastard! He can't do that."

"McConnell or Machik?"

"Both! Either!" Angus's eyes flashed a brilliant blue. "That externship program has served almost every inmate at the prison at one time or another. They can't just cut it off."

"Widener's going to step in."

"The hell they are! That's *my* program! What about my students? Those kids?" Angus pointed at the door, wincing as he tried to get up from the bed. "They benefit from representing inmates there. They came to us because of the clinic!"

"Don't get upset." Nat felt for him. "Lie back. Let me get you some water."

"No, thanks." Angus smacked the bedsheets in frustration. "I have to get out of here. I'm so cut off. My cell phone died. I lost my BlackBerry in the crash. I'm lying here like a fish, and they're undoing everything I've done."

"We'll take care of it when the dean gets back." Nat went to the bedside tray table, poured water from a tan plastic pitcher into a Styrofoam cup, and handed it to him, which was when she noticed a wetness in his eyes, a sheen that he blinked rapidly away. Her heart went out to him. "Here you go."

Angus nodded and accepted it, drinking thirstily. He cleared his throat, keeping his head down. Nat remained silent, standing over him. She couldn't see his face from this angle, only his tawny strands of hair. She let her gaze travel to the muscular roundness of his heavy shoulder, the cut of a thick bicep, and the freckles covering his arm, then felt her throat catch with a distinct, albeit unwanted, thought:

What a beautiful man.

"Thanks." Angus recovered and handed her the cup.

"You're welcome," Nat answered, getting back in control. "More water?"

"No. Thanks."

"Feel better?" She set the cup on the table, and suddenly Angus reached for her free hand. His hand felt warm on top of hers, connecting them, and she didn't move her hand away.

"Natalie, listen," he said, his voice husky. He looked up, his eyes dry and intensely blue. "I have to tell you—"

"Excuse me?" came a female voice from the door.

Angus dropped Nat's hand, and they both turned. It was Deirdre, leading the Mongol horde of students. She looked from Angus to Nat and scowled.

"Sorry to interrupt, but your dinner has arrived."

"Dinner?" Angus checked the wall clock. "It's only five o'clock."

Natalie, listen, I have to tell you . . . what?

"The trays are here." Deidre helped the orderly slide a full tray of food from the tall rack and brought it to the bedside table herself. "Dinner is served," she said. "Roast chicken, peas, and a salad. Yum."

Rrring! Rrring! Nat startled. It was her cell phone. She pulled it from her purse.

"You can't answer that here," Deirdre said. "Cell phones aren't allowed."

Thank you, India. Nat checked the display, praying it wasn't Hank, not here. But she didn't recognize the phone number. She opened the phone.

In the background, Angus was saying, "I'm sure it's fine, Deirdre. We won't bust Professor Greco."

"Hello?" Nat put her hand over her other ear and walked toward the door, while a woman's voice came on the line.

"Ms. Greco? This is Barb Saunders."

Nat turned and caught Angus's eye, mouthing "Barb." Into the phone, she asked, "How are you?"

"Not great. Can you come over tonight?" Barb's voice sounded so choked that Nat almost felt like crying herself. "I need to talk to you. There's so much I want to know, about, you know, the end."

"Yes, I'll come. What time?"

"How long will it take you to get here? I'm sorry about the short notice, but I can't risk another headache."

"I'm halfway there now. It'll take me half an hour or so."

"Thanks so much. See you soon," Barb said, and hung up.

Nat flipped the phone closed.

"You gonna go?" Angus asked, and Nat didn't hesitate.

"Yes."

"Please wait until I can go with you," he said, and the students looked back and forth, like stepkids between Daddy and New Mommy.

"She can't wait. Sorry."

"Then be careful." Angus looked disapproving. "Look out for black Ford pickups. Call me here as soon as you can."

"Okay," Nat said, grabbing her bag, as Deidre and the students closed the circle.

Natalie, listen.

CHAPTER 22

Nat steered the Volvo along the last stretch of country road on the way to the Saunders house. Raindrops pounded on the hood of the car and sliced the night in front of her headlights, which froze them like a camera flash, making vision difficult. She'd checked for pickups on the way, but none had a Delaware plate. Still, she was relieved to finally reach Barb Saunders's house. She parked, grabbed her purse, and, putting it over her head, got out of the Volvo and ran up the driveway to the front door. She rang the bell. The door was opened quickly by Barb's sister Jennifer.

"Come in! It's pouring!" she said, hurrying Nat inside. "Can I take your coat?"

"Yes, thanks." Nat slid out of her coat, trying not to get water everywhere, and while Jennifer left to hang it up, she scanned the living room. Duct tape crisscrossed the couch cushions where they had been slashed, and the computer workstation looked bizarre without the computer, like an eye socket without an eye. The children's books and DVDs had been returned to the shelves, but one of the drawers in the credenza hung by a screw, broken.

It's under the floor.

"I know what you're thinking," Jennifer said, returning, and Nat looked over in alarm.

"You do?"

"You wonder what's wrong with people. To burglarize a house during a funeral. It's sick."

"I know." Nat could see that the family had tried to put the room back together. Soft yellow lights shone from a remaining lamp, the TV played on mute, and sharp red Legos and large Tonka trucks were strewn across the shag rug. From the kitchen came the shouts of little boys and the homey aroma of boiled hot dogs.

"How bad is the rain?" Jennifer asked.

"Bad."

"Thank God it's not snow. These kids *have* to go back to school next week. We couldn't take a snow day." Jennifer flared her eyes comically. "Between her three and my two, I'm going crazy." She picked up a yellow rain slicker from the couch. "I'm taking my nephews out to the movies, so you and Barb can talk in peace."

"Thanks." Nat felt a familiar dread. She'd been waiting to do this for days but still felt unready. "How is she?"

"Hanging in, for the kids. She's a great mom." Jennifer leaned closer, zipping up her coat. "If she gets a migraine, call my house. I left my home number on the table. My mom is there, with my kids."

"Okay. Thanks."

"Come with me," Jennifer said to Nat, heading for the kitchen and calling out, "Anybody in here wanna go to the movies and eat too much candy?"

"Yes!" "Yeah!" "Aunt Jen!" the three boys shouted together. "Let's go! Can I get Milk Duds?"

The cacophony took Nat back to the Greco household, so long ago. Or maybe Monday night.

"Hello, Nat." Barb rose from her knees, where she'd crouched to help her youngest son with his coat. Her eyes were a tired hazel and her blond hair had been brushed back into a loose clip. She wore a black cardigan and jeans and managed a shaky smile. "Thanks for coming back. I felt so bad about last time."

"Don't worry about it." Nat waved her off. "Hi, guys," she said to the kids, who were zipping their coats with complete absorption.

"Say hello to Professor Greco." Barb tapped the boys on their puffy shoulders.

"Hello, Pefefe Greco," the older one said.

"I want Milk Duds," said the middle one.

"Okay, kids, see ya later." Barb bent down and kissed her sons on their smooth cheeks, making a cute little grunt each time. "Be good for your aunt. One candy apiece and that's *it*."

"See ya, honey." Jennifer gave Barb a quick kiss, waved to Nat, and packed off the kids, who toddled out the door in their thick coats, their SpongeBob mittens dangling from clips on their sleeves. The door closed behind them, and the house fell abruptly quiet.

"Whew." Barb sighed, mock-collapsing at the knees. "They're funny, aren't they?"

"They're adorable." Nat marveled at the tag team of women taking care of five children between them. "I can't imagine what this has been like for them, and you."

"They did okay at the service. I was proud of them. They don't understand much, really. Now, the burglary, they understood. Someone messed up their *Bob the Builder*." Barb made a child's frown. "That they cried over. It was like it all got to them, all at once."

Nat felt for them. "Moms don't get enough credit, do they?"

"That's the *truth*." Barb crossed to the coffeemaker. "Would you like a cup?"

"If it's no trouble. Can I help?"

"Sit down. It's all made. All I do is make coffee. Jen handles everything, between the cops and the TV people." Barb picked up the glass pot and poured coffee into an ivory mug that read, West Chester University. "How do you take it?"

"Black is fine."

"Great." Barb brought the coffee to the table, which was covered with a white tablecloth of wipe-clean plastic. A line of Chips Ahoy and Fig Newtons sat on a plate like fallen dominoes. Barb stood, hovering. "You want something to eat? If you don't like cookies, I have grown-up food."

"No, thanks."

"You're sure? The roast beef was a big hit."

"No, that's fine." Nat waited for Barb to sit down, then realized that she was stalling. She wanted to know and didn't want to know, just like Nat wanted to tell and didn't want to tell. "Sit down, Barb," Nat said softly.

"Okay." Barb sank slowly into a chair across the small table, folding her hands at the edge of the table. There was a glass of water at her right, which Nat knew she would need.

Don't pretty it up. "Would you like me to tell you what happened, or do you want to ask me questions?"

Barb swallowed, visibly. "I want you to tell me everything, and then I want to ask you questions. I do have some, if you don't mind."

"Of course I don't mind." The kitchen was quiet except for the pounding rain outside. A warm golden light emanated from an overhead lamp. Nat lay her hand down on the table. "Gimme your hand, and we'll get through this together."

Barb put her hand in Nat's.

"Good girl." Nat began the story from when she saw Graf coming out of the staff office, then noticed that Ron Saunders was still alive on the floor.

"Did he . . . suffer?" Barb interjected, her voice wavering.

"No. I don't think so."

"Thank God." Barb blinked tears away. "Thank you, Jesus."

Nat waited for her to recover her composure.

"You tried to save him, I know," Barb said, after a moment.

"I did." Nat felt a stab of guilt. She described what she did, then brought the story to her point. "He did give me a message for you."

Barb gasped. "He did?"

"Yes."

"Did he say he loved me?"

Tell the truth. You're just the messenger. Nat answered, "Honestly, he could only get a few words out, and he had another important message for you."

"He didn't say he loved me?" Barb's lower lip puckered, and tears welled in her eyes. She grabbed a napkin and dabbed at them, smudging her mascara. "Not anything? Not even my name? The boys?" She held the napkin at the corner of her eye.

Nat squeezed her other hand. "Barb, do you have any doubt in this world that your husband loved you and the boys?"

"No. We were happy."

"Then feel it. Know it. Because he told me a message you *don't* know. I promised him I would tell you."

Barb lowered the napkin, her eyes reddish. "Okay, what?"

"He said, 'Tell my wife, it's under the floor.'"

"What?" Barb frowned, her forehead a network of premature wrinkles. "What's under the floor?"

"I don't know. He didn't say."

"I don't know what that means. What floor? What's under it?" Barb ran a trembling finger-rake through her hair. "What kind of message is that?"

Nat didn't know if she should go further. "Can you handle it if I tell you something that's worrying me?"

Barb kept frowning. "Sure."

"I'm worried that the burglary here wasn't coincidental. Since the cushions were slashed, it looks like it wasn't a real burglary. It looks like—"

"Somebody was looking for something? That's what my mom said, too."

"Do you know what it could be?"

"No idea." Barb blinked, mystified, but Nat didn't have the heart to tell her Angus's suspicions.

"Barb, was Ron friends with Joe Graf?"

"Sure, Joe was his best friend. We went out with them all the time." Suddenly, Barb's blue eyes rounded. "My God! I know what Ron means! I remember now!"

"What?" Nat asked, then caught herself. "Wait. It's not my business." Still, she was dying to know what was under the damn floor.

"No, no, it's okay," Barb said excitedly. "Ron has a workshop in the garage. He used to keep things under the floor there. It was like his hiding place. We put our wills in there, which we got after Timothy was born, and also life insurance papers, because it's fireproof."

"Do you think that's what he meant? Was he talking about your wills?"

"No. We both knew where our wills were. My sister knows, too. He must have put something else there for me. Something I don't know about." Barb leapt to her feet, full of new purpose. "Come on!"

Nat rose, and Barb was already in motion, leaving the kitchen.

"I have to warn you," she said, over her shoulder. "There's a video we made there, too. Nothing hardcore, just dumb stuff, for us. We put it there so the kids wouldn't find it." She giggled, then her smile faded. They hustled through the living room to a door. "That can't be what he meant, can it? Why would anybody want to find that?"

Nat lingered at the threshold while Barb opened the door, flicked on a panel of fluorescent lights, and hurried to a corner of the garage and rolled aside a green Rubbermaid trash can on wheels. She bent over and moved a box of old rags aside to reveal a large door in the floor, which had apparently been installed when the concrete had been poured.

Nat held her breath as Barb moved the heavy lid aside.

CHAPTER 23

The two women stood over a square hole almost as big as a safe. The hole stood empty, and its contents sat stacked on the concrete floor—a videotape labeled, Barb and Ron's Excellent Adventure, two life insurance policies, a joint last will and testament in a blue backer, and four old copies of *Playboy*.

It's under the floor? Nat couldn't explain it.

Barb looked over at her in confusion. "There's nothing under the floor. What's going on?"

"I have no idea."

"Maybe there's something in the magazines?" Nat picked up the magazines and thumbed through them, like a flip book of flesh tones. Subscription cards blew out and fluttered to the floor. She picked them up, examined them for good measure, then stuck them back in one of the magazines. "Nothing."

Barb moaned, covering her face with her hands. "Ron, what do you mean?"

Nat went over and touched her back, spiny in the thin knit. "Is there another floor hiding place?"

"Not that I know of."

"I'm so sorry. I don't know what he meant."

"Neither do I." Barb lifted her face, now tinged with red. "That's a great message, lemme tell you."

"I'm so sorry. Maybe I misunderstood." Nat flashed on Saunders dying. "What else could he have said? 'It's under the door?' Do you have a door we could look under?"

"No."

"Core? Shore? Boor? Sore? Tour? Fore? More? Lore? Any of that make sense to you?"

"No. Thanks a whole helluva lot, Ron!" Barb said, her mood darkening. She gritted her teeth. "Great message, hon! *Not* that you love me! *Not* that you love our kids!" She picked up a *Playboy* and threw it at the wall, knocking into one of the levels hanging there. "Just look under the floor. For your friggin' *porn!*"

"Maybe it's here but we're just not seeing it."

"Like where?" Barb whirled around on her sneakers.

"Anywhere." Nat surveyed the room, looking for a clue. It was a garage used for a workshop and storage area. Hammers and saws hung neatly on a brown pegboard on one wall, next to a tall metal toolbox on wheels, stacks of tiny plastic drawers, and a Craftsman workbench. Kids' toys and bikes, balls and Wiffle bats, and a plastic Little Tykes three-wheeler sat stowed in boxes toward the front of the room, against the metal garage door, the kind that slid up. The rain thundered outside, the room uninsulated from noise and cold.

Barb eyed the place, her hands resting on her hips. "I suppose I could look some more. He was so handy. He could have hidden something here. Or even in the house."

"I'll help you. We could search pretty thoroughly, together. Let's start here, then if we don't find anything, we'll look in the house, under some rugs, okay?"

"Okay." Barb sighed, pushing up the knit sleeves of her sweater. "We've got three hours before the boys get home."

"Then let's get busy."

• • •

It wasn't until ten o'clock that Nat hit the road, driving home through the dark countryside in a continuous downpour. Hard rain pounded the car's roof, and the wipers worked frantically to clear the windshield. There were only a few other cars on the road, but she drove cautiously in the storm, too nervous to call Angus or Hank. She wanted to be alone with her thoughts anyway, which tumbled over themselves in confusion.

She and Barb had searched everywhere, but they hadn't found anything under the floor, much less money from drug sales or otherwise. Maybe the burglars had taken whatever they were looking for, or whatever it was was never there in the first place. Maybe Nat had misunderstood Saunders, or he had been delirious, in extremis. Either way, she felt terrible for delivering a message that made no sense, and for linking the message to a burglary that may have been just a burglary. She had been playing sleuth and failing miserably. She was a lousy Nancy Drew.

Rain fell so hard that the wipers couldn't keep up. The headlights fought the mist rising from the melting snow and were losing the battle. Ice and slush pooled along the side of the winding road, spraying from the Volvo's tires. She accelerated only gently and passed a homemade orange sign that read, CAUTION—HORSE AND WIFE CROSSING. Somehow it made her think of Angus.

Natalie, listen.

Suddenly light flooded the Volvo, from headlights blasting behind her, and she felt a reflexive tremor from the accident last night. She'd been too preoccupied to check for black pickups. She looked in the rearview. It wasn't a pickup behind her, but a state police cruiser. Flashing lights on its roof flickered red, white, and blue in the storm. She checked her speedometer. Forty-five miles an hour. What had the last sign said? Thirty-five?

Damn. She'd been speeding. The cruiser flashed its headlights, illuminating the interior of the Volvo, and she pulled over, cut the ignition, and braked. She went into her purse and retrieved her wallet while the familiar wide-brimmed silhouette appeared at her door. She wondered if it would be Milroy or another trooper she knew. She lowered the window, blinking against the rain spraying inside, but she didn't recognize him. She couldn't see much of his features, only his profile, visible in the headlights from the cruiser. Droplets dotted his steel-rimmed glasses, and a plastic cover, like a shower cap, protected his hat.

"You're going too fast for these conditions, Miss," the trooper said, his voice almost drowned out by the rain. "License and registration, please."

"Sorry," Nat said, hoping for a warning. She handed her ID and registration through the open part of the window, and the trooper stuck them on his little clipboard, where they could get soaked.

"Please wait here." The trooper went back to the cruiser, and Nat slid the window up, fighting a free-floating anxiety. What if he wasn't a real trooper? She'd seen reports like that in the news. She hadn't asked him for ID. She twisted around in the seat, shielding her eyes from the high beams. The multicolored lights on his roof were still flashing. It was a real state police car.

Stay outta Chester County.

Nat felt a tingle of paranoia. No one knew she was here. She rooted in her bag for her cell phone to call Hank. She pressed his speed dial, but he didn't pick up, and she didn't leave a message. She went to Plan B, holding the phone up to the light to see the numbers for information, then asked for the hospital's phone number. The call connected after a minute, and the hospital operator picked up.

"Angus Holt, please," Nat said, just as the trooper reappeared at her window, with his clipboard and a long white ticket book. She flipped the phone closed and put it back in her purse, then lowered the window.

"Please step outside the car, Ms. Greco."

"In the rain?"

"Step outside, please."

Nat felt oddly nervous. She reached for her purse and fumbled for her cell phone, but it must have slipped to the bottom of her purse. She groped for it but couldn't find it in the dark.

"Ms. Greco? Now."

Calm down. Nat opened the door and got out in the storm, and the trooper stepped aside and faced her. She still had her coat on but cold rain poured onto her head. She tensed her shoulders so it wouldn't run down her neck and covered her head with her hands.

"Please wait a minute," the trooper said. He switched on a black flashlight and aimed it inside the Volvo's front seat, where the beam danced a jitterbug over the front seat.

"Will this be long? This is torrential—"

BOOM! Suddenly there was an earsplitting blast. Something exploded from the cop's head. Warmth splattered across Nat's face. The trooper's hat flew off in the air. He dropped the flashlight and crumpled to the wet street.

Nat screamed. She whirled around in the pounding rain. A silhouette in a black ski mask stood on the far side of her car, out of the cruiser's headlights. He held a gun, smoke snaking from its barrel.

"Run, bitch!" said the figure.

Nat felt stunned for a split second, then bolted across the street in terror, as hard as she could in the pouring rain. She began screaming but rain drowned the sound. She tore into a dark field of snow and mud. She sprinted forward in the darkness, pinwheeling her arms to keep her balance. Slush churned up around her, soaking her boots. A dark tree loomed in front of her. She darted to avoid it. Branches tore her cheek. She couldn't see a thing in the rain. She ran with her hands in front of her. There were no buildings or lights. She didn't even know if she was running in a straight line.

She glanced back. The Volvo sat on the road, lit up by the police cruiser. Freezing rain slaked her face and soaked her. Her lungs felt about to burst. She panted with exertion. She tried to think through her panic. What was happening? Was he coming after her? There were no houses around. Her cell was in the car. She kept running.

A loud neighing cut through the rain, a sound so piercing she felt it in her chest. Suddenly horses were galloping around her, massive shadows speeding in the dark. They snorted and blew, their hooves crunching through ice and sucking mud. Nat stood stock still, too terrified to move, screaming as they stampeded past. A heavy haunch bumped her in the shoulder, spinning her around, and she fell down in the muck. Hooves pounded around her, spraying mud. She got up as soon as she could, checking behind her.

The two parked cars were far away now, their lights like dots. The herd of horses passed, their hooves pounding ahead of her. She couldn't stop to catch her breath. She kept going, wiping mud and rain from her face. Then she saw it. A large building with a tiny light on.

"HELP!" she hollered, hurling herself forward toward the building. She ran to a three-rail fence and half flung herself, half fell over the top, landing on her butt in the freezing snow. She scrambled to her feet and ran to the building, feeling her boots strike something hard. Gravel. A driveway. She spotted a metal handle. A door. She found the handle, yanked with all her might, and the door rolled aside. She bolted out of the rain and into the dark building.

"HELP ME!" she yelled, and her own terror echoed in the darkness.

CHAPTER 24

Nat felt beside the door for a switch, then stopped herself. If she turned on a light, he would know where she was. Rain thundered on the metal roof, louder than outside. She spun around, wiping her face clear of rain and muck. She was in a cavernous, dark space. She smelled sawdust and rubber, then spotted white poles lying on the ground. It was an indoor riding ring.

She went around the perimeter, feeling the walls, looking for a phone. She found the outline of a doorway and hurried inside, her hands outstretched. She was in a small office. She almost fell into a desk chair while she felt around on the desk, scattering papers and a stapler. A phone would be on the right; most people were right-handed. It was, one of those big multi-line phones. She grabbed the receiver and punched in 911.

No dial tone. She tried again. Still nothing. She hit buttons until she realized what was wrong. The electricity must be out because of the storm. The phone didn't work without the power. She looked around for a cell phone. Maybe someone had left one behind. She felt around the desk. Were there keys to a car? A truck? She knocked over a mug of office supplies, grabbed a pair of scissors, and shoved them in her coat pocket. She ran out of the office, tore across the riding ring like a thoroughbred, and bolted for the door. Then she stopped, panting. Rain poured from a black sky. There were no lights anywhere. Now she knew why. No power. No moon. No nothing. She squinted, trying vainly to see anything. Back toward the road stood the dark outline of another structure, hidden behind a line of trees.

She took off, barreling through the field. Maybe it was a barn. All these horses had to live somewhere. Maybe there would be a barn manager. A cell phone. A car. Rain thundered down. She couldn't see her hand in front of her face. Where was the shooter? Why had he told her to run? Was he coming after her? She ran closer to the structure. The roof had a peak like a star. A barn, Amish-built. New hope drove her forward, half sprinting and half falling. There had to be a house, didn't there?

She ran across the field, reached the barn, and caught her breath under the overhang. She hurried through an empty horse stall, rolled aside the door, and hurried into a center aisle. She looked right, then left. Rain pounded on the roof. She darted down the aisle, looking for civilization. She opened a closed door. A line of trash cans glimmered in the faintest light. She ran out, found another door, and flung it open. It felt warm inside. The smell of old leather filled the room. Saddles sat on racks on the wall. How could one family have so many saddles? Then she realized. It was a riding school. That's why no one was here. There would be no house. She almost burst into tears.

She bolted out of the room, down the concrete center aisle, and found no more doors. She went back to the last stall because its window overlooked the dark pasture. She'd have a clear view if the killer had run after her. In the corner of the stall, a large horse lay still in a bed of hay, its gray white coat glowing softly in the dark.

"Ho, fella," Nat said softly, surprised that the horse didn't move. She entered the stall. She could see the Volvo through the window, not far from here. The horse nickered, and she heard congestion in its breathing. No wonder it hadn't moved. She stroked its muzzle, and it leaned against her hand like a big dog, begging to be scratched.

"Are we gonna be okay?" Nat scratched the hard bone between its dark eyes, feeling herself begin to calm down and think more clearly. The killer wasn't coming after her or he would never have let her go. It could be a while before anybody drove along and found the trooper. Getting back to her car was her only hope. She gave the horse a final pat, then let herself out of the stall.

She plunged back into the storm, racing for the Volvo. She pounded through mud and slush, her heart pumping hard against her chest. There was no noise but rain. She ran until she couldn't run another step, up the hill to the road. The Volvo was parked, its engine still running. She could see the murdered trooper, his arms lying askew in the street. She intentionally didn't look at his head. She darted across the street to her car, flung open the door, jumped inside, and hit the locks, shaking and dripping.

She floored the gas and reached for her purse at the same time, digging for her cell phone as she tore down the road. She found the phone and pressed speed dial for 911, but in the next minute, the Volvo interior was bathed in headlights. Police sirens erupted behind her, and she almost cried for joy. She slowed to a stop, parked, and threw open her door.

"Help! Police!" Nat practically popped out of the car.

"Hands in the air! Get your hands in the air!" Two troopers jumped from the police cruiser, one from each door. Suddenly, a second cruiser careened around the corner and sprayed to a stop in front of the Volvo, sandwiching her in between. Sirens screamed. High beams blinded her. Two more troopers jumped out of the second cruiser.

"Hands in the air!" they shouted, advancing toward her with guns drawn.

"Don't shoot!" Nat shouted back, raising her arms. "I was calling you—"

"Against the car!" a trooper bellowed, and two others grabbed her by her forearms and threw her facedown against the Volvo, wrenching her wrists behind her back.

"No, wait!" Nat yelped in pain. Steel handcuffs were clapped onto her wrists. Hands ran up her legs to her crotch, then down her hips and waist. She tried not to panic. "This is crazy! I was just calling you! This man came out of nowhere—"

"What's this, a knife?" The trooper bumped her against her car and shoved a hand in her coat pocket.

"Scissors. What are—"

"We're taking you in for questioning in connection with the murder of Trooper Shorney."

"The trooper?" Nat felt her heart beginning to pound. "No, wait, I saw the guy who shot him. I can tell you—"

"And for the attempted murder of Barbara Saunders."

"*What?*" Nat felt stricken. Rain thundered down. She couldn't believe she'd heard him right. "Did you say, Barb? What happened to Barb?"

"Do we have your permission to search your car?"

"Go ahead, just tell me what happened to Barb."

"You have the right to remain silent. Anything you say can and will be used against you in a court of—"

"Wait, why are you Mirandizing *me*? I didn't do anything!" Nat shouted. "I saw the man who killed the trooper! I would never—"

"—law. You have the right to a lawyer and to have a lawyer present during questioning. If you cannot afford a lawyer, one will be appointed for you."

"I didn't do it! I didn't do anything!" Nat shouted louder, as the other troopers searched the front and backseats of her car.

"Let's go!" Two troopers flanked her and hustled her to the patrol car. Two others were searching her backseat, shining their flashlights inside.

"You're making a mistake! I'm a law professor!" Nat howled against the rain, and she didn't stop until they shoved her into the backseat of a cruiser.

And sped off into the dark, drenched night.

CHAPTER 25

An hour later, Nat found herself at the Avondale barracks of the Pennsylvania State Police, chained to a wall. It was unreal. She was in a small, windowless room that looked like a normal office—except that one entire wall was covered with stainless steel from floor to ceiling. She sat on a stainless steel bench built into the steel wall, with her wrists handcuffed to a steel rail at arm height, and her legs, in boots, manacled to each other and looped through another steel rail, at ankle height. She was filthy, wet, and exhausted, and could barely process that the trooper had been killed before her eyes, and that Barb had been shot.

Be good for your aunt. One candy a piece, and that's it.

Nat couldn't get her thoughts together. She felt tears come to her eyes and didn't try to wipe them away, even if she could. Barbara was a mother of three. Her boys could be orphaned. Who would have done that? Why? Was it connected to the burglary? To the prison riot? It had to be, but Nat was too stunned to piece it together. Water soaked her coat, mud covered her boots. Her hair dripped filthy water, and the warmth that she'd felt spatter her face was the trooper's blood.

Please, step outside the car, Ms. Greco.

Nat tried to think. This would turn out all right. The troopers would come in and unlock her cuffs and leg irons, understanding that she'd had nothing to do with either of these crimes. They couldn't seriously suspect her of murdering a cop. They would realize their mistake in bringing her in. She would go home to Hank. She closed her eyes but his wasn't the first face that came to mind.

Natalie, listen.

Suddenly the main door opened, and a heavy-set man in a brown suit jacket, brown print tie, and khakis came in, smiling at her in a professional way and pulling over a metal chair. "Hello, Ms. Greco," he said warmly. "I'm Trooper David Brian Mundy." He sat down and gestured to the manacles. "Sorry the patrol officers had to lock you up like this. I know it's uncomfortable."

Nat felt her temper flare. "Trooper, new shoes are uncomfortable. Handcuffs and leg irons are another thing entirely."

"Fair enough." Mundy nodded. "Sorry about that, but it's procedure. Security." His voice was unusually soft for such a large man, and he had shoulders as wide as a defensive lineman's. His face was open and honest, with the heavy cheekbones of a Native American, and his eyes were brown, his nose short and wide, and his complexion uneven. He asked, "Would you like some coffee?"

"No, thanks." Nat had no idea how she'd hold it anyway.

"You're not missing anything. It tastes like motor oil." Mundy chuckled and eased back into the chair, his heavy thighs spreading in his slacks. He was about forty-five, judging from the lines around his eyes. He took a minute to appraise Nat, with evident empathy. "You're quite a sight. My wife would say it's a bad hair day."

"Can I just ask, how is Barb Saunders?"

"The last I heard, she was still unconscious and in intensive care. She took two bullets to the chest."

No. Nat regretted not asking for coffee. She needed something. She felt like crying but knew she had to watch her step. She didn't know if

this was an interview or a custodial interrogation, but the leg manacles were a tip-off. If it went south, she'd invoke her right to counsel.

"Would you like some water, or anything from the vending
machines? Bag of chips?"

"No, thanks," Nat answered, as another man entered the room. He
was as tall as Mundy but leaner, in a dark gray suit and striped tie. A
strip of graying blond hair ringed his bald head, and he had narrow
blue eyes and thin lips. He didn't smile, but nodded in Nat's direction.

"I'm Trooper Edward Duffy. We're both detectives here."

"Nat Greco," she said, as Duffy sat down in a far chair and put a
steno pad and pen in his lap. He didn't even look up. You didn't have
to be a professor to know who was the good cop and who the bad.

"So how do you know Barbara Saunders, Ms. Greco?" Mundy
asked.

"She's the widow of a prison guard, a C.O." Nat straightened up on
the slippery bench. "Why don't you tell me why I'm locked up?"

Mundy nodded again. "Okay, well, it wasn't long after Barbara
Saunders was shot that Trooper Matt Shorney was shot dead, not far
from her house. We have reason to believe you may know something
about his death. He stopped you and called in your plate, so we can
place that time, exactly." Trooper Mundy paused. "Look, we saw the
ID in your wallet, so you're obviously an educated person. You have
no criminal record. You teach at a law school. Penn, right?"

"Yes. I teach *law*. I study *law*. Do you really think I would kill a state
trooper?" It was so absurd that Nat could barely control her tone.

"Nobody's saying that yet."

"Then why am I chained to a wall?"

"Like I said, it's standard procedure." Mundy glanced in Duffy's
direction, but the other trooper was taking notes. "I gotta tell you, I
can't figure you out. You don't fit the profile. Not in the least."

"Of course I don't. It's unthinkable."

"But if you have information for me, you can help us both by talking to me. Come on, meet me halfway." Mundy's eyes softened. "Tell me what you know about Trooper Shorney's death. I'm here to listen. You said something to the troopers about a man you saw shoot him."

Nat wanted to trust him, but couldn't. Red flags were waving from all quarters. "So I'm not a suspect?"

"Professor, let's not play games. You're smart enough to know that you'd be making it easier on yourself if you talked to me. If your story about the man is true, you're a material witness. Tell me what happened."

"So I'm not a suspect," Nat said, and Duffy, on the other chair, sat staring, stone-faced.

"You're a person of interest," he interjected, his tone cold.

Wrong answer. "Then I want to make my phone call," Nat said evenly.

They unshackled Nat, led her down to the basement of the barracks, and deposited her in a small white interview room with a few black chairs on either side of a fake-wood table, a stained gray rug, and a Panasonic videocamera in the corner, which was turned off. A phone sat on the table. She punched in Hank's cell number again. She didn't know any criminal lawyers, but they could find one together, and she wanted him to know what was going on. If the trooper's murder had made the TV news already, he could have recognized the red Volvo, with its Penn Law parking sticker. She waited four rings, then he picked up.

"Hello?" Hank said, and Nat felt a warm rush at his voice.

"Babe, it's me."

"Nat? I can't hear you too well. We're in the middle of a game here. Lemme call you back."

"No, wait—"

"Call you later. Love you."

Great. The dial tone came back on. Nat tried again, but no answer. She checked her watch. Almost eleven o'clock. She had to get a lawyer, tonight. She thought of Angus. He'd been in the back of her mind anyway, taking up permanent residence. She called information for the hospital again, dialed his room, and he picked up. "Angus?"

"That you, Natalie? I've been calling your cell for the past hour. What happened with Barb?"

"How long you got?" Nat collected her thoughts and told him the story tersely. He listened in shocked silence. Then she got to the point: "I think I need a criminal lawyer."

"Of course you do! Jesus, God. Listen, don't worry. I know everybody in criminal defense. I wish I could be there myself." Angus cursed in frustration. "You know the drill, though. Don't say a thing."

"Of course."

"Not a thing! Don't try to convince them, because you can't."

"I won't."

"God knows what's going on out there. I can't believe this."

"And Barb? Can you imagine?" Nat felt sick inside, but she'd had time to think. "Somebody must want whatever it is she has. Did they try to kill her to get it? Or did she find it after I left, and they took it and shot her?"

"We'll sort it out later. In the meantime, focus on yourself. I'll have one of the best criminal lawyers in town there in an hour. Sit tight."

"I don't have much choice."

"Natalie, everything's going to be all right," Angus said softly, which was exactly what she needed to hear.

An hour later, back in the interview room, the initial shock had worn off, and Nat was wrapping her mind around her own predicament. They couldn't connect her to the murder, simply because there would be no evidence. She hadn't done it, so she had nothing to worry about. Reason reigned, even in Chester County. The next time the door to the interview room opened, Trooper Mundy stuck his head inside, then admitted someone else.

"Ms. Greco, your attorney is here. We'll give you a few minutes with him, then we'll be back."

"Thanks." Nat rose as Mundy shut the door, leaving her alone with a balding, preppy sixty-year-old in rimless glasses. He wore a red paisley bowtie and a black topcoat that looked like cashmere, and he carried a leather envelope with an expensive patina. He was hardly what she expected, but top criminal lawyers made great money and appearances could be deceiving. For example, she was covered in horse manure.

"Hello, I'm Carter Brooke," the lawyer said. He extended a hand, then stopped in midair with a slightest sniff. "Too bad they didn't let you wash up."

"They couldn't."

"Why not? It's just rude." Brooke's eyes glinted gray as Nantucket Sound.

The question only confused Nat. "They'll have to do a residue test on my hands, to determine if I fired a gun. Though the mud will mask the fact that I haven't, so the lack of residue won't prove my innocence. That's not good." She eyed her filthy hands with dismay. "They want everything according to procedure because they think I shot a cop, which of course, I didn't."

"Right. Let's get down to brass tacks. We don't have much time." Brooke slid out of his topcoat, revealing a full-dress black wool tuxedo with satin lapels and red paisley cummerbund.

"A *tux*?" Nat asked, astounded.

"I was at dinner."

"In a tux?"

"A firm dinner." Brooke folded his topcoat carefully, then set it on the cleanest chair he could find, which was none.

"What firm are you with?"

"Dechert."

"Really?" It was one of the best firms in town. *For bankers.* "They do criminal cases?"

"I do, most of them. I've represented major clients in antitrust probes and SEC investigations, from target letter to trial."

But all white-collar work. "Have you ever tried a murder case?"

"Well, no." Brooke pulled over one of the broken-down chairs. "But this shouldn't be too difficult tonight. We'll get co-counsel if they charge you. By the way, I hear you're a fellow Yalie."

Nat was stumped. "Angus said you were one of the best criminal lawyers in town."

"Angus who?" Brooke withdrew a black Mont Blanc from inside his tuxedo, just as the door opened and the two troopers reentered the interview room.

"Okay, folks, let's get this show on the road." Mundy pulled up his chair, and the other trooper took a chair off to the side, but Nat wasn't finished with her conversation.

"Angus Holt," she said to Brooke. "He sent you here, didn't he?"

"I don't know any Angus, except steak." Brooke sat down, brushed off his tuxedo pants, and extracted a fresh legal pad from his leather envelope. "I was called by your father. Greco Construction has us on retainer."

Oh no. Mr. Tuxedo must've gotten here before Angus's lawyer. "How did my father even know I was here?"

"I don't know." Brooke expertly twisted off the gleaming top of his pen between thumb and index finger.

"Wait, hold on." Nat turned to the troopers, raising her hand like a nervous 1L. "Trooper Mundy, this isn't my lawyer."

"What are you talking about?" Mundy glared at Brooke, who stiffened defensively.

"Yes, I am."

"No, I have another lawyer coming. I want to wait for him." Nat turned to Brooke. "I'm sorry. It's nothing personal." *But the other guy will know what he's doing.*

"We're not playing games here," Trooper Duffy interjected, his eyes hard. "You have a lawyer present and he's more than qualified. We can't wait anymore, and as long as you're represented, we have no legal obligation to wait." He turned to Brooke. "Are you willing and able to serve as counsel?"

"Certainly." Brooke looked matter-of-factly at Nat. "Maybe I'm not whom you expected, but the sooner we get this started, the sooner you can get home."

Nat considered it. She could probably represent herself at this stage. Hell, even Jelly could represent her at this stage.

Way to go, Dad. "Okay, let's proceed," she said, then braced herself.

CHAPTER 26

Nat went through the preliminaries as if they were happening to somebody else. She mechanically signed the statement that said she'd been informed of her Miranda rights and had given consent for the troopers to search her car, which had already been impounded. She watched silently as Trooper Duffy set up the black videocamera and aimed it at her, as she sat opposite Trooper Mundy, who was trying hard to reestablish their love connection. He had already brought her a cup of hot coffee.

"Told you," Mundy said, when she took a sip. "If you want me to get you a sandwich that tastes like sawdust, I can do that, too."

Nat shook her head. Brooke settled next to her and started writing on his pad, as did Duffy, who took a seat to Mundy's left, on his side of the fake-wood table.

Mundy began, "Well, I don't pull any punches, Ms. Greco. You're a direct person, and so am I. How about I tell you what we know at this time, and maybe you'll tell me what you know."

"We're listening," Brooke answered, for both of them.

"By the way, may I call you Nat?"

"No," Brooke answered again, and Nat thought maybe he'd work out after all. Her gaze shifted to the black lens of the camera, then shifted away. It was making her nervous.

Mundy continued. "Okay, tonight at around 10:35 p.m., one Barbara Saunders was found by her sister, shot, when the sister got home from the movies. Mrs. Saunders was found in the garage, lying on the floor. The sister called 911 immediately, and they appeared quickly on the scene, though Mrs. Saunders had lost a lot of blood."

Nat sensed from his pained expression that he'd been to the garage. She imagined Barb lying there and prayed the kids hadn't seen her.

Mundy continued, "The sister told us that you had been there to see Mrs. Saunders that night. She also told us that you'd been trying to see her since her husband's death. You told Barbara Saunders that you had a message for her."

The week unspooled through Nat's brain, an awful rewind. Next to her, Brooke took rapid notes on his legal pad.

"We looked around and found a large hole in the garage floor." Mundy made a big square with his hands. "In the hole was a will, a videotape, some magazines, and some money. About nine hundred and fifty dollars."

Money?

"We also found some pills on the ground, OxyContin. They were scattered, like somebody had dropped them on the way out." He exchanged a glance with Trooper Duffy, who kept taking notes. "The money was scattered on the ground too, like it had been left behind in a big hurry."

Nat's mind reeled. She fought to keep her mouth shut.

"We searched your car, and we found twenty-three thousand dollars and two bags of OxyContin in your trunk."

"*What?*" Nat blurted out. "In my car?"

"Did you take those things from the house?"

"Of course not!" Nat responded, getting scared. "This is crazy!"

"Is it? Tell me why."

"Look I didn't shoot anyone, much less a state trooper, and when I left the house, Barb was alive and there was nothing in the hole but a will, magazines, and a videotape."

Brooke looked over at her, frowning. "Nat, please don't volunteer additional information."

"So you went to the house, that much is true?" Mundy asked, and his frank brown eyes searched hers, as if he really wanted answers.

Brooke said to Nat, "I'm instructing you not to discuss this."

She kept her mouth shut, but it was killing her. The money and the drugs connected her to a crime she hadn't commited.

Duffy interjected, "If we wanted, we could book you right now for the Oxys. Unless you got a doctor you want us to call."

Nat shuddered. Drug charges. Murder. She would be ruined. She clammed up.

Brooke cleared his throat authoritatively. "It would be imprudent to make an arrest on a drug charge at this juncture, before you had investigated the other crimes."

"Aren't you going to tell me what happened, Ms. Greco?" Mundy asked, but it was Brooke who shook his head.

"No, she isn't. Are we free to go? This is a waste of her time."

Nat flushed red, and Mundy eyed her gravely.

"Let me tell you one thing, before you go. Some people say a murder case is a puzzle, and they talk about pieces we have to put together. Other people call it a game. It's never those things, not to me." Trooper Mundy shook his head. "I'm a simple guy, and to me, it's simple. You know something I don't. To me, it's about a young man, Trooper Matt Shorney, who was killed. We both knew him, Duffy better than me." Mundy gestured behind him, where the other trooper bent his bald head over his notes. "I want to know what happened to him because it's my job. Simple as that. No puzzle, no game. Just work. If you know what happened, I'm asking you to tell me. The rest, it's all bullshit."

Brooke said, "I repeat, my client won't be making any statements."

But Nat felt touched by Mundy's words. He was right. This was about something more important than her hide. This was about the truth, and about Shorney and Barb. If she could tell the troopers what she knew, maybe they could still find the killer tonight.

"Trooper Mundy," she said, "before he died, Barb's husband told me to tell his wife there was something under the floor. I went there to tell her, and we looked all night, but we couldn't find what he meant."

"That's enough now." Brooke touched her arm, but Nat shook it off.

"Let me talk to him. I know what I'm doing." She faced Mundy, with the black camera lens over his shoulder. "I saw a man shoot Trooper Shorney."

"You really saw him killed?" Mundy recoiled slightly in surprise, and his eyes widened.

Duffy's head snapped up, and Brooke squeezed Nat's arm. "Please don't say any more," he said firmly.

"A man in a black ski mask shot him. He shot once, then he told me to run, and I did."

"Could you see his face?"

"No."

"What could you see? Anything?" Behind Mundy, Trooper Duffy had stopped taking notes and was folding his arms.

"I don't . . . know," Nat stammered. Gruesome images flashed through her mind. The trooper's hat flying off. The ski mask.

"What do you remember about his build? Tall? Short?"

"Nat, please," Brooke interrupted, but she waved him off again.
"Average."

"What kind of coat did he have on?"

"I don't know. Dark." Nat tried to remember. The only recurrent image was a figure in the rain, behind a gun. "I don't remember."

"Was he white, black, Hispanic?"

"I don't know."

Brooke interrupted again, "Please, what you're doing is against my express legal advice, do you understand?"

"Yes," Nat answered, patting his hand. She could see he'd had the fear of Greco put into him. "Please. It's okay."

"You said the shooter spoke to you?" Mundy asked, regardless. "What did he say? What did it sound like?"

"He said, 'Run, bitch.' He had a normal voice."

"Did he have an accent?" Mundy asked, and behind him, Trooper Duffy's eyelids fluttered, just short of an eye roll.

"No," Nat answered.

"Where did he come from?"

"I don't know. He came out of nowhere, in the rain."

Duffy looked away, but Mundy leaned forward. "What kind of car was he driving?"

"I didn't see a car. He came up behind me, on foot. He shot the trooper over my shoulder. I turned around and saw the gun in his hand." Nat's thoughts raced ahead. "He must have been the one who shot Barb. He must have been the one who put the pills and the money in my car."

Duffy interjected, "You didn't say he had anything in his hand but the gun."

"He didn't."

"So how did he put twenty grand in your car? And the Oxys?"

Nat felt momentarily confused. "I don't know," she answered, as Mundy fell silent.

Duffy took the lead. "And where'd it come from then, if he didn't have a car?"

"I don't know. I have to think."

"He couldn't run around with that much money, not in the rain. It's quite a bundle."

"I'm not sure how he did it. I have to think." Nat couldn't wrap her mind around it fast enough.

"The cruisers are equipped with an MVR tape, a mobile video recorder," Duffy said with a slight smirk. "But it sure doesn't corroborate your story."

Nat was nonplussed. "That's impossible. I mean, he was there."

"Not according to the camera, he wasn't. The camera shows your back, you facing Matty—I mean, Trooper Shorney—and him going down. It shows no third party, ski mask or no."

Nat tried to understand. "Does the camera show just the driver's-side door?"

"Yes, and the back of your car and your license plate."

"But this man, the killer, wasn't that close. He was on the other side of the car, near the curb. He must have been standing out of the camera range."

"Oh yeah?" Duffy cocked his head. "The camera has audio too, and we didn't hear anybody say, 'Run, bitch.'"

Nat's mouth went bone dry. "He said it. I heard it." Then she remembered. "The rain was so loud, maybe the audio didn't pick it up." She began to feel scared, desperate. "Look, I didn't take money or drugs from Barb's house. I didn't put them in my car. I would never have shot Barb, Trooper Shorney, or anybody." Her words sped up in a panicky way, as Duffy's voice grew colder. "I mean, really, look at me. I'm a law professor. Why would I kill innocent people, or steal drugs and money?"

"I don't know yet, but I've got a couple guesses."

"Like what?"

"For one, you work at a major university. You can sell pills to the students. It's just the kind of candy corn the kids like nowadays."

"That's ridiculous!"

"Is it?" Duffy lifted a sparse eyebrow. "Here's how I see it. Saunders was dealing, on the inside, at the prison. He knew he had a stash

"Right, that was it." Nat figured her makeover was working. "I saw a Phoenix trailer at the prison just the other day, when I drove past."

"Sure, that's our job. How can I help you, honey?" The woman bent over and straightened the magazines on the coffee table. "We're not open today, but I have to come in. The filing never ends."

Nat thought fast. "Funny, that's what I came about. I need a job, and filing sounds great to me."

"Really?" The woman burst into a smile, then reached out her hand and shook Nat's warmly. "Pleased to meet you. I'm Agnes Grady Chesko. What's your name? I didn't even ask."

Uh. Nat's gaze fell to the magazines. *Car & Driver.* "Carr. Pat Carr."

"Well, Pat, I manage the office, do the books, and keep a whole crew of crazy guys paid. I'm what they used to call 'chief cook and bottle washer,' but you're too young to know that expression." Agnes eyed her. "You still in high school?"

"Uh, no. I had a year of college. I was an art major."

"That's nice. Where?"

Somewhere far away. "University of Wisconsin, but I'm taking a leave. During the week I have a regular job."

"What do you do?"

Something believable. "I work at a bookstore in town."

"Oh, I never go into Philly. It's too far, and I hate to pay for parking."

"I could really use a Saturday job, just for the extra money."

"We couldn't pay much. Maybe minimum wage."

"Tell you what. Please, give me a tryout, for free, today. If you like what I do, then keep me at minimum wage."

Agnes brightened. "So, you want 'pin money,' we used to say."

"We call it tuition money."

"Good one!" Agnes clapped her on the back, and Nat almost hit the wall. "I like a good sense of humor. You'll need it when you see that filing."

"I can handle it. I'm good at the alphabet."

"Hallelujah, looks like my prayers have been answered." Agnes laughed again and threw up her hands. "Come back into my nest, and I'll show you the ropes."

Yay! Nat felt a tingle of excitement. They walked down a short hallway with an office and another door to the right. Nat looked over. "Is that the boss's office?"

"Yep, he's not in much. He's always out at jobs. We've got twenty-three employees including me, full time, and we sub out the rest. Here's my den." Agnes gestured at a cramped office with a single window and a funny smell. A black metal desk covered with knickknacks sat against the back wall, and gray filing cabinets lined the interior wall, along with a messy shelf of black notebooks of building codes. Agnes stepped over to her desk, which held a large cardboard box, full of papers. "This is my filing, a year's worth."

Yikes. "Yikes." Nat went to the box and peeked inside. There had to be invoices in there from the Dumpster company at the prison. In fact, there should be a file on the prison job somewhere in this office, if the place worked the way Greco Construction did. "I assume every job has its own file."

"Right." Agnes took the top invoice from the pile, which read, John Taylor Residence, then crossed to the drawer and pulled out a manila folder labeled, Taylor Residence, John. "This is obviously the job name, so you put the invoice in the job file. It's not rocket science."

"Gotcha. Residential jobs go by first letter of the last name, and commercial jobs go by the first letter of the company?"

"Exactly. You catch on quick."

It's that Yale law degree.

"I'll get to work and catch up on my payroll. It'll be nice to have somebody else to talk to back here, especially another girl."

"Great." *Rats.* Nat had been hoping Agnes would leave her alone with the files. She slid off her coat, set it on the back of a chair, and picked up the filing box, getting a stronger whiff of that funny smell.

She looked down and almost jumped. A ferret slept on its back, on a net stretched over a blue plastic box. Its back legs flopped open pornographically. "Is that a ferret?"

"Sorry, I should have introduced you." Agnes sat down at her desk and pulled her keyboard closer. "That's Frankie, my loverboy. Isn't he so cute?"

"*So* cute." *But is he gonna close his legs anytime soon?* Nat picked up the filing box and set it nearer the file cabinets. "I'll get this off your desk so you can work."

"Good idea." Agnes switched on a black Sony boombox on the credenza behind her. "Hope you don't mind the oldies station. I'm talking the fifties."

"Fine with me," Nat said, until a woman started singing that she'd die if a man didn't call her. No wonder women were so messed up. It's a wonder we could even walk.

"I'm a big Frankie Valli fan. He sang 'Sherry' and 'You're Just Too Good to Be True.' You know those songs?"

"Yes, sure." Nat went through the top papers. Another bill for John Taylor Residence, then some lumber ordered from Tague for the Shields Family Addition. She took both bills and went to the correct drawers, starting with the Ts, in case Agnes was watching her.

"They did a show about them on Broadway. *Jersey Boys.* I went with my girlfriends. Oh, did we have fun." Agnes's fingers flew across the keyboard, pounding like a rainstorm. "My friend Danielle threw a bra on the stage."

"Was it hers?"

Agnes laughed, and Nat kept her distracted.

"Is Frankie the ferret named for Frankie Valli?"

"Aren't you the detective!"

One can only hope. "No, I'd be a bad detective. I'd be a great construction worker, though. I used to think it would be fun to do the demolition part, like where you take apart rooms."

"Yeah, get all your aggressions out."

"Right. Do you have employees here that do that? Maybe I can get a transfer."

"Ha! The Mexicans do that, mostly. They don't even speak English."

Damn. "It still sounds like fun, except for the cleanup. Where do they take all that stuff? Throw it in Dumpsters, right?"

"Now *that's* not a job you'd want."

"You do that yourselves or you have a Dumpster company?"

"We use a company, whichever one's local to the job."

"So how long have you had Frankie?" Nat went back to the box, took off the top few papers, and held them close to her chest as she went over to the C drawers, for Chester County Correctional Institution. She wanted that job file.

"Five years, and I don't have him. He has me."

Aw. "I used to have a cat, so I know what you mean." Nat checked the Cs, which were spread over two drawers, C–A to C–I and C–I to C–U. She went for the bottom drawer. "I don't know much about ferrets. Educate me."

"First thing you have to know is ferrets aren't rodents. They're cousins of weasels, otters, and skunks."

Nat slid open the bottom C drawer as Agnes typed and talked.

"Ferrets are closer to dogs, more like dogs than cats. They make wonderful pets. Here's a fun fact. Ferrets are illegal in California."

"Why?" *The stench?* Nat thumbed through the C files. Chester County Dance Studio Addition, Chester County Petting Zoo, Chester County VFW Post. No Chester County Correctional file. Why?

"Discrimination, that's why. Discrimination and misinformation. The California legislature thinks that ferrets will turn feral, but they misconstrue the species." Agnes typed away. "Did you know that dog bites send a million people to the emergency room each year? But dogs aren't illegal. Ferrets are just plain discriminated against."

"That's not fair." Nat thumbed through the folders again, looking for the Chester County Correctional file. No luck. She searched the rest of the second drawer in case it was misfiled, but still no luck.

"Feral cats are lawful, and isn't that just so ironic? That's one of our arguments." Agnes's voice grew urgent, and she typed even faster. "I'm a member of Ferret Fanciers of America, and we petitioned California to legalize ferret ownership. Governor Schwarzenegger just isn't responding."

"That's too bad." Nat closed the drawer and went back for another set of papers. Where could that file be? She picked up some papers and rifled though them. "By the way, do you keep copies of these receipts at the jobsites, too?"

"No, all the paperwork is here at the office. It would get lost on site. These guys would lose their heads if they weren't attached."

"For every job?"

"Yes."

Hmm. So the prison file wouldn't be in the construction trailer at the prison. "That makes sense."

"There are a few special job files in Jim's office, though. He started keeping the real active jobs in there, since he's always referring to the files. If you have filing and can't find the job file, just give it to me and I'll go in to his office."

"Okay. I don't yet." Nat turned away with the papers. So that answered her question. "Now, you were teaching me about ferrets."

"Well, the Latin name of the domestic pet ferret is *Mustela furo,* and it's not a wild animal. They've been domesticated for a long, long time. Two or three thousand years."

"Really?" Nat filed the last few invoices, thinking of a way to get into the boss's office for the file.

"They're often confused with their cousins, the North American black-footed ferret, or *Mustela nigripes.*"

Nat checked her watch: 12:05. It gave her an idea, and she straightened up. "By the way, have you eaten lunch? I haven't."

"It is that time, isn't it?" Agnes looked up from her keyboard, her eyes bright. "Goody! Let's go to McDonald's. I'll bring Frankie in his Ferret Ferry. I wear it on my shoulder, and it looks exactly like a purse."

Bet it doesn't. "I have too much filing to go out on my first day. Either you could go out if you wanted a break, or I could go out and bring you something back."

"Oh, right." Agnes thought a minute. "I should stay here to do payroll, so it would be great if you ran out and got the food. Do you mind?"

"Not at all. I'm the gofer."

"Gophers are in the *Geomyidae* family. Ferrets are in the *Mustelidae* family. We're ferret fans, here." Agnes laughed, and Nat smiled.

"Now, what would you like from McDonald's?"

"Do you know where it is?"

No. "Yes."

"Good. A Big Mac with a Diet Coke. Thanks."

"Okay. It'll be my treat, since you're giving me a chance today."

"You're too nice." Agnes smiled, and Nat grabbed her coat guiltily.

"Hang in. I'll be right back."

"We'll see you soon."

"We?"

"Me and Frankie."

"Right." Nat looked down at the ferret. His legs were still open. *Okay, him I won't miss.*

She hurried from the office and made noisy footsteps to the door, then opened the door so the chimes would ring and let it slam loudly, as if she had left the building. Then she hurried back, as lightly on her feet as she could, holding her breath as she slipped past the open doorway to Agnes's office.

She took a quick left, stole down the hall, and darted into Jim Graf's office, her heart pounding. She scanned the room in a flash. Desk, computer, TV, building codes. File cabinets behind the desk. She ran for them, opened the cabinet quietly, and thumbed through the manila files. Albemarle Residence, Boston Pizza addition, Chester County Correctional Institution.

There! Nat slid the folder out, shoved it under her coat, then closed the drawer silently. She ran out of the boss's office, tiptoed past Agnes's doorway, and hurried out to the front door—where she stopped, stumped. If she ran out, the door chimes would go off. It wouldn't take Agnes long to figure out which file was missing, and if she linked the prison file to Nat, her bleached-blond cover could be blown. She opened the door and closed it again, letting the chimes go off, then walked back noisily to Agnes's office and poked her head in the doorway.

"I forgot your order," she said, faking a frown.

Agnes looked up from the keyboard. Frankie slept soundly in his net, and somebody on the radio was wearing blue velvet. "Big Mac and a Diet Coke."

"Got it. Sorry. See you," Nat said, and took off. She couldn't wait to get out of there and read the folder.

It was almost Too Good To Be True.

Half an hour later, Nat parked the Kia behind a Wawa, sipped a fresh, hot coffee, and inhaled half of a turkey hoagie with provolone while she opened the Chester County Correctional file. It was at least three inches thick, and the top invoice was from CCWM, for Chester County Waste Management.

Bingo! She went through the entire file and pulled out all the CCWM invoices. There were four, and she set them side by side on her lap. An invoice was sent in June, September, November, and February. This month. Four Dumpsters hauled off, at a cost of $1,749.00. The February Dumpster had been taken away the day after the riot. She considered the pattern. Four months for the first Dumpster. Four for the second. One for the last. It stunk worse than ferrets. She reached for the borrowed cell phone and pressed the number for CCWM, but the machine said they were closed on the weekend.

Nat sighed, then noticed an icon on the phone. She'd gotten a message from Angus's number. She used the password Bill had given her, got to voicemail, then recognized the caller's voice, with a tiny fluttering.

"Natalie, it's Angus, and I got your message at my office." He sounded anxious, and urgent. "Call me as soon as you get this. The D.A.'s looking for you. They found the murder weapon in a field."

Nat felt sick to the pit of her stomach.

"They want you to turn yourself in."

Nat gathered the papers, threw the rest of the hoagie aside, and started the engine.

CHAPTER 33

Nat tore out of the parking lot, turned onto the main road, and headed for Route 202, speeding south to the state line. Pennsylvania police didn't have jurisdiction in Delaware, and she'd be damned if she'd turn herself in. She wouldn't get bail, not for the first-degree murder of a cop. It was a charge that carried the death penalty. She made the decision in a blink, for once not overanalyzing something. She'd always believed in, and even loved, the law. But if she submitted to the law, she'd never get justice. And neither would Trooper Shorney or Barb Saunders. The cops weren't going to hunt for the man in the ski mask. No one else was trying to find out what had really happened.

She flicked on the radio, already tuned to the all-news station, and didn't have to wait long until she heard her own name. The announcer said, "University of Pennsylvania professor Natalie Greco is being sought in connection with the homicide of Trooper Matthew Shorney of the Pennsylvania State Police and the attempted murder of Barbara Saunders of Chester County. Mrs. Saunders remains in intensive care, in a coma, following her injuries."

Nat shuddered, for Barb. Her stomach clenched like a fist and she hit the gas. She passed strip malls and gas stations, an Arby's and a

McDonald's, a Staples and an Office Depot, jockeying as well as she could in the traffic of Saturday errands in the suburbs. She picked up the cell phone and pressed buttons until she got to the number Angus had called from, then hit Send. "Angus?" she said, when the call connected.

"Natalie." It was all he had to say, and she felt her throat catch. "They're looking for you. They want to arrest you. Where are you?"

"On the way to Delaware." Nat passed another strip mall with another McDonald's.

"You must be terrified."

"Basically, yes." Nat ran a hand through her shorn hair. "I'm worried that the doorman is going to tell the cops that he lent me his car. If the police are charging me, then he's an accomplice after the fact, and sooner or later somebody will tell him so."

"Natalie, slow down. You borrowed a car?"

"Yes, and as soon as he tells them, they'll have an ID on the car and a warrant for the cell phone. They could be looking for the car right now, and if they are, my disguise isn't worth a damn. I could be pulled over and arrested any minute."

"Disguise? You're wearing a disguise?"

"A good one, too."

"Natalie, listen. Bennie says you should turn yourself in. The cops said you could turn yourself in to her. I respect her opinion."

"What do you think?" Nat listened hard for his answer, pressing the phone to her ear.

"I'm not an expert. I don't want to give you the wrong advice." Angus's voice softened. "Right now, Bennie's opinion matters more than mine."

"Not to me."

"Honestly?" Angus sounded almost pained, and Nat bore down. Somewhere inside, her heart wanted to know what this man was going to say to her, right now.

"Honestly."

"For me, I think you'd be crazy to turn yourself in, to her or anyone else. I think they'll crucify you. I think you should let me meet you in Delaware. We can figure out the best thing to do, together."

Nat almost cried, with gratitude. "Are you well enough to drive?"

"I'll get to you. Tell me where to go."

"Call you when I get there. Bye." Nat closed the phone and in time saw the blue sign ahead, WELCOME TO DELAWARE. Her heart lifted, and she made a beeline for the border. She remembered that some cell phones had GPS in them, so she found a pen in the car, scribbled Angus's cell number on her hand, then powered down the phone. She'd have to get rid of the car, too. Another strip mall lay ahead, and she pulled in.

People milled everywhere around the lot, families with kids in winter gear, carrying plastic bags and pushing oversized shopping carts. She drove around the back of the big-box store, so she couldn't be seen from the main drag. She toyed with the idea of parking the car around the back, with the license plate against the wall, but cops would come back here eventually. She wanted the car disappeared and she couldn't go out in the middle of nowhere to dump it or she'd never get back. Then it struck her. She shouldn't hide the car at all. There was only one way to get it disappeared instantly and still make a clean getaway.

She drove around to the front of the store, where customers were coming and going, and found just what she was looking for. Signs. NO PARKING. NO STOPPING. VIOLATORS WILL BE TOWED AT OWNER'S EXPENSE. She parked in front of the store, gathered up the prison file, grabbed her purse, and got out of the Kia and walked quickly away. On a busy shopping day like Saturday, the car would be towed within an hour, hopefully before Bill got wind that she was wanted for murder. She walked calmly out of the parking lot to the street, watching the traffic for a bus or a cab.

Fifteen minutes later, she was still waiting nervously when a blue tow truck that read Bill's Tow-the-Line steered past her and into the mall's parking lot. She turned and watched with satisfaction as the Kia was tugged away, hanging from the chain like a minnow on a fishing line. She finally spotted a cab, hailed it, climbed inside, and told the older driver she needed a cheap, out-of-the way motel.

"I know just what you mean," the driver said, with a knowing wink, and Nat didn't disabuse him of whatever notion he had. The cab lurched into traffic and eventually steered into the outskirts of Wilmington. She felt suddenly as if she were leaving her life. Speeding away from her home, her city, and the job she loved. And Hank and the family who, as annoying as they were, at least didn't believe she'd killed anybody. There was no way she could see them now.

She was officially on the run, a law professor turned fugitive. She didn't know how it had all gone so wrong, or how she could set it right. She knew only that it wouldn't be as quick a fix as a box of Beach Blonde and CVS eyeglasses. And that Angus would help. She felt like he *got* her, in a way no man had before. She felt as if he'd fight for her, and help her fight for herself. And she loved what he'd said:

I'll get to you.

Because she knew he already had.

CHAPTER 34

Nat hit the cheesy motel room, threw her stuff on the bed, crossed directly to the curtains, and yanked them closed. She went to the TV, grabbed the greasy remote, and clicked through the channels, relieved not to see her face on the screen. She left the news on, muted, so she could monitor the cops. She was on edge, keeping fear at bay by sheer denial. Academics were ill-suited to life on the lam, and she felt disorientated, lost in time and space.

I thought you wanted space. Which is it, space or time?

Nat thought about calling Hank, but he'd tell her to turn herself in.

We can figure out the best thing to do, together.

She went to the phone, double-checked the number on her palm, and called.

Nat showered, dried off, and put the same clothes back on, having no other choice. She brushed her teeth with a finger and combed her hair so it was less Bart Simpson, then put on some makeup, pretending that she wasn't wanted for murder. Her eyes looked back at her from the mirror, a darker brown against the contrast of the blond. They looked worried, too, but that had nothing to do with Revlon. She banished all negative thoughts. She had work to do.

She went to the bed and picked up the prison file, but a packet of blueprints fell onto the patterned rug. She got the packet and took it to a little veneer table, where she spread it out so that it dropped over the sides like a tablecloth. A hanging light with a gold-toned shade hung over the table, casting a circle on a floor plan of the prison, before remodeling.

On the plan, she could see the entrance of the prison, the control center, the cafeteria, the classroom where she'd been attacked, and, on the other side, the room in which Saunders and Upchurch had been killed. She turned to the second page, which was HVAC, then turned to the third page. It was the electrical plan, the schematics that showed the wiring.

She eyed them, then looked closer. She could see the straight black lines that would have been wiring for the security cameras, because they went to a central spot in the ceiling, which she gathered was the silver orb Angus had mentioned. She compared the wiring in the room where Saunders and Upchurch had been killed. There was no such wiring. No security camera.

Nat double-checked. She could see the wires going to the other security cameras, but the room where Upchurch had been killed had no such pattern of wires. She followed the black lines of wiring to the other staff rooms on that side of the hallway. There were three staff rooms, and they all had wiring for security cameras, except for one at the end of the row nearest the RHU pod.

She mulled this over. She didn't ask Graf why he and Saunders had taken Upchurch into that room in particular. She had assumed it was because it was the security office, but maybe it was because it didn't have a camera. Graf had to have known that. If he didn't know it before the remodeling, he would certainly have known after. His brother had the schematics, and even a professor could read them.

She felt as if she were onto something. So Graf knew that what-ever he did in that room wouldn't be recorded. It suggested a degree of premeditation that gave another lie to Graf's version of events. So either Upchurch had been involved in dealing drugs, or he'd simply found out that Graf and maybe Saunders were. So what did Upchurch do exactly that merited execution? His killing seemed like an overreaction to skimming profits or a double-cross of some kind. Why bother killing him, given the risk? Why not simply make his life miserable?

Nat felt stymied. What if Mrs. Rhoden had been right, and Upchurch was a quiet little guy who never bothered anyone? A victim of teasing, first by schoolkids and later by Graf. It forced her to re-analyze the problem, which led her to a startling question: What if Upchurch wasn't the intended victim that morning? What if it was *Saunders* whom Graf had intended to kill? What if Graf merely used Upchurch as an excuse, to catch Saunders unawares?

She tested her theory. Could Graf have killed both Saunders and Upchurch? Was it even physically possible? She went through the steps in her mind. Say Graf brings the knife in. He kills Saunders, then Upchurch, then makes it look like Upchurch killed Saunders. Graf tells the lie to cover up his crime. So it was possible. If it was a cover-up, how high up did it go? At least to Machik, for all of the foregoing, as the lawyers say. But why would Graf have killed Saunders, his best friend? And if it happened that way, why hadn't Saunders told her that before he died? His keeping mum shot her whole theory.

Nat jumped at the sound of a knock, then walked over and peeked through the peephole. She couldn't deny the fluttering inside her chest at the sight of the familiar shaggy ponytail, thick gray sweater, and jeans. She opened the door.

"Natalie," Angus said softly, scooping her up into an embrace that lifted her off her bare feet, then quickly setting her back down. "Okay, that hurts. Sorry."

"My, jeez." Nat tugged her sweater down, flustered. *That was a definite hug, wasn't it?*

"Look at your hair! You're blond!" Angus ruffled her spikes with a hand.

"It's my disguise."

"You look so cute, like a little puppy! A little yellow puppy!"

Great. "I'm a felon, not a Labrador."

"It's a totally great disguise." Angus set a brown shopping bag on the bed. "I never would have known it was you at all."

"Good."

"You're still so pretty." Angus's eyes locked hers for an awkward moment, and Nat squirmed in the silence. It seemed too much, all of a sudden. A motel room with a bed, and the two of them alone together. She, newly single, and he, terminally sexy. Nat gestured to the bed . . . er, bag.

"What's in there?"

"Good stuff!" Angus seemed to snap out of the moment, his characteristic good cheer returning. He went to the bed and opened the bag. "I've got you everything you need to be a proper outlaw. Ready?"

"Sure."

"First, for the fugitive who has everything, *voilà*!" Angus pulled a pink toothbrush out of the bag.

"My favorite color!" Nat laughed. It was fun to be silly, after today.

"I knew it. Blondes love pink."

"That's me, Fugitive Barbie."

"Now, for my next trick, check it out." Angus's hand went back in the bag and retrieved a twelve pack of king-size Snickers. "Nutrition!"

"Yummy!" Nat took the Snickers, the sight of which actually made her hungry. "Just the thing for the girl on the go. Literally."

"Snickers are one of the four basic food groups, which are pizza, The Strokes, California rosé, and"—from the bag, Angus pulled a red-and-white Verizon box—"a new cell phone."

"Yay!" Nat took the box. "I'm back in business."

"Get ready." Angus held up a three-pack of Hanes white cotton underwear, bikini style. "Ta-da!"

"You bought me *underwear*?" Nat burst into astonished laughter, grabbed the pack, and swatted him.

"I'd never run from the law without clean underwear."

"So if they shoot me dead, I won't be embarrassed?" Nat eyed the package. "Size two? You think I'm a two? I can't fit my hand in a two!"

"What do I know?" Angus shrugged. "I don't want you thinking I spend lots of time imagining your adorable little butt, which I do. Just don't tell your boyfriend."

Nat stopped smiling. She felt guilty standing with Angus, holding undies.

"What?" Angus asked.

"We broke up."

"Am I supposed to act sorry?" He cocked his head matter-of-factly. "Because I'm not. I'm better for you, and we both know it."

Whoa. Nat hit him with the packet again, and he turned back to the bag.

"But that's beside the point now, because you're in jeopardy. There's a time and a place for everything." Angus plunged his hand in the bag, then turned around with a white bank envelope, which he presented to Nat. "My mother always said a girl needs mad money, and I haven't met a girl I'm as mad about in my life."

Gulp. "Are you serious?"

"About the money or you?"

Me. "The money."

"Absolutely."

Nat opened up the end of the envelope, exposing a thick stack of stiff new bills. "Yikes, how much is here?"

"A thousand dollars. Luckily my bank is open on Saturday. I had about three bucks on me when you called."

"Angus, I can't accept this."

"Yes you can, and you will." He closed her hand around the envelope, and Nat couldn't deny the effect of his touch. "Pay me back whenever. Now, I have one last item in your going-away kit. Hold on." He turned away, dug in the bag, and handed her another envelope. "This is a one-way ticket to Miami, on a train that leaves early tomorrow from Wilmington. It's the earliest I can get you out of here. I'd fly you, but you need ID for that. I'll take you to the Wilmington station tomorrow morning."

"No. If I accept a ticket from you, you're an accomplice. You're aiding and abetting."

"I can't think of anybody I'd rather do that to. With. Whatever." His gaze was direct and even, meeting Nat somewhere in the middle of the space between them, which she could sense growing smaller by the second.

"Angus, I can't do that to you."

"Just go, and we'll see what to do next."

"Why Miami?"

"Because it's as far away as possible and I have a good friend there, a great criminal lawyer."

"I'll get away on my own."

"You have to take this, for me. For us."

Us? Nat didn't know what to say.

"We have a chance if you get through this. I'm being selfish here."

Nat's heart quickened and before she could protest, Angus leaned over and kissed her softly, his beard still cold as it brushed against her cheek. He explored her mouth, and she kissed him back, tasting his warmth until he pulled away and met her eye with frank desire.

"I love you, I do," Angus whispered.

Nat fell speechless, feeling everything at once.

"I want you to be safe and sound, away from here. I don't know if it's legally right or wrong, I only know that I love you and want you safe." He leaned down and kissed her again, his blue eyes still open, clear as sky, and Nat kissed him back, eyes open, too, exposing herself to him. Their gaze and kiss connected them, one to the other, and she knew in her heart that even though it was too soon, she was stone crazy about the man.

"Angus, I—" Nat began to say, but he kissed her again, more urgently, probing, and she felt herself enveloped in his scratchy sweater.

"I knew it would be like this," Angus murmured, stroking her face, then cupping the back of her shorn head, pulling her mouth to his again.

Nat surrendered to the feeling, enjoying the sweetness. He kissed her again and his hands traveled down her back to her hips. He picked her up in both hands and gentled her onto his lap, easing them both backward onto the bed. She found herself climbing onto him, straddling him in her jeans, in a way she hadn't done ever before, and his arms gripped her waist, pulling her down onto him. He kissed her deeply, and she wanted to wrap herself around him in every way, feel herself take him inside, and when she couldn't stand it any longer, he seemed to know and began to take off his sweater, laughing when he got it stuck on his head. "Help!"

"It's caught on your beard." Nat laughed with him and helped, and when Angus's face finally reappeared, flushed with effort, she looked into his eyes and touched his beard with wonderment, running her fingertips over its reddish gold strands, feeling its softness and coarseness at the same time. He yanked off his T-shirt, revealing a thick, muscular chest covered with dark gold hair and a long ponytail snaking over the bulge of his shoulder.

Nat stirred at the sight of such a natural man, kissing him deeply as he put his hands under her sweater and guided it upward, smiling with pleasure as she pulled it over her head and let it fall away.

"My poor baby," Angus said suddenly, and Nat saw his face change. Then she remembered, ashamed. Her chest. The scratches. Her hands flew to cover herself, but he caught her hands and kissed them.

"No, it's okay. Let me see," he said, his eyes troubled, and he gentled her hands apart and eyed Buford's handiwork.

"Let me make it better," he murmured, while he kissed each scratch, then sent a shiver down her spine as he placed his hands warmly on her shoulders and slid down the straps of her bra. He reached around and unfastened the bra, and she wriggled out of it and tossed it aside, both of them giggling as if they were children at play. He pulled her close to him, and she felt the strength in his shoulders and back as they kissed again, harder and with need, and everything changed, darkening and deepening, as soon as skin met skin and his chest pressed against hers.

Angus lifted her in his arms and laid her back on the bed, quickly unbuttoning her jeans, pulling down her zipper, and tugging her pants off, then standing over her and sliding her panties down. Nat shuddered with arousal as he put his hands behind her knees and slid her to the edge of the bed, and then they suddenly stopped being children at play and became again adults, a woman and a man.

About to love each other.

CHAPTER 35

Afterward they lay happily together in the dark, and Nat rested her head on Angus's chest, playing with the ends of his hair. "I've never slept with a ponytail before," she said.

"I match my dog, you know."

"What do you mean?" Nat was remembering the obedience school diploma on his wall.

"She's a rescue dog, part Afghan, part golden retriever. She looks like a wacky lion." Angus sounded completely relaxed. "My ponytail is exactly the length of her tail."

"I don't want to know how you measured that."

"No, you don't. Everybody thinks my hair is a political statement, but it's just to match Miss Sally." Angus cradled Nat closer. "God, you are so *little*. How does so much woman fit into such a tiny package?"

Giving new meaning to Gnat.

"I *love* your body."

Nat smiled, too shy to say that she loved his, too. It turned her on that he was so much stronger and bigger. He made love outside the rules. She mentally replayed her favorite scene, and it almost brought her to another orgasm. Nat had just learned that she was a total sexist in bed, which is the kind of thing you realize when you sleep with a caveman.

"God, that was great. Don't you think?"

Nat liked a Cro-Magnon who needed reassurance. "We both get As."

Angus laughed softly. "I knew it would be terrific. I *called* it."

Nat shifted happily on his chest. "So how premeditated was this seduction?"

"Not very. To be honest, it usually takes more than a toothbrush to get a woman into bed."

"But you brought a condom." Nat lifted her head to see him grinning in the dark.

"Correction. I brought three condoms."

"You're an optimist."

"Oh yeah? Talk to me in twenty minutes."

Nat laughed, and Angus hugged her close.

"You know why it was so great?" he asked.

"No. Why?"

"Because it's love."

Nat hesitated. "You think?"

"I know. I told you, straight up. I love you."

"It doesn't feel too soon to you?"

"It's an emotional reaction, Natalie. You can't time it or analyze it. Yes, of course, it will grow and blah blah blah, but it's there right now. The important part, the *wow*. That's love."

The wow. Nat soaked in the words. She knew what he meant. Had she ever felt the wow with Hank?

"It's okay if you don't know it yet, but you love me, too." Angus sighed. "I swear, I am so tired. It must be the meds they gave me. You must be exhausted, too."

"I am," Nat said, but she was already planning her next move.

"Don't worry. Everything's going to be all right."

"Let's sleep now. We're both tired."

"I'll get you out of here in the morning, and you'll be safe."

No way. "Okay, you've convinced me." Nat had wanted to tell him about the floor plan and her new theory, but the less he knew, the better, for his sake.

"I already set my cell to wake us up," Angus said. "We can't miss the train. You need anything?"

"Hush, now."

"Me, too," Angus said. His furry chest rose with a deep breath, and in the next minute, she heard his breathing even into slumber.

She waited until he began to snore, then got up and hurriedly put her clothes back on. She gathered her files as quietly as possible, then grabbed her purse and coat and went looking for the money and cell phone he'd bought her. She found the money in the dark, but didn't find the cell phone amid the clothes and shopping bag. She couldn't risk waking him, so she gave up.

She tiptoed to the door, pausing to look at Angus's sleeping form. She hoped he'd understand why she was running out on him. She opened the door a crack, slipped out, and closed it behind her with a whisper.

Wow.

Nat hurried into the frigid night air, pulling her coat around her and patting her purse for the tenth time, making sure the thousand dollars was staying inside. She needed to get away and fast, in case Angus woke up. She scanned the rundown street, which was lined with twin houses and small businesses. There was no traffic, no cabs or buses, and no pay phone in sight. An auto tag place looked closed, as did a tarot parlor with a flickering neon hand in its window. A takeout pizza joint stood on the far corner, and a few old cars were parked in a small lot in front—which gave Nat an idea.

She put on her pink glasses and NASCAR cap, and hurried to the restaurant. She threaded her way through the parked cars and opened the barred door, greeted by a steamy interior and the mixed aroma of oregano, cooked pepperoni, and cigarette smoke. The storefront contained only a few red tables, and one held a trio of teenagers hunched over a hamburger pizza with a pitcher of Coke. They looked up when Nat walked over.

"Excuse me, guys." She pushed up her glasses. "Do any of you want to sell me your car?"

The teenagers burst into raucous laughter. The tallest one, a good-looking kid with a fake diamond earring, said, "Yo, dude, you for real?"

"Yes. I need a car, now. I'll pay cash."

"Cash *money*, dude?"

"Yes."

A second kid, who had bad skin, said, "That's not legal. You don't have no title."

A future lawyer. "That's okay with me. I don't care." Nat turned back to the tall kid. "Name your price, pal."

"A million dollars."

Or not. Nat turned to the shortest one, who wore an Eagles knit cap. "What do you say? You got a car?"

"An '86 Neon. Got 120,000 miles and no radio, but it runs good." Eagles Fan cracked a lopsided grin. "S'my stepsister's car."

"I like Neons. You like cash?"

"Yes." Eagles Fan's eyes glittered. "And I totally hate my stepsister."

"*Sell* it, dude!" the others shouted. "They're gone the whole frickin' weekend!"

"This is your lucky day, my friend." Nat took the envelope from her purse, flashed the crisp bills, and counted them off. "I'll give you three hundred bucks for the car, right now. Yes or no."

"Three hundred dollars?" Eagles Fan's young face lit up.

"Three hundred, dude! We can party all weekend!" They all laughed, and Eagles Fan was giddiest of all.

"Dudes, my stepsister will be so *pissed*! She'll *burn*! She'll *freak*!"

"Do it, dude!" the tall kid yelled. "They won't even know 'til Sunday night!" They all slapped each other five over the table, yelling, "Excellent!" "Awesome!" "We rock *hard*, dude!"

"I'm doin' it!" Eagles Fan grabbed for the bills.

Fifteen minutes later, Nat hit the road in an old blue Neon that had a perfumed powder-puff and a graduation tassel hanging from the rearview mirror. She drove past strip malls and houses, traveling as far away as she could before she found another cheap motel and pulled in. Angus wouldn't find her here, and neither he nor the cops knew about the Neon. She locked the car and went inside to get a few hours of sleep before dawn.

She'd need energy to set her plan in motion tomorrow.

CHAPTER 36

The sky was still black, and starbursts of frost remained on the Neon's windows when Nat pulled into the Wawa parking lot. She checked the car's clock. 5:30 a.m. So she was ahead of schedule. A couple in ski clothes got out of a black Jetta next to her, kissing and putting their arms around each other, and she shook off thoughts of Angus. He would already have awakened without her, and she hoped he'd understand. She thought of last night's lovemaking, which had only improved with age, then put it out of her mind.

She looked around, making sure the coast was clear before she got out of the Neon. No cops were in sight, and only a few people were gassing up at this hour. She grabbed her purse, stepped out of the car, and headed into the convenience store in her pink glasses and NAS-CAR cap, startling at the front page of the thick Sunday newspapers on the front rack.

LAW PROF RUNS FROM LAW, read the headline of the *Daily Local News*, and the lead photo was Nat with long, dark hair, from the law school's website. She lowered her head. At least they didn't have a shot of her in her disguise. She picked up a copy offhandedly, grabbed a cup of coffee, a bagel, and the sunglasses she should have gotten yesterday, then paid and hurried back to the Neon.

She read the article as soon as she got in the car, starved for news. Vice Dean McConnell was reportedly "shocked and surprised" at her criminality, and Nat felt sick inside. What would her students think? Carling and Warren? She could kiss tenure goodbye. Her parents, the "wealthy Greco family," had no comment, and her heart ached for them. They had to be worried, too. She thought about calling them from a pay phone, but couldn't risk their phone lines being tapped. They'd just have to trust her. She was on her own.

She skipped to a sidebar that reported that drugs and "a substantial amount of cash" had been found in her car, at the scene of Trooper Shorney's murder. She raced through the rest of the article, which was so long that it had knocked all other news off the top half of the page, including Philly's escalating murder rate, the federal prisoner whose trial was starting on Tuesday, and the war in Iraq. She set the newspaper on the passenger seat, twisted on the ignition, and drove out of the lot. She had lost one job, but gained another. Catching a killer.

She headed north in only sparse traffic to West Chester, while the sun tried and failed to sneak up on the sky, betrayed by splashy streaks of rose and violet. She had gotten the address she needed last night from information. She hit the gas and drove an hour, and by the time the sun was low in a cloudless sky, she had reached a winding street of white townhouses in a development called Heaven's Gate, which proved hyperbolic.

She cruised past the sign at the entrance. Each townhouse sat stacked like a child's tower of three blocks, with the garage door underneath a living room with a picture window. Minivans and other kid-friendly cars sat in the driveways. She double-checked the address she'd written on her hand and drove to the street. The Neon was the only car on the road, and she held her breath as she spotted a sign on the black mailbox of one of the houses. THE GRAFS.

Nat suppressed a bolt of fear but kept driving, facing straight ahead in the sunglasses and NASCAR cap. She found a parking space down the street, near the development's Exit sign. It afforded her a full view of the Graf house in her outside mirror. She parked by the curb, determined to watch the house. Sooner or later Graf would have to show his hand, and if she wasn't there when he did, nobody would be. And he wouldn't be worried about her anymore; he'd assume she was on the run, trying to save her own hide. Only a lousy fugitive would be crazy enough to come back to Chester County.

She sipped her coffee and ate the bagel, keeping an eye on the outside mirror. When she finished breakfast, she reached for the Chester County Correctional file she'd stolen from Phoenix Construction and read through it. It contained lots of invoices for construction materials; cinderblocks, two-by-fours, sheets of drywall, bags of cement, and more two-by-fours. Her heart sank as she finished the last page. The file told her nothing more. The Dumpsters were her best hope, and she couldn't check them out until tomorrow. She set the file on the seat and watched the house in the cold car.

Hours passed, nine to ten o'clock, then to eleven. Families drove in and out of the exit, in cars packed with kids. Nat kept her head down in the cap, fake-reading the newspaper. She flashed on Graf outside the Saunders house. She could believe him capable of murder, especially of a black man. But one question plagued her. Why hadn't that been the first thing Saunders said to her, in his very last words on earth?

Suddenly, the front door of the Graf house opened, and a man stepped outside. It was Joe Graf. He was wearing his same quilted vest he'd worn at the Saunders house, on top of a flannel shirt. He paused to light a cigarette, cocking his head and cupping his hand, while the door opened again. A child emerged in white pants and a blue snow jacket.

Nat could tell even at this distance it was a boy. The child's hair blew like a black fan in the wind, and his small legs churned as he ran to keep up with Graf. Graf caught the child's hand and walked him, jumping along, to a black Bronco. He opened the car door and lifted the child inside, then presumably fastened him into a car seat. It wasn't exactly the actions of a cold-blooded killer, and Nat figured this was either the dumbest or the smartest thing she'd ever done. She started the engine, drove out the main exit road, and waited a distance from the Heaven's Gate sign. If Graf were leaving, he'd have to go out this way. In a minute or two, his black Bronco traveled out of the exit and onto the main road. Nat let two cars pass in front of her, then took off after him.

She tracked the black Bronco as it made its way through the sub-urbs, in increasing traffic. They wended their way through a busy Ship Road, then to Routes 100 and 113, a tangle of big-box stores, tanning salons, Office Depots, Toys "R" Us stores, and strip malls like the ones she'd seen the day before. The whole time, she kept her eye out for police cars. She followed Graf as he eventually switched onto an even busier Lancaster Avenue, going west, and at one stoplight she got so close she could see the child waving his hands in the backseat. She dropped back and let a truck get between them. In Paoli, the Bronco pulled off of Lancaster Avenue and took a right turn into a strip mall with a Dunkin' Donuts, a Radio Shack, and, at the corner, yet another Wawa.

She pulled to the far side of the Wawa lot, so it would be hard to see her from the Bronco, and watched as Graf parked in the strip mall and emerged from his car, lighting another cigarette. He took a few puffs before he went around to the backseat of the car and opened the door. The cigarette clamped between his lips, he lifted the child out. Nat could see that Graf had an adorable little boy, no doubt a mix of his mother's Asian blood and his father's bad blood, not that she was jumping to conclusions.

Graf took the kid's hand and walked him around the side of the strip mall to a storefront she hadn't noticed when she pulled up: Kwan's Karate Studio. She slumped behind the wheel of the Neon, dejected. She'd pegged Graf for a killer and all he was doing was being a great father. She eyed the traffic nervously. She was risking apprehension for karate classes? Graf went through the front door, disappearing inside the karate studio, and Nat settled in for the duration.

Suddenly the door to the karate studio opened, and Graf emerged. Nat ducked instinctively as he hurried to the strip mall, jumped back into the Bronco, pulled out of the space, and took off fast.

Go! Nat started the ignition and followed as Graf made an illegal U-turn on Lancaster Avenue, then headed east. The two cars drove, with four cars between them, all the way back to where they'd come from. She hoped Graf wasn't going shopping. She told herself to remain calm as she followed the Bronco and ten other cars into the parking lot at the Exton Square Mall, at the bustling intersection of Routes 30 and 100. She drove slowly, at the end of the line, as Graf parked the Bronco, jumped out, and hustled into Houlihan's in front.

She pulled into a space at the back of the parking lot. What was going on? From Paoli to Exton, they had passed tons of other places to eat. Why hadn't Graf stopped at one of them? Was he a Houlihan's freak? Was anybody? She watched the door to the restaurant. A well-dressed older couple went inside, followed by a quartet of high school gymnasts in blue-and-white sweats.

She couldn't see through the dark glass of Houlihan's from this distance. She waited but he didn't come out. What was he doing in there? He couldn't be eating; it made no sense. He wouldn't have enough time if he was going to pick up his son. She had to risk getting closer, to see. She straightened her cap, pushed up her sunglasses, and got out of the Neon. She walked toward Houlihan's, lingering near the mall entrance, then peered inside.

Nat spotted him after a minute. Graf was seated at a small table near the window. He had a soda and appeared to be looking out the window. He had to be waiting for someone. Was he meeting that nice wife of his? Was he cheating on her? Nat kept her head down, under the hat brim. People walked by Graf's table, but he kept looking out the window. In the next second, he checked his wristwatch.

Who was he waiting for?

"Excuse me," said an older man in a leather coat, walking past on the way to the mall.

"Sorry." Nat shifted over to let him pass, but he didn't move.

"You a NASCAR fan? Me, too!"

"Sorry, it's not my hat," Nat answered. She didn't want to be remembered or draw attention to herself. The man moved on, unblocking her view of a bright red pickup that was just pulling into the front of the parking lot. A black man in a Sixers cap and black down coat got out of the truck, hustled to Houlihan's, and made a beeline for Graf's table.

Nat squinted behind her sunglasses. Something about the man looked familiar. Were they friends? Did the man know Graf was a bigot? The man sat down opposite Graf, and they started to talk, their heads bent together. She kept watching. She figured that they couldn't talk long because the karate lesson couldn't last more than an hour. It had taken half an hour to get to here from the karate studio, in traffic. Graf didn't have much time. That meant neither did Nat.

She pulled down her cap and went back to the Neon, walking past the red pickup. It was an F-250. The license plate was from Pennsylvania. She strolled casually around the back of the truck—which was when she saw it. A little Calvin decal. Where had she seen that before? A blurry picture flashed through her mind. Darkness. A patch of ice. The Ford F-250. The side of the driver's face barely visible through the dark glass. Then she knew where she'd seen the man. He was driving the black pickup that had crashed into her and Angus.

Was it possible? She rechecked the license plate. It was Pennsylvania, not Delaware. But license plates could be switched. Pickups could be painted. It had been a few days. Could it be the same pickup? It couldn't have looked more different from the black one. It was a loud cherry red, with shiny white pinstripes running along the sides. On the back of the truck bed was a memorial, painted in flowery white letters. It read,

IN MEMORY OF ANJELA REYNOLDS, 2002–2006.

Still. Was it the same truck, painted red? Was it the same driver who had crashed into them? She looked around, but nobody was watching. Shoppers walked quickly because it was so cold. She reached into her pocket for her keys, stepped up to the side of the pickup, and walked between it and a Dodge Caravan, making an inch-long scratch in the side of the truck. A jittery black line appeared out of nowhere. The pickup was black underneath the bright red. It was the same truck and the same driver.

Whoa. Nat turned and walked away, trying to act casual as she headed for the Neon. Questions clicked away in her brain, and she felt all her senses on alert. How did the pickup driver and Graf know each other? Had Graf had anything to do with the crash? Why would this guy have wanted to hurt her and Angus? Was he part of a drug ring? She wished she could talk it over with Angus, but she'd left the damn cell phone. She had to figure it out herself. It gave her a new plan. She would follow the pickup driver, not Graf, when he left Houlihan's. She had almost reached the Neon when she heard a woman's voice, shouting shrilly in the parking lot.

"Help!" a woman cried. "Help, somebody!"

Nat turned on her heel reflexively, and to her surprise, an old woman was pointing at *her*.

"Stop that girl!" The old woman had an open cell phone in her other hand. "She keyed that man's truck! I saw it! I called 911!"

Nat froze, taking in the scene all at once. Shoppers stopped in their tracks and turned to her. The pickup driver and Graf came out of Houlihan's. The old woman hollered to the pickup driver, waving her cell phone. He and Graf turned toward Nat. Graf's expression changed after a beat, when he recognized her.

And came running at her.

CHAPTER 37

Nat turned and ran for the mall entrance, its twin doors clearly marked. Shoppers walked in the parking lot in all directions, and she bolted around a mom and a little boy with a balloon, then a flock of little girls in party hats. She blew through the glass doors like an explosion. Her hat flew off. Her purse bumped against her side. Her heart pounded with exertion and fear. She ran down a wide beige-tiled corridor flanked by Houlihan's and Jos. A. Bank. Whitney Houston sang about somebody to love. The hall ended in a glitzy fountain, and Nat veered to the right, almost slipping, then glanced back. Graf was coming on strong, closing the gap between them, knocking a man out of his way.

She flew down the corridor, past a jewelry store with sparkling window displays, looking for a way out of the mall or a store to hide in. Two women leaving Kitchen Kapers looked aghast, and Nat realized that they were seeing a terrified little woman being chased by a big burly man. Three women came out of Lane Bryant and frowned at the sight, obviously thinking the same thing, and behind them two pregnant women stood talking outside of Mother Maternity.

They were in a mall. In other words, girl country.

"Help!" Nat screamed. "My husband's trying to kill me!"

"My God!" one of the older women cried, closing ranks behind Nat. "Security! That poor woman, her husband's chasing her!"

"Stop that man! He's abusive!" The pregnant women joined the outrage. "Stop him! The bully!"

Nat screamed, louder, running down the shiny mall corridor. "Save me from my husband! He's going to kill me!"

"Watch that!" "Look!" "Check it. That jerk in the flannel's going to beat up his wife!" Horrified shoppers stopped to watch. Some shouted for security. Others pointed. In no time Nat had the complete attention of the crowded mall, and they were all on her side. She rounded the corner in front of JCPenney and almost plowed into a throng of teenage boys in blue football jackets.

"Guys, please!" Nat yelled. "My husband's trying to kill me!"

"Hurtin' a *chick*?" one of the players said.

"That's *so* not cool," said another, as they formed an offensive line. Still fleeing, Nat looked back to see Graf running into the football players, who tackled him to the ground. Converging on the fracas were two security officers, running down from the second level.

She was too terrified to look back again, but there was no way Graf could catch her now. A sign showed an arrow to the exit. She took a fast right and streaked down another hall, past startled shoppers. She had to get out of here. Sooner or later Graf would explain everything and call the cops. She burst through the exit doors, hit the cold air running, and darted across another busy parking lot, trying not to get hit by a car. She sprinted through the parking lot and came to a road and another building. The sign out front read, Chester County Library.

A library? They wouldn't come looking for her there. They would expect her to escape to her car, but if she did that now, she'd be spotted. She ran to the large library, which was all tan stone, modern sloping roofs, and smoked glass windows, and when she got near the entrance, slowed her pace, arranged her clothes, and slipped inside.

She exhaled in relief the moment she stepped inside, finding the hushed atmosphere a sanctuary. The library was large and modern, with a thick gray-blue carpet, a wide entrance aisle, and double-sided bookshelves down the middle. The circulation desk was on the right, with brown signs that read, Payments, Returns, and Library Cards. Patrons collected around the desk.

Nat turned right, passed the desk, and down a wide aisle, where she could see that the foot traffic was less. She ducked into the stacks to hide. Books surrounded her, and she felt at home among the plastic covers and Dewey decimal system. A line of red skulls on the spines signified that the books were mysteries, her favorite. Then she caught her breath, noticing a lineup of computers on the other side of the room. The reference section. Almost no one was there.

She left the stacks and crossed to that area, passing up rows of computers for the back of the room, where modern wooden carrels held more computers and green-bound periodicals guides. The only other patrons in the area were a gaggle of teenage girls, talking and giggling away, undoubtedly hiding out for their own reasons. Nat was short enough to pass for one of them, if she acted the part. She made a beeline for the seat next to them, took it, and hunched over the computer keyboard, keeping her face down. They were all gathered around a computer monitor, so she did the same thing, logging onto the Internet. She cruised online and giggled when the girls did, keeping her head down.

The blondest teenager was saying, "I can't believe he put that picture of her on his MySpace page because he IM'd me and told me that he didn't like her and he was only taking her to prom because he wanted to show me—"

Sitting at the computer made Nat think. She logged onto Google and typed Anjela Reynolds and Pennsylvania, and in a nanosecond, the screen gave her the results. She clicked on the top entry. **Anjela Reynolds, age 76, was crowned Mrs. Senior Golfer today** . . .

The blond teenager was saying, "I tried to IM him and you know what? He *blocked* me. Can you believe it? He's such a poser. So I used my mom's screen name and saw that he was online when he told me he was gonna be at the movies with his parents and—"

Nat clicked the next entry. A headline popped on the screen. **CHILD KILLED IN CROSSFIRE**. She skimmed the article:

The death of little Anjela Reynolds is a classic story of someone being in the wrong place at the wrong time. The only
difference is that this time, the person was four years old.
Little Anjela slumbered peacefully in her blue Graco stroller
when gunfire broke out between rival drug dealers in front of
her mother's rowhouse in Chester. Police estimate that it was
the third shot that ended Anjela's tragically brief time on this
earth.

Nat skimmed the article, but it didn't tell her anything about the man whose pickup bore a memorial to Anjela. She looked at the picture on the webpage. A crestfallen family at a graveside, sitting behind a tiny white coffin. A grief-stricken woman slumped on the shoulder of a man with cornrows. Nat recognized the man instantly. The driver of the pickup. She checked the caption of the photo.

Mourning baby Anjela Reynolds are, left to right, mother Leticia Reynolds, father Mark Parrat of Chester. . . .

Mark Parrat. He was the pickup driver. Nat's thoughts raced ahead. Had it been Parrat in the ski mask, too? Had he been the one who shot the trooper and Barb? She went back to Google, typed in Mark Parrat, Chester, PA, and read the headline.

MARK PARRAT FREE ON BAIL.

Parrat, free on bail from what? She was about to read the article when she heard a commotion behind her and peeked over the girls' heads. A security guard was talking with the librarian, who was wearing a long corduroy skirt and snow boots. Nat kept her head down, praying he wouldn't see her.

The blond teenager continued. "So then I texted him and didn't tell him I knew he was online and I asked him what restaurant was he at because me and Kimmy were—"

Out of the corner of her eye, Nat saw the security guard turn and leave. She picked up the article quickly where she'd left off:

> Mark Parrat of Chester was set free on bail today, pending resolution of drug distribution charges and weapons offenses. Parrat is said to be second-in-command to alleged drug kingpin Richard Williams, who is charged with the murder of six rivals in the Bex Street massacre. Williams is being held without bail pending the resolution of drug distribution and conspiracy charges. The trial is set to start in Philadelphia this winter.

Nat blinked. Richard Williams. That's where she'd heard the name. He was the federal prisoner on courtesy hold at Chester County. He was coming up for trial on Tuesday. It all jibed with her theory. Graf and Machik must have been dealing drugs to the inmates, in league with Parrat and Williams. Saunders must have found out about it, and Graf had to kill him to silence him. Upchurch was just the cover to get Saunders into the room without the security camera. It would have worked perfectly, but for the prison riot and Nat running into the room.

The teenager was going nonstop. "So I told Courtney that we should have a pity party, and we had ice cream and made popcorn and put real butter on it and rented *Miss Congeniality II*, even though I saw it like forty gillion times—"

Nat rose quickly, turned without a sound, went back down the stacks, and peeked around the corner. The librarian with the long skirt was talking to another librarian in hushed tones, and they were standing too close to the door to let her pass unnoticed. She ducked back in the stacks and peeked out through the top of the books. In the next minute, the librarians walked back to the circulation desk, and she left the stacks, walked toward the door, and slipped outside.

Nat's adrenalin was pumping so much she hardly felt the frigid air. She kept her head down and scanned the parking lot for Graf or security. Nothing. Just two women with blue canvas tote bags going to the library and shoppers carrying multicolored bags from the mall. The Neon was parked on the other side of the mall. She kept up her pace, walking along the outside of the JCPenney, looking constantly for security guards, feeling exposed without the NASCAR cap. She hurried to the end of the store, turned the corner for the parking lot and mall entrance, then froze.

A black-and-white East Whiteland Township police car idled in front of Houlihan's. Its back door was open. The old woman who had complained about the keying was sitting in the backseat of the cruiser, cradling her arm. A patrol officer bent over her, talking with her. It was too far away for Nat to see what was going on, but an ambulance pulled into the parking lot and turned toward the cruiser. Nobody was looking in Nat's direction. She kept her head down and stayed on course for the Neon.

Two women passed her, talking. "Can you believe that?" the one asked the other. "That black guy knocked that old lady right over and drove away. He almost hit her with that truck."

Parrat. Nat kept walking. Graf's black Bronco was still parked in its space, which meant that he could reappear at any second. It had been only fifteen minutes since the chase through the mall. Enough time for Graf to explain to the local cops she was a fugitive. She tucked the fear away. She couldn't afford to freeze up again.

The ambulance pulled up next to the cruiser. The cop was focused on helping the old lady to the ambulance. Nat hustled across one line of parked cars and ran around a moving Lexus SUV. She kept an eye on the ambulance. Its driver was getting out and talking to the old woman and the cop, blocking their view of her.

Three lanes of parked cars lay between her and the Neon. She had to go faster. A dirty white Tahoe barreled past, and Nat hustled around it. Only two rows to go. A minivan slowed to park, and she hurried through the parked cars. One row left. She scooted up and finally reached the Neon.

Yes! She got out her key with a trembling hand and shoved it in the lock, opened the door, jumped in, and started the ignition. She hit the gas and was pulling out of the space when a black Hummer came out of nowhere and stopped just short of her front bumper with a loud *scchhreech*.

Nat gripped the wheel, waiting for the impact that didn't come. She must have pulled out in front of the Hummer in her panic.

HONK! HONK! The Hummer driver pounded his horn in protest. The massive chrome grille blocked Nat in. The Hummer driver started shouting at her, but she ignored him and looked at the cruiser. The noise had drawn the cop's attention, and he was looking over, shielding his eyes from the sun. The ambulance driver was supporting the old lady on his arm, and in the next minute, she started pointing at the Neon with her free hand.

Nat yanked the wheel to the left, floored the gas, and jumped the curb to get out of the lot. Cars stopped at a traffic light and clogged the exit lane. She accelerated onto the median like a stunt driver, then banged down and tore out of the entrance lane, almost sideswiping a minivan. She veered right onto Lancaster Avenue and kept the pedal down, straight ahead.

A police siren started blaring, but Nat didn't have time to look back. Traffic filled Lancaster Avenue, and she switched onto the shoulder and ran in that lane, increasing her speed to seventy miles an hour, then to eighty. Drivers turned to watch, their mouths dropping open. She kept the hammer down. The Neon blasted down the shoulder of the road. She checked the rearview. The police cruiser roared out of the mall lot.

And came straight at her.

CHAPTER 38

Nat had to think fast. The cop could outrun her on a straightaway. The Neon was no match for the cruiser's big engine. The siren sounded louder, the cruiser getting closer. Cars were already pulling over to make way.

She swerved onto a suburban back street and tried to keep her wits about her. She gripped the wheel and gritted her teeth, turned left, and sped to the end of the street. She turned right randomly and focused on the road. Houses, trees, and cars flew past. An old man putting out his trash shook his fist at her. A woman walking her poodle scooped him up. The police siren blared. The cruiser popped into the rearview, swung a wide turn onto the back street, and barreled ahead.

Nat's heart lodged in her throat. She turned onto the next street. A gray Mercedes was driving toward her. She drove up on the curb to go around it, then hit the road with the rubber burning. In the next second, she heard another police siren, farther away, joining the first. The cop must've called for backup.

She hit the gas. She couldn't see the cruisers but she could hear them. She saw nothing but the road. In the next second, she swerved to avoid a Taurus station wagon pulling out of a driveway, with kids in the backseat.

Dear God! She didn't want to kill anybody. She didn't want to get killed. She had to get out of this neighborhood. She took a right, skidding around an icy patch at the end of the street, then saw a sign. Route 100.

She raced down the street, followed the signs, and bombed down the road for the on-ramp. The cruiser veered around the corner, right on her tail. The straightaway gave the cops the chance to close the gap, the cruiser's grille a gleaming maw. They zoomed together onto the highway, pursuer and pursued. The second siren blared closer. Traffic cleared at the blaring of the siren, and Nat rammed down the middle lane, with the cops right behind her. It was now or never. She gritted her teeth and jammed the pedal to the metal.

The Neon speedometer climbed to ninety, ninety-five, then hovered at one hundred. Nat streaked down the shoulder, spraying ice and gravel. The steering wheel wobbled furiously in her grip. It took all her might to hold it still. Suddenly she saw a ragged shred of tire tread lying ahead on the shoulder. She barely had time to react. She heard herself shout as she turned the wheel, jerking the Neon into the left lane. The back end fishtailed but she held on tight and kept control of the car, her concentration so intense it could only have been powered by fear.

Boom! A huge crash sounded. Nat glanced in the rearview. The police car was spinning like a pinwheel, an alternating flash of black and white. The police must have hit the tire tread. No other cars were around, so she could see in a flash that the cops wouldn't collide with anyone.

She blew down the highway, switching to the shoulder so she wouldn't crash. She couldn't stay on the open road. The other cruiser would see her. They'd catch her on the straightaway. Then she figured out where to go. Someplace they'd never look for her. She saw the sign that read Brandywine Valley Museum and knew she was on the right road. She aimed for the exit, dead ahead. She could still hear the second siren getting closer. She took the exit, steered around a car waiting at a red light, and barreled forward.

HONK! Nat ignored the sound and took a right turn, then a left, getting closer. She slowed her speed and whipped around the winding route into more rural territory and drew her first breath for the first time in what seemed like ages. She took the next curve at speed, then another switchback, cruising around the country road.

On the way, her brain went into overdrive, functioning in emergency mode. She'd have to ditch the Neon. The cops knew the license plate. They'd find her as soon as they put out an APB, calling in more cars. A cop killer in a bright blue Neon wouldn't be joyriding for long. She was maybe twenty minutes away, then ten, then five. She reached the vicinity and eyed the stone barns, sheds, and outbuildings, assessing them for her purposes. She drove by a well-maintained house, then spotted a decrepit stone barn and slowed to a stop.

A faded sign read, Property For Sale. The barn was encircled by muddy acreage, snowy in patches. Its stones crumbled into white dust, and its green door was peeling, showing graying boards. A gravel road led from the road to the barn door, and only a busted electrical fence bounded the property. In short, it was perfect.

She jumped out of the Neon, ran to the fence, and pressed the wire down with her feet, then jumped back in the car, maneuvered it into the driveway, then drove over the fence. She jumped back out of the Neon, ran to the fence and righted it, jiggling one of the weathered posts. She hurried back to the car and drove down the old driveway, careful to stay on the gravel so her tire tracks wouldn't betray her.

She reached the barn and leaving the car in idle, got out and yanked on the rusty door handle. Finally, the door slid to the right on a rust-laden track. She wedged herself inside the door and shoved it open the rest of the way, clammy with flop sweat under her coat. She looked quickly inside the dark barn. Cobwebs draped from the rafters like her mother's swag curtains, and moldy-smelling hay sat stacked next to an array of trashcans. An old tarp partially covered a dusty workbench and a greasy old red oil tank. Against the filthy stone wall, a chain harrow slumped on a floor covered with dirt, old hay, and rocks.

Nat hurried back to the car, drove it into the barn, then cut the ignition, and climbed out of the car, stuffing the construction file inside her purse. She hustled to the door and rolled it closed behind her. It was dark inside the barn, which had only sideways slits for windows. She remembered the blue tarp on the workbench and made her way there until her eyes adjusted to the darkness. She grabbed the tarp, went back to the car, and threw it over the top, managing to cover the bumpers on both sides.

Her heart lifted for the first time all day. She might have escaped both the cops and Graf. She never would've thought she had it in her. Her father would never have believed it, either, though she wasn't sure how proud he would have been. But that didn't seem to matter so much anymore, for some reason. She stepped backward to inspect her handiwork, which was when she heard the unmistakable sound of wood creaking somewhere.

And before she realized what was happening, the floor gave way beneath her feet and she was falling.

CHAPTER 39

Nat had no idea what happened. She sat splayed at the bottom of some sort of dark, narrow hole. She had fallen on her butt, which hurt. She looked up, shaken. The floorboards had splintered, about five feet over her head. She was ten feet underground, or more.

She scrambled to her feet, wincing in pain, and picked up a small piece of wood that had tumbled inside and landed on top of her leg. Its rough surface felt light and porous to the touch. She broke it in two with her hands; it snapped with ease. Rotten, worm-eaten, or maybe gnawed by termites. A terrifying thought struck her. Was the Neon going to fall in on her?

She flinched and covered her head reflexively, as if that would have done any good. She looked up, cringing. It was dark in the hole, and the only light came from its mouth, jagged with splintered wood, broken in the center. The Neon was parked to the right of the hole. She looked ahead and couldn't see anything. Her back was to a wall, and she turned and felt it. Cold and wet to the touch. Dirt. She pulled her hand away and smelled it. Earth. She turned back and couldn't see anything.

She figured out the situation. Dirt and rock covered the barn floor, but the part of the floor nearer the door was made of wood.

She'd weakened the old floorboards when she drove over them, breaking them just enough so they'd give way under her weight. The Neon must have been parked on the solid dirt floor, so it wouldn't fall in.

Great. At least I won't get hit by a car. In a hole.

Nat put a hand out and felt the wall directly across from her. It was as if a hole had been dug in the earth, tall and skinny, but big enough for a person. She visualized it as being made by an index finger poked down into topsoil, as if to plant a seed. But she had to get out. She jumped up but couldn't reach that high. When she came down, her feet slid a little, but didn't touch dirt on the other side. Why?

She peered down at her feet, but it was too dark to see anything. It creeped her out. What was down there? A horror-movie image of a snake pit slithered into her mind. She tried to edge away but there was nowhere to go. Her back was literally to the wall. She jumped again but kept slipping when she landed. The floor of the hole was uneven. She couldn't see a thing. Then she remembered something. The key ring for the Neon had tons of stuff on it, the typical keychain of a teenage girl.

She reached in her coat pocket and pulled out the keys. The keyring held a pink plush heart, a small pink Swiss army knife, and a tiny pink penlight. Nat flicked the penlight on and aimed it at her feet. No snakes, just dirt. The penlight cast a faint, almost translucent, circle of light on the dirt wall opposite her, and she gasped. The wall on the other side of the hole didn't go all the way down, as she had assumed. It stopped at about thigh height, and the bottom half appeared to lead to another underground hole.

"Hello?" she said, but there was no echo. She crouched down as much as she could in the narrow hole and aimed the light inside the other hole. The light didn't reach far enough to reveal what was down there. Images of treasure chests full of gold doubloons and skeletons chained to walls popped into her head. She sat on her butt, then stuck her feet in the hole and aimed the light down her body. She could see a dirt bottom not far under her feet.

Nat let herself slip down like a kid on a muddy sliding board and tumbled into the bigger hole. She yelped, and dirt muffled the sound. She cast the light around the new hole. It was dirt on all six sides, rich brown earth veined with burnt-orange clay. Stones stuck out from the dirt. The ceiling was tall enough to stand up in, if you were as short as Nat, and like the walls, was reinforced by old wooden boards.

Could these boards break, too? If they do, will I be buried alive? And what about oxygen? I've grown fond of oxygen.

Nat banished the negative thoughts. She was standing in a man-made room of some kind. It seemed too elaborate for a root cellar. She cast the penlight on one of the boards in the back, then noticed some carvings. She made her way over and shone the light on the boards. Carved into it were the initials c.j., and underneath, t.j. She ran her fingers over them. They had been etched by a crude knife. She cast the light elsewhere on the wooden board. There were more initials: l.m., c.m. Then a date: APRIL 28, 1860.

"My God," Nat said aloud. She couldn't believe her eyes. 1860. She knew what it had to be, because she taught it every year. She must be seeing a stop on the Underground Railroad. A series of holes, hidden trap doors, and secret hiding places for slaves escaping from Maryland and points farther south. Some of the stops were homes with hiding places, but many more were in outbuildings, to make escape easier if the slavecatchers came. Chester County was dotted with historic houses that hid runaway slaves, houses that still existed today. Nat knew the houses by heart, taking a historian's delight in the old-fashioned names: Moses and Mary Pennock's house. Eusebius and Sarah Barnard's house. Mordecai and Esther Hayes's. Isaac and Thomazine Meredith.

Nat stood, marveling. This hole must have been one that no one had found yet. One that hadn't been discovered until now, perfectly concealed for almost a hundred years. The secret hiding place for so many poor, desperate souls. Nat had taught the History of Justice, and now she was inside it. She felt tears come to her eyes and blinked them away, running her fingertips over the boards. She wondered how many of these courageous people had made it north to freedom. How many had turned back. How many have been captured, beaten, or even killed.

This was sacred ground, and so were its boards, blanketed with initials and dates, which Nat read by penlight. L.B., AUG 1859, M., 1862, LU, 1861. Some of the slaves had written their names: JANUARY GRANDY. HANNAH CLEMEN. Some had numbers next to their names, which Nat guessed were their ages:. JED, 19. MARY, 9. Many of the initials were no longer visible, but she could feel them with her fingertips. She remembered telling Angus about the Underground Railroad that day in the Beetle, on the way to the prison. She couldn't wait to tell him about the secret hole hidden under the floor.

Nat blinked. *A secret hole hidden under the floor.* People used it to escape to freedom. She flashed for the umpteenth time on Saunders's last words.

Tell my wife. It's under the floor.

She thought about it, as she had thought about it so many times before. But this time she looked at it in a different light. Saunders had said, "It's under the floor." When he'd said that, he'd been lying in the security room, the one without the videocamera. Maybe he hadn't meant that whatever "it" was was under the floor at his house. Nat had thought that only because the "tell my wife" part came first. But for a second, she set aside the "tell my wife" part. What if Saunders had meant that "it" was under the floor right where he lay—in the prison itself? And what would be under the floor at a prison?

A tunnel?

"Whoa," Nat said aloud, in the dark hole. It could be true. It wasn't crazy. Tunnels could help people escape. She was standing in one. But who would a tunnel in a prison be for? It only took a minute to come up with the answer.

Richard Williams.

Williams was the drug kingpin being held at the prison for almost a year. He'd want to escape before his trial, because with his charges, he'd go to prison for life. And he'd have the dough to get a tunnel built for him. He could have paid Graf to do it. Then Graf could have gotten his brother the contractor in on the scheme. It could easily have been disguised as part of the renovations. If Phoenix, or at least Jim Graf, had been digging at night, when his brother Joe Graf was on duty, nobody would have been the wiser. Especially if Machik were in on it, too.

Nat had an epiphany. The scam wasn't drugs. It was something far more lucrative, and far worse. It was letting a dangerous killer escape through a tunnel under the floor. How much would Williams pay to beat a federal rap? A couple million, maybe more? No wonder Machik got rid of the rugs in that security room so fast. The rugs had covered the mouth of the tunnel, and any inspection of them would have shown dirt on the underside. No wonder they had remodeled the room when Nat and Angus started asking questions. They had to keep hiding the tunnel. No wonder there had been orders for so many two-by-fours in the construction file. The two-by-fours had reinforced the length of the tunnel. It had taken them a year to dig, and they were about to put it to use—and get away with setting a ruthless murderer free.

Nat gasped as she realized the implications. Saunders was killed because he had discovered not a drug conspiracy, but an escape conspiracy. Upchurch was still the sacrificial lamb. Then Nat realized something else. If the murders of Saunders and Upchurch had been to conceal the escape, maybe the prison riot wasn't random at all. It had been staged at one end of the prison as a way to distract everyone from the killings at the other end. A riot in the RHU would have been the perfect way to keep everybody occupied while Saunders and Upchurch were being murdered in the security office.

Her thoughts clicked away. It all made sense. She'd had to fight upstream to get help that morning. All the SWAT team guys and C.O.s were running the opposite direction, toward the RHU. It was only by chance that she'd been attacked, run the wrong way for help, and discovered the slaughter in the security room.

She felt astonished at the ambition of the conspiracy, then flashed on the newspaper that she'd seen today. Williams's federal trial was scheduled to start this week. She remembered that the article had said that his trial would be on Tuesday. It jibed with why Graf would be meeting with Parrat today at Houlihan's. They would have been discussing last-minute plans. Williams would be moved to Philly tomorrow.

That meant that Williams would have to escape from prison *tonight*.

And Nat was the only one who knew.

CHAPTER 40

Nat stared stunned at the carved initials illuminated by the penlight, pale and thin as moonshade in the dark. She tested her theory and it sounded right. But what could she do about it? How could she tell someone? She had no cell phone, nothing. She checked her watch, the numerals glowing an eerie green, anachronistic in this historic place. It was 4:10 p.m. They'd wait until dark to let Williams escape. They'd need cover of night. She had to stop them and she didn't have much time.

First, she had to get out of the hole. She shone the penlight on the wall leading out to the first hole. The stones that had looked random before had been wedged into the wall in an ascending pattern, makeshift stepping-stones from so long ago. She marveled at the ingenuity and heart of these benighted people. She put a foot on the first stepping-stone, and it held strong and stable, then used the others to make her way slowly to the first hole, where she figured out a way to get out. She'd dig out footholes for herself on the side of the wall. She could do it, now that she saw how it was done. She even had a penknife to scoop them out. She whispered a prayerful thanks and started digging.

Almost two hours later, she came out of the hole with a plan and no time to waste. She brushed dirt from her pants and coat, ripped the blue tarp off the Neon, and yanked open the barn door. A lone car traveled down the road, headlights coming and taillights going. Sunday night traffic would be light. She'd be more exposed, vulnerable to the cops, but she didn't have any choice. At least it was dark out, a frigid night so piercingly clear that the stars scattered across the night sky looked like diamonds on a jeweler's black velvet.

She jumped in the car, started the engine, and reversed out of the barn and down the driveway to the road, where she ran over the broken electric fence and drove forward. She hit the gas and tore up the road. She'd need a phone. She slowed past one house and considered asking to use theirs, but rejected the idea. She couldn't take the risk. She kept driving and up ahead spotted the single light of a country store, but it was closed. She traveled down the road, passing houses until she finally found a gas station with a pay phone.

She pulled in, parked with her license plate away from the road, jumped out of the car, and ran into the phone booth. She left the door partway open so the light wouldn't go on and used the penlight to call 911. The call connected, and Nat said, "I want to report that there's going to be an escape at the Chester County Correctional Institution tonight—"

"Who's calling?" the dispatcher asked.

"It doesn't matter. I know for a fact that an inmate named Richard Williams is going to escape from—"

"Miss, where are you calling from?"

"Please, just listen. If you don't, a very dangerous criminal will escape from prison."

"Miss, I'm sorry, what is the nature of your emergency?"

"It's at the prison."

"You're at the prison, Miss?"

"No, there's about to be a crime committed at the prison. You have to send the police—"

"Are you in any danger, Miss?"

"No, but there's going to be a crime—"

"I'm sorry. This line is for emergency services only. If you wish to report a crime, please call—"

Nat repeated the number, hung up, and fished another quarter out of her pocket, then called the State Police station. When the call connected, she disguised her voice, just in case Milroy, Mundy, or one of the other troopers happened to answer the phone. "Is Trooper Mundy there?" she asked.

"No, he's not. Who's calling?"

"I can't say. There's going to be a prison break tonight at Chester County Correctional and—"

"Ginny, honey, who are you kidding with that voice? You sound like a rookie tranny." The trooper chuckled. "I told you, stop with the prank calls or it's your last sleepover. Now cut it out."

"No, please listen. I'm not Ginny. It's the truth."

"Who are you then, if you're not Ginny?"

"It doesn't matter, just listen to me. Send a car over to the prison right away."

"Ginny, I told you to stay off. Cut it out." He hung up.

Nat held the dead phone, desperate. Who else could she call? She watched the road nervously. A minivan went by. She dialed information for the number, fished another quarter out of her pocket, then placed a call to the federal marshals in Philly. When the call connected, she said, "I'm not sure whom I should be speaking with, but I have information that there's going to be a prison break—"

"Excuse me, who is this?" the marshal asked.

"I can't say. Please, you have to believe me. You have a car guarding Richard Williams at Chester County Correctional, right?"

"Who wants to know?"

"Okay. There's going to be a prison break there tonight. There's a conspiracy between a C.O., the assistant warden, and a drug dealer to get Williams out—"

"A conspiracy, huh?" The marshal sighed. "How do you know about this conspiracy?"

"I figured it out. I was in a hole from the Underground Railroad and—"

"I'm very sorry, Miss, but we're busy here. I urge you to seek professional help."

"No, I'm not crazy! Please, listen, Richard Williams—"

"Please, seek help." The line went dead.

Nat hung up the phone. She didn't know what to do. She aimed the penlight and read the inky cell phone number she'd written on her hand, fainter since her shower, and called Angus. She watched another car going down the road as the phone rang, feeling her emotions well up. The call connected, and she was about to speak, but his voicemail came on. She bit back her feelings and waited for the beep.

"Angus, I don't know where you are or when you'll get this." Nat paused. She considered telling him about the tunnel, but she didn't know what he'd do. "Bye."

She hung up, emotionally shaky. Something made her want to call her father, which was palpably insane. But she couldn't go backward, so she had to go forward. She had to stop the escape and if she couldn't get anyone to help, she'd have to do it herself. But she didn't feel brave enough to go into the belly of the beast. It wasn't like her, and she knew it. They were right, when they said that, all of them. She was a scholar, a historian at heart. This wasn't just bleaching your hair and wearing dumb hats. This could get dangerous.

Her thoughts strayed to the hidden room under the ground and all those carved initials, each one a person who had summoned extraordinary courage. They fought for justice, in far worse circumstances. If they could do it, she could do it. She'd been teaching the History of Justice for three years, and she had never understood why before. It was for history to repeat itself. Right now.

She set her jaw, left the phone booth, and hurried back to the car. She drove with an eye on the rearview mirror and slowed when she turned the curve and spotted the prison, set in the middle of a field of melting snow. She drew closer and saw the razorwire and the lights, and near the entrance door, the dark sedan of the federal marshals. She couldn't get to them without going past the guardhouse, but she couldn't do that. She had no idea which C.O.s were in the conspiracy, and Graf might have one of his guys on lookout, since tonight was the night of the escape.

Nat eyeballed the prison layout as she drove past at a reasonable speed, not wanting to draw undue attention. The building was located far from the road and she couldn't sneak up to it on foot. The prison's design ensured that anyone who tried to break out of prison would be exposed; of course, any idiot who tried to break *into* the prison would be exposed as well. She figured that the tunnel had to run from the prison to the road, or at least near enough to it. Digging the tunnel would have been doable in a year's time, or less. She had to assume Parrat would be here tonight to make the pickup, wherever the tunnel ended. Graf and Machik would be on duty, too, and they'd undoubtedly make up some story in the morning about how Williams had escaped. And overnight, they'd become rich men.

She drove by the entrance to the prison, looking for any sign of a tunnel's exit. She followed the curve of the road around a grove of evergreen trees, then traveled uphill, using the blue water tower as her guide. The grade steepened, and she drove around the back of the water tower, then slowed when she got to the back of the prison. She looked through the trees.

She didn't see the tunnel's exit, but in the next minute, she saw another way to execute Plan B.

Nat had to work quickly. She drove farther up the road until she found a break in the evergreens, then pulled the car onto high ground, using the trees on the right as cover from the guardhouse. She opened the glove compartment and ransacked it. Old Trident gum pieces, loose CDs, two condoms, a tube of Bath & Body hand cream, and a pack of matches fell onto the passenger seat.

Bingo. But she needed a few more items. She got out of the car and started looking. It was dark but she pulled out the penlight and cast it around the side of the road. Gravel, melting snow, and mud appeared in the penlight's circle of moonshade, but no luck. She kept looking, then saw a large grayish rock. She kicked it hard with her foot, once, then again. She succeeded only in shifting it slightly, which meant it would do fine. She got down on all fours and clawed at the snow around the rock until she finally unseated it, then lifted it up with a tiny grunt and hurried back to the car as fast as she could.

She retrieved her purse, with the construction file still in it, and slung it over her shoulder, then picked up the rock, edged out of the driver's seat with it, and set it on the floor of the car. She gathered all the stray branches, old leaves, and sticks she could find, stuffed them in the passenger seat, then took the manila folder from the construction file and set it in the middle of the sticks. She struck a match and lit the folder, which caught fire quickly. Then the kindling began to flame, too.

Last, she assessed the condition of the field. Much of the snow had melted, but the ground was still cold enough to stay firm. Dark gray smoke filled the car. Fire warmed her face. It was time. She steeled her nerves and got her target in sight. Near the prison, off by itself, sat the row of white propane tanks, next to one of the construction trailers. She felt her heart thudding in her chest. The propane tanks were too far from the road to endanger the houses on the street and too far from the prison building to endanger it, either. She was taking a page from Graf's book. If he could create chaos, so could she.

She double-checked that the emergency brake was engaged, then rolled the heavy rock onto the gas pedal. The engine gunned in angry response and the tires spun in protest, spraying mud, wet snow, and gravel. She counted to three and released the emergency brake, and the Neon took off like a shot, heading downhill for the propane tanks. The car zoomed into the field at speed, with orange flames leaping from its windows. The guard ran out of the guardhouse, but he was too late. In the next minute, the Neon smashed into the propane tanks, knocking over the tall white tanks like so many bowling pins.

KABOOM! KABOOM! The tanks exploded with a deafening blast, sending a geyser of orange flame shooting into the night. Sparks flew skyward like fireworks. Bits of metal spiraled into the air. Smoke billowed from the flames. KABOOM!

Nat hid behind the trees. Emergency sirens erupted from the prison. Floodlights sprang to life and blasted cones of light on the perimeter fences. The guard came running to the fire. Two marshals leapt from the dark sedan in the parking lot. C.O.s poured from the prison. The scene looked every bit the bedlam of the prison riot. But Nat couldn't make her next move yet.

Suddenly, she heard shouts behind her and turned. Front doors were opening in the houses on the other side of the street. Residents were stepping outside to see what was going on. A middle-aged couple hurried down their front walk and across the street.

"Look!" Nat said, pointing. She kept her face to the fire. "The propane tanks exploded at the prison!"

"My goodness gracious!" The woman wrapped a blue quilted coat closer around her and looked down the hill, orange flames dancing in her hooded eyes. Her graying husband came up behind her in a long parka, and she turned to him. "George, shouldn't we get our propane tanks checked?"

"Nah, they don't spontaneously combust, honey."

"Then what causes that?"

"God only knows," Nat answered, fake-watching as other neighbors walked toward her and the older couple, beginning to collect in the street. When would the police come? What was taking so long? She couldn't risk being spotted. Her hair was so bright it glowed in the dark. She couldn't wait another minute. She started to walk toward the field and ignored the new shouts behind her.

"Hey, wait!" a man's voice yelled. "That blonde! I just saw her near a car when I took out the trash."

No! Nat heard a scuffing noise behind her, and turned just as an angry middle-aged man grabbed her jacket.

"Get back here. What were you doing anyway?"

"Lemme go!" Nat wrenched herself free and took off down the hill. She couldn't let anybody stop her now. Not after she'd come this far.

"Stop!" the man shouted, chasing her downhill toward the prison. In the next minute she heard the blare of distant sirens. She ran as fast as she could across the field, her feet churning in mud and snow, barely ahead of the man.

"Stop right there! I'm calling the police!"

Nat screamed, as suddenly her collar got yanked back, throttling her. The man grabbed her, jerked her backward off her feet, and threw her to the wet snow. Her head hit the cold ground and she lay almost choking as the man stood over her. She kicked him in the leg as hard as she could.

"Ow!" the man doubled over and crumpled to the snow, and Nat scrambled to her feet and started running. The sirens grew louder, closer. Police. Fire. Help was on the way. The blaze raged at the propane tanks, burning into the sky around the blackening shell of the Neon. She raced past the heat and toward the prison while all hell broke loose.

More C.O.s streamed outside the prison. The SWAT team ran at the fire with portable extinguishers. The Neon blazed away. The air smelled like burning rubber. Everybody shouted warnings and directions and ran this way and that. In the emergency, nobody noticed the little blonde streaking for the prison entrance.

Nat kept running. In the next minute, she saw a trio of state police cars zooming down the road from the right. They tore around the curve and drove up the prison driveway. Two yellow fire trucks powered right behind them, their red lights flashing and sirens screaming. She bolted to the prison entrance. Floodlights blasted the driveway around the entrance, and she recognized the familiar figure of a woman C.O. Tanisa. Nat ran to intercept her.

"Tanisa, it's me, Angus's friend!" she shouted over the din, grabbing Tanisa's arms. "Williams is going to escape tonight! Graf's behind it and Machik, too!"

"You?" Tanisa's eyes focused on her face in astonishment, then outrage. "You shot Barb Saunders!"

"No, I didn't! It was Richards, he's—"

"You killed that trooper!" Tanisa shrieked, about to punch her, but Nat bolted away. Tanisa called to another C.O., "Stop her! Catch that blonde!"

Nat darted ahead in the melee. Police cars pulled up, their sirens screaming. Uniformed troopers leapt from the cars. Firefighters in heavy canvas coats jumped from the fire trucks and unrolled hoses. People hurried in all directions, a stricken crowd.

Nat bolted for the entrance in the mob scene but noticed a uniformed cop on the other side of the crowd, also running to the entrance. She caught a glimpse of the side of his face. She recognized the face and the cornrows. He had on a gray uniform but he wasn't a trooper.

It was Mark Parrat, the pickup driver. The man in Houlihan's and probably in the ski mask, too. She was about to scream when she got tackled from behind by a pair of strong arms. Before she knew what was happening, she was falling face first to the hard, wet driveway with someone on her back. Her forehead exploded in pain.

"You're not so smart after all, huh, professor?" a man said in Nat's ear.

Just before she lost consciousness.

CHAPTER 42

Wake up!" a man was saying. "You're fine, kid. Walk it off, walk it off."

Who let my father in?

"Wake up! Come on, I didn't hit you that hard."

Nat felt someone patting her cheek. Her forehead thundered, her ears rang. The tunnel. The escape. She flashed on Saunders, bleeding on the floor. She heard herself say, "It's under the floor."

"Wake up, professor. You're gonna be fine."

Nat opened her eyes. She found herself flat on her back on the prison driveway. Noise surrounded her. Firefighters, cops, and C.O.s ran and shouted. Shadows shifted everywhere around her. One face hovered above her, his features clear in the floodlights. Trooper Mundy.

"Good morning, professor. Now that you're awake, you're under arrest."

"No, please, listen." Nat felt herself hoisted to her feet. She fought the fog in her head. Warm blood ran down her face. She struggled to stand on wobbly knees. "There's a tunnel under the floor. They were gonna get Williams out tonight. Parrat is here. He's gonna—"

"You're coming with me."

"Trooper, just check it! There's a tunnel under the floor! I started the fire to stop them! I messed up their plans! Parrat is going to get Williams out!"

"*You* started the fire? You're a disgrace!" Mundy thundered, pulling her through the crowd. "I stuck up for you with Duffy. You made a fool outta me."

"He's wearing a fake cop outfit!" Nat writhed in Mundy's grip, pummeling his arms, using every ounce of strength to get back to the entrance. "He killed the trooper! He shot Barb!"

"Fake cops now? You've lost your mind."

"No, I swear, Graf is in on it, with Machik and—"

"I heard you called my office, asking for me, pretending you were a man. I don't know your deal, but you're effin' crazy!"

Mundy kept pulling Nat away, but she couldn't let this happen. God only knew what Parrat was doing now. She would lose her chance. Williams would go free. She couldn't make Mundy listen. She couldn't make anybody listen. Not her students, not her family, not her father. She felt a wellspring of anger bubble to the surface. Rage that had been building her whole life, spontaneously combusting. Gnat. Book smart. Why couldn't she make anybody hear her?

"WILL YOU ALL LISTEN TO ME FOR ONCE?" Nat screamed at the top of her lungs, so loud that her voice broke. She felt like the mouse that roared. "PARRAT IS GOING TO GET WILLIAMS OUT! THERE'S A TUNNEL UNDER THE FLOOR! SAUNDERS DIED FOR IT! I'LL SHOW IT TO YOU!"

Suddenly the *pop pop pop* of automatic gunfire crackled from the prison like an electrical current. The crowd exploded into movement. Cops and C.O.s ran for the prison from all directions.

"That's Parrat! He's inside!" Nat shouted amid the melee, and Mundy's eyes looked bewildered, then furious.

"I cannot effin' believe this!" he shouted, then he picked Nat up, threw her over his shoulders like a sack, and carted her to an empty police cruiser. He opened the back door and started to shove her into the backseat.

"No, lemme go, you gotta listen!" Nat writhed but she was losing the battle. Mundy stuffed her into the backseat, and when the car door almost slammed on her, she summoned all her courage and kicked him in the shins. Mundy hopped back for a split second, and she seized the moment to jump out of the car and take off toward the prison entrance. The trooper ran after her and clamped his hand on her arm.

"Don't you ever *stop*?" he asked, exasperated, and just then a shout came from the front of the prison. The crowd edged backward, suddenly hushed. Nat was too short to see anything, and Mundy shoved her behind his broad back, but she peeked out.

And witnessed a nightmare.

CHAPTER 43

"Say hello to the warden, everybody!" shouted a brawny inmate. He emerged from the prison and appeared in the spotlight, pressing a black Glock to his hostage's temple. The inmate's dark eyes were slits, his mouth a scarred sneer. It had to be Richard Williams, his malevolence evident even in his T-shirt and blue scrubs. Williams shouted, "Don't nobody move a muscle, or Mr. Warden McCoy's gonna get his head shot clean off, right in front of y'all."

Nat watched, aghast. Warden McCoy, in a tie and jacket, had gone grim with fear. His blue eyes stayed glued to the gun at his temple. His mouth stretched in a grimace. Williams used the warden's body as a human shield, wrapping a tattooed arm around the other man's torso and walking him along in front of himself. The C.O.s, police, and firefighters on the driveway froze, a tableau of law enforcement personnel rendered instantly impotent. The car fire raged in the background.

"Now, here's what's gonna happen, folks. Ya'll's gonna stay cool. Me and my boys, we gonna take a little walk down to our car. If our driver gets hurt, or one of us gets hurt, these good people goin' *down*." Williams pushed McCoy ahead of him down the driveway. A black sedan with an ADT security badge on the door idled halfway up the driveway. It couldn't get closer because of the fire trucks. The crowd of cops and C.O.s stood paralyzed, a captive audience to the thug's little show.

Williams continued. "We already lef' you one body, a C.O. who let me outta my cell. Don't make me leave you any more. We don't want no more heroes tonight."

There was a new commotion at the entrance to the prison, and suddenly, someone else emerged from the doorway, behind Williams and Warden McCoy. It was Parrat, the pickup driver. He walked out in his fake-cop uniform, his gun to the soft cheek of another hostage. Nat gasped when she caught a glimpse of his victim.

Tanisa. The C.O.'s mouth stayed grimly closed, but her eyes had gone still with fright. The C.O.s in the crowd stood riveted when they saw her. Parrat had Tanisa's arms pinned behind her back and he shoved her in front of him, The two of them walked closely behind Williams and the warden, like a horrifying parade.

A C.O. in the crowd shouted, "Let her be!"

Parrat didn't respond, but Tanisa did. "Shoot him!" she hollered, her voice ringing clear and strong.

"Bitch, shut up!" Parrat shouted, shoving his gun into Tanisa's ear. Nat felt her heart cry out.

Williams walked on, with McCoy in front, saying, "Now, now. Folks, stay cool, calm, and collected. Everything's gonna be all right. Just stay cool. We got one more comin' with us, then we outta here."

Nat looked at the prison entrance. Another figure was walking outside with a hostage. Graf stepped into the spotlight in his C.O. uniform, his eyes cold as gunmetal and his revolver trained on Machik. A ripple of shock shot through the crowd at the sight.

A C.O. called out, "You're scum, Joe! You're *worse* than scum!"

Graf ignored him, and Nat was the only one not surprised at his treachery. The only trick was that Graf had Machik as a hostage. But that fit in, too. No one knew Machik was in on the conspiracy except for Graf and her. In effect, Graf was smuggling out a confederate, right under everyone's noses.

A second C.O. shouted, "You won't get away with it, Joe!"

Mundy stirred, and when he did, Nat felt something hit her hand. She looked down. There was a bulge in the back of Mundy's jacket, around his belt. *A gun.*

"Very good job, folks," Williams was saying. Warden McCoy looked terrified, the gun boring into his temple. "Y'all doin' a very good job, and I'm mighty proud of you. Don't nobody do nothin' stupid and we all gonna be all right."

Nat eyed the crowd. Nobody was moving. They couldn't take the chance. Williams was getting away. The warden's brow sweated in the lights. Anyone's movement could trigger the murder of the warden and Tanisa. Nat couldn't be seen behind Mundy's back. She was too short, and for once, it was an advantage. She had to do something. She stayed perfectly still except for her hand, which she slipped under the back of Mundy's jacket. If the trooper felt anything, he was too smart to let it show. The unfolding scene was proving her right. He must be letting her take it. She reached the handle of the gun and pulled. But it didn't come.

"Me and my friends gonna take these good people wit' us." Williams's voice grew closer. He must have been directly in front of Mundy. "We gonna drop 'em off, good as new, when we're clear. So stay cool and nobody gets hurt."

Nat tried the gun again but it didn't move. Was it stuck? No. It must have been in a holster. Her fingers found some kind of latch over the gun handle. She fumbled and felt a snap, unfastened it, and finally slid the gun free. It was warm from Mundy's body heat, and its barrel caught the dark light.

Okay, I'm not shooting anybody. The teachers can't do everything around here.

Nat took the gun and eased it slowly under Mundy's right hand,

and she felt an almost physical tingle when he accepted it from her, betraying no movement.

Williams was saying, "Y'all stay—"

Suddenly Mundy swung his arm up and fired the gun. It exploded in an earsplitting *pop pop pop*, setting off a horrifying fusillade. The shooting happened in a sickening blur. A red hole exploded in Williams's temple. He crumpled. The attack startled Parrat, and Tanisa turned and elbowed him. He fell away and was instantly cut down by the cops in the crowd, his body spinning with the impact of the bullets.

Graf aimed for Mundy, but flew backward when he was shot himself, his gun spraying bullets. One hit Machik in the head and he went down, dropping on the spot. The crowd surged forward, almost knocking Nat over. She let them rush past, squeezing her eyes shut against what she had just seen. She couldn't believe that it had happened.

She half-stumbled and half-walked away, breathing in fresh air. She bent over and leaned on the huge, cold bumper of one of the fire trucks, praying to keep nausea at bay. In the next minute, she felt a large hand on her shoulder and turned around. It was Mundy, slipping the gun back into its holster.

"You okay, professor?" he asked.

"More or less." Nat smiled shakily. She couldn't believe it was finally over. "Okay, less."

"You did nice work. You got guts. Sorry I gave you such a hard time."

"S'okay." Nat didn't say I-told-you-so. It didn't feel like a victory after so much carnage.

"You wanna show me that tunnel?" Mundy threw a comforting arm around her shoulder.

Nat nodded, wiping away a tear that came from nowhere.

CHAPTER 44

Nat sat in her chair in the dingy interview room, recorded by the black videocamera and fueled by a cup of bad coffee, and explained to Trooper Mundy, Trooper Duffy, and an assistant D.A. everything that had happened since the last time she sat there. She included her discovery of the stop on the Underground Railroad, but they seemed less excited than she about the historical angle. After she had finished, the three of them left her in the interview room, to confer. She thought of calling a lawyer, but decided against it. She felt newly competent, happily.

Nat waited and took inventory. They'd put a Band-Aid on her forehead, and her neck hurt from when that man near the prison had pulled her down. She brushed off her pants, ripped at the knee. Her clogs were soaked, and she couldn't remember the last time her toes had been dry. She thought about Angus, but hadn't called him or her parents yet. This interview had gone on longer than she thought it would. She checked her watch just as the door opened and Mundy came back alone.

"Bad news," he said, closing the door softly behind him.

"I'm going up the river?"

"No." He smiled tiredly, then pulled out a chair and plunked down so hard it skidded. "We sent somebody out to pick up Jim Graf, from that construction company."

"Phoenix."

"Right." Mundy leaned on his heavy thigh and looked at her with his frank brown eyes. "He's dead. Hanged himself in the bathroom."

Nat felt it in her gut. She wondered how Agnes, Graf's secretary, would react. She reached for the coffee and took a cold gulp.

"He was going down and he knew it."

"That's awful." Nat set down the Styrofoam cup, and Mundy ran a hand through his hair.

"So where we go from here is that we'll start our investigation, verifying what you told us. I think it'll square with your story." He shook his head. "That tunnel sure was something else."

"It was." Nat couldn't believe it herself. A football-field-long tunnel, more a crawlspace than anything, that began from the new staff room and ended in the middle of the evergreens, away from the houses. The tunnel had been reinforced with two-by-fours, like the one she'd seen on the Underground Railroad, but less well made. Graf and his pals lacked the brains, and the heart, of those people.

"We also got troopers canvassing on the street, and two neighbors reported seeing a cop car parked there tonight. They always see cop cars around the prison, so they didn't report it."

"They didn't know it was Parrat, in the fake copmobile."

"Right." Mundy arched an eyebrow. "Quite a plan. Most bad guys aren't that smart."

"Williams was a smart bad guy. The CEO of bad guys."

Mundy chuckled, checking his pad. "'Course we're not bringing charges against you for Matty, or the attempt on Barb Saunders."

"How is she?"

"No change."

Nat felt a twinge.

"We'll be talking with the warden and his deputy, but we don't think they're involved at this point. Machik is as high up as it went."

"Not everybody would be. It was an unwieldy conspiracy to start out with, between bad guys and good guys. At least formerly good guys."

"But we can't prosecute the dead. So it's all over, at least the legalities."

"Somebody should follow up with Upchurch's aunt, Mrs. Rhoden. She deserves at least to be compensated for what happened to her nephew, as if that were possible."

"I got that."

Nat thought of Machik getting shot, and of Graf. Then Graf's cute little boy, skipping to his karate lesson, and his nice wife. "Don't these men consider their families when they do stuff like this?"

"Honestly, no. Families aren't as important to them as money. Speaking of which, I'm supposed to tell you that you do have some things to account for, young lady." Mundy checked his pad and slid a yellow pencil from his breast pocket. "You vandalized public property."

"What?"

"The propane tanks and the fence."

Nat scoffed. "Gimme a break."

"My hands are tied."

"Are you serious?"

"This is a charging decision by the D.A." Mundy made another check. "Also, they're charging you with criminal mischief."

Nat snorted. "For keying the pickup?"

Mundy blinked. "What?"

Oops. "What for?"

"Setting fire to the Neon."

Nat didn't object, and Mundy looked up, surprised.

"You okay with that?"

"I like thinking of myself as mischievous. It's my new thing." Nat stood up and brushed off her pants. "Anyway, this sounds like fines."

"A *lot* of fines."

"Then, can I go. I've heard enough." Nat didn't even want to fuss at him. She was tired and sad, and she'd fought hard enough, for long enough. "Can I use a phone? My parents must be freaking."

"Sure." Mundy stood up, pulled a cell phone from his pocket, and handed it to her. He added, "By the way, the media's already out front. I'm supposed to tell you that the D.A. would appreciate it very much if you didn't talk to the press. He'll draft a press release." Mundy eyed her with a dark twinkle, more straight man than trooper.

"Tell the D.A. that I would appreciate it very much if he waived my fines, in view of my service to the community."

"You're learning, prof." Mundy smiled, and so did Nat. She pressed her parents' phone number into the cell, as he patted her on the back. "Come on out when you're finished. I'll give you a ride home."

"Thanks." Nat called her parents at home, but they didn't answer, so she tried her dad's cell. It rang and rang. She was about to hang up when she heard his voice. "Dad? It's me, Nat."

"Where are you?" Her father sounded stressed. "We've been calling your cell."

"I'm fine. I'm at the police station again, but it's all over now."

"Nat, listen. We're at the hospital, at Penn. Can you come?"

"What? Why?"

"Paul had a heart attack."

CHAPTER 45

Nat entered the hospital room in intensive care where Paul lay still in a bed, his eyes closed and his color grayish. A transparent greenish tube ran from his nose, an IV snaked from his arm, and a white plastic clamp hooked up to a fingertip, connecting to a vital-sign monitor that showed an unmistakably erratic line of hills and valleys, in glowing blue. In a night of so many awful sights, this was the worst.

"Nat, come in," her father said, meeting her and enveloping her in a hug. His cheek scratched like sandpaper instead of being character-istically clean-shaven, and he didn't smell of his beloved Aramis. He released her, holding her off, his eyes a sad and shiny brown, until they traveled, bewildered, to her hair. "Why'd you change your hair?"

"It's a long story. What happened?" Nat looked past him to the bed, which was flanked by Junior and Tom on one side, and her mother and Hank on the other. They all looked red-eyed and exhausted.

"He was playing basketball with Hank, and he just went down." Her father's voice cracked with emotion, a sound Nat had never heard from him. "He had a defect in his heart, his aortic valve."

"But he's twenty-six," Nat said, as if her father didn't know.

"They must've missed it when he was little, and the cold medicine he was taking made it worse, somehow. The shortness of breath wasn't a cold, it was his heart. I don't understand it all." Her father scratched his head, heartbroken. "They had to repair the valve."

"He had heart surgery?" Nat was reeling. She'd missed the whole thing. She couldn't take her eyes from Paul, lying motionless, his hands at his sides. She felt awful for not having taken his condition seriously. She almost couldn't bring herself to ask the question. "He's gonna be okay, isn't he?"

"They don't know." Her father's shoulders slumped, soft in his blue dress shirt. "They said we'll know in a few hours if he's outta the woods."

"This isn't possible." Nat couldn't wrap her mind around it. Paul was the one with the most life, of all of them. "When did it happen?"

"Last night, around seven o'clock."

Nat thought back. She had been in bed with Angus. Her brother was collapsing on a basketball court while she was having sex. She pressed the thought away. "You've been here since then?"

"Yeah. We slept in the chairs in the hall. It's against the rules, so they hate us."

Nat had recognized their coats when she'd hurried down the hall. "Don't they have a waiting room for intensive care?"

"It's too far from the room. Screw their rules." Her father smiled. "Come say hello to your mother." He led her to the bed, where her mother reached out and gave her a bony, still fragrant, hug.

"I'm so glad you're back. Was everything okay?"

"Fine."

"What happened to you, Nat?" her father asked, and it struck her that they had no idea about the prison. She'd had to fight her way through the reporters and cameras outside the police barracks, and the sensational story had been all over the radio news. But her parents and brothers had been here, not caring about TVs or newspapers, with Paul their sole focus. Their world had changed in a heartbeat, without much thought for her—which was exactly right and proper.

"It doesn't matter now what happened," Nat answered.

"He's gonna be all right, sweetie, I just know it." Her mother patted her on the back, weary and puffy-eyed. All her makeup had worn off, and she had on a blue track suit she normally would never have allowed herself to be seen in in public.

"I know he is, Ma. I guess you were right, all along."

"It happens." Her mother winked, but she looked stripped down and so did Nat's father, the two of them reduced to their real selves, the way she'd seen them only on Christmas mornings. It was an odd thought, and she felt almost ashamed now for having it.

"Hi, Nat," Hank said. He stood next to her mother, and she met his eye only briefly.

"Hiya."

"Good to see you." He returned her look, equally uncomfortably, then stepped forward and gave her a perfunctory hug. His embrace felt almost the way it used to, strong and warm, and she broke it quickly, her emotions welling up because part of it wasn't the same, and part of it was exactly the same, a sensation she couldn't parse or experience right now.

"Hey, Nat," Junior said somberly, across the bed, and Tom managed a smile for her.

"Nice haircut."

"Thanks." Nat felt as if she had stepped into some topsy-turvy world, where twenty-six-year-olds had heart attacks and brothers complimented you. She wanted to go out and come in again, so Tom could make fun of her and Paul could break a lamp. Paul. Her little brother. His feet made soft white tents at the foot of his bed, and she reached out and rested her hand on a toe, as if she could keep him tethered to the world that way.

"His color looks better, don't you think?" her mother asked, eyeing Paul, and her father cocked his head, doing the same.

"I think you're right, Di."

"I can hear him breathing, too. It's stronger than before." Her mother leaned close to Paul's face, her hair almost falling forward into his cheek. "I hear him. John?"

Her father nodded, brightening. "I hear it, too. Like he's using his chest more."

They all leaned over, listening. Nat had nothing to compare it to, but Paul's breathing sounded normal to her. "He sounds good to me."

"I think so, too, Ma," Junior said.

Tom agreed. "Most def."

But Hank chuckled softly. "This is the quietest Paul's been in his life."

Her father arched an eyebrow.

Her mother blinked twice.

Tom and Junior looked up.

You did not just say that. We *can joke about Paul, but* you *can't joke about Paul.*

Nat didn't have to look at Hank to understand why he'd said it. She knew he was uncomfortable with her here and with whatever terrible thing had happened to Paul, and the fact that it had happened while they were playing basketball. And, sadly, these things had combined to make him say the wrong thing at the worst possible moment. He would never know where or when everyone remembered that he wasn't really a Greco, but Nat knew that it was right here and right now.

"They let us stay only fifteen minutes every hour," her father said, letting the moment pass. "We got only three minutes left. That pain-in-the-ass nurse comes in like clockwork."

"They're into their rules, huh, Dad?" Nat asked, still holding onto Paul's toe.

"Your dad made them let all of us in," Hank added, with a sideways smile.

"Good for you, Dad." Nat felt tears come to her eyes. She wondered how many people he'd threatened with litigation, grievous bodily harm, or both. Something happened to her then, when she thought about Tom and Junior, and her mother and father, flanking her brother's bed like human guardrails, standing beside him day and night, for a lousy fifteen minutes every hour, determined to prevent anything or anybody from hurting him or taking him away, as if they were a little suburban army. They did it because he was one of them, and they were each the most important thing in the other's lives.

And in that moment Nat understood, with a certainty that went as deep as bone, something she had never realized before. That each of these people would have done this for her, from the day she was born to the day she drew her last breath on earth, bound by their common name and their very blood. And if the price to be paid for that profoundly human service was the occasional cruelty, thoughtless comment, or simple disregard, it was worth every single penny.

Because they were family.

CHAPTER 46

Ms. Greco, look over here!" a photographer shouted, one of the mob outside her apartment building the next morning. "Ms. Greco, any comment?" "Nat, what did you have to do with stopping Williams's escape?" "Ms. Greco, please! Any comment?" "The Chester County D.A. says you were integral to their law enforcement efforts. Can you explain?"

Nat raised a hand as she hurried into her building. She'd slept about two hours at the hospital, but nothing could get her down today, not even the press. Paul was out of the woods this morning. She entered the lobby lighthearted, until she reached the security desk, manned by Bill in his uniform.

Oops. Nat had completely forgotten. He had lent her his Kia for a day, a few days ago, and his cell phone, too. She had no excuse. *I was on the lam?*

"Professor!" Bill rose, smiling expectantly, and Nat felt a wave of guilt.

"I'm so sorry. I'll get you your car and your phone today. I was kind of busy."

"That's all right. I know. You caught the crooks. You're famous!" Bill beamed at her with new regard.

Nat blushed. "Not really."

"Really!" Bill gestured to the press outside. "They been out there all night. They interviewed me about you, and I told 'em how nice you are, how smart. You're a hero!" He extended a hand over the desk. "Put 'er there."

"Aw." Nat shook his hand, and Bill tugged her close to the desk.

"Tell me somethin.' Did ya use my car to make a getaway?"

Nat winced. "Frankly, yes."

"Great! Then my wife says we could sell it on eBay." Bill made a finger frame in the air. "For sale, Getaway Car."

Hoo boy. "Glad to help out, Bill." Nat crossed to the elevator and pushed the button. "See you later."

"Would you autograph the car for me, like they do on Jay Leno?" Bill called after her, but Nat pretended not to hear as she stepped into the elevator and the doors slid closed. She had to shower up, change, and check in on her job, if she still had one.

And she wouldn't mind seeing Angus, either.

Nat opened the heavy front doors of the law school and entered the Great Hall, whose vaulted cupola of eggshell white, tall Palladian windows, and glistening marble staircase testified to the school's old-Ivy creds. Students milled around, talking and laughing between classes, and a few turned as she walked in. Her navy pumps clacked across the polished floor of rose-and-tan marble. She was wearing a conservative navy suit with her white punk hair, sending the sartorial equivalent of mixed signals.

"Hi, Marie." Nat waved to the guard as she passed the security desk.

"Stop right there, Miss," the guard called out, her voice echoing in the hall. "I need to see your ID."

Nat turned. "It's me, Marie. Nat Greco."

"Professor Greco?" Marie broke into a grin of recognition. "Sorry,

I didn't see your face! Well, welcome back. I knew you didn't kill anybody."

"Thanks." Nat cringed, and the students started turning to her, one by one.

Marie reached for her newspaper and waved it in the air. "You stopped that gangsta from escaping. I read all about you, on the first page. Will you sign your picture for me?"

"Maybe later," Nat answered, but when she turned to go, she found herself surrounded by a ring of students, gawking with admiration. She recognized a few of the faces from her first-year classes, and Warren, Carling, and Chu from her seminar, gazing at her with new eyes.

"Did you really blow up a car, Professor Greco?" Warren asked, as they all gathered around. "That is *so* cool."

"I didn't—"

Chu corrected, "No, she blew up oil tanks."

"Not, really, I—"

"We didn't know you were such a *badass!*" Carling grinned and raised a palm. "Come on, gimme some!"

"You got it!" Nat slapped him five and suddenly understood why guys slapped five all the time. Because it was fun.

Just then the door to the faculty lounge opened, and Vice Dean McConnell walked out, some papers in his hand. As soon as he spotted Nat, his face froze like an academic ice sculpture.

"Professor Greco," he said, walking toward her, and the students fell silent, watching.

"Hello, Jim." Nat thought he might strangle her until a thatch of thick gray hair popped out behind him, followed by a trademark red bow tie. It was Dean Samuel Morris, back from the African veldt, and not a moment too soon. His hooded eyes flew open behind his tortoiseshell bifocals and he broke into a characteristic grin.

"Nat, here you are!" Dean Morris, an adorably chubby man, threw his arms around her in a hug that smelled of pipe tobacco. "What am I hearing about you?"

"It's a long story, Sam." Nat enjoyed his aromatic embrace until she spotted McConnell over her shoulder, his eyes narrowing. Dean Morris released her just enough to slip an arm over her shoulder, scoop her out of the crowd, and propel her from the Great Hall into the school lobby.

"You must tell me all about it. I've been fielding calls all morning from the media, and I should tell you, I have been in touch with the police. They faxed me your statement, at my request."

Gulp. Nat couldn't tell from his tone whether she was about to be fired or praised, and he wouldn't show his hand in front of the students anyway. They were collecting in the lobby, smiling at her and even waving as she passed. Melanie Anderson, from her seminar, began clapping, and the other students burst into spontaneous applause, which echoed in the cavernous lobby. Nat acknowledged them with a happy nod, and Dean Morris flashed them an official smile as they rounded the corner on the way to his office.

Vice Dean McConnell fell into step with them. "Sam, we can't just say, 'all's well that ends well.' I expressly forbade Nat here from going out to the prison, and she went anyway."

"That's where the bad guys are," Nat said lightly, but Dean Morris seemed not to hear as he swept them down the hall, where more students turned to gawk, then started buzzing and finally clapping.

McConnell continued, "We've never had a law professor charged with murder, whether or not the charges were dropped. It's unprecedented. I warned her many times last week—"

"Not here, Jim." Dean Morris silenced him with a hand chop and turned to Nat. "We do need to speak in private."

Nat's heart sank. What bothered him? Theft? Fraud? Arson? *Pick a felony, any felony.*

Vice Dean McConnell frowned. "I would like to be included in this meeting. As you know, Professor Greco is up for tenure this year and—"

"Thank you, but that won't be necessary." Dean Morris whisked Nat from the vice dean, past the secretaries looking at her starry-eyed, and into his office, where he gestured her into the seat across from the desk. "Please, sit."

"Thanks," Nat said uncertainly, and Dean Morris shut the door behind them and turned to her, his expression somber.

"I'll get right to the point. The police statement said that you hid out in an underground tunnel, used for the Underground Railroad. Is that true?"

"Well, it was more like a hole," Nat answered, surprised.

"This hole was previously unknown? You discovered it yourself?"

"I think so. It was covered with boards."

"Amazing." Dean Morris leaned on the desk, his gray eyes blazing with intellectual zeal. "Once this is out, we'll get calls from every history department in the country. This is a coup for our law school."

"Really?" Nat said, then corrected herself. "I mean, really."

"You're going to publish on it, of course."

I am? "Of course. The wood shoring up the hole had carved initials and names, from the era, and I plan to trace some of the names." Nat was freewheeling, but it was her passion, even if nobody else had cared about it until this very minute. "There are records, you know, of different slave families and the routes they took from Maryland and points south. I teach it in my seminar."

"Wouldn't that be a dandy article?" Dean Morris beamed.

"Except that Vice Dean McConnell isn't sure I can keep teaching the seminar, as much as I'd like to. I'd do it in addition to my other classes, as I have been."

"Oh, you must keep teaching it now. About the article, could you expand it into a book, perhaps?"

"I sure could." Nat relaxed. She wasn't going to get fired if she wrote a book. How hard could it be? Lots of clowns wrote books. She was a bookworm before she became a bad-ass.

"There's so much we can do with this find. The sky's the limit."

"I could even take my students out there for a field trip."

"A field trip—in *law school*?" Dean Morris's smile faded.

Nat decided not to push her luck.

At least not yet.

Ten minutes later, Nat was hurrying down the sunny hall through crowds of excited students, who asked her questions, patted her on the back, and congratulated her on, inter alia, saving the day, bleaching her hair, and blowing things up. She thanked them all, bursting with relief and happiness, so that she was almost completely full of herself by the time she went downstairs to the clinic and opened the glass door, where the omnipresent crowd of students were gathered around Angus in his ponytail, ratty sweater, jeans, and boots. Even as scruffy as he was, he was still the most beautiful man she had ever seen.

Wow.

"Natalie!" Angus hollered the moment he saw her. He burst into a grin, and his bright blue eyes lit up. He cut through the students, swept her into his woolly arms, and planted on her lips the same soft, warm kiss she remembered from when they'd made love. She kissed him back as he held her close, blowing their cover even as the students began to shout and hoot, and when they kissed again, Nat felt a warmth that burned soul-deep, spread inside-out to her skin, and told her that she was, finally, safe.

CHAPTER 47

Weeks later, Nat had started the next chapter in her life, seeing Angus and teaching with new confidence. Her celebrity status had intensified, with more news articles every day and reporters from the *New York Times*, CNN, and Court TV sitting in on her classes, bringing cameras that made even Chu raise her hand. Paul was on the mend, eating a restricted diet and even talking more softly, but she didn't feel completely happy until she heard that Barb Saunders had recovered and left the hospital, too.

Nat took a sunny Sunday afternoon to see Barb for the first time, driving to her house with the window down, the wind ruffling her short hair. It felt great to have her old color back, though she didn't think she'd grow her hair long again; it was the wrong proportion for her height. Her bruises and cuts had healed, and the evil scratches on her chest were long gone. She felt like herself, in jeans and a black cotton T-shirt, with a green Barbour for warmth. Her life had come back together, and she had made amends, too, restoring the Kia and cell phone to Bill and writing the Neon owner a fat check. It was money well spent, and she put it all behind her, enjoying the cool breeze coming in the window, carrying the earliest scents of spring.

The snows of winter had melted, and the dull browns of the Chester County countryside were vanishing before her eyes. New grass sprouted in patches of kelly green, bushes burst into leaves of forest green, and the buds of the trees were the tart hue of Granny Smith apples. Horses that had been blanketed during the winter showed their gray dapples, chocolatey browns, and rich chestnuts, making painterly splotches as they grazed in the fields. It was a lovely drive, and she couldn't wait to see Barb. Angus couldn't come because of work, but she preferred the visit to be girls-only, anyway. It had started with her and Barb, and it should end that way, too.

She took a different route to avoid driving past where Officer Shorney had been killed. She didn't need the reminder, today or ever. The bad guys had gotten theirs, and everybody called it justice, but Nat knew better now. Justice didn't compensate for the loss of human life. Justice was an intellectual concept, inevitably trumped by emotion. Justice was the word we used when we couldn't have what we really wanted, which was everything back the way it was. Justice was only a consolation prize.

She reached the house, pulled up in front, and parked, delighted to see Barb sitting in a plastic beach chair on the lawn, laughing as she watched her boys ride trikes, bikes, and Razors in the driveway. Barb had lost weight in the hospital, and it showed in her face, her cheeks sunken slightly. Still she looked happy. Her blond hair was clipped back and she wore a light blue windbreaker over her jeans.

"Hello, gorgeous!" Nat grabbed her stuff, got out of the car, and walked across the brown-green grass, which was lumpy and soggy under her loafers. "You catchin' some rays?"

"Damn right. It's the life of Riley." Barb patted an empty chair next to hers, with a grin. "Jen's inside, making us all dinner. Pot roast and potatoes."

"What a good sister."

"She's doing the laundry, too. I'm milking this for all it's worth."
Barb laughed, and so did Nat.

"These are for you." Nat handed her a bouquet of flowers, and Barb
sniffed them with a sweet smile.

"Thanks so much. I love roses."

"Me, too. How're you feeling?"

"Better, day by day." Barb set the roses on her lap and gestured at
the boys. "They're doing better, too. We'll get through this."

"I know you will." Nat had come to say something. "I'm so sorry
for what happened to you."

"No need to apologize."

"That night, they followed me." Nat's throat caught. "I led them to
you."

"Stop. You didn't do anything wrong. You had a message to deliver
and you delivered it, for Ron. Now, that's enough." Barb patted her
arm.

Tell my wife. It still bugged her why he had said that, but she wasn't
about to bring it up all over again. "It seems so long ago."

"I know." Barb managed a smile, and Nat couldn't wait any longer
to give her a surprise.

"By the way, I have a gift for you and the kids. It's from the students
and faculty at the law school." Nat reached in her purse, retrieved an
envelope, and presented it with a flourish.

"What's this?" Barb opened the envelope, and her eyes widened at
the check. "My God! I can't take this."

"You have to or we'll sue you."

"It's too much." Barb's eyes glistened, and Nat swallowed the lump
in her throat.

"It's for the kids. Take it, please, from all of us."

"Thank you so, so much." Barb folded the envelope and put it in
her pocket, and both women fell silent a minute, holding back feelings. They knew it was the time for going forward.

"I got oatmeal cookies for dessert," Nat said, handing Barb the Whole Foods box.

Barb grinned, the awkward moment gone. She undid the tape and opened the lid. "These look awesome."

"They are. I eat three in a sitting."

"Life is short. Have dessert first." Barb picked up a cookie and took a big bite. "Grab one before the little monsters do." She called to the kids, "Cookies, guys!"

"Thanks." Nat took a cookie, and the boys jumped off their bikes and came running.

"Mom, mom! Can I have a cookie?" the littlest one yelled, running up in too-big jeans.

Barb caught his arm before he jumped into her lap. "Calm down, mighty mite. Say thank you to Professor Greco."

"Thank you!" the kids called out in unison, wisely dispensing with the professor part and grabbing the cookies.

"You're welcome," Nat said, laughing. They ran back to their bikes and hopped on, then tried to eat and ride at the same time, crashing into each other. "Multi-tasking, I see."

"Always." Barb shielded her eyes with her hand, watching the littlest one, whose red trike was heading for the curb. "That's far enough!" she called out, weakly.

"You want me to yell for you? I'm a teacher."

"That's okay." Barb watched him, her eyes flinty with sunlight and concern, and Nat watched with her, eating the sweet, oaty cookie. At the end of the driveway sat a few large rocks, painted white, and the little boy was on course to plow into one. Barb made a megaphone of her hands. "Honey, don't ride there. That's Daddy's garden, you know that."

"Okay," the little boy shouted, sticking the cookie in his mouth and freeing his hands to steer back onto the driveway.

"What's Daddy's garden?" Nat asked, and Barb broke off a piece of cookie.

"A flower bed that Ron made with the kids. Tulips and daffodils, bulbs that come up. He used to say it was his special garden because it grew automatically." Barb spoke sadly. "It wasn't true, though. He spent plenty of time weeding it. He painted those rocks, too, with our house number."

Nat eyed the rocks, which were white. She hadn't seen them in the winter because they'd been covered by snow, but now they stood out, by themselves.

"Ron was always worried that an ambulance would get lost out here. He painted the numbers really big, and the paint's reflective."

"Excuse me a minute." Nat was already standing up. She walked toward the white rocks, acting on the strangest hunch.

"What?"

Nat walked around the rocks and stared at the numbers: 524. Each number was painted in black on its own rock. *Tell my wife. It's under the floor.*

"Nat?" Barb was walking over.

Floor. Four? Nat squatted down, reached for the rock with the black four, and wedged it out of place.

"What are you doing?" Barb asked, but by then Nat was looking in astonishment at the large circle where the white rock had been, clearly outlined by a ring of earth. Lying in the center of the circle was a large Ziploc bag, which held a yellow manila envelope.

Nat felt her heart start to hammer.

"What's that?" Barb asked, amazed.

"I don't know, but it was under the *four.*"

"*What?*"

"Remember what Ron said? 'It's under the floor.' He must have said, 'the *four.*' I must have misheard him."

"I should have thought of that!" Barb's hand flew to her mouth, and Nat retrieved the plastic bag, brushed off the wet dirt, and read the name on the outside envelope, written in ballpoint, a man's hand. It said, *Barb*. Touched, Nat rose and handed it to her.

"It's for you. This must be what he wanted you to have."

Barb accepted the plastic bag as her boys played in the background, making motor noises with their mouths. She pulled aside the blue plastic zipper on the bag, then extracted the envelope, and opened it. She took out five or six typed pages, with other white papers stapled to the back. On top was a shorter piece of blue paper, a handwritten note that Barb read to herself, then looked up with tears in her eyes.

"He says, 'I love you,'" she said finally, her eyes welling and her lower lip trembling. "He says, 'I love you and our boys with all my heart.'"

Nat blinked back tears of her own, remembering that night, when Barb had been so upset that his last words hadn't been about her. And after all this time, they *had* been. As tragic as it was, Nat had a sense that they had come full circle.

"Then he says, 'If you're reading this, it means I'm gone.'" Barb's voice broke, but she continued reading aloud, hiding her tears from the kids. "'I would've put it in the garage but I wanted it as far away from you and the boys as possible, in case anyone came looking for it. Turn the rest of these papers over to the police as soon as you can, and they can catch these men. Let them take it from there. Stay safe, and know that I love you and our boys, even now.'"

Nat swallowed hard, then suppressed her emotion at the words. Saunders had been killed for what he knew, but in the end he had triumphed, putting the proof under a rock. It must have been what they were searching for that day, after the funeral. Not drugs or money. Evidence.

"I'm so happy to have his note," Barb said, wiping her eyes. "Thank you so much for finding it. It's the greatest gift you could have given me." She detached the note from the papers, then handed them, the envelope, and the Ziploc bag back to Nat. "Please take these. Give them to the police."

"You sure?" Nat accepted the pages.

"My head's already starting to hurt, and I don't want the kids to see me upset."

"I'll make sure you get a copy. You can read them when you're ready."

"Great, thanks." Barb shielded her wet eyes and held the note close. "This is all that matters to me. That my husband loved me and his sons. That we were his last thought."

"I understand," Nat said, just as Barb's lower lip buckled.

"I'm going inside. Can you watch the kids a sec?"

"Sure." Nat's heart went out to her. "Can I help you in?"

"No, please, keep an eye on the kids." Barb turned away and went to the house, her head down. "Be right back, boys. Stay outta the street. Mom's got a little headache."

"You gotta my-grate, Mommy?" the little one called out from his bike, and Barb blew him a kiss.

"Hope not, tiger. Be right back. Hold on with two hands!"

Nat watched her go, making sure Barb reached the door, and then she turned to the pages that Ron Saunders had written.

And what she read brought her to her knees.

CHAPTER 48

N at sat parked along the side of the road and slumped in the driver's seat, behind the steering wheel. A pale afternoon sun shone in a faint blue sky, and old, dry leaves spun frantically across the road in a gust of wind, the last frantic dance of winter. The scene was as bucolic as ever, but she couldn't appreciate it anymore. Not after what she'd read in Saunders's pages. She'd begged off on dinner in favor of delivering them to the police, and both Barb and Jennifer had understood.

But Nat had lied to them. She hadn't gone to the police. She was still sitting in the Volvo, parked at a crossroads. The road to the right led to the state police barracks. The road to the left led home. She wasn't sure yet which one to take. Ron Saunders's pages, a narrative based on overheard conversations and amateur sleuthing, described the conspiracy to help Williams escape exactly as Nat had figured it out. Except for one thing she'd missed.

She read the first paragraph again, but it kept coming out the same way:

On April 28, last year, I was on duty and I took Angus Holt to meet with Richard Williams in the courtesy-hold area. I thought Williams wanted to ask Holt to be his lawyer. Holt thought that, too, because he said so. We were having a rat problem at that time, so I had to put poison everywhere, including the heating ducts. I overheard Williams ask Holt to set up an escape. Williams said he had "one of his boys," Mark Parrat, who would handle paying Holt to get Williams out before his trial. Holt asked why Williams was asking him to help, and Williams answered because the warden would let him meet with a lawyer without anybody suspecting anything, but he couldn't go meeting with C.O.s and he didn't know which C.O.s were "safe" to approach.

Nat rubbed her face. She couldn't believe it. Angus hadn't mentioned that he'd met Williams, either the day that she first went with him to the prison or any day thereafter, even more recently. But Saunders had had no reason to make it up. The rest of the pages contained details of the finances and other plans, which Saunders had overheard and recorded. So much of the narrative was right, but could this part be wrong? Angus could never have been involved with Graf and Machik. She'd seen them fight with her own eyes. And if he was really part of the conspiracy, why would Parrat have hit him with the black pickup?

Nat reread the next paragraph, which picked up the narrative:

Holt said no, but Williams kept upping the money. They agreed on three million dollars up front and a million more when Williams escaped. Holt said the construction might "present some opportunity" to get Williams out. Holt said he knew all the C.O.s and he knew which C.O. to "hire" for the job, maybe Graf. Holt also said they would need somebody higher up, too, maybe Machik. Holt said he would take care of it and get back to Williams.

Nat felt sick to her stomach. It was awful even to contemplate. Angus had dedicated his life to law that served the public interest. He would never have done such a thing, and he didn't care about money. His apartment was as no-frills as his office, his wardrobe was nonexistent, and his biggest asset was the Beetle. She had never met anybody so uninterested in material things. Could she have been so wrong about him? She knew him. She *loved* him.

She read the last paragraph that pertained to Angus:

After that, Holt met two more times with Williams, but I couldn't listen in on them the way I could on Graf and Machik. I am attaching copies of the visitor logs to show that Holt visited Williams three times, and the logs prove that Holt was there. It's true I don't have any proof that Holt followed through. I leave that to you guys. I do think they are covering it up, big-time, because last week I checked the log and the pages about Holt were gone. It's a loose-leaf notebook, so there was no sign they were ripped out, but I knew they were there before, and the copies in here show that.

Nat flipped to the back of the pages, where photocopies of visitor logs had been stapled. There were three separate dates. She ran a finger along the signatures. Sure enough, it was Angus's signature. She knew his handwriting from cards and love notes he'd stuck in her briefcase. From shopping lists, even. They were practically living together. He had his own key. He'd be home later, to spend the night after she got back from her dinner with Barb Saunders.

She set the papers down on the passenger seat and watched old leaves blow across the road, so dry they'd disintegrated into dirty brown fragments. Or it could have been her state of mind. There was no proof that Angus had stayed involved in the conspiracy. What if he had originally agreed to it, then changed his mind? Maybe he had simply pulled out in the end. Of course he wouldn't admit to ever having been involved in the first place, because he'd be too embarrassed and ashamed.

She considered the crossroads. She could go to the left, meet Angus at home, and ask him about the pages. Give the man she loved the benefit of the doubt. She trusted him, and he'd give her the same consideration.

Or she could go to the right, drive to the cops, and turn him in. Show them the pages. They would call him in for questioning. There would be handcuffs. The interrogation room. The media. The electronic flashes. She knew what it would do to him, and to his reputation. She had been there. The accusation equaled the conviction, especially at a law school. He still didn't have all his outreach programs reinstated. It was driving him crazy. And a betrayal like this, from her? It would break him. And break them up.

Nat looked at the crossroads and considered her choices. Left or right? Right or left?

She twisted the key in the ignition and hit the gas.

CHAPTER 49

H oney, I'm home!" Nat called from the doorway. It was their standard greeting, and she was trying to keep things as normal as she
could before springing the pages on him. But in the next second, she
heard the unmistakably festive *pop* of a champagne cork.

"Hey, girl!" Angus came out of the kitchen beaming and holding a
bottle of champagne in one hand and two crystal flutes in the other.
He was wearing a workshirt she loved with jeans, and he looked so
at home in her apartment, with the lighting soft and the books surrounding them both, a perfect backdrop for two law professors. The
sight made her heart ache, and she prayed he had a good explanation,
one that would make it all go away.

"Champagne?" she said.

"We're celebrating. I settled that case with the city today." Angus
gave her an exuberant hug and a warm kiss, but Nat made herself stay
on task.

"You did? That's great!" She managed a smile, slid out of her coat,
and put it and her purse on the chair.

"The city solicitor gave up the ghost. We proved that the poorer
sections of the city don't get waterlines repaired as quickly as the
middle-class sections."

Nat remembered the details. He cared so much about that case. It had kept him up for nights on end.

"We had two great experts submit reports and they compared response times to water main breakages in Philly with those in other major cities. When we flunked, the city guy caved in." Angus set the two glasses on the coffee table and poured champagne into one. "We got a very nice settlement and a consent decree, so we can nail their asses for the next five years if they step out of line." He handed Nat the full glass, then poured himself one. He looked at her with a slight frown. "You look a little down. Was it tough, seeing Barb?"

"Well, yes. Kind of."

"First, a toast." Angus raised his glass, his smile so kind and his eyes the softest blue, focused, as usual, on her. "To you, who inspire me to great things."

"To you, too," Nat said quickly, then sipped the champagne, because it would be easier to swallow than the lump in her throat.

"So tell me." Angus sat down and rested the glass on his thigh. "Come sit next to me and tell me how it went."

"Uh, not yet." Nat remained standing, gathering her nerve. "I have a strange question."

"Sure. But no sitting?" Angus patted the couch.

"Not yet."

"Okay."

"Did you ever meet Williams? I mean, before?"

"What do you mean?" Angus frowned. Not deeply, just simply. Puzzled.

"I mean, did you ever meet Richard Williams at the prison?"

"Let me think." Angus cocked his head. "No, not that I remember. Why? Did Barb say I had? How would she know?"

Oh, no. "Well, she wasn't sure. She just said she thought so." Nat hadn't thought he'd deny it, so she had nowhere to go right away. "She said she heard that you were going to be his lawyer at some point."

"Me?" Angus chuckled. "Me, represent a gangbanger like that? I don't think so."

Nat felt her face grow hot. "But you represent other inmates. You do criminal work."

"Not guys like Williams. They're a specialty. I'm not in the pinky-ring set."

Nat didn't get it. He was denying it. Why would he deny it? She sank into the chair opposite him.

"What?" Angus blinked. "Is something the matter? Are you sick?"

Heartsick.

"What's the matter, sweetie?"

"I don't understand." Nat set down the glass, went to her purse, and got the papers. "I have to ask you some questions, and I need you to tell me the truth. Because I love you, and I trust you."

"Okay," Angus said quietly. "Is this a game?"

"No." Nat kept the papers on her lap. "I found these papers at Barb's house. Her husband wrote them. Ron. He says that you met with Williams three times. He made copies of the sign-out logs to prove it."

Angus remained still. His expression didn't change.

"Now do you remember seeing Williams about being his lawyer?"

"No, honestly I don't." Angus held out his hand. "Can I see the papers? There must be a mistake."

"Wait a minute." Nat kept the papers on her lap. "He said that he overheard you and Williams make a deal to get him out for three million dollars. He thinks that you were in the conspiracy with Graf and Machik and Parrat."

Angus's eyes flared an outraged blue. "That's *absurd.*"

"I know it is, which is why I didn't go to the police. I love you, and I know it's absurd, and I wanted to give you a chance to explain. Because I know you would never do anything like that."

"I didn't. I would never! I can't believe you're accusing me of this."

Me, neither. "I know. I feel terrible, but then why did you meet with Williams? Your signature is in the logs. I have the photocopies right here." Nat heard the desperation in her own tone. Angus's mouth pursed, buried in his dark blond beard.

"Let me see the logs. There must be some mistake."

"Okay." Nat opened the papers and gave him the photocopies of the logs. He rose to take them, reading them over the coffee table. After a minute, he sat back down.

"What are the other papers?" Angus gestured. "In your hand."

No.

"Natalie?"

"Just answer the question. I'm giving you a chance. I love you."

Angus looked down the logs, then looked up again, his features suddenly drawn. His smile had gone. His eyebrows sloped down.

"Tell me. I came to you. I want to know."

Angus took a gulp of champagne, then set the glass down.

Nat waited, breathless. *Please have a good explanation.*

"Okay, Williams asked me to get him out. I thought about it, but I said no. I would never have done it, you know that."

Nat felt her throat catch. "You met with him three times."

"I guess I did."

"Why did you lie about it, just now?"

"I was embarrassed."

Nat felt a twinge. "So, why did it take you three times to tell Williams you didn't want to represent him?"

Angus's eyes flashed. "You're accusing me. You really are."

"Just level with me. We've talked all about this, and you never mentioned to me that you considered representing Williams. Why?"

Angus met her eye over the champagne, forgotten now.

Nat waited.

"This is over, Nat. Let it lie."

No. "No. You couldn't have been involved in a conspiracy like that, Angus. We figured it out together."

"We did. We love each other."

"I remember talking in the car, about what happened in that security office. You said it was Graf who executed Upchurch." Then Nat realized. He had kept her off the track. Deflected the focus away from Saunders. "You even said they had videotapes from the day of the riot." Then it dawned on her, too. "You sent me on a wild goose chase, didn't you?"

"Nat, no—"

"And in addition to everything else, you put me in danger when you took me to the prison that morning, to your class!"

Angus paused a minute. "I do love you, you know."

"Tell me you were not involved in this conspiracy." *Please, say it.*

"I didn't know Buford and his pal would be in my class. I would never let you get hurt. *Never.*" Angus locked eyes with her over the table. "I love you. You know that."

Nat's mouth went dry. "But you knew there would be a riot?"

"I thought it would be contained, in RHU. It was supposed to be."

Nat couldn't believe her ears. "It was a diversion from the murder of Ron Saunders."

"It was never supposed to get that far. They let it get that far, and they had to do it. It wasn't my idea. I didn't want to know anything about it."

Nat felt her mouth drop open.

Angus closed his eyes, still sitting there.

"Angus." Nat felt her own heartbeat. The apartment was so quiet that she swore she could hear bubbles popping in the champagne. "You did not take money to get Williams out of jail. That would be illegal."

Angus opened his eyes. "It would be illegal, but it wouldn't be unjust."

Nat couldn't speak. She felt as if she had entered some alternate universe. Her world had gone topsy-turvy again. She loved this man, and he had lost his mind.

"You remember when we talked about the difference between law and justice, the day we met?" Angus asked, his tone calm. "This is a perfect example. When Williams first asked me, I thought, of course not. But he kept throwing these numbers at me, and I thought, I could do so much good with that money." Angus's eyes glittered in the soft lamplight. "I could fund programs, hire expert witnesses, help people. Those experts I just hired in the case against the city? They cost twenty-five grand. Where else would I have gotten that money? I helped the very people that Williams hurt. With *his* money. It's reparations."

Nat felt herself go numb.

"I've almost spent a hundred grand of it, this year. We bought fifteen experts in an array of civil cases. Taken *days* of depositions. Hired a first-rate co-counsel. Staged the level of litigation that only big firms can. I've gone to war for my clients and I've won cases with that money. That's justice. Even if it's not law."

"Ron Saunders died, and Upchurch, too," Nat whispered, barely finding her voice.

"I didn't expect that. I didn't know that. I thought Williams would get away and they'd pick him up again in a few months. They always do. A scumbag like that, he's always in trouble. In fact, I considered diming on him myself."

"But he kills people. Kids. They die in crossfire. Men like him destroy communities."

"He was the means to an end, and the end was worth it to me."

Nat felt tears come to her eyes. "But this can't be true. They tried to kill us with that pickup that night. Parrat crashed into us."

"I know, and I was totally pissed. They wanted me out. They didn't need me anymore. I only brokered the deal." Angus took a step toward her. "See, I wasn't really in it, Natalie. They wanted me to kill you, but I didn't. I couldn't. I fell in love with you. It's real."

Nat's heart stopped. *"Kill me?"*

"That night in Delaware, in the motel. They told me to kill you, but I didn't. I wasn't going to kill you. I was going to get you out of town."

Oh my God. Nat thought back to that night. The night she ran out on him. He'd found her to kill her. Would he have done it? Was he telling the truth?

"You believe me, don't you?"

I think you're crazy. And I'm crazy for falling in love with you.

"Don't look at me like that. I wasn't in deep, like they were. I just acted as a go-between between the two parties, like any lawyer."

"Like any lawyer? You took money to break the law. To release a dangerous man into the world. You looked the other way when they killed Ron Saunders and Simon Upchurch. You—"

"Let me see the papers," Angus said impatiently, reaching out his hand.

"No."

"Natalie, give me the papers."

"I can't."

"What do they say? What proof did he have? He couldn't have proof. There wasn't any proof. I was careful."

"Angus, please." Nat felt a tear spill down her cheek. "Take it back. Take it all back. There's still time."

"Give me the papers!" Angus grabbed the papers from her, then looked up. "These are blank!" A sheaf of empty pages fluttered uselessly to the rug. "What's going on here?"

Suddenly the apartment door burst open and four troopers exploded into the living room, their guns drawn. "Hands up!" they yelled. "Get your hands up now!" Troopers filled the hallway.

"What?" An astonished Angus put his hands in the air.

Nat stood by, wet-eyed and stricken. Saunders had been right. It had all been true, but it hadn't been enough to convict. She'd known it, and so had Mundy and the D.A. So they'd hooked her up with a wire, which she wore underneath her T-shirt. She had gotten Angus to confess, and his own words would send him to prison for years and years.

The very notion made her want to curl up and die.

CHAPTER 50

S orry, I'm late!" Nat called out, letting the door slam closed behind her and walking into her parents' elegant entrance hall. It still seemed empty without Jelly to greet her, but this wasn't a day to think about bad things.

"HAPPY BIRTHDAY, NAT!" Paul called out from the kitchen. When she reached him, he slapped her a high five, with a resounding *whack*!

"Thank you, bro! What'd you get me for my big day?"

"A KITTEN."

Nat's heart jumped up. "For real?"

"NO, LOSER." Paul burst into laughter, and Nat gave him a shove. "HEY, WATCH IT! I'M A HEART PATIENT!"

The scene was the usual Sunday afternoon craziness. The July sun streamed through the windows, flooding the kitchen with lemony light, and her family, in pastel golf clothes, shifted around the room like suburban shadows. Her mother chopped cantaloupe into chunks to make her trademark melon and prosciutto, her father poured himself a Heineken, and Tom and Junior arm-wrestled at the granite island next to two tall Pilsners of beer.

"Tom's gonna win," Nat said, tickling Junior in his side.

"Hey, yo, no fair!" Junior stayed in the fight, and Nat caught the Pilsner glass before it spilled.

"Happy Birthday, honey!" her mother called out, coming over with the paring knife and giving her a brief squeeze, followed by Big John Greco, who gave her a bear hug. He was still damp under his white polo shirt from that afternoon's game.

"Happy Birthday, kid," he said, raising his glass with a grin.

"Thanks, Dad. You win?"

"NO, *I* DID!" Paul interjected, coming over. "BY TWO STROKES! THE KING IS DEAD, LONG LIVE THE KING!"

"You got lucky," Nat and her father said at the same time.

Her father said, "Great minds."

Nat smiled. "Exactly."

"Hank said to tell you 'Happy Birthday.' I saw him last week."

No regrets. "Say hi for me, too, would you?"

"Gotcha!" Junior shouted behind them, winning the arm-wrestling match.

"YOU GOT LUCKY!" they all said, then laughed.

"Happy Birthday to you, too, sis," Junior said, grinning crookedly, and Tom came over and gave her a quick kiss on the cheek.

"Thanks for the assist, professor."

"No sweat." Nat smiled. "By the way, I have some good news—"

"DAD, YOU SCREWED THE POOCH IN THE SECOND HOLE. IT WAS ALL DOWNHILL FROM THERE."

Tom shook his head. "That's not where he went wrong, you idiot. It was on the fifth, the second shot. I told him. The ball always takes a funny roll on the fairway there."

Junior snorted. "Wrong again. It was the sixth. I told him, go with the eight iron, but he went with the nine. I made twenty-five bucks and let him off easy. *Easy.*"

"Shut up, everybody. You're all wrong." Her father raised his hand, and the boys fell silent.

Nat waited for Big John to pass judgment. The wrong iron. The wrong hole. The wrong whatever.

Her father said, "I think your sister was trying to say something. All of you boys shut up and let her talk."

Whoa. Nat blinked. For a minute, she forgot what she was going to say.

"SO TALK ALREADY!"

"Paul," her father warned, frowning, and her mother looked up.

Nat knew that look. *Don't yell at Paul, dear.*

But her mother said, "What's your news, honey?"

Nat looked from her mother to her father, and back again. *Who were these people?*

"Nat?" her father asked.

Nat eyed him with suspicion, but from all outward appearances, her father was listening. Eyes alert, face turned toward her, lips parted expectantly. She had seen people listening on TV, so she knew what it looked like. Even her mother had her head cocked, and held the knife poised over the melon. In fact, they were *all* listening. To her.

Nat answered, "My book about the Underground Railroad is going to be published. I submitted the outline and three chapters, and they made me an offer."

"That's terrific, kid!" her father said, giving her another big hug, and her mother came over for another one, too, this time without the knife.

"An author in the family!" she said. "I'm so proud!"

"Way to go, sis!" Junior said.

"Congratulations, Nat!" Tom called out, but the last word belonged to Paul.

"GREAT. NOW ON THE SECOND HOLE . . ."

AUTHOR'S NOTE
AND ACKNOWLEDGMENTS

I'm big on research, but this time I went to extremes. Whether it was because of my newly empty nest or a wish for a different intellectual challenge (yeah, right), I've begun teaching at the University of Pennsylvania Law School. That's right, Nat Greco's school employs me as an adjunct professor (read, Faculty Comic Relief), and her huge lecture hall is my own. My course isn't The History of Justice, but a course I developed called Justice and Fiction, which traces images of law and justice in books, movies, and TV. As a result, I know exactly what it feels like to stand before a class of students who are way smarter than me. (Surprisingly fun.) I hope that *Daddy's Girl* benefits from my walking in Nat's pumps and experiencing firsthand just how wonderful, and how difficult, it is to be a teacher. I am never more bone tired than after I teach, and it's given me renewed respect for every teacher I've ever had—and furthermore, every teacher on the planet. So my deepest thanks here go to teachers, for their sacrifice, commitment, and love. I'm glad to make a teacher my heroine, because they are heroes every day. This book is dedicated to them.

I also want to make clear where reality ends and fiction begins, so here comes the disclaimer. The University of Pennsylvania Law School is real, but all of the law school faculty, staff, administration, and students in this novel are completely fictional. The real law school dean, Dean Michael Fitts, is a brilliant legal scholar who has a genuine warmth and enthusiasm for the school, its faculty and staff, and the students. Dean Fitts redefines the modern law school dean, and the faculty and administration exemplify legal education in the United States. The real vice dean is my friend Jo-Anne Verrier, whom I hope forgives the bad press her job gets here. The administration and faculty have been nothing but kind to me, and no reader should mistake any of the fictional characters in *Daddy's Girl* for anyone at Penn Law. And as an alumna, I know it's the best law school in the country.

Equally important, the students in *Daddy's Girl*, while adorable, aren't the students in my class. Frankly, my kids rock. They're interested in learning and participate in class all the time, which has nothing to do with me and everything to do with their innate intellectual curiosity and the articulate expression of their own ideas. I did teach them *The Merchant of Venice*, for the reason Nat does, and they got the point instantly. Apologies and thanks to my students. You know I love you guys.

Because so many readers get their ideas about law and justice from fiction, it's important to me to get my facts straight. I couldn't do that without lots of help, cooperation, and time from experts, and any mistakes in the novel are mine. And again, in the disclaimer department, the so-called Chester County Correctional Institution in the novel is completely fictional, as are its staff and administration. To give verisimilitude to my fictional prison, I did research at an actual prison, Chester County Prison in Pocopson Township, and I want to thank the very professional and kind Major Scott Graham, Director of Security. He gave me a tour of the prison and helped me generally understand how county prisons work, even during my fictional riot herein, and I appreciate that so much. There is no such job as Assistant Warden, and none of the fictional personnel in this novel reflect any of the professional and caring administration or corrections officers at Chester County Prison. Of course, the inmates in the novel are fictional, too.

Thanks to an array of other law enforcement professionals in Chester County. Thanks to Lieutenant Brian Naylor of the Pennsylvania State Police, Embreeville Barracks, and a big hug of thanks and admiration to Sergeant Jill McKone, Avondale Barracks, who took the time to give me a complete tour, correct my trooperspeak, and explain in detail what would be obvious to anyone else. And thanks to Nicholas J. Casenta, Jr., Chief Deputy District Attorney, and Patrick Carmody, First Assistant District Attorney, both of the Chester County District Attorney's Office, for their time, expertise, and warmth. Thanks, too, to Detective Sergeant Jeffrey S. Gordon of the Chester County Detectives Office, for helping me understand local police procedures.

Thanks, as always, to my old friends Glenn Gilman, Esq., and retired detective Art Mee, for legal and police expertise. And thanks to new friends, the lovely and brilliant Dr. Felicia Lewis and my lifesaver Dr. John J. O'Hara. And to book maven Joe Drabyak, who always goes the extra mile—for books.

SPOILER ALERT: I owe an important thanks here, but you shouldn't read on if you haven't finished the book yet. What follows is a complete and total spoiler and will reveal a PLOT TWIST, so please don't read it now or it will ruin the surprise. In fact, cover the rest of the page with your hand because it would kill me if this was ruined for you. But I have to thank this person in print and want to explain why. So go finish the book and then come back. Please.

Thanks to historian Mary Dugan who educated me on the Underground Railroad in Chester County, Pennsylvania, and who devotes so much of her time to the Kennett Underground Railroad Center in Kennett Square, Pennsylvania. Let me take a minute to provide some background for those of you who need a short refresher on American history, or those from another country. The Underground

Railroad existed and was most active from 1835 to 1865, during an awful chapter in American history when the slavery of African Americans was legal. Slaves were "owned" by many in the southern states, though it became illegal in the northern states. Slaves were often cruelly treated—forced to perform backbreaking labor and endure physical punishments and worse—and their families and children were often divided and sold to other owners. In time, many slaves became desperate for their basic right to live free and ran away to the northern states, placing themselves in legal and lethal jeopardy. They became fugitives from the law and were subject to punishment and even death if they were caught.

The term "Underground Railroad" was supposedly coined by a slavecatcher, who, failing to find his prey, said, "There must be an underground railroad somewhere." The term is misleading because there was no actual railroad under the ground, with rails, train cars, and such. Instead, the Underground Railroad was a series of people willing to hide the fleeing slaves in their homes. Those who hid the slaves were called "station masters" and their homes were "stations" or "stops." The stations tended to be no more than eight to fifteen miles apart, the length of travel on foot in one terrifying night. There are no reliable estimates of how many slaves escaped to freedom, because records were not kept for fear of being used as evidence. Estimates have ranged from 30,000 to 100,000, and according to William Switala's *Underground Railroad in Pennsylvania*, 13, (2001), a report given in 1864 to the Freedman's Inquiry Commission in Washington, D.C., estimated that 30,000 to 40,000 slaves reached the north.

Chester County, Pennsylvania, did play a very active role in the Underground Railroad. The "central route" or "Eastern Line" of the Underground Railroad began in Maryland and Delaware, ran north through Chester County, and traveled farther to Norristown and then Philadelphia. Chester County residents helped many former slaves escape northward because the county lay just over the Mason-

Dixon Line and was home to a committed and courageous network of free African Americans and abolitionist Quakers. Quakers of the Progressive Meeting in Longwood and the Marlborough Friends Meeting in Pocopson hid the slaves in their homes, at great personal risk. Many of the homes still stand, and interestingly, surround what would later become Chester County Prison. Levi Ward, Eusebius and Sarah Barnard, William Barnard, Joseph and Ruth Dugdale, Mary and Moses Pennock, John and Hannah Cox, Isaac and Thomazine Meredith all lived in homes surrounding what is now the prison and hid slaves in their homes.

Historian Mary Dugan took me to some of the county's "stations" and showed me hiding places in outbuildings and private homes, for which I am very grateful. In fact, the names of the Quaker "station masters" in the novel are completely authentic, and so are the slaves' names and initials, taken from actual names I found in my research. I cannot begin to describe here how much I admire the bravery and heart of these former slaves, whom the law had treated so cruelly, as well as the people who helped them escape. They risked everything for justice.

For those of you who want to read more about the Underground Railroad, there are several books which informed this novel, and many of them contain original source material, which make for fascinating reading. Do take a look at: William Still, *The Underground Railroad* (1872) and R. C. Smedley, *History of The Underground Railroad in Chester and the Neighboring Counties of Pennsylvania* (1883). Both of these works bring history to life, and William Still's is a wide-ranging must-read. Mr. Still was an African American who was chairman of the Pennsylvania Abolition Society's Vigilance Committee and he interviewed fugitives whom he helped hide, creating a first-hand account of the life of slaves, including which farms and plantations they worked, who "owned" them, and how they escaped. More recently, you can read Fergus Bordewich, *Bound for Canaan* (2005);

David Blight, ed., *Passages To Freedom* (2004); William Kashatus, *Justice Over the Line: Chester County and the Underground Railroad* (2002); and William Switala, *Underground Railroad in Pennsylvania* (2001).

End of the spoiler, back to pure love.

Thanks to those of you who selected *Daddy's Girl* for your book club. I appreciate you letting me join, and I have posted discussion questions on a special webpage for book clubs at my website, www.scottoline.com. I think you'll find the questions fun and thought-provoking, and I hope that the historical backdrop to the novel will inform a lively and emotional debate. Raise a glass of wine for me, and enter the Third Annual Contest for book clubs. It's a random drawing and if you win, you get a visit from me and I take all of you to dinner. (And second prize is . . .)

Thanks to the following people, who gave generously to an array of worthy causes at silent auctions to have their name appear in the novel: Adele McIlhargey (benefiting Gwinnett County Library, Georgia), Bill Sasso (YMCA of Philadelphia), Jennifer Paradis (Key For the Cure), Elizabeth Warren (by Bruce Mann for the Equal Justice Foundation), Clare Cracy (by Marian Staley to benefit the Fox Chase Cancer Center), Agnes Grady Chesko (by Pat Chesko for The ARC of Chester County), Max Bischoff (by Paul Roots for the Miami Valley Literacy Council, Ohio), and Melanie Anderson (bought at the terrific Turn the Page Bookstore in Boonsboro, Maryland), and my old friends Sam and Carolyn Morris (French & Pickering Land Trust).

And this is in loving memory of David Brian Mundy, bought by my friend Debby Mundy, his wonderful sister, and also in memory of Professor Edward Sparer, a terrific professor at the law school, remembered by all of us and especially by my classmate Alan Sandals, to support the Equal Justice Foundation. And finally, in loving memory of Edward Duffy and Marilyn Krug, remembered by Janet

Moore and Steve Werner in support of Family Services of Chester County.

Finally, thanks to everyone at HarperCollins, my one and only publisher for the past fourteen years and fourteen books. Thanks to Carolyn Marino, my extraordinary editor, who encourages my flights of fancy like teaching, even when they take away from my writing time. And big thanks to the great team at Harper: CEO and role model Jane Friedman, Brian Murray, Michael Morrison, Jonathan Burnham, Kathy Schneider, Josh Marwell, Christine Boyd, Liate Stehlik, Maureen O'Brien, and Wendy Lee, who work so hard on publishing my books and do such a terrific job. I know how lucky I am, guys.

Thanks to Molly Friedrich of The Friedrich Agency, who is quite simply the best literary agent in the world, as well as the equally talented (okay, so both are the best) Paul Cirone. Thanks to superagent Lou Pitt, who represents me so well in Hollywood. Love and thanks to Andy Marino, writer and musician. And love and a special thanks to Laura Leonard, who helps me in so many ways, from being a sounding board for book ideas to being a great girlfriend, which, as everybody knows, is the most valuable person in the world.

Thanks and love to my family, because they are my heart.

And love to my late father, who made me a Daddy's Girl, forever.